RB
The Widow Maker

by
C. C. Colee

AmErica House
Baltimore

First printing

ISBN: 1-58851-378-5
PUBLISHED BY AMERICA HOUSE BOOK PUBLISHERS
www.publishamerica.com
Baltimore

Printed in the United States of America

Dedication

To our families: Thanks for all the support you have given us
Chris and Cody

Dr. Kiely:
Welcome to our world
on the high seas. We
hope you enjoy ...
until the next
adventure,
Cody Lee
(Debbie Rosenbrans)
9/18/01

Chris Cole

Chapter 1

It was an unusually pleasant day in London, England in the spring of 1720. Aubrey Malone loved the market place and its crowds. She could lose herself in the masses and the array of goods always took her mind off her problems at home. As she moved to the table of books, she made a face at her thoughts. Home. It really was not home for her and it never would be. Since the death of her parents during an epidemic two years before, she had been in London with her maternal uncle, Jonathan Hacker.

Aubrey picked up one book and then another. To anyone around, it appeared as if she was looking at the titles, but in all actuality, she saw nothing. She was remembering the first time she met her uncle. Jonathan Hacker had not even taken the time to greet his young niece himself at the docks that day. He had sent his manservant instead. He was middle-aged and so very 'proper' that his demeanor had quickly put a damper on her spirits that day! 'Yes Miss, No, Miss, Very well, Miss.' Those few curt words seemed to be the extent of his vocabulary and she had come to hate those words before the day was through.

She had been thoroughly excited over her journey by ship from Liverpool to London. It was not so much that she wanted to come here, but the ride on the ship. She loved the large vessels. The very thought of the majestic sailing ships brought a small smile to her countenance as she continued to 'browse' over the table of books, lost in her own little world.

Aubrey moved to another table of books and perused the books as she did before. She remembered the carriage pulling up to a huge house near the park. Her eyes roamed the three-story brownstone structure and the large draped windows that seemed to glare down at her. She was taken to the drawing room and told to wait as her uncle wished to have a word with her.

With an exasperated sigh, Aubrey turned away from the books to a table that held small porcelain figurines. Her eyes scanned the table as her brain registered the shapes of little girls with kittens, girls with parasols, girls with bouquets of flowers, little boys with dogs, little boys atop horses and others of the like. The happy scenic poses made her smile once more, just for a fleeting moment. But then, a dark look crossed her young face again as she remembered her uncle's entry into the drawing room where she had been left to wait for over an hour.

Jonathan Hacker had entered the drawing room like a raging bull. She had stood up from the sofa quickly as he had walked up to her purposefully.

Aubrey stood stoically still as he eyed her from head to toe and then back up again, 'So you are the one. Thank God you look more like my sister instead of him! At least that is reassuring. There may be some hope for you yet.' His emphasis on the word 'him' made Aubrey flinch and it left her speechless. Her father had been Irish, 'a ragged Celt', as her uncle referred to him with much disdain. When she made no comment, her uncle had stepped a bit closer and said abruptly, 'Well, do you not speak, child?'

In a near whisper, Aubrey had replied, 'Yes, Uncle, I do apologize. I would like to thank you for allowing me to...'

Turning from her and throwing out one fine manicured hand as if in dismissal as he walked away from her, he interrupted her by saying, 'Allowing you to stay here? As if you had another place better to live!' Facing her again he added, 'It is my duty as your mother's only kin to take responsibility for you. God knows what heathen ways you would learn from the other side of your so-called family! No, it is time that you learn the ways of a proper young lady.'

Aubrey's head shot up from her reverie when the chimes of a nearby clock tower sounded the late hour. She put down the figurine she was holding and quickly made her way through the crowd towards home. No, her uncle's house, she corrected herself. The thought of correcting oneself made her smile and soon a soft but audible giggle escaped her.

He had watched her moving from one table of books to another and then to the table of figurines. It was her auburn hair lit up around her in the afternoon sunshine that had caught his eye. The sight had literally made his heart swell. He glanced at the clock tower when she gazed up at it in a startled fashion.

"Late for home," he mused aloud, smiling to himself. As she made her way out of the marketplace, he followed.

That evening, Aubrey took pains to dress for dinner. She knew she was about to meet yet another fine gentleman suitor of her uncle's choosing. As she sat at her dressing table looking at herself in the mirror, she saw hazel eyes gazing back. Pushing her lower lip out and exhaling, Aubrey watched as the few wisps of her hair fluttered.

She awaited the summons of her uncle to dinner. He did this every time! She thought to herself, rolling her eyes. He had to set up his next rich prospect before meeting the package he was about to buy. Aubrey tapped her foot with the growing tenseness she was feeling. How she hated this! This was like selling her off to the highest bidder! Of course there were no other bids. Not when they found out that she had the Irish blood mixed with the revered English blood.

Aubrey always managed to let that knowledge out before the evening was through. Why make them go any further in their 'courtship' when nothing would come out of it? Besides, they were always men much older than she was, and she shuddered at the thought of being wed to some old man. She smiled at her reflection as she mentally congratulated herself for such ingenuity of letting that fact be known. Uncle would have had it kept a secret until it was too late. She never used the same tactic two times in a row, so her uncle could never tell when she was about to 'spring' the unfortunate news on them.

There was a knock at the door and the door opened to reveal the housekeeper, "You are to come along now, dear," the kindly woman told her with a smile. Mrs. Tanner had always been nice to Aubrey, even when her uncle would send her to her room as punishment for some infraction, and there was always some infraction!

"Thank you, Mrs. Tanner," Aubrey stated sweetly as she returned the smile.

She was led into the drawing room and met by her uncle who was standing with a smile. Beside him stood another man who was nearly as old as her uncle, or older. The man was not as tall as her uncle was and although he was elegantly dressed, he had quite a belly. His face was slightly blotched with red marks and he seemed winded just standing there. Aubrey took a deep breath and entered into the lion's den.

"Ah, here she is. Franklin, this is my niece, Aubrey. Aubrey my dear, allow me to introduce you to Mr. Franklin Adger. Franklin is an old friend of mine from our school days, is that not right Franklin?" her uncle was saying as she stood trying to look pleasant.

Franklin Adger's eyes slowly took in Aubrey's face, and then he feasted himself on the gentle swell of her breasts that her gown allowed to show. Aubrey felt repulsed by the man's gaze and felt the room become warm. She knew that this was going to be another long evening ahead of her.

"What? Oh, ah, yes, yes, that is right, Jon. Old friends, yes indeed." Aubrey thought that this Mr. Adger might faint from the lack of air. He had turned even redder in the face and could not seem to catch his breath. Faint? Well, that might be too much to hope for! Aubrey thought to herself. Her face did not betray her thoughts as she graced him with a smile, knowing that her uncle expected it.

"Dinner, sir," came the monotone voice of the butler.

"Good! Shall we, Franklin? I am sure Aubrey would not mind being escorted into the dining room by you, would you Aubrey?" Her uncle was decidedly a cruel man. She feigned a smile and nearly jumped out of her skin when Franklin Adger took her arm with one of his meaty hands.

"You are more beautiful than your uncle has let on," he whispered in her ear.

Aubrey had to force herself not to wipe her ear as she felt an irresistible urge to do so. She knew that her uncle had heard the comment because the whisper was nothing of the kind and she watched as her uncle smiled. Arrogant ass, she thought of her uncle as they all paraded into the dining room.

During dinner, she barely tasted her food. She listened intently to the conversation between the two men. She knew that her uncle would say something soon about her parents and their irresponsibility of letting her stay unmarried at this advanced age of ten and nine years. The men talked of business, of old acquaintances and then politics. If they did not move on to the matter at hand, Aubrey thought that she might just fall asleep sitting up.

"Exactly, Franklin. The problem with our society is there are so few well-educated young ladies available for men such as ourselves. Who on earth would chose a wife from the countryside and then expect her to be readily accepted into our society, I ask you?" her uncle was saying.

"Oh yes, I, ah, agree with you, Jon. Such a union is destined for disaster! The idea of expecting us to be pleased with such ill-mannerisms," Franklin Adger stated, then spooned a mouthful of pheasant into his already bulging cheeks.

If I were to be married to this example of well mannerisms then I would surely throw myself into the path of a carriage. Aubrey thought to herself. The man was absolutely repulsive! She nearly shivered, but caught herself, and in good time, for she found her uncle watching her. With a show of family unity, Aubrey smiled at him. Franklin did not miss this play as he caught her smile and was pleased.

"Exactly Franklin, such an atrocity for the rest of society to endure."

Aubrey decided that with this topic she should let Mr. Adger in on their little family secret.

"Well, unfortunately some may even be part Irish and not the full bloodied English, proper or not," she carefully added to the conversation.

"Franklin, my good man, would you care for more liver pudding? You seem to have little left to go with your meal," her uncle interjected over her words.

Franklin looked up to his friend and nodded. When he made no reply, Aubrey thought he did not hear her over her uncle. Jonathan Hacker, however, did, and by the look he bestowed on her, Aubrey knew that he would have words with her after his friend left. Jonathan looked to the serving maid who was already in route to their guest's plate.

"This is delicious, Jon. I commend your cook," Franklin stated, not looking up from his plate. Aubrey sighed inwardly. This old man missed her statement. Now she could see how this man was so grossly misshapen. His plate was still full and they had been eating for over half an hour.

"Thank you, I will pass the compliment along." A few more moments passed in silence as they ate.

Franklin delicately dabbed the sides of his mouth before stating, "Am I to understand then, Jon, that Miss Aubrey is part Irish?" Since he still did not look up from his plate, he missed the startled gazes of uncle and niece as their heads shot up to look at him in unison. Then the two looked at one another. Aubrey wondered how to answer the question without further gaining her uncle's wrath. Her uncle wondered how to answer the question without further curiosity from the man.

"Well," Aubrey started at the same time her uncle was saying, "Franklin," Franklin Adger looked up to first gaze at his friend, and then he turned his gaze to Aubrey. When neither one spoke further, he stated, "I see."

"Actually my friend, I was not sure how to approach that particular subject. But my niece is still going through finishing school and apparently has not schooled herself in the proper etiquette of conversation," her uncle stated with a small laugh. Hacker dabbed his mouth with his napkin and continued, "It really is not anything to concern yourself over. Trust me my friend, my niece will provide you much comfort and ease in your future years." Aubrey looked to her plate, not daring to look up at either man for fear that her disgust and revulsion would be clearly written on her face.

When Aubrey finally looked up, she found her uncle watching her and Aubrey knew he would not tolerate this tactic of hers any longer.

The evening meal ended early and Aubrey escaped to her room. But she was not to cherish this solitude for long. Her door flew open and slammed against the wall. Her uncle stood in the doorway, then in quick strides, he was upon her, grabbing her shoulders, "You little chit, I have had my fill of you and your little games!" he scolded.

"At least he should know what dowry I bring with me," Aubrey replied calmly.

Her uncle shook her hard. So hard, that her carefully pinned hair fell about her shoulders. "You will learn to keep quiet! I am expecting another suitor for dinner tomorrow evening. Until then, you are to remain in this room." He tossed her aside and Aubrey fell into her settee at her window. He left the room, slamming the door behind him.

Aubrey took a deep breath. At least he just shook her this time.

"But of course he did, you idiot. How would it look to have company tomorrow evening and present yourself with a bruise or black eye?" She spoke aloud to the empty room. She glared at the door before turning to open the window. She breathed deeply of the fresh scent of the garden below and looked up to the stars, "Oh, Mama and Da, I am trying so hard to be brave, but the thought of, ugh! I cannot even say it. Please help me!" she whispered to the night sky.

How long she had set gazing at the stars, she did not know. Her eyes filled with tears at the thought of how her life had changed so drastically. She looked to her lap, but it was blurred with tears. Aubrey felt certain that she would not be able to endure too much longer. Glancing about the room she made plans. She would gather a small satchel of belongings and at the first opportunity she was leaving. With that decided, she took a deep breath, stood up and reached out to shut the window. As she stretched to catch the window handle, she felt her bracelet slip from her wrist.

"Oh!" she exclaimed as she tried to catch it but missed and it fell to the garden below. Leaning precariously out, she tried to see it below, hoping that the chain would catch a beam of light from the windows of the house but it was too dark. I'll look tomorrow, she thought and then shut the window and got ready for bed.

He was about to leave from his covert watch on the house when he saw her at the window. He had hidden in the garden since he noticed the pudgy man leave the house earlier. He was not even sure that she would have a room on this side of the house, but he thought with the garden as a view, what woman could resist? He saw light in the room and the shadow of a man, but no young woman. He was about to look elsewhere when she was suddenly sitting at the window. Something about the way she sat was not right, and he could not place a finger on what nagged him about that. At least now, he knew which room. He looked at the side of the house and found no help there as to how he would climb up. He grimaced at the thought of climbing down with her in his arms. Surely they would both fall. He looked around and found no tree limb nearby. His shoulders slumped in defeat and he rolled his eyes. Damn! He looked up at her again from his hiding place, watching her as she gazed at the stars. She was definitely coming with him when it was time to leave, and the time was drawing very near.

He continued to watch her as she bowed her head. His brows knitted in a frown as he watched her brush at her face. Tears? Was she wiping away tears? Why was she crying, if she was crying? He thought. As he watched her stand and reach to close the windows, his keen eyes caught sight of the glint of the falling object. He followed its descent as best as he could into the darkness of the bushes below. Then he looked up to see her lean over the windowsill looking at it as well. He stayed in his hiding place for a while longer; watching her window even after she had closed it and the light of her room was extinguished. He listened for any sounds before slowly standing.

He stealthily approached the house to where he saw the object fall. Judging his position from under her window, he moved as if watching the object fall again. Then he got on his knees and searched the ground. After a few seconds, he felt it. Picking it up, he held it to the moonlight. It was a bracelet with a capital 'A' dangling from it. In the eye of the 'A' was a small pearl. He fingered the bracelet, then, remembering where he was, stuffed it in his pocket. Quietly, he made his way out of the garden as he had come in. With one last look at her window, he smiled and was gone.

Across the street waited another man. When he approached him, the man asked, "What in the hell took so long?"

"You worry too much," he scoffed with a hushed voice as he stepped back into the shadows. A carriage went past the house somewhere out front and the two men fell silent. Finally, as the horse's hooves could be heard striking the cobblestone further down the street, he took hold of the lapel of the other man's heavy jacket, "You stay here and watch this place. If that young lady comes out again, you follow her." The directive was given with a raised finger as it pointed to the house and then into the second man's face.

"What? I," Gibbs began.

"Do as I say! Do you understand? I will not be pleased if I hear you have lost her, Gibbs." The last statement was said in such a way that Gibbs knew he would never be heard from again if he lost the girl. Looking from the house and then to the man who held him, Gibbs nodded in reply. With that, and with one more look to the dark and silent house, the man left Gibbs alone in the bushes.

Chapter 2

The next morning Aubrey awakened early. A bird sang happily outside as she went to the window and opened it to let the fresh air in. She listened to the bird for a few moments and she envied its happiness. Resting her palms on the sill, she leaned out of the window to peer below to see if she could locate her lost bracelet.

"Too high up," she muttered. The door came open behind her in the room and Aubrey heard a gasp.

Mrs. Tanner stood in the doorway, "Aubrey! What in God's name are you doing? Get back in here before you fall!"

With a sigh, Aubrey pulled herself back into the room and turned toward the woman, "I will not fall, Mrs. Tanner."

"Perhaps not then, but you should not be exposing yourself so at the window like that. You are in your nightclothes. Suppose some man should be walking by and see you out there so scantily dressed? He would think that you were advertising like some common harlot! Your uncle would be beside himself if he knew!" Mrs. Tanner went on to scold as she made up the bed with all its volumes of linens and comforter.

Aubrey made a face at the scolding. Nothing of her showed in this nightdress, it covered her from her neck to her toes! Uncle Jonathan beside himself? Oh dear, what would the world be like with two of him? Aubrey let a little giggle escape at the thought and she quickly squelched it behind her hand as Mrs. Tanner turned a stern eye upon her. The older woman moved to the armoire and took out a dress and laid it across the bed. As Aubrey began to unfasten the long row of buttons down the front of her nightdress, she looked objectively at the dress on the bed. Pouting at the plain looking thing there and then looking at her reflection in the mirror across the room, Aubrey wished that she had a fine day dress that fastened up the front with tiny buttons.

"Mrs. Tanner, why does Uncle not let me have dresses like the other young women of my age wear? They all dress in the latest fashions from Paris. When I am away to school, I feel, so plain, so—unattractive," Aubrey ventured as Mrs. Tanner helped her off with the nightdress by pulling it up over her head and upraised arms.

"Oh dear, you are not plain and unattractive—and clothes do not make the person," Mrs. Tanner pouted in comforting reply. "Your uncle is just—very British and very old fashioned. Your beauty will surpass any style or fashion."

Aubrey listened dejectedly as the older woman kindly swept Aubrey's desperate plea for a change away like some dust under the carpet. All dressed and with a tray of breakfast served to her on the little table in her room, Aubrey was left alone by the housekeeper to drown in her own thoughts. She clicked her tongue at the plate of eggs and sausages. Making a face as she looked around the room, Aubrey nodded. She was decidedly confined to her room by her uncle, just like his fits of anger had come down upon her so many times before. Now she knew how the people in prison must feel. Aubrey picked over the food with her fork but ate very little.

He was out early as well, as it was his habit to be up before the dawn. Upon his return, he sent a sleepy Gibbs away. He had come back here in the light of day to this place, hoping to better see the lay of the house, the garden, the location of her room. To better see her. Suddenly she was there at the window. She was dressed in a long-sleeved, white dressing gown–she looked like an angel up there in the sunlight. His heart skipped a beat as she leaned out the window to peer below. He stepped farther back into the shadow of trees at the edge of the garden, looking around to see that no one was about.

When he looked back up, his eyes wandered down the front of her. The material of the dressing gown was pulled taunt against her young breasts. Why did someone so beautiful dress like such a little girl? He wondered as he frowned at the dressing gown and remembered the dresses he had seen her wearing at the market. Then, suddenly, she vanished back into the recesses of the room.

"Soon," he whispered, as if he were making a promise. He watched the window, hoping she would come back. A small smile stole across his face as he spied from the recesses of the room, arms in the air and the white dressing gown coming up over those arms. He could see nothing else, but even that much gave him mental images that caused stirrings deep within him. Dressing for the day no doubt. What price he would pay to see her out and about today, he thought to himself as he sighed deeply. He heard the clock in the square chime the six o'clock hour and he would have to be getting back soon. There was work to be done in preparation for departure.

There was a light tapping on the door to Aubrey's room. She opened it to Mrs. Tanner.

"I came for your tray, dear, but you have not eaten a bite of your breakfast," the housekeeper frowned.

13

"I will eat down in the kitchen at lunch, I promise. Tell Edward that I have a taste for his delightful mutton stew," Aubrey smiled lightly.

Mrs. Tanner crossed her arms over her chest, "I am sorry dear, there will be no lunch in the kitchen today, your uncle has directed that you will take your meals in your room, all of them except dinner, of course."

"Dinner?" Aubrey echoed with a distressed look on her pretty face.

"You have another suitor coming this evening," Mrs. Tanner said stiffly. She was not pleased with the way that her employer treated his niece and she certainly did not approve of the men that he brought in as potential husbands. Mrs. Tanner's hands were tied in the matter though. All she was doing was carrying out her orders.

Aubrey frowned. Meals in her room all day until the next suitor inspects the prize. The old Franklin Adger came to mind. The very thought made her stomach churn. How in the world could she possibly eat now? She smiled wanly at the older woman, "Thank you, Mrs. Tanner, but I am not very hungry."

"Nonsense, child, you have to eat, or you are going to be sick," Mrs. Tanner scolded sweetly.

"What difference would it make?" she pouted. Mrs. Tanner looked at her with a sad smile as she brushed a gentle hand at Aubrey's auburn locks.

"I will try and eat a little," Aubrey said. Just as Mrs. Tanner turned to leave, Aubrey stopped her, "Mrs. Tanner, I dropped my bracelet in the garden yesterday. May I go look for it?"

"Aubrey, you know that you are restricted to your room. Your uncle is working in his study just below," Mrs. Tanner said firmly.

Aubrey dropped her chin to her chest, "Very well." She would never find her bracelet—some bothersome squirrel would most certainly find the shiny treasure and steal it. Or perhaps even one of those big ravens would come by. Da had always told her how the big black birds were attracted to shiny objects. One would most certainly sail in and take her bracelet then sail away on the winds!

"Here," Mrs. Tanner was saying, breaking into her thoughts. Aubrey looked as the housekeeper laid a hoop with Aubrey's sewing in it close to her tray.

"This has to be finished before you return to school, does it not?" the woman asked.

"Yes," Aubrey replied quietly. Mrs. Tanner stood in silence for a moment before she turned on her heel and left the room.

Aubrey pushed away her breakfast and picked up the sewing. She looked at the work she had done so far. Another few diligent hours and the project would be finished. Getting up from the little table, Aubrey moved to the settee by the window where the light was strong. She spread the piece of work out on her lap and traced the carefully stitched lines of various styles and colors with her forefinger. Proper manners, proper speech, politeness. Finishing school was going to kill her with its boredom! The only thing that Aubrey did enjoy about it was the needlework.

Nearly an hour had passed and Aubrey's attention was drawn to the sound of the door at the back of the house closing. She peeped up over the ledge from her settee and watched as her uncle strode down the walkway through the garden and to the alley behind the house. He tugged at his waistcoat and tapped his top hat onto his slightly balding head. Aubrey watched as he stopped momentarily to chat with a passing constable before Hacker moved on down the alley to the street.

He had seen her briefly at the window and then she was gone again. He watched carefully and thought that he saw the top of her auburn head every now and again just below the ledge. What must she be doing indoors on such a lovely day? Why was she not at the market, or down in that garden below her windows? In his musing, he nearly leapt out of his skin when the older man came abruptly out of the back of the house and started down the walkway. Ducking behind a large tree, he barely missed being seen by the constable who wandered through the alley swinging his truncheon idly. The last thing he needed was to be arrested! The two men met at the end of the walkway and chatted for a short time; then finally they parted.

The moment her uncle turned the corner, Aubrey was out the door of her room. She closed the door quietly and began her careful journey down the hallway to the broad staircase. Aubrey had this down to a fine art now. At least three times a month, she managed to sneak out in this way to go to the freedom of the marketplace and she would be able to sneak back in most times without being detected. Aubrey crept by the dining room, pausing to hide against the side of the grandfather clock as Mrs. Tanner came out to go to the kitchen. Then she crept out the back door to the garden.

He looked back to the brownstone house after the two men had moved on in their separate ways. To his delight, she was coming out the doorway at the back of the house. She appeared to be moving in a very covert fashion as she carefully shut the door and crouched down low to pass along under the windows. A broad smile crossed his face as he watched her. She was dressed in a light brown silk dress with long tight-fitting sleeves and a high collar. Although the neckline was high, the material of the dress fitted to her young form perfectly, hinting of the treasures beneath. She was in among the bushes under her window, resting a small hand against the stone house and looking up toward her room.

The sun fell directly on her and he thought that she looked like a wood nymph among the garden greenery. The sunlight glinting off a ring that she wore on the middle finger of her right hand caught his eye. But then, his eye followed the arm down and he ran his eyes over her slim figure. He watched every move of her body as she bent down to brush aside the branches of the bushes and clumps of flowers.

She was looking for her lost bracelet. He fingered the tiny thing in his pocket. You will get it back, some day, he thought to himself. Aubrey finally gave up her search and he watched her flounce on a bench.

"Lost, I am sorry, Da." He saw her lips move, but she spoke so quietly and from this distance, he could not hear the words. A gift? A gift from whom? Surely not that stuffy old English bastard who was the Lord of the house! he thought as he watched her. She was framed against the green backdrop, her hair ablaze in the early morning sun as it fell loosely about her small shoulders. How he yearned to go and sit with her.

Finally, with a deep sigh, Aubrey glanced around the garden and spied a squirrel poking around in the grass.

"Did you take my bracelet?" Aubrey asked aloud abruptly. As if it understood what she had said, the squirrel sat up on its haunches and looked at her. Exhaling forcefully, she looked around in the grass at her feet, swishing them to and fro, hoping to turn up the lost object.

The man in the bushes took the opportunity of her inattention to move a bit closer. Ducking stealthily behind a larger tree, he nearly beamed with pride. He was only a few meters away from her now. Close enough that he could rush forward, grab her and carry her away. As he mused on this vision of abduction, her head raised and she seemed to be looking directly at him. She remained silent for a few moments; her face was devoid of all expression. He held his breath and willed himself not to move a muscle.

"What are you lookin' at?" Aubrey asked flippantly. The man's throat went dry. Had she seen him? As if in answer to his question, the answer came in the form of a loud 'caw' from just over his head in the tree. He followed her gaze to see a large raven on a branch just two meters above his head.

"Was it you? Did you steal my bracelet? Ya beggin' thief!" Aubrey went on to scold. Oh, listen to that sweet Irish drawl, he thought to himself.

"What did you do? Did you lose it? Did you carry it away to your nest?" Aubrey went on to scold the bird. The scene was just too irresistible, for here she was looking like a wood nymph and she was conversing with the animals! He looked up at the large black bird as she talked to it. The bird squawked again gruffly in reply and it cocked its head to look at her as if in question.

"Give me back my bracelet," Aubrey demanded as she rose from the bench and stomped a small foot. The bird flapped its dark wings in arrogant reply. He remained hidden in the bushes, stifling a laugh behind a gloved hand at the tantrum.

The door behind her snapped open abruptly and Mrs. Tanner's scolding voice came to her.

"Aubrey! What are you doing out here? Get back into this house immediately!" Aubrey spun around quickly to face the woman. He caught his breath as he watched her hair swirl in the sunlight. Tomorrow she would be with him and he would relish the feel of the silken masses as they slipped through his fingers. He watched as the object of his desire went dejectedly into the house while the older woman held the door for her then she was gone. The clock chimed the seven o'clock hour. He had to go, too.

"Aubrey, for her auburn tresses," he breathed as he was walking along. The abrupt sight of the raven suddenly drew his attention as it came to rest on the road in front of him. The bird ruffled its feathers and squawked at him loudly. He made a face at the big black bird and muttered, "Go away, she is mine. I saw her first." The bird hopped off to the side of the road and cocked its head, watching him walk on by.

Chapter 3

Mrs. Tanner escorted Aubrey back to her room. The young woman sighed as she was being pulled along like a child.

"I simply do not understand why you do these things, Aubrey. Suppose your uncle had come back? Suppose it had been he who caught you out of your room after he explicitly said that you were to remain in here? Do you want him to get more angry with you?" Aubrey sat on her bed, her head dipped in shame.

"I just wanted to find my bracelet, the one that Da..."

"You will have to look another time," Mrs. Tanner said briskly cutting her off.

Aubrey's lips twisted with the hint of impending tears, "I am sorry, Mrs. Tanner." The older woman's heart swelled immediately and she cradled Aubrey's head against her stomach.

"Oh Aubrey, my dear."

"I am so lonely, I miss my Da and Mama," Aubrey said as the tears came. After a few moments, Mrs. Tanner dipped her head to look into Aubrey's tear-stained face.

"You will need to have a new dress tonight, for your company. I will have Andrew bring around the carriage and we will go down to the dress shop."

"But Uncle Jonathan said that I have to stay in my room," she retorted.

"If we hurry, he will never know we have gone, and he does not know your wardrobe, so a new dress will not be new to him. Besides, you need a new dress to meet company this evening," the matronly woman said with a smile. Dress the lamb up for the slaughter, Aubrey thought.

"Can the dress have buttons down the front?" she asked. High time you dressed like a woman, instead of a little girl Aubrey Malone, she thought, especially if she was to be wed off to some old man. Mrs. Tanner eyed her a bit unsure. Jonathan Hacker was very strict about how his niece was presented in her attire.

"Well, we will see," the older woman finally said carefully as Aubrey followed her.

Aubrey would much rather have walked, but Mrs. Tanner said that it would take too long today. As they rode along in the carriage, she looked out the window at the passing city. Her mind was filled with thoughts of her plight in life, as she knew it now, a plight wrought by a love between two people from two very different backgrounds.

The fact that her mother, Jonathan Hacker's sister had married a Celt, and then bore the man a child was beyond all reason to him. For that reason, he had never forgiven Aubrey's mother. Although Aubrey had never done anything bad or wrong, Jonathan Hacker looked upon her as an embarrassment. Aubrey was not of the high quality of breeding that Jonathan had expected from his younger sister. Just as he now marketed for a suitable husband for Aubrey, Jonathan had done the same for his sister who had been two and ten years younger than him.

Now it was his duty to marry off this child. Many potential suitors had been introduced to Aubrey. They had all been men of good family stock. He was tiring of her continued rejection of the men he brought in to court her. It was Hacker's intent to marry her into a rich British family and to collect a fine dowry. Then he would also be free of all obligations to her. Aubrey, on the other hand, was disinterested in the whole idea. None of the men suited her.

As she listened to the noise of the carriage on the cobblestone streets, she recalled their last argument on the subject. Her uncle had suggested that perhaps if he brought home a 'ragged Celt' from the Moors, that she might marry him, like her mother had done. It was the most hurtful thing that he had ever said to her. Aubrey had taken a great risk and told him that she hated him and wished that he had died instead of her father. Hacker had laughed at his niece and then he had given her a sound beating with the strap. It was two days before she was allowed to leave her room and Uncle Jonathan had ordered that she was to receive no meals as part of the punishment for her disrespect.

Mrs. Tanner and the kindly old cook had brought food to her without their employer's knowledge. Even after she was permitted out of her room, Aubrey stayed in the house, ashamed and embarrassed. She had a black eye for a week and the other bruises took even longer to fade.

Aubrey wondered how old this new suitor would be. Only a couple of times had her uncle entertained men her age. They had acted like children and clung too closely to their mothers. The last thing Aubrey wanted was a bossy mother-in-law. The older men that were entertained were fat and ugly to her just like Mr. Adger. But she was to provide them with 'much comfort and ease' in their future years.

Finally they were at the dress shop. It was a tiny shop down by the docks with a glassed-in front. Aubrey gazed out the window at the big ships moored at the wharf. They fascinated her. How she would love to take a journey on one of them!

"Aubrey dear, come along now and get your dress, we must be getting back," Mrs. Tanner said.

She tried on several dresses, and finally found one that suited her. It was light green with buttons down the front. Mrs. Tanner looked at it objectively for a few moments. It fit her snugly with long tight sleeves that were cuffed at the wrists.

"Well, I suppose it will be alright," she finally nodded. Aubrey beamed with happiness. This was most certainly the very best dress she had ever owned!

When he had left the house, he had searched out Gibbs and had sent him back to resume the watch. Gibbs had almost lost the two women when they took the carriage ride to the market place. He was a stouthearted man, but the warning he had gotten the night before frightened him. Gibbs knew that the other man would dispose of him in an instant if he failed at his assigned duty.

As he started past one of the shops, Gibbs searched the streets for the young woman. He nearly bowled over Mrs. Tanner as she was coming out of the doorway. Stopping short, he tipped his hat to her apologetically. She merely regarded him with an air of disgust. As he backed up to let her pass, he ran against someone behind him. He heard a small cry of alarm and there was the sound of cascading boxes.

"You clumsy oaf!" Mrs. Tanner spat. Gibbs turned to look and see whom he had run into. His heart leapt. Here was the very young woman that he had been told to keep an eye on, and she was right here under his nose, within his grasp!

He stooped to help her pick up the boxes she had dropped, "Pardon me, Miss," he said.

Aubrey cast her eyes down in embarrassment as he continued to gather her packages. One of them had come open. As he reached for the object that had fallen from its box, he directed his gaze at Aubrey and wondered if perhaps he should snatch her up right now and take her to the other man.

"You should watch where you are going, sir." Mrs. Tanner scolded the man sharply, pulling him out of his thoughts. Aubrey made a face of sympathy for him, for it had been an accident.

"Pardon," he said again as he rose with a silken undergarment in his hand.

Mrs. Tanner suddenly reached forward and snatched it from his gloved hand and said indignantly, "Give me that!" He gave Aubrey a sweeping bow with his hat in his hand.

"Pardon me, Miss."

"Come along, dear. We cannot be late, or your Uncle will discover our deception and we both know what that will call down," Mrs. Tanner said as she took Aubrey by the arm. They got back into the carriage. Seeing Aubrey watching him, Gibbs tipped his hat a second time and sighed heavily as he watched the carriage clatter away.

"I hate carriages," he mumbled to himself as he began to walk as quickly as he could back in the direction of the park and to the brownstone house.

Halfway down the street, near the docks for the merchant ships, he ran into the man.

"What in the hell are you doing back here? I told you to stay at the house and watch her," the man asked sharply. Gibbs sighed again. He was tired of running into people and tired of being snapped at today.

"She was just here, with the housekeeper or whatever the old hag is."

"Here? At the docks?" the man asked suddenly, his countenance lightening up at the mention that she had been so near.

"Aye, she was at that dress shop right down there. I had her right under my hands, I could have gotten her for you then," Gibbs told him.

As he finished his narrative, the man snatched Gibbs up by the front of his shirt, "Did you touch her?" His voice was angry.

"No, I did not touch her. What the hell, let me go," he stammered angrily as he tried to pry himself free of the man's vice-like grasp.

"You never mind 'getting' her for me–that is my concern. You just do as I told you, keep an eye on her. But do not dare touch her," the man was warning in a low growl.

Gibbs made a face, "Christ, I hope she is worth all of this! What is she, some kind of a Duchess or something?"

"Never you mind what she is. Go, and heed my warning. I will kill you outright and they will never find your body, do you hear me?"

"All right, but you better let me go, because I was following them. They are traveling by carriage," he replied.

"Go, then," the man said as he practically threw Gibbs. As he watched Gibbs running to his appointed task, the man straightened his jacket and pulled his gloves on a bit tighter.

"She is worth it, I am certain."

"Good Lord! And to think that the nasty man had this in his filthy hands!" Mrs. Tanner was complaining as she arranged the contents in the box that had fallen.

"Such things as this are only to be seen by the person who wears them, or that young lady's husband!" Aubrey knew the box contained her new chemise. At the mention of the word 'husband' and the very thought of a man seeing her in her underwear, Aubrey shuddered. A dress with a modest neckline might not be too bad, but her undergarments? Mrs. Tanner continued to fuss about the clumsy nasty man for several minutes as Aubrey stared out the window of the carriage. Finally, Aubrey said, "It was an accident, Mrs. Tanner. I am sure he meant us no harm. He seemed very nice."

Mrs. Tanner snorted in a very unladylike fashion, "Nice indeed! You have no idea of the kind of men who loiter about at the docks, my dear."

Aubrey nodded and remained quiet.

Chapter 4

Dinner that evening was as boring as usual. To maintain control of the topics of conversation at the table, Uncle Jonathan had sternly ordered Aubrey to keep her mouth shut and to only answer when she was spoken to. She was to offer no more information to the conversation than what was asked of her. Uncle Jonathan retired after dinner to his study with the latest prospect's father for a cigar and brandy. Thankfully there was no mother to deal with this time.

Aubrey was uneasy with being left alone in the sitting room with this new suitor, but Uncle Jonathan had insisted on it. It would give them the chance to get acquainted, he had told her. Aubrey watched as the young man strolled about the room. He was dressed in a finely tailored gray waistcoat and trousers. His crisp white shirt bubbled with ruffles up to his sharply chiseled chin. Reginald William Peyton was an attractive young man. His long, sable hair was fashionably pulled back from hazel eyes. Looking at him in hesitant glances, she noted that he was a good bit taller than she was and he was of trim build. But his attitude made him quickly undesirable in Aubrey's eyes. Not to mention that he sat entirely too close for a stranger, and the way he looked at her.

He told her that he was the eldest child in his family of seven siblings. He was also ten and nine years of age. He had been chattering on about himself and his family for about three-quarters of an hour now. He asked her questions, but did not give her time to answer before he would interrupt and ramble on out of control, usually about himself. Aubrey looked at him with worry in her eyes as he did so.

"My father is very rich," he boasted as he easily slid himself a bit closer to her.

"That is very fortunate for you and your family. What business does he do?" she asked as she stood up from the settee when his hand that rested behind her on the back of the settee had slipped down to lay flat on the cushion very near her rump.

"He owns the largest shipping line in London," he said getting up and following her.

"Merchant ships? Do you sail on the ships?" Aubrey asked in new interest as she turned to him. Aubrey's fascination with the sea and ships had been instilled in her by her father. He had always spoken of the seafaring ways, having worked in the shipyards in Ireland as a boy, and later on in his adult years in both England and Wales. She remembered him telling her, 'Someday me darlin'', when you get older we will go on a trip on one of the big merchant ships like the ones I used to help build.'

'When, Da?' she asked.

'When you are ten and eight, me darlin',' he replied.

But when she reached that age, Da was two years gone. The only trip she had taken was from home to here and Uncle Jonathan told her she would never go back to Ireland as long as there was breath in his lungs.

She came out of her reverie to find that Reginald Peyton was standing close to her. He was almost touching her. Aubrey started to move away, but he grabbed her by the wrist, "Do not go away, Aubrey, look here, if you let me kiss you, I will give you this," he said in low tones as he hovered over her and held up a gold pocket watch. Her hazel eyes watched the timepiece twirling idly at the end of the fob for a few seconds and then she snatched her arm away from him.

"You are very rude, sir. I do not know you well enough for you to call me by my first name. You have no business putting your hands on me either. We have just met this evening." Peyton made a face and tucked the watch back into his vest pocket. Aubrey smoothed the cuff of her dress where he had caught her by the wrist and went on.

"I most certainly will not let you kiss me either! If you do not take care, I will call my uncle."

"My father says that we are to be married. In that case, I have every right to call you by your first name. I also think that a kiss is in order to seal such a grand union," he said smugly. Noting the look on her face when he made reference to the kiss and their grand union, he smiled almost lewdly, "It would please me immensely to sample the sweetness of my future bride's lips tonight, and then I will most certainly taste of them again on the big day and much more there after. We will sail to Africa for our honeymoon, my father's ships go there all the time. Father is going to give me a ship of my own, and as her captain I will sail all around the world. While I do so, conducting business for the lines, you will be home taking care of our family." Aubrey looked at him in surprise as he carried on the conversation of plans.

Finally, when he paused to take a breath from his long speech, she blinked her eyes at him and retorted, "I am not going to marry you!"

Reginald Peyton made a face like a spoiled child, and then with much sternness he said, "If my father says that I will marry you, then I will. When we get married, I assure you that you will not talk to me in such a manner; it is not proper."

24

She shook her head in disbelief, and pointing a finger in his face she spat, "Oh no, sir, you are quite mistaken." Aubrey strode from the room with him quick on her heels. She stopped outside the study and knocked. It was decidedly a great risk she was taking by disturbing her uncle, but glancing back at young Peyton, she knocked once more.

Jonathan opened the doors with a forceful jerk. He stood red-faced, and glaring at her demanded, "What do you want, child?"

"Uncle, young Mr. Peyton said that I am to marry him," she began, almost in tears. Reginald Peyton had stepped up to stand so close behind her that she could feel the heat of his body on her back. There was no stepping forward to make distance between them, as her uncle blocked the way, Aubrey was hopelessly trapped for the moment.

"He is being very rude also," she added in a whine, casting the wretched brat a scornful look over her shoulder.

"Stop tattling like a little child. We will discuss this later," her uncle hissed.

She had embarrassed him, and she knew that she would pay for that later. Behind her, the young Master Peyton snickered as he stroked a long finger down her spine. Quickly she whirled on him in a flurry of skirts with the thought to slap him for his lewdness. Her hand came up halfway and Hacker caught her by the wrist from behind.

"Mind your manners, child," he growled as he squeezed her wrist in a vice-like grasp. Aubrey turned her attention back to her uncle now. Behind her uncle, the senior Mr. Peyton stood watching the scene. He puffed on his cigar and cast her a disapproving look.

"It would seem, Jon, that someone has definitely spared the rod and spoiled the child," he said with a grunt through a cloud of cigar smoke.

Jonathan Hacker glared at Aubrey with cold eyes, "Well, William, she has come to me from the isle–after my sister's death. I fear she has a great deal of her father in her." Aubrey's gaze dropped to the floor at his condescending tone about the man she had loved so dearly.

"You are excused to your room, young lady. Tell Mr. Peyton and your betrothed good night," Hacker hissed as he released her.

She glared angrily at the three men. Her betrothed? She had been given no choice in this matter at all. She was not happy at all with this situation, she did not care how wealthy his father was, or how many ships he owned and she did not care how handsome he was or how handsome he thought that he was. She was not going to be wed off to this spoiled, lewd and rude upstart.

"Aubrey!" her uncle hissed in warning.

Grasping the sides of her skirts, she offered a slight curtsey, "Excuse me, Misters Peyton and Uncle. Thank you for your visit. Good night." Reginald Peyton caught her by the wrist again in her passing, and he held her back for a moment. Aubrey glared down at her wrist and then at her uncle who stood watching as if there was no problem at all. When she turned her head back to face Reginald, she discovered that his face was just inches from her own. His hazel eyes followed the line of her nose and came to rest on her lips as he said softly, "I will come calling tomorrow evening at dusk. We will take a ride in my carriage around London. It will give us the opportunity to get–better acquainted without the old men around." Aubrey shivered in his grasp and twisted her wrist free of his grasp. Without another look back, she very nearly ran to the broad staircase.

From the interior of the study, she heard the elder Peyton say, "Let her throw her little tantrums now, Jon. They will stop once she is wed to my son. Reginald will set her to rights–rest assured on that fact!"

"Indeed I shall, Father," the young man chuckled in reply as he turned to watch her in her ascent. Aubrey stopped and looked down toward the drawing room doorway where he stood. Reginald gave her a curt bow. With an exasperated huff, Aubrey caught up the skirts of her green dress and hurried up the stairs out of sight.

An hour later, Jonathan Hacker burst into Aubrey's room without so much as a knock. Aubrey emitted a yelp of alarm. She had just slipped her nightdress over her head and was smoothing it into place over herself.

"You thought to thwart my mission of marrying you off, did you not?" he began as he slammed the door shut behind him. Aubrey stood frozen in fear.

"Well, Miss Aubrey Malone–your days of delaying the inevitable are over. By the end of next month, you will be out of this house forever and my reward will be great. You choose not to participate in your future–so I have chosen for you." He stood before her proudly as he spoke so harshly.

Aubrey's mouth dropped open in stunned surprise for a moment. Then she took a chance and stepped forward half a step, "Choose? Choose from what, Uncle? Ugly old men–little boys who are still tied to their mother's apron strings?"

Hacker advanced on his niece, causing her to step back, "Damn you, you ungrateful little," Aubrey flinched as she saw his hand go up. The man held back, deciding this time not to strike her. "Reginald Peyton is the same damned age as you! He is destined to be one of the wealthiest men in the Colonies. His father has set up business across the Atlantic and Reginald will be taking over the office business there. After your honeymoon in

Africa, you will both be sailing to your new home in the Colonies."

"The Colonies?" she echoed forlornly. He raised his hand again as if to strike her; she threw up her arms to fend off the blow. He ground his teeth and still held back from hitting her.

"Tomorrow, Mrs. Tanner will be taking you to the dress shop to get your wedding gown, and not to that appalling dress shop where that piece of trash came from either!" he growled as he pointed at the green dress that Aubrey had lain carefully over the back of the settee.

"Your wedding dress is finished and waiting for you at the finest dress shop in London. It cost me a great deal, but it was a small price to pay to be rid of you. You will be married the end of next month, the church has already been reserved, and all preparations have been made as of my meeting with Mr. Peyton, Senior tonight. Your engagement dinner will be next week. If it were not for all of this I would beat you soundly for embarrassing me. Instead, I will just be thankful to have you out of my house." Jonathan Hacker turned on his heel and slammed out of the room in very much the same fashion as he had come in. Aubrey threw herself across the bed in a flood of tears.

The clock in the downstairs hall chimed twelve and Aubrey finally raised herself up from the bed. Going to the mirror, she looked at her reflection. Her face and eyes were puffy from crying. In a fleeting memory, she recalled the look in Peyton's eye when he had promised to come back the next night for the carriage ride. She shivered violently. Looking around the room, she moved to the closet and took down her small traveling bag. She would not be here for that engagement dinner, she would not be here for the wedding, and the lewd young man would be waiting at the altar without her. In fact, she promised herself that she would not even be here for breakfast tomorrow.

Chapter 5

The next morning when the maid called on her for breakfast, Aubrey was not in her room. The young woman went to the dining room, clasping her hands nervously in front of her to report to Jonathan Hacker. He wiped his mouth and looked at the woman with an air of indifference, "She is no doubt out roaming the garden. No matter then, if she misses her breakfast, it will be her own fault. She will have to wait until the noontime meal to eat. Then she will be punished severely for not being present for the meal as she is expected."

Aubrey hurried along the street to the market place. It would be the last time she would visit the place she had grown to love so much. She sought out the ticket office of the merchant lines of Mr. Peyton the senior. It was not hard to find it, because the young amorous Master Peyton was strutting around out in front of the tiny building. Sighing, Aubrey made a face then ducked into a doorway before the young man saw her. How could she ever book passage with him there?

She watched him from her hiding place and shuddered at the thought of being married to him. He leered at every young woman who passed by and tried to engage them in conversation to which they flippantly shrugged him off. She smiled at the thwarts to his lewd advances. Oh yes, what a fine husband Master Peyton would make. He would no doubt be off with other women while his wife was at home wondering where he was and what he was doing! Aubrey thought to herself.

From his place on the ship, he could see Gibbs down on the docks. Watching something intently, he caught the man's attention and gave him an angry look. Gibbs merely pointed in the direction of a doorway near the ticket building. Following the pointing finger, he saw her. His heart swelled with passion. He watched her from his place on the ship. His auburn haired beauty would look in the direction of the ticket office and then duck quickly back into the doorway. Hiding? He thought with a frown as he watched her.

He noted her attire. She wore a beige colored dress that was very plain and he made a face. The dress did not flatter her at all. Even from this distance, he could tell that the material of the dress was cut from a rough weave of wool. But despite the uncomplimentary garments, he looked upon her with a desire that was growing by leaps and bounds. Upon further

28

inspection of her, he noted that she carried a small plain purse and bag as well. Traveling, he deduced. Then with a smile he motioned for Gibbs to join him on the ship and moved to meet the man halfway. Gibbs approached him and he spoke to the man without taking his eyes off the auburn haired beauty, "If she is buying a ticket, purchase it for her. Make sure it is passage for this ship. Apparently she is trying to avoid someone. Hurry."

"Purchase it for her? With my money?" Gibbs whined. He quickly found himself snatched up by the front of his shirt, his face just inches from the other man's, "If that is the only way to get her on this ship, then do it that way."

"Aye, sir," Gibbs said in quiet disgruntlement.

Aubrey watched Peyton as she stepped back out of the doorway and backed into someone. Looking around she noticed the same man whom she had run against the day before.

"Pardon me, Miss," he said as he tipped his hat to her.

She turned back to look at the ticket office and clicked her tongue at the sight of Peyton. Gibbs eyed her.

"Can I help you?"

Aubrey hesitated only a moment. After all, she was in dire need of assistance. Sizing him up she looked back at Peyton. Surely the little worm would not give this man a hard time. Then she looked to the ship that was tied up to the docks beside the ticket office. If there would ever be a time for her to be brave, this would be the time, "Where is that ship going?"

"She sails for Africa, Miss" he advised.

"Are you a passenger on that ship?" she asked.

"No, I am one of the crew." Gibbs said with a small smile.

She looked at the ticket office again and found Reginald Peyton was still strutting about like an obnoxious fool. Aubrey made a face as she thought that this must be his normal demeanor, then suppressed the urge to giggle at her own thoughts. Putting on her best serious face, she asked, "Do you think that there are any more places available on board?" Gibbs looked her over. From this proximity, it was clear to him why she had taken the eye of the other man. Then he cast his look toward the ship to see the man was standing at the railing, watching him closely and a cold chill ran down Gibbs' spine.

"If you wish to book passage, I can help you, Miss. That little fellow there, the son of the owner is a difficult little," he said nodding toward Master Peyton and letting his sentence trail off. She made a face.

"Indeed."

Gibbs was puzzled at the reply and then she asked, "How much does it cost?"

"Wait here and I will check for you," he offered, looking to the man on the ship again. Aubrey nodded and waited patiently in her hiding place as Gibbs went to the ticket office. She sighed and hoped that she was finally on her way away from this place and her overbearing uncle.

Gibbs lingered covertly near the ticket office for a few minutes but it seemed like hours to Aubrey and to the man on the ship as they both watched him from their respective places on either side of the dock. The man on the ship cast a longing glance in her direction. She would be on this ship tonight, at any cost. Finally Gibbs returned to her, his hat in his hands, a look of dismay on his face, "Miss, all that is left on board are cabins in the first class. They are costly." He could not hide the perusing look he gave her. Why was she dressed so poorly?

"How much?" she asked quickly, her voice denoting desperation now as she reached into her small purse.

"Ah, one hundred pounds," he said with a painful look.

She stood for a moment in apparent deep thought. She searched in her small purse then laid a hand on his arm, "Will you wait here for me? I promise that I will return with the money directly. If I give it to you, will you purchase my ticket?" She paused and looked past him to the office where Peyton now stood with his hands on his hips. Dropping her voice, she looked up at Gibbs with pleading hazel eyes. "That man, the one at the ticket office frightens me."

"Certainly, Miss," Gibbs nodded, glad that it would be her money for the ticket and not his. He arched one eyebrow in curiosity. That little bastard frightened her and she was traveling alone? Aubrey left him in a flurry of skirts and flowing auburn tresses.

He looked back to the ship, and as he suspected, the man on the deck glared at him coldly. The man must certainly think that he had scared her away. Gibbs put up his hand in a gesture to tell the man to remain calm and wait. The man shot Gibbs a warning look and then searched the nearby market place for her.

Aubrey was at a table where people sold and traded items. He watched intently as the auburn haired beauty exchanged something for money. He whistled lightly at the exchange, even from this distance he could see that she had gotten a stout wad of bills for the item. She put the money into her purse and moved back toward the doorway where Gibbs waited patiently.

"Here sir," she said as she pressed the money into Gibbs' gloved hand.

"Please book passage for me on that ship, the one going to Africa. What is she called?"

"She is the *Gull*, Miss," Gibbs replied as he closed his fist around the wad of money.

"Very well then, please book me passage in the first class section of the *Gull*," she went on as she pointed to the very ship the man who was watching her stood upon. Gibbs looked from her to the money in his hand. His eyes wandered to the ship where the man watched intently.

"Aye Miss," he nodded as he put his hat back on. He left her in the doorway again to go to the ticket office. She watched as young Master Peyton ignored Gibbs while he was in the process of purchasing the boarding pass. Finally both she and the man on the ship exhaled in relief as Gibbs was in receipt of the pass and he returned to Aubrey.

"Thank you, sir. You are a life saver." She smiled up at him as he handed her the pass. He nodded his head in reply to her, thinking of his own life that he had just spared as he cast a glance to the ship.

"The *Gull* sails with the afternoon tide," Gibbs told her.

"The tide?" she echoed.

"Half past three," he translated.

"Can I board now?" she asked.

"I suppose, if you wish. I think that it would be boring for you. It is quite early and you would have to stay in your cabin because of the loading of supplies and goods into the hold."

"I have to board now. I would not mind staying in my cabin," she began. Gibbs pursed his lips and rolled his eyes.

"Come along then, I will escort you," he said.

"Thank you, sir," she replied. She looked again to the ticket office then placed herself so that the large man was hopefully between her and Reginald Peyton. Gibbs frowned down at her as she walked along practically mirroring his movements.

"Is there something the matter, Miss?" he asked, thinking back to how she had been lurking in the doorway.

"He is an ugly little character. Could you see that he does not accost me as I board?" She asked as she indicated Peyton with a pointing finger. Gibbs rolled his eyes. This task of getting her on board for the other man was getting far too tiresome. Looking at the ship, he saw once again the man who had set him on this task in the first place. The man was standing there, with his arms folded and watching them.

"I am at your service, Miss," Gibbs finally said.

A broad grin lit up her beautiful face. "Thank you, sir. I will surely let your Captain know of your polite services and help today."

31

"That will not be necessary; the Captain is a very busy man, please do not concern yourself," Gibbs said suddenly. The man on the deck smiled as he watched the young woman moving closer to him. Aubrey ascended the ramp and handed her pass ticket to the man seeing to the checking of cargo and the boarding of passengers. She passed a short distance from the man who had been watching her for days. He followed her with his eyes as she followed the young steward to her cabin. As he had observed in the market place, she was completely unaware of his attention on her.

Gibbs stepped up to him and sighed deeply, "She is on board; will you leave me alone now?"

"No, go down to that table and find out what she sold to get passage on board this ship; then buy it back," the man said. Gibbs looked at him with his mouth hanging agape.

"Christ! Do ya know how much money she spent to come aboard this ship?"

"I do not give a damn how much money she spent, Gibbs. Get down there and get that item back. Now!" The man spat. Gibbs rolled his eyes once more and trudged away to the task he was given.

"Cheer up, Gibbs! I will get your money back to you." The man called after him with a smile. Gibbs merely waved a gloved hand in reply as he stepped down on the dock and proceeded to the table, cursing under his breath. Within moments he was returning and slipped the object into the man's hand. Gibbs stood waiting patiently until the man finally asked, "Why are you hovering over me, you fool?"

"To get my money," Gibbs replied stiffly.

"How much?"

"One hundred pounds."

"I will give it to you later," he replied as he pocketed the object and walked away.

Aubrey was brimming with excitement, but the rush of adrenaline that had coursed through her as she avoided the young Master Peyton and approached a stranger for help had run its course. Now she was exhausted. She locked the cabin door, and lay across her small bunk.

"Africa," she breathed tiredly and closed her eyes. She dreamed of her father and the stories he had told her of tall sailing ships, seeing different and foreign shores. She was awakened by the sound of a light tapping on her cabin door.

"Miss, the noonmeal will be served in twenty minutes. The Captain has requested that you join him in the great cabin. We will be departing shortly thereafter in case you have anyone to say your farewells to," came the voice of the nice young steward.

"Thank you" she called, brushing her hair into place. As she looked at her reflection in the mirror, she smiled sadly, "There is no one at the docks to bid you farewell, Aubrey Malone. There is no one out there who cares where you are going. You are all alone."

Aubrey sat in the Captain's quarters with the other first class passengers and had a fine meal which she ate with much gusto. Two of the other passengers were elderly women and they fretted over her traveling alone. She managed to avoid their worrisome questions as to whether a fine young gentleman was awaiting her in Africa to marry her. After dinner, she joined the rest of the passengers, first class and others traveling less expensively on the deck to watch London disappear into the fog as they cast away from the dock and down the Thames. She made sure not to stand too close to the edge so it was not possible to be seen by either of the Peytons from the ticket office.

He made sure to stand just near enough to her to watch her face in the fading light of the lamps at the dock and watched as the wind caught wisps of her hair and made them dance.

London was gone from her life and she breathed a sigh of relief as she stood relishing the freshness of the twilight night air in her face. Aubrey stood at the railing now, unafraid of anyone seeing her. Hiding a yawn behind her hand, she turned from the railing to go back to her cabin. The ship lurched slightly on a wave and she accidentally ran against a man on her way to the steps that led to the decks below. She looked up at him in mild alarm as he caught her gently, "Pardon me, sir," she said in a small voice. He looked down on her and tipped his hat in silent reply. Aubrey moved on toward the companionway and did not notice the man watching her until she disappeared out of his sight.

He looked into the fading light and breathed the salty air that he loved so well and said in a low voice to himself, "At last I have you on the sea with me, and we will be together soon."

Chapter 6

The first day out, Aubrey had risen early and stayed by the railing at the bow nearly all day. She was unconcerned that she was alone and headed to a strange new land. She was free. She watched the sailors as they went about their daily duties and even searched out the faces for the man who had helped her get her pass, but he was nowhere to be seen. He would have been a familiar face, someone perhaps that she could talk to on the long trip, a friend. She deduced that he must have been working somewhere below. The captain strolled by and engaged her in small conversation. From the conversation, she learned that this captain was new to the trade and this was his first trip to Africa.

"How do you know that you sail in the correct direction?" she asked him in wide-eyed wonder.

He chuckled at her, "Do you see that young man up there by the helm?" Aubrey followed the pointing finger. The man at the helm was tall with light brown hair that lay at his collar in waves and was busy over the charts. She nodded to the captain.

"He is a very experienced and capable navigator. He will make sure that we go the way we are supposed to. He knows the ocean," the captain told her. Aubrey watched the man for a moment. The navigator glanced down at them and she found herself staring intently into steel blue eyes. He offered her a handsome smile and Aubrey dropped her eyelashes, blushing in reply.

"Ah yes my dear, the navigator knows the way. He will not steer us wrong," the captain said as he tapped the brim of his hat lightly and moved away on his rounds about the deck of his ship.

The *Gull* was a week out from London and Aubrey had awakened early everyday to enjoy the sea. The weather had been excellent to them, winds to push them along quickly during the day and at the night a light wind continued to hasten their journey. This morning Aubrey dressed in her pale green dress–the new one she had just gotten before she left London. She breathed a deep sigh of relief as she watched the water as it coursed by the bow. As she looked out upon the waters, she wondered for a brief moment if Uncle Jonathan had even noticed that she was missing from his home. She frowned a bit when she thought of how distressed Mrs. Tanner would be. Then, she stood in quiet remorse for the loss of her parents. Her personal reserve was broken by the insistent calls of the man in the lookout as he summoned the attention of the captain.

Aubrey turned to watch in new interest as the captain moved to the bottom of the mast on which the man was posted high in the air in the crow's nest.

"What is the problem, Mr. Briggs?" the captain called up.

"A ship sir, she is trailing us," came the reply.

"Are you quite sure? We are in the trade lines and she could be another merchant. What flag does she fly?" the captain asked as he reached his hand out to take an offered long glass. There was extended silence from above as the man peered out with his own long glass. Aubrey squinted against the sun and tried to see what the man was seeing.

"Well?" the captain called in annoyance, unable to see the ship from his position. Aubrey watched in keen interest as the captain moved up to the quarterdeck to look again.

At the same moment the man leaned over the edge of the bucket and said in a desperate voice, "She flies the Jolly Roger, sir."

"Pirates," the captain breathed as he looked around the decks of his ship and summoned his quartermaster with a slight wave of his hand.

"Call all hands to stations, we are being pursued by pirates. Have every man on board armed. Get these women off the deck and below to safety," he ordered. But the order was given too late as a cannon blast rang out from the ship that chased them. The ball splashed into the water halfway between the pirate ship and the *Gull*.

Aubrey had heard the exchange between the men. She turned to look back at the fast approaching ship in alarm. It was larger than the *Gull* and dark in color, three masts held her sails. With all its sails unfurled and the wind pushing them out stiffly, it was the most ominous thing she had ever witnessed.

"Pirates?" she echoed to herself. Da had told her about them too. He told her about their ways of coming up on unsuspecting ships and stripping them of all they carried. He had told her of how they delighted in torturing and killing the crew and passengers of the ships they overtook. He had also been gentle in hinting that they took young women for their pleasure. He spoke of how they would eventually kill the people after looting the ship and then they would send the ship to a watery grave. Suddenly she felt all alone and small in the world. An insistent tug at the sleeve of her dress made Aubrey turn quickly to see the young steward standing next to her, his face ashen.

"Miss Malone, I must insist that you come below with me." Her eyes darted back to the captain and the navigator who had come down from his post and was speaking to him.

"She is very fast, sir. She is no doubt heavily armed," the navigator began as he watched the oncoming ship with his piercing blue eyes.

"We are heavily laden with trade goods and supplies. We are slow and we are not gunned for a fight, which makes us no match for her," he continued on. Aubrey listened closely to the conversation and ignored the gentle tugs of the steward on her arm. The captain nodded as he watched the other ship approaching.

"What do you suggest we do? Surrender to them?" the captain asked incredulously.

"It might be advisable–it would be a less dangerous route to take," the navigator said as he watched the oncoming pirate ship.

"I cannot let them take my ship, I have women aboard–you know what they do to women!" the captain said firmly and suddenly as he saw the faces of the men around him.

"With what do you propose to fight them?" the navigator asked as he raised his eyebrows in mild disbelief. Aubrey looked around to see that the sailors and the male passengers were all armed now.

The steward still tugged at her arm, he was almost whining now, "Miss, please, come with me."

"I will go to my quarters and lock myself in, yes," she finally nodded, trying to be rid of him.

The navigator glanced her way and then said to the captain, "Surrender and perhaps they will let us go. We most certainly cannot fight them. We will all be killed." His tone was firm now. A loud cracking sound emitted from the ship that pursued them. Aubrey turned to look at the pirate ship.

"She is firing warning shots, they intend to board us," the navigator reported with an eerie calmness.

"I will not surrender my ship, damn you! We will fight them with what we have and we will put out all sail to try and outrun them. Get back to your post." the captain spat. It looked to Aubrey as if the navigator wanted to laugh at the man for the suggestion that they could outrun the quickly approaching ship.

"We are too heavily laden," he repeated tightly instead.

"Get us all the speed you can, Mr. Hollis!" the captain yelled up to the man at the helm.

"Get that young woman below, damn you! Will we advertise to their lookout what we have aboard?" the captain then growled at the steward.

"No, sir. I am trying, sir. Miss Malone, you must come with me and I will hide you in my quarters. They would never think to look there. But they would most certainly find you in yours," the steward was saying to her as he

36

pulled her along the deck.

"I have no money," she argued as she looked with frightened eyes back at the oncoming ship.

"It does not matter. Money is not all that they seek, especially from the women. Please Miss, into hiding you must go," the steward insisted, visibly embarrassed for his comments to her. She cast one last glance at the captain who was checking his pistol and still shouting orders. Turning, Aubrey allowed the young man to pull her along to the companionway. As he did so, she ran against the navigator who stood watching the ship with one hand resting on his hip.

"Pardon me, sir," she breathed with a gasp as the steward pulled her past the man and down the companionway steps.

"Go to your post, or I will have you clapped in irons and put below!" the captain growled at the navigator.

With one last disagreeing look, the navigator took the steps to the quarterdeck two at a time hissing under his breath, "Stupid fool."

Aubrey's face was masked in worry as they hurried along the corridor. In the journey to hide her, Aubrey and the steward passed Gibbs in the companionway.

"Are they upon us?" the young man asked.

"They are already here," Gibbs replied tightly as he moved on in the opposite direction.

Aubrey glanced back over her shoulder at Gibbs as he moved along to the companionway steps. In the next moment, she found herself being pushed into a small cabin.

"Stay here. No matter what happens, do not come out. I will come back for you when all is clear," he told her, then opened a closet and pushed her into it. The door shut in her face and she was left in the closed darkness. She heard the door to the cabin shut as well. As the steward moved along the corridor he passed the navigator.

Aubrey stood in the tiny space, barely breathing, listening to the commotion on the deck. There was a much louder sound of guns now, much closer this time. The *Gull* seemed to shudder under Aubrey. There was shouting from above but she could barely make out the words, only that it was something about the ship being hit by a blast from the pirate ship. Aubrey's legs felt weak, and to ease their shaking, she slid down into a sitting position in the floor of the closet. She huddled there, her breath catching in small gasps.

Above, the pirate ship continued to intimidate and damage the *Gull* with cannon fire from the large cannons on her port side and smaller guns on her railings. The Captain of the *Gull* looked upon the dark predator of the ocean in unbridled fear now. Men from the pirate ship threw grappling hooks attached to ropes across between the two sailing vessels and soon the *Gull* was pulled up tightly against the dark ship. The bump of the two ships coming together jostled Aubrey in her hiding place and she looked around in new fear, clamping her teeth tightly to keep from crying out. The footfalls of the heavily armed men could be heard above as they came aboard the *Gull*. The pirates fell upon her crew and the few male passengers who had armed themselves. In a short time, the *Gull* was relinquished to the pirate crew and those who resisted were killed.

Just as she sat wondering and worrying about the two old women on the ship, she heard an argument break out in the corridor outside the doorway to the cabin in which she hid. One man was speaking with a French accent and the other man was British but spoke French as well. A shot rang out over the angry voices and she heard the sound of something falling heavily upon the floor. Then there was silence outside the cabin. Aubrey emitted a small cry of alarm and then silenced herself with her own hand. Tears sprang into her eyes and she prayed that the pirates would not find her. Horror seized her heart as the door to the steward's cabin could be heard opening abruptly. She closed her eyes tightly, holding her breath.

Aubrey could hear someone moving about in the cabin and then the door to the closet snapped open abruptly. Another yelp of fear escaped her as she clamped her eyes shut tightly. She quickly opened her eyes as she heard the voice of the sailor who had purchased her boarding pass. Extending a gloved hand, Gibbs said, "Miss, you will come with me, now."

"Where is the steward? How did you know I was in here?" she asked in wide-eyed fear despite the familiar face. He leaned down and caught the hem of her dress in his hand.

"It was not hard to find you." Aubrey swallowed hard, pulling it out of his grasp, realizing that her hiding place had been given away by the small oversight that the dress had caught in the door upon closing. But why was she afraid of this man? He had been so kind to her and helped her get on board.

"Are the pirates gone?" she asked in hope.

"No, they are not. Come with me," he repeated as he now reached into the closet and took her by the arm.

She looked at him in uncertainty now, pulling back into the recesses of the small space. "No, the steward told me to stay here."

"That little boy is dead," Gibbs said stiffly as he pulled her to her feet. She looked him over and became further distressed to see that he was heavily armed with weapons that she had not seen him with the day he had purchased her ticket for her.

A gasp caught in her throat and she tried to extract herself from his grip. "You are one of them? You are a pirate?"

"Yes," came the curt reply as he led her to the doorway and into the corridor.

"Let me go! I have no money; all the money I had I gave to you to purchase my ticket." Her voice held a tremor of fear, but it fell on deaf ears as he brought her up onto the deck.

He took her to the railing, "You will remain here, Miss, stand right here in this spot. Do not try to run away. There is no place for you to go," he advised as he moved away.

The deck of the *Gull* was a mass of confusion. Aubrey stood where Gibbs had placed her along the port side railing. Fear-filled hazel eyes watched as angry-looking men from the pirate ship were still spilling over the railing and onto the deck of the *Gull*. Glancing around the deck in distress, Aubrey now saw that the captain lay dead a few feet away with his throat cut. The young steward had been murdered as well in the same fashion. She stared in horror at the two men, unable to tear her eyes from the sight. Then at last she looked away as she heard the terrified screams of one of the elderly women. A pirate was fighting the old woman for her purse. He struck her with a heavy hand and she fell, hitting her head on the corner of the hold. Aubrey could tell by the way the woman lay so still that she was dead. The pirate then proceeded to relieve her of her purse and the expensive-looking jewelry that she wore.

Searching the deck again, she met eyes with the navigator as he stood at his post. He locked her in his blue-eyed stare for a few moments, then he was looking past her. In the next instant, she felt a heavy hand grasp her by her hair and she found herself being dragged back and sideways into the arms of a tall man. One of the crew had managed to break free of his captors, catching up a pistol that lay on the deck and pointed it at the pirate who held Aubrey. The powder merely flashed in the pan as the man pulled the trigger.

Still holding Aubrey by the hair, the pirate pulled a pistol of his own from the sash about his thin waist. He pointed the pistol and shot the man point blank in his chest. Aubrey responded with a terrified yelp. Tucking the weapon away, the pirate grasped her firmly under the chin with his free hand and he tilted her head forcefully to turn her face up to his. She struggled against him, pushing at his chest with both hands as the man chuckled heartily. Her resistance was in vain while he effortlessly lowered his head towards hers in an attempt to kiss her.

At that moment, there was the sound of a deep resonating voice calling out in French. The man who held Aubrey released her so suddenly that she stumbled away from him and went down onto the deck on one knee. Quickly regaining her footing, Aubrey searched the decks for the owner of the authoritative voice as she scrambled away from the reach of the pirate. Aubrey now turned to see a man coming toward her from the stern of the ship. He was tall, thin and dressed entirely in black. Striding forward from a haze of smoke from spent cannons that lay over the deck, the sight of him struck fear even deeper into Aubrey's already pounding heart. Long dark brown wavy hair fell from beneath the black-plumed hat, touching his shoulders. There was a scar on the left side of his face from his eye to the middle of his cheek. Over his left eye, he wore a black satin patch.

Aubrey scanned him nervously as he scanned her with keen interest. He was heavily armed with rapier, dirk and two pistols. He smiled at her without parting his lips but the look in his eye caused her to tremble. In French and with the same deep throaty voice that she had heard a few moments before, he glanced around the deck, calling out what sounded to her like commands to the pirates. She suspected that this must be the captain of the dark ship.

The man looked to Gibbs now and spat a command at him. The latter stepped up to Aubrey and took her by the arm once more. As he pulled her toward the starboard railing, and ever closer to the pirate ship, Gibbs put a strong arm around Aubrey's waist and caught a line from the other ship. The man in black had already crossed the expanse between the two ships and had touched down easily on the deck of the dark ship. Gibbs grinned at her with a toothy smile, "Hold on, little one," he drawled. Before she had time to think, they were swinging out over the chasm between the two ships. Aubrey clutched fearfully at the front of Gibbs' shirt and emitted a shrill cry of alarm that made him chuckle. They touched down lightly and he released her.

Aubrey looked back to the *Gull* gasping in dismay as Gibbs moved away. The pirates were coming back to the dark ship and were bringing all types of goods with them. She heard a shrill scream and turned her frightened eyes toward the sound. The other older women had been dragged up on deck from wherever she had been hiding. A pirate struck her savagely with his fist and the woman crumpled to the deck.

The deep voice of the man in black drew Aubrey's attention once more. He was calling to his men and pointing the rapier that he held in his hand toward the *Gull*. Most of the men were busy with the loot that they were stealing from the ill-fated merchant vessel. Suddenly a loud argument broke out on the deck just a few yards away. With one fluid motion, the dark haired captain pulled his pistol from a sash about his waist and pointed it at the two men. There was a loud report and a puff of smoke from the weapon as the captain pulled the trigger. One of the men fell into whatever goods he had been arguing about.

Aubrey let out a yelp of alarm and exclaimed, "Sweet Mary Mother of Jesus!" A faint Irish brogue laced the outburst. In the back of her mind, Aubrey could hear Uncle Jonathan scold her dearly for the blasphemy and moreover the Irish drawl which he hated so much. Turning to look at the captain now, she noted that he merely received the reaction with an amused look on his face and a deep-throated chuckle. He handed the weapon off to Gibbs who set to the task of reloading it as the captain advanced on Aubrey in long, smooth strides. She stared at him in mind-numbing fear. Some of the men nearby stopped in their business of pilfering and watched their captain as he advanced on the auburn-haired woman. Catcalls and lewd-sounding remarks rippled through them in rapid French but she was at a loss to understand it. Her eyes shifted from the hypnotic stare of his uncovered eye to look at the men who were jeering. She began to tremble violently and the words spilled from her mouth, "Please, sir. I have no money, no jewels, I have nothing."

He stopped within arms reach of her and watched her face in continued amusement as she stammered on.

"I–I do not speak your language, please. Can you understand me? I have nothing of value to offer you."

Aubrey found that in her fear, she had been unconsciously backing away from the man toward the stern of the ship. He continued to hold her eyes in his dark stare. Suddenly she was against the steps to the quarterdeck and could go no further. With a small cry of alarm, she dropped unceremoniously down onto one of the steps in a sitting position. A flush of embarrassment lit up her cheeks as a wave of chuckles, more catcalls, and guffaws went through the men who watched the scene in keen interest. The captain shot them a warning glance that commanded silence.

Gibbs moved forward and he handed the weapon back to his captain, who slipped it easily back into his sash, then he came to a stop just a few steps in front of Aubrey, who was still sitting on the step. She looked up the small set of ladder-like steps and reached a hand, curling her fingers over the edge of the step as she climbed up a few steps. Aubrey looked back to check his advance. He did not follow, but merely stood with his arms folded over his chest, watching her. Just as the escape route looked promising, Aubrey heard heavy footsteps on the wooden floor of the quarterdeck above her. She looked up to what she had thought would be freedom but it was blocked by

41

a man, the very one who had come from behind her on the *Gull* to catch her up, smiling down at her. With a desperate squeak, she stopped and looked back to the captain.

He was at eye level to her now, yet she noted that his gaze was not on her but at something above her head. Aubrey followed the gaze to see that he stared at her hand that clung so tightly to the step above her head. The small silver and emerald ring that she wore on the middle finger of her right hand glinted in the late afternoon sun. It had been a gift from Mama. It was an heirloom passed down from many generations of her maternal family and the only thing she had left that she could hold in her hands and link to her past with Mama and Da. To part with it would break her heart.

Aubrey looked back to the man who stood so patiently before her, eyeing both her and the tiny treasure. Her eyes shifted in uncertainty back to the ring. Her life was in danger. Perhaps if she gave the ring to the pirate, he would spare her. Perhaps if she gave it to him, he would put her back onto the *Gull* and let her go on her way unscathed. Quickly pulling the ring off her finger, she thrust her hand out to him palm up, offering the ring and gasping desperately, "Please, sir, I did not lie to you. It was a mistake–I forgot that I had this. It is yours, sir. You may take it. I am sorry that it is so small, but the stones are real perhaps they will bring a small sum of money to your pocket. Please do not hurt me."

With an amused chuckle, he plucked the ring from her palm, his touch evoking another squeal from her as she snatched her hand back as if she had been burned. The captain turned to his crew, brandishing the small prize, and with a laugh that rumbled deep from his chest he said something to the men in French. The men all laughed heartily in reply. Aubrey's eyes scanned them nervously then looked back to the man as he turned on her again.

"Please, sir, forgive me," she breathed, pressing herself against the steps as he came closer. He regarded her for a moment, taking her in with a sweeping look of the dark eye. The eye followed the line of tiny buttons at the front of her dress. Aubrey wished now that she had not been so insistent on having a dress like this, so womanly–perhaps her little plain dresses that hinted of a young teenage girl would have been better. Aubrey felt as if her heart was going to leap out of her chest.

With a wave of his gloved hand, the captain signaled to Gibbs. He stepped up quickly and nodded as he received instructions from his captain. With one last fleeting smile to her, the darkly clad man pocketed the ring then, turning on his heel, walked quickly away toward an opening near the center of the deck that looked dark and foreboding. She exhaled forcefully, and she drew a cleansing deep breath of the fresh sea air as if the presence of him before her had cut off her air supply. Apparently her offer had been taken–she was safe. Her entire being felt weak as the energy drained from her body. All too soon, the hysteria came back as Gibbs stepped forward and put out his gloved hand to her as he had in the steward's cabin.

"Come down from there," he commanded.

"No," Aubrey breathed. She unthinkingly reached up for the next step again. Gibbs' eyes drifted up above her and she followed the gaze. The man was still there, smiling down at her, nay–leering. She turned her attention back to Gibbs as he caught her by her free wrist.

"I said, come down from there."

"Why? Are you taking me back to the *Gull*?" she asked trying to hide the fear in her tone and trying to free herself from his grip.

"No, she is gone." he replied as he held her wrist despite her efforts to pull back from him.

"Gone? What do you mean she is gone, sir? Why she sits right there!" Aubrey argued as he pulled her down from the steps. She was at least three feet off the deck and now she found no footing under her. Throwing out her free hand, she clutched at his jacket with a sound of alarm. Gibbs caught her about the waist with his free arm. She flew into the defensive, kicking and grabbing at his hands.

"Let me go!"

Gibbs grunted at her little onslaught of energy and then he set her down on her feet firmly. He was beginning to tire of this little woman now. Keeping a firm hold on her wrist, he began to pull her along.

"Be good. You go to the captain now."

"But the *Gull*–I must," she argued again as she cast her eye back to the merchant ship. Aubrey frowned as the ship seemed to be a bit farther away than it had when she had left it. A quick glimpse up into the sails of this ship she was now aboard offered her a view of canvas full of the wind. To her new horror, she realized that the pirate ship was pulling away from the *Gull*.

"You must take me back. They are leaving me," she muttered in distress.

"Aye, but not under sail." Gibbs nodded with an evil smile down at her. At that very instant, the deck under their feet shuddered with the reverberating movement and sound of cannons firing. Aubrey looked down to the decks of the pirate ship. Men were touching fire to the cannons and as soon as they had belched their charges of fire and smoke, the men were pushing in loads again. Aubrey's eyes darted to the merchant ship. The *Gull* shuddered as she took the hits on her port side. Deck planking flew up into the air and fires broke out all over the ship in the wake of the cannon shot.

The main mast broke midway up and it fell with a loud crash onto the deck, burying the bodies of the dead and dying passengers and crew under a sea of wood and sail. Aubrey could not help but cry out in alarm at each hit that the ship took from the pirate vessel.

"In you go," Gibbs was saying as he opened a door under the quarterdeck and pushed her inside the darkened interior. Aubrey let out another yelp and turned to exit as quickly as she had been thrust in. The heavy wood door shut soundly in her face leaving her to stare at the knotted and pocked wood panels as more cannon fire could be heard from outside.

Chapter 7

"Sweet Mary!" she whined to the door. How on Earth could she have been so stupid to trust that man back at the docks? He was a stranger. She had given this stranger money to book her passage, to aid her escape from Uncle Jonathan. Now she was a prisoner of another kind. In her terrified thinking, she did not think to try the door for escape from the darkened place into which she had been thrust. Suddenly the sensation of being watched came over her.

Aubrey turned slowly to face the area behind her. Her eyes slowly adjusted to the darker interior area as opposed to the brightness of the sunlit deck. A large window commanded the view of the ocean beyond. She was afforded a complete view of the now furiously burning *Gull* as she drifted further and further behind. It was like looking at some morbid portrait. As her eyes became more adjusted, Aubrey noted a floor to ceiling bookshelf full of volumes of books that were tucked behind little ledges to prevent them from being pitched off the shelves in the event of rough seas.

From behind a desk that was set off to one side of the great gallery of windows, the darkly clad pirate captain watched her passively. Aubrey drew a quick breath, pressing herself against the door, staring at him in return. He leaned back and reached into his vest pocket. Her eyes quickly scanned the rest of the cabin. In the center of the room there was a long wooden table surrounded by six chairs. In a far corner, the darkest in the room, there was a large bunk, neatly made under a heavy quilt.

Aubrey looked back to the man behind the desk. He was holding her ring between his forefinger and thumb as if to display it to her. She flew into nervous chatter.

"I am sorry sir–I have nothing else of value–nothing to offer you. I have no money–no valuables." She paused in her blithering and looked to the floor. All that I had with me in this world is on the *Gull*. Her eyes sought the ship outside the window. It was sinking.

"I–have–nothing," she stammered as she looked upon him pleadingly. The one dark eye met with her frightened hazel ones.

"I must sound so very stupid to you, sir, but I do not speak your language. How can I make you understand?" she went on. The man stood from behind the desk and tugged at his waistcoat and vest, putting the ring on his left pinkie. Despite the scar and eye patch, he was dashingly handsome. Smiling at her now, he spoke to her.

"Detendez-vous, Mademoiselle. I know that you have no money. You have used all of your funds to book your passage on the *Gull*. A first class passage I might add. What an eloquent way for someone so young, so beautiful and so alone to travel." The voice was deep and rumbling. Although it was heavily laced with a French accent, the English was perfect.

"You–you speak English?" she stammered as he drew near. He chuckled and stopped right in front of her. In a fit of bravery, she retorted, "I was not traveling alone."

"Oh, indeed, but you were–my man has told me so. So you see, I find now that you are not only very beautiful, but you are a menteur as well–a liar. Unfortunately, you are not a very good one," he said as he caught her by the front skirts of her dress and pulled her out and away from the door. His hand grasped her skirts dangerously close to a part of her body that no man should touch–especially a stranger.

Aubrey immediately brushed feverishly at his hands to break his grasp on her clothing. He laughed at the rebuke and let go of her dress. Out in the open now, he was free to circle her slowly, surveying her. She held her breath as he walked around her like a shark circling its prey. Stopping in front of her again, he took up a lock of her hair.

"Quel est votre nom?"

Aubrey frowned up at him in question to the foreign language.

"I am Rene Black, Captain of the *Widow Maker*," he offered with an air of boasting. She remained still and silent, but visibly trembling.

"I asked you your name a moment ago. Will you be rude and not tell me?" he asked as he twirled the lock in his slim fingers. Aubrey easily and nervously brushed the hand away.

"I am Aubrey Malone, sir," she said in a quiet voice. She debated on whether she should curtsy in the presence of him as Uncle Jonathan had expected her to do in the presence of all his stuffy friends in the past. She caught nervously at the sides of her dress as if to do so. She was alarmed when he reached out and took her chin in his hand, turning her face from side to side as he surveyed the young woman before him.

"A Celt. I have never–had a Celt before," he said thickly. Aubrey caught her breath again, the tone of his voice was giving her chills, what did he mean–never had a Celt before?

"Breathe s'il vous plait, Mademoiselle, before you fall out right here on my floor in a dead faint," Black chuckled. Aubrey fingered the sides of her dress nervously as he surveyed her from this close proximity.

"How old are you, Aubrey Malone?" He asked.

"Ten and nine years, sir," she breathed.

46

"Ten and nine years," he echoed slowly in a breath as well. She watched him as he seemed to drift away in his mind. Finally, dropping his hand from her chin, he sighed and abruptly turned away from her.

"Make yourself comfortable, Mademoiselle. You will be sailing with us, now," he told her with a wave of his hand.

Aubrey remained in place as he moved to the front of his desk to toy idly with objects on top of it. With a hint of hope in her tone, Aubrey took a step forward and asked, "You will be taking me on to Africa then?"

The room was filled with a rich deep laughter as he turned toward her with a smile. Leaning up against the edge of his desk with one hip, he said, "Surely not, we do not sail the waters off that continent. Our home waters are those of the Caribbean."

"But–this is not the Caribbean," she found herself arguing.

"I stand corrected then; we also frequent the waters off the coast of the Colonies, traveling north sometimes to the Azores," he said smugly at her parried correction.

Aubrey exhaled. "But–I paid passage for Africa."

Captain Black shook his head with another small smile, "You are very naive, Mademoiselle. You did not pay us to convey you to Africa. We are not in the business of conveying passengers to and from their destinations. You are with us now, therefore–you will not be going to Africa. You will remain with me, on this ship. You are part of a prize taken from the *Gull* and I claim you for my own," he said informatively. Aubrey received the information with a look of disbelief and an odd sensation coursed through her at the last statement in his speech. Da's stories of pirates flashed through her troubled mind. Black smiled at her, "Pray do not distress yourself, Mademoiselle. I assure you, that if you are very good you will be treated with the utmost of care and affection. Indeed how could we possibly let you go? Aside from the fact that you have no ship to sail on other than this one, once off this ship, you would be a great threat to us."

Aubrey's hazel eyes had begun to fill with tears, which she blinked back and with a puzzled frown she asked, "How on earth could I be a threat to you and your crew, sir?"

Shrugging his shoulders, he came towards her again.

"How? Because you are witness to the demise of the *Gull*. You have witnessed the murder of her captain, her crew, and the other passengers aboard her. If we set you free, you would inform the authorities. Then we would all be hunted down and if caught, we would be tried and hanged."

"I promise, Captain Black, I would not tell anybody. I give you my word, sir. I would carry the secret of this day to my grave, sir," she whispered thickly.

"Indeed, you will not tell anyone—you will not be in contact with anyone to tell," he nodded as he hovered over her. Aubrey swallowed hard and stared up into his face as he continued.

"Have you ever seen a man hang, Aubrey?"

"No sir," she whispered again.

"And I pray that you never shall—it is not a pretty sight. At one moment he is standing there, staring out at the crowd and the next moment, he is suspended in the air, his face turning red and then blackening with the lack of air as the noose cuts into his throat," he said in an ominous tone, made all the more ominous by the natural deepness of his voice. Aubrey stared into the one good eye and the black satin eye patch and blinked her own eyes quickly in fear. A tear slipped from each hazel eye simultaneously as she did so. There was a loud ringing in her ears and a sick feeling in her stomach.

"I—do not feel well, sir," she croaked as she put a small hand to her stomach.

Traveling by ship had not daunted her constitution in the least, but this picture that he painted in her mind gave her the sensation that she might very well retch right on the spot!

"Then sit, s'il vous plait," he said as he took her by the elbow and guided her to the table where he seated her in one of the high-backed chairs.

"Perhaps you are hungry—it is very nearly dinnertime. Are you hungry?" he droned on brightly as he moved back to his desk and sat down. Hungry? How on earth could anyone eat after such a description?

"No, sir, I am not hungry," she replied weakly. "I want to go home," she added mournfully.

"This is your home." He smiled as he took up his quill and opened a book on the desk before him.

After a brief silence, she looked up hopefully, "May I go to my cabin then? I do not feel well. I would like to lay down."

"This is your cabin. There is the bunk. By all means, stretch right out there," he said, as he waved a hand at the bunk tucked in the corner of the cabin. A retort sprung to her lips but was squelched by a knock upon the door. She shot a look in the direction of the door through which she had been thrust into this cabin as Black called out, "Entre."

The door did not open, but she heard the opening of another one behind her. Aubrey was afraid to turn around and see what horror would be presented next. She dropped her gaze to the top of the table and struggled with a sob. The smell of food wafted into the room and a large man accompanied by a young boy of about four and ten years began to set plates, eating utensils and dishes of food on the table before her. She stared now at the fine porcelain dishes and silverware, stolen from some other poor unfortunate ship, no doubt.

Black seated himself at the end of the table and took up the wineglass at her place setting. He poured it full of the dark liquid and set it beside her plate. Aubrey did not look up to even acknowledge his offer. She sat, instead, with her hands folded in her lap, her fingers working nervously against one another as she pondered their previous conversation. Finally he cleared his throat as if to command her attention. She raised her eyes to meet his and he stared at her pointedly.

"Thank you," she finally said stiffly.

"Merci. The French word for thank you is merci," he corrected.

"I am not French," she said quietly.

"But you will learn to speak it," he said as he began to dish food onto his plate. Aubrey watched him and noted that his gaze had lifted to look behind her. She swallowed hard again. What in the world could possibly happen next?

"Ah, Jean Luc," he drawled with a slight smile. Dropping his gaze back to Aubrey, he said, "Aubrey Malone, allow me to introduce my quartermaster and my good friend, Jean Luc Pierne."

Aubrey drew a deep breath for courage when she saw the man's hand come into her line of vision. She continued to stare at the table before her as a slightly deep voice though not as deep as that of the captain, but was deep and commanding nevertheless, greeted her, "Enchante, Mademoiselle Aubrey."

Aubrey turned her head slowly, fighting the cold chills that wracked her body at the thought of what this person may look like. Hopefully it was not the animal that had taken her in hand on the deck of the *Gull* and tried to kiss her! Her eyes slowly followed the masculine figure up as she carefully placed her hand into his. As she raised her eyes, he raised her hand to press his lips upon the back of it in a gentlemanly fashion. A pair of piercing blue eyes met hers as she looked upon the face of this new person. Just as his lips brushed the back of her hand, she snatched it away from him. "You!" she gasped.

Chapter 8

Black chuckled as he raised his glass to his lips, watching the scene in mild amusement. Jean Luc merely raised a brow at her in question.

"I take it that you two have met?" Black asked in a chuckle.

"This man is the navigator of the *Gull*," Aubrey spat as Jean Luc seated himself to Black's right placing him across the table from her. Aubrey quickly took in all the features of the man that she had not noted before. His rugged handsome features were broken only by a deep cleft in his chin that accentuated a certain boyish charm about him. In his left ear he wore a silver earring.

"Non, Mademoiselle, I am the quartermaster of the *Widow Maker*," Jean Luc was saying with a small smile in his thick French accent. It was decidedly the closest he had ever come to her in all of the many days that he had been watching her in London and on the *Gull*. He took the opportunity to drink in every inch of her beauty. Staring intently into her hazel eyes, he could even make out the green flecks in the iris of them.

"Mademoiselle Malone wishes us to take her to Africa, mon ami." Black chuckled again as he handed Jean Luc the bottle of wine.

"But we do not sail those waters, Rene," Jean Luc replied conversationally as he poured his wine and then began to put food on his plate.

"As I have told her," Black nodded. He put out his hand toward her plate saying to Aubrey, "Hand me your plate."

Aubrey merely looked from him to his outstretched hand to the plate. Her tone was quiet as she said, "I am not hungry, Captain."

Black clicked his tongue and rolled his eye. In the next instant, the plate was in the hand of the quartermaster and he was giving it to his captain, "Poor nutrition can be deadly aboard ship, Mademoiselle. You should eat when the opportunity presents itself." Jean Luc told her.

"Africa is a wild place, full of frightening things," Black went on to say as he filled her plate with food. Aubrey merely watched him quietly.

"The Caribbean is much more beautiful," Jean Luc nodded as he cut the meat on his plate.

"You were on the *Gull*," Aubrey said quietly as she cast Jean Luc a hurtful glance, completely ignoring the content of the men's conversation.

"I did not deny that I was. I merely correct that my rightful position is aboard this ship as her quartermaster," he said pointedly with a smile. He was delighted that although she was most certainly terrified of her present situation, she still found the courage to be obstinate in the face of it. She was exactly as he knew she would be of temperament when he had first seen her at the market.

"Jean Luc was aboard the *Gull* to ensure that she sailed into our path," Black boasted from his end of the table.

"He and another man," Aubrey corrected.

Jean Luc cringed at the reference to Gibbs. He hoped that she would not disclose any more information about him to Black. Jean Luc had performed a 'setup' within a 'setup' by using Gibbs to get her on board the *Gull* so that she could be rescued at sea with him when they had their rendezvous with the *Widow Maker*. But his plan had gone slightly awry for he was unable to be there at the precise moment to claim her—and Rene had been in just the right spot.

"It is a very cruel trick, sir," Aubrey said quietly as she shot a glance from her plate to the captain. Black made a small face of humor and exchanged glances with Jean Luc as the latter filled his fork with food.

"What do you know of navigation, Mademoiselle Aubrey?" Jean Luc ventured to ask.

"Nothing, sir—I know only that I saw you with the charts at the helm of the quarterdeck. It was Captain Wilson who told me that you were the navigator," she replied quietly.

"So you do not approve of our ruse?" Black asked of her as he ate his meal. Aubrey looked from Black to Jean Luc.

"It is cruel," she reiterated.

"Are you well-traveled by ship?" Jean Luc asked.

"No," came the curt reply coupled with a scathing look from the hazel eyes.

"Well, you speak of the 'helm' and the 'quarterdeck' as if you are quite familiar," Jean Luc shrugged, making any reason to converse with her.

"My Da taught me," she said flatly.

"Indeed?" Black asked in new interest.

"Yes sir, he worked on ships."

"Where?" Black queried on.

"Wales, Ireland, and England," she reported as she thrust out her chin proudly. Black and Jean Luc exchanged amused smiles at her display. Jean Luc continued to watch her, a deep desire smoldering in him.

"Wales? Then perhaps your pere was a pirate. Many a fine pirate has sailed from those waters," Black said informatively.

Stressed to the point of an unthinking outburst, Aubrey came out of her chair like a shot, "My Da was not a pirate! My Da was a good man!"

Black clicked his tongue and raised an eyebrow at Jean Luc, saying in French, "Apparently I have hit a sore spot."

Aubrey's face had gone ashen at the realization that she had made such a remark to these two men who were pirates. Many times just such an outburst had earned her a cuffing at the hand of Uncle Jonathan. She seated herself slowly as they watched her. Black easily stood from his own chair and came to stand behind hers. She cringed, closed her eyes, and bit her lip. She waited for the familiar pain of a striking hand for her impertinence.

Jean Luc watched with a frown at her reaction then his blue eyes drifted up to watch Black who could cut quite a looming form when he felt the need to do so. Black liked to intimidate and bully the crew, his prey and, sometimes, his women. He had been quite successful of late, in all campaigns with the exception of one.

The navigator recalled another young woman about this age. Black's intimidation and bullying had not daunted her in the least. She had merely mirrored it back to him and this had delighted the dark haired man, causing him to fall in love with her for being so strong.

Jean Luc's attention was drawn back to the present when Black spoke to Aubrey.

"Are we to understand then, Mademoiselle, that you do not approve of our methods of obtaining our fortune, and that you consider us, who are pirates, to be bad men?"

"Forgive me, sir. I do not think before I speak," Aubrey whined as she practically cowered in the chair.

"Rene, she is our guest," Jean Luc scolded in French over his wine, hoping to spare her the added fright. Aubrey's eyes now searched Jean Luc's face worriedly. She had not understood the remark, but the calm tone denoted his defense for her. Black merely shot him a perturbed look, holding him in the dark stare for a moment. Jean Luc returned the stare stoically, saying nonchalantly in French, "You evoked the retort from her, Rene."

"Decidedly so, I want to see what she is made of," Black replied.

"It is obvious, Rene, that she is not like..." Jean Luc parried back as he set down his glass and cut more meat on his plate.

Black's eye narrowed as he growled, "She will be left out of this, Jean Luc, and you above all know better than to bring up the subject of her," Black cut in, laying his hands on Aubrey's shoulders, slipping them up under her hair to the back of her neck. Aubrey's gaze dropped to the plate before her. She remained quiet, waiting for certain impending punishment.

"Rest assured, Mademoiselle, if we were bad men, you would not be sitting at this table right now. Have we mistreated you in any way?"

Jean Luc watched with clenched teeth as Black caressed the object of his desire. Aubrey shuddered under his hands.

"No Captain. Please forgive me. And you also Mr...." she began as she shot a glance to Jean Luc.

"Pierne," he said easily, trying to hide the jealousy.

"Mr. Pierne. I am sorry. Sometimes I speak before I think! Please do not punish me now for that mistake. Please do not hurt me." Her voice fell away with a fearful sob.

"I accept your apology." Jean Luc nodded quickly and he looked pointedly at Black, for the scene before him was killing him. Black removed his hands from her and went back to his seat.

"Why do you act like punishment is something that you are accustomed to?" Jean Luc had to ask with much suspicion. His mind recalled the night he had seen the man up in her bedroom window and then he had seen her at the very same window some moments later–crying.

"Are you a bad girl? Do you cause your mama trouble?" Black chided from his end of the table as he poured himself more wine.

"No, sir, my mama is–dead sir." She said quietly as she wiped away another tear that had slipped out.

"Hmm. Do you fuss with your siblings?" he went on to ask.

"I am an only child, sir," she replied as she sat before them, still not touching her meal. Jean Luc had a pang of hurt in his heart as he watched her fold her arms over her chest, hugging herself like a child.

"Why then were you punished? In what manner? Were you deprived of pretty things? Were you made to go to your room without your supper?" Black asked. Jean Luc sighed deeply, muttering in French.

"Rene, leave her be."

The captain graced him with a dark stare, asking in French, "Would you care to be excused?"

"No, Rene, I would like to finish my dinner–in a manner that promotes good digestion," Jean Luc replied with a sneer as he took a sip from his wineglass. Both men's attention was drawn to Aubrey as she began to speak.

"I was not afforded many things anyway, sir, so the depravation of such would not have mattered in the least. I did, however go many nights without a meal. I spent a great deal of my time in my room. I–was–also beaten." Both Black and Jean Luc looked upon her with expressions of shock as she finished her narrative in a hushed tone. They exchanged glances and in Black's eye, Jean Luc could see the light of remembrance, but the dark haired man remained quiet.

"Beaten?" Jean Luc found himself asking carefully.

"Yes, sir," Aubrey nodded dutifully.

A hush of silence fell over the table and Jean Luc watched her as she dropped her head in embarrassment, a tear sliding down the alabaster cheeks again. Black cleared his throat asking, "Did anyone know that you were on the *Gull*?"

"No sir. I–was–running away. No one knows where I am, nor do they care," she replied hesitantly. A smile crept over Jean Luc's lips and he had to put up his napkin to hide it. His observation of her at the docks was correct.

"Running away from your abuser?" Black asked.

"Yes, sir," she nodded. Jean Luc frowned. The man from the brownstone house?

"Surely not your papa?" Jean Luc asked, digging covertly for information.

"No sir. My maternal uncle, my legal guardian. My Da is–dead also." She replied.

"Where did you get the money to book your passage? First class requires a very large sum of money. How could you have been aboard without being signed in on the manifest? Did you travel under an assumed name?" came the flurry of questions from Black.

"I stole something to get the money for my passage, a gold pocket watch. I was traveling under an assumed name," she replied quickly. His inquiry was forcing her to lie to him. Aubrey frowned because she had no idea how the man had gotten her aboard the ship other than the fact that he had purchased the pass for her. Had he made up a name? He certainly did not know hers.

Black chuckled and he looked to Jean Luc.

"We have a little thief on board with us, mon ami! Imagine that! A thief aboard a pirate ship!" Jean Luc returned the chuckle and was delighted to see a small smile fleet over Aubrey's tempting lips as well at the folly. The smile vanished as soon as Black turned his gaze back upon her. His tone was almost stern, "From whom did you steal the watch? Did you take it from your uncle or perhaps from a lover?"

"I did not steal the watch from my uncle and I have no lover, sir. I took the watch from the son of the man who owns the merchant lines from which the *Gull* sailed," she offered smugly.

"Indeed? And how did you do that?" Black asked.

"He was intended by my uncle as a suitor. I stole it from him when he visited us," Aubrey said easily. Black laughed heartily and Jean Luc was forced to chuckle as well. Especially when he thought back on seeing the young man at the docks. A boastful fellow like that would sorely miss such a treasure. Jean Luc's smile faded as he looked upon Aubrey. Such a treasure, and he had nearly lost her to the little British bastard.

"Eat," Black said gently as he indicated her plate with his wineglass. Aubrey cast a glance to Jean Luc and he returned a nod of his head in agreement of Black's command. She carefully picked up her fork and just as she poised the utensil over the plate, there was furious knocking at the door to the outside. Aubrey nearly jumped out of her chair, her fork clattering onto her plate. Even the two men were startled.

"Captain! Captain! There is a ship astern!" came the alarmed voice of the cabin boy outside. Black and Jean Luc both turned their heads instinctively toward the quarter gallery window. They could see nothing from this vantagepoint. The sky was darkening with the onset of nightfall.

"Mon Dieu," Black spat as he rose from his chair and threw his napkin onto the table.

"Go see what it is." He ordered of his quartermaster. The latter stood quickly as well, and throwing his napkin upon his plate, he hurried from the cabin, slamming the door behind him. Aubrey was immediately thrown back into a panic at their reactions.

"You remain here. Eat your dinner," Black ordered as he gathered his weapons from his desk and clapped on his hat, then exited the room as forcefully as Jean Luc had. Aubrey sat in the empty cabin, her eyes rolling fearfully in her head as she looked over the vacant table and heard the running footsteps of men overhead.

Chapter 9

On the forecastle of a fine brigantine a good distance behind the *Widow Maker*, two men watched the dark pirate vessel intently in the last rays of daylight.

"See her?" came the British-accented voice as the man lowered his long glass and looked at the man next to him.

"Aye," came the thick Scottish-accented reply.

"Who do you think she is?" the first man asked again.

"Judging from that debris we saw earlier, and given the waters we are in, tis no' hard ta guess," came the tight reply.

"Shall I alert the captain?"

"Nay, leave the captain alone. They are far enough ahead that they are no threat to us. We will have our time later." The reply was cutting now as the man snapped shut the long glass.

"I think we should let the captain know," came the British tones as he looked through his long glass again.

"I said nay!" the Scotsman said through clenched teeth.

The other man shrugged with an air of indifference. "Well, you are the quartermaster."

"Damn right I am, and dinna ye forget it," came the angry Scottish voice.

"What do you see?" Black asked in French as he approached Jean Luc on the quarterdeck.

"Nothing," came the reply.

"What did he see?" The dark haired man queried on as he nodded up toward the lookout in the crow's nest.

Jean Luc snapped shut the long glass and sighed, "A twin mast ship, some distance back."

"Flag?" Black asked as he put his long glass up to his eye.

"Solid red," came the reply. Black lowered the long glass and frowned.

"Solid red? With the evening sky hues the fool has mistaken a Union Jack for solid red."

Jean Luc offered a shrug and watched his captain move away from the railing.

"Keep a keen eye. They may have seen the debris of the *Gull*."

"Without a doubt, Rene," Jean Luc growled.

"Better debris then witnesses, mon ami. We got our just rewards," Black replied smugly. Jean Luc watched the man as he turned away in the growing darkness. You got my reward Rene and she sits at your table as we speak. With a silent curse into the wind, Jean Luc turned back to watch the water to their stern. The moon was beginning to rise, and his own anger.

Black entered the cabin to see the table vacant. Aubrey's plate was undisturbed–not a morsel seemed to have been taken and her wineglass sat full. Clicking his tongue, he put his weapons and hat on his desk, then turned to her. She stood with her back to him, looking out at the rising moon beyond the quarter gallery windows.

"I told you to eat," he scolded as he neared. Her posture took on a sudden stance of apprehension, but she did not turn.

"I am not hungry, sir," she said stiffly.

Black stood in silence for a moment and then he stepped closer to her, easily trapping her between him and the ledge of the broad-sill of the window.

"What are you thinking about?" he asked quietly.

"Please, take me to Africa," she whined.

"Does a beau await you there?" he asked as he turned her to face him. She pulled back instinctively, but he held on to her.

"No," she replied as she stared forward into his chest.

"Then why would you want to go somewhere like that to be alone?"

"Why did you take me from the *Gull*?" she said, with tears in her voice as she looked up at him.

"You saw her, she was sinking. Had I left you on board, you would be dead now and what a terrible waste," he smiled as he lowered his head towards hers. She turned her face away uncomfortably.

"Your mere and pere are gone, what a tragic loss for you. Your uncle, by your own word, mistreats you and so you run from him. He will not find you here. I will take care of you now," he said thickly as he turned her face with his hand to look up at him again. Lowering his face he pressed her lips in a kiss. Aubrey fought to free herself of the embrace, but he held her in place. She gasped as he broke from the kiss, her face emblazoned with embarrassment. Chuckling low in his throat, he asked, "I thought that you told us that you had a suitor in London? Did he not caress you and kiss you like that?"

"No, sir, I do not know any man in that manner." she gasped.

"Ah, then your uncle had presented you for an arranged marriage." He nodded as he took her hand and led her to the table.

"Yes, sir," she nodded as he seated her at her place.

"Eat your dinner now, the alarm of earlier is of no concern to me. My men will take care of matters up there," he directed as he pushed in her chair and laid her napkin in her lap. Finally sitting in his chair, he waved his hand at her glass.

"Drink your wine."

"I am not allowed, sir. My uncle allowed me only water. He said I was too young to partake," she said meekly.

"Nonsense! A foolish rule set by a foolish man. We French are weaned on it. Water is a dear commodity on board ship, and with us, you will learn to drink wine," Black scoffed. Aubrey tentatively picked up the glass and brought it to her lips.

"It is an excellent vintage, comes from Marseilles, the home of my quartermaster," Black informed her as he drained his own glass once more and refilled it.

Aubrey tasted the libation. It was sweet and it gave her a warming sensation as it went down.

"Your dinner is most certainly cold now, but eat, s'il vous plait," he pressed on. Aubrey eyed him as he leaned back in his chair and propped a booted foot up into Jean Luc's vacant chair. Aubrey looked at the food on her plate and she was beginning to get hungry.

"You are very polite," he commented.

"My uncle demanded it, sir," she informed him stiffly as she finally picked up the fork and began to push the morsels of food around on her plate.

"Did he send you away to finishing school as well?" Black asked with a small smile.

"Yes sir, he did," Aubrey nodded.

"They did not teach you French at this school?" he asked in surprise.

"No, sir. I was being schooled in–proper English." She said with an apologetic face as she put a piece of the meat into her mouth.

"Proper English, humph!" Black snorted as he took a drink of his wine. "They go to school for everything–even the proper way to put on their drawers and wigs!" He added with an additional snort.

Aubrey tittered in laughter, then caught the tiny outburst behind her napkin. "Forgive me, sir."

Black smiled at her reaction. She appeared to be relaxing. In subtle encouragement of her change in demeanor, he said, "Oh, by all means, your laughter delights me. I was beginning to wonder if you knew how to smile at all. I was afraid that perhaps like the British, you were frightened that your painted face may crack if you smiled," he said with a grunt. The additional insult to the British made her giggle all the more. Despite that it was the heritage of her mother, she had begun to hate the British.

She looked down at the plate to pick up another bite of food, saying quietly, "I do not make up my face, sir."

"C'est bon, for it would hide your singular beauty," he said with a nod.

Aubrey ate in silence and Black watched her. His mind drifted in the relaxed waves of the liquor he had consumed. The young woman before him was attractive, but as Jean Luc had pointed out, she did not possess the beauty or strength of...

"I am finished, sir. Where will I sleep? I am very tired," Aubrey said quietly, breaking into his wandering. The ship bell sounded twice.

"Ah, it is nine o'clock–no wonder you are tired, it is bedtime." He nodded as he set aside his empty glass and stood. Aubrey stood nervously as he approached. His hands went directly up to the small buttons at the front of her dress, "This is a very pretty dress, Mademoiselle, but it will be far too uncomfortable for sleeping."

Aubrey stepped back with a gasp and brushed at his hands. "I–I can sleep in my dress, sir. It is not a problem."

"Nonsense, I will give you something more comfortable," he said with a wave of his hand as he moved toward the bunk. Stooping to pull out a drawer at the base of it, he produced a fine white silk shirt. "Here, this should do nicely for now."

Aubrey found the shirt being placed into her hands and she stared down at it. The silk was so fine it felt like liquid in her hands.

"I–this is far too expensive, sir. I cannot wear this."

"Will you insult me by turning down my gift to you?" he asked.

She looked down quickly, "No, sir. Thank you."

"Merci," he corrected.

"Merci," she said quietly.

"Put it on." He smiled down at her and put his hands on her shoulders. Stroking her exposed collarbone through her dress with his thumbs, he lowered his head once more and kissed her. When he released her again, he chuckled and began to unbutton his jacket.

"You are much in need of schooling in the fine art of amour. You may change there, if you are adverse to changing in front of me."

Aubrey looked in the direction he had waved. There was an ornate dressing screen in one corner of the cabin. Then she looked back toward him, watching in silence as he moved to the bunk pulling off his black jacket. "I will turn down our bunk." The shirt slipped from her grasp and landed into a small pile at her feet, "But–I–cannot sleep with you."

Black watched her in amusement as she turned full circle, looking around the cabin.

"I will sleep there, sir," she finally said, as she pointed to a settee placed along one wall. He regarded her for a few moments with a frown, pressing his lips tightly together. Then he went back to pulling down the covers.

"Very well, Mademoiselle, as you say but only for a short time. I will not tolerate your sleeping on the settee forever–it would ruin my reputation. The Captain's woman sleeps in the Captain's bunk."

As Aubrey emerged tentatively from behind the wall, Black was sitting at the foot of his bunk, shirtless. He cast his eye over her and stood. "My shirt fits you well."

Aubrey stepped back nervously as he approached. He closed the distance easily and caught her by the wrists, pulling her up against him and dipping his face into the side of her neck. She fought to free herself, whining, "Captain–please."

"My name is Rene," he cooed as he once more lowered his mouth on hers. He could taste the wine she had with her meal as he kissed her deeper.

"Bonsoir, Precieux," he purred as he released her and pushed her toward the settee. Aubrey guardedly curled herself onto the piece of furniture as he moved to the bunk and pulled a blanket off for her.

Moving back to the bunk, he blew out the lantern and got in. Stretching out his long frame, he laid in the darkness, smiling in approval. The sight of the rich silk of the shirt hanging over her young body had been pleasurable. Then the image of another woman in one of his white shirts came to mind and the smile disappeared. Mentally shaking the memory off, Black listened to silence from her side of the cabin and deduced that she was already asleep.

Chapter 10

Jean Luc propped a booted foot up on the starboard gunwale of the quarterdeck. She was just beneath him in the captain's cabin. He had dreamed of her being with him—but this part did not fit into his plans. Jean Luc had spent many hours imagining her in his arms as he kissed and caressed her.

A pang of remorse stabbed at his chest as he recalled the way she had looked at him this evening when she had recognized him from the *Gull*. He would need to gain her trust in order to get close to her. But once he did, she would see a love and devotion the likes of which she had most certainly never seen before. The day's events played in his mind as he watched the stars appearing one by one in the sky.

Someone approached him from the shadows and he turned suddenly, laying a hand on the butt of the pistol he kept tucked in the red sash about his waist. Gibbs stumbled back in fear at the sight of Jean Luc's hand on his weapon. "Pierne, it is I." Jean Luc made a face at him and turned back to the sea. "I did what you asked—I got her aboard the *Gull*," Gibbs said in a hushed voice.

"Indeed, you did," Jean Luc nodded.

"Beaufort had his hands on her. I had nothing to do with that, I had no control over that."

"I know." Jean Luc nodded again, not turning to look at the man in his prattling.

"I am done with it now, you hear me, Pierne. The captain has her now, and I want no part of it," Gibbs hissed close to his ear.

"You watch out for her—if Beaufort so much as casts a lewd eye upon her and you see it, I want to know," Jean Luc hissed back as he fingered his pistol again.

"No!" Gibbs argued.

"Oui!" Jean Luc spat as he turned to face Gibbs.

"Stupid fool! Black will have you drawn and quartered!" Gibbs spat back.

Jean Luc shoved at the man forcefully. Gibbs stumbled backward as the quartermaster growled, "You are the fool. You will do as I say and you will tell no one of my plans back in London, or I will cut out your tongue and feed it to you." Gibbs looked at the angry face of his quartermaster in the light of the moon. He knew the man's anger and he knew that he would come

61

through with his threats. With a grunt, Gibbs moved away, leaving Jean Luc to stand alone once more at the railing.

The next morning, Aubrey stretched and inhaled deeply. She opened her eyes to the sight of the cabin glowing red with the morning sun streaming into the windows. The sky beyond was streaked with clouds that varied in hues of pinks and reds and the background sky was the bluest of blues. Tucking her hands up under her chin she watched the show before her. The sound of the door opening caught her attention. She watched with bated breath as it swung silently open. Black came into the cabin quietly and crossed to his desk. Aubrey sat up easily, clutching the blankets to her chest. "Good morning, Captain Black."

He turned toward the sound of her small voice, and much to her dismay, her greeting enticed him to come toward the settee.

"Bonjour. Did you sleep well?"

"Yes sir."

"Bon, put on your pretty green dress now and I will take you to the galley for the morning meal," Black said as he moved away from her with an air of boredom.

The galley was literally crawling with dirty, ugly and disheveled men. Her first reaction to it was one of stark fear then she drew back in revulsion. Black patted her hand soothingly, "You are fine." He led her to a table in the back of the room and seated her. The burly cook appeared and set plates in front of them heaped with smoked ham and potatoes. Aubrey made a small face and wondered if this was all they ate on this ship.

"What is the reason for such an ugly little face, Precieux?" Black asked with a small grin.

"I cannot eat all of this, sir," she said stiffly.

"Then eat what you can, I am sure that one of these monsters would gladly eat the rest of it." He chuckled. Aubrey looked around in mild alarm. Some of the men spoke in low tones as they looked at her. She shivered violently.

"Please sir, take me to Africa," she pleaded once more.

Another low chuckle rumbled in his throat as he cut a piece of meat on his plate. "I told you, we do not sail those waters."

Aubrey dropped her head and poked at the food on her plate.

The quartermaster appeared on the scene and took a chair across from her.

"Bonjour, Mademoiselle, and to you also, Rene." Black nodded to the man, but Aubrey did not look up.

"Are we cross this morning?" Jean Luc asked in French of Black as he nodded toward Aubrey.

"She is still asking to be taken to Africa," Black said with a slight chuckle in English.

"Perhaps she does not understand how very far away it is–and how long it would take to get there. Let me show her on the charts." Jean Luc chuckled in the same language now.

Aubrey glanced at him as he spoke. Then, looking around the room again she asked of the captain, "Sir, are there no other women on this ship?"

"No," Black said after a brief moment of thought, and cast a look to Jean Luc.

"Why?" Aubrey asked.

"Do not concern yourself with that," Black said stiffly.

"But where are these men's wives? Their sweethearts?" Aubrey asked in distress. Black and Jean Luc were forced to chuckle at her question.

"Every whore in port is their wives and sweethearts," Black reported as he ate. Aubrey's face blanched at the reply. The two men began to converse in French and Aubrey ate in silence.

After a short time she became uncomfortably aware of someone standing very close behind her. She looked across the table at Jean Luc and found his eyes looking above her. Turning slowly, Aubrey found herself staring up into the face of the very man who had caught her up on the deck of the *Gull*. A cold chill ran down her spine. From this closer proximity, she was afforded a better view of him. His eyes were gray and close-set in his face. Stubble of beard and mustache covered his face and his hair hung in wavy strings, looking as though it was very much in need of washing.

As the man began to speak to his captain, Aubrey dropped her gaze back to her plate. Black wiped his mouth and listened to the man intently as he spoke in their native tongue.

"Fouquet is in the crow's nest this morning. He has spotted a ship trailing us, Captain," the man was saying. Black looked at him in question and the man answered, "She flies a solid red flag."

"There is that red flag again," Black muttered, reaching out and catching a lock of Aubrey's hair in his fingers, then twirling it idly, making her freeze in place. Black's toying did not seem to register in her mind, as her attention was more on the man who seemed to press in on her from behind. Jean Luc watched Black's slender fingers in their play.

"Who is that?" Black asked of Jean Luc.

The latter shrugged slightly, "How would I know, Rene?"

"Keep an eye on her, Beaufort. I will be up directly. Have the men prepare for engagement. She trailed us last night, and now she has shown herself in the light of day. Perhaps this red flag is some sign of some crazy rogue British fleet that the Crown has sent upon the waters to be a thorn in our sides," Black said as he dropped the lock of Aubrey's hair and picked up his napkin.

"Aye sir," the man called Beaufort nodded.

The conversation sounded important and the men's voices denoted a hint of unrest. Aubrey shot a look to the captain as he exhaled hard. Wiping at his mustache, he said to her in English, "Well, are you finished with your breakfast, Precieux? It is time for you to return to the cabin. We have some pressing business to attend to."

"Yes sir, I am finished," she nodded meekly.

Black stood and put out his hand to her. She tentatively placed her hand into his and looked to the man who had been standing so closely. He now blocked her exit as he looked down at her from his height of at least six feet. The quartermaster had stood as well.

"Move, Beaufort, can you not see that the lady is leaving?" Jean Luc snapped curtly.

"Ah, pardon, Mademoiselle," the man began, offering her a mocking bow as he backed off only slightly.

Black gently pulled Aubrey from her chair and he looked upon the man with a flash of fire in his dark eye, growling, "Move, damn you."

"Are you here just on business or are you here for a meal as well?" Jean Luc asked in French with a hint of hatred in his tone toward the man.

"A meal," Beaufort replied gruffly.

"Then get it and get to your post."

"I have finished my watch," Beaufort growled as he watched Black lead Aubrey away.

"Then eat and get to your hammock," Jean Luc sneered as he moved from the table to follow them.

With a grunt, Thomas Beaufort sat down at the table next to the captain's. Watching as his captain left the galley with the young woman in tow, Beaufort turned his attention to the plate of food at her place on the other table. It appeared nearly untouched. With a lewd smile, he reached over and took the plate to set it on the table before himself. Then he took up her fork as well and poked it into the pile of meat and potatoes. As he proceeded to eat her breakfast, he looked back to where he had last seen her and he chuckled. Holding up the fork and looking at it thoughtfully, he licked it lasciviously and purred, "Yum."

"Where is this phantom ship?" Black called up as he stepped out onto the main deck.

"Gone now, just like last night. She must be a fast one," Fouquet called down from the crow's nest. Black grunted and shook his head.

"I think that you have all been out to sea too long. You are beginning to imagine things now."

"I did not see a thing, Rene," Jean Luc offered with a boyish batting of his blue eyes.

Chapter 11

It had been nearly a week since Aubrey had been taken on board the *Widow Maker*. She had been treated and fed well. Black appeared to be a gentleman most of the time, although his advances came often. The day was clear and the sea had rolling swells as she stood in the quarter gallery looking at the ocean. She watched the water with fascination while Black had gone topside, leaving her to herself. When Aubrey heard the door open behind her, she ignored it thinking that it was only the captain returning.

Suddenly, she was grabbed from behind and thrown on the floor. She hit it hard and was momentarily stunned. Looking in the face of an unknown man, Aubrey tried to scream but he covered her mouth with his hand while he tore at her dress with his free hand. He spoke to her rapidly in French as he sat astride her. She struggled with all her might to get free and managed to bite his hand, causing him to curse and temporarily remove his hand from her mouth. She cried out desperately as he tore open the front of her dress and the tiny buttons flew like shot from a pellet gun. Aubrey screamed again before the heavy hand clamped down on her mouth once more.

Up on deck, Black was speaking to Jean Luc as they worked over the charts. Suddenly his head turned in the direction of the doorway to the cabin below. For a fleeting moment, the two men looked at each other. A desperate scream was heard and they sprinted for the doorway under the quarterdeck. Black was in front when they reached the cabin. He saw Aubrey struggling on the floor, her dress torn open and a man was on top of her. Throwing caution to the wind, Jean Luc moved past Black and yanked the man off of Aubrey.

Free from the man, Aubrey scrambled to her feet clutching her torn dress together. Within moments the fight was over as Jean Luc's fist connected with the man's chin. The man dropped to his knees. Turning, Black moved to help Aubrey but she scrambled away from him as well. Jean Luc straightened and looked to Aubrey.

As Black approached her again, he was surprised as she reached toward him and pulled his pistol from his belt. He ducked low, thinking that he was her intended target. Instead she fired over his head and he heard a heavy thud behind him. Whirling around, Black saw the man on his back, quite dead with a neat hole in his chest. Jean Luc straightened again, a look of surprise on his face as he too had ducked from her aim. Both men turned their gaze upon the young woman who stood in the corner, still holding the smoking pistol. Black took the weapon from her trembling hand and handed it over to Jean Luc before gathering Aubrey up into his arms. She now clung to him in terror as she stared over his shoulder at the dead man on the floor. Black smoothed her hair and spoke quietly in her ear in French. She did not understand his words, but his tone of voice was soothing. Jean Luc looked on in despair, wishing that he could hold and comfort her.

"She knows how to shoot? They teach more at those finishing schools than we imagined, n'est-ce pas?" Black asked of his quartermaster in French.

Jean Luc shrugged, smiling lightly despite the situation and said easily, "How would I know, Rene? I do not usually frequent them." Black frowned down on the man in the floor now, for he did not recognize him.

"Raoul Fouquet. He was new on board," Jean Luc said, identifying the man with a nod of his head.

"Get him out of here," Black said in French with vehemence in his voice.

Jean Luc dragged the body to the corridor where it was unceremoniously dropped. Signaling for two men who were passing by, Jean Luc ordered them to dispose of the body.

In the cabin, Black took Aubrey to the settee and settled her there.

"Here then, let me see. Are you hurt anywhere?" He tried to look her over but she pushed him away, trying to hold the torn clothing together to cover herself. He surveyed the damage as she fumbled with it. The dress was torn beyond repair. Casting his eyes about the floor, he noted that the tiny buttons were strewn everywhere. Aubrey wore undergarments, but the chemise had been ripped at one shoulder as well, leaving her uncomfortably exposed.

"I am afraid that we will have to find something else for you to wear, Precieux, your pretty green dress is no good now," Black said easily. Aubrey gave him a look that hinted of tears.

"Are you injured anywhere?" Black asked.

"My head hurts a little from when he knocked me down," she said, quietly rubbing at the back of her head with a free hand. He looked her over objectively.

"The cabin boy on board, Henri, is about your size in body, though a bit taller. Perhaps we can get him to donate some clothing to you."

"Boy's clothing?" she whispered hoarsely.

"I am afraid so," he replied with a chuckle.

The cabin boy brought her britches and a shirt. Black moved to his desk and sat down while Aubrey changed behind the dressing screen. Black was surprised when she came to stand very near his desk, her hands wringing nervously as hazel eyes darted around the room.

"You are not going to leave me alone anymore, are you?"

"Well, there are times when I must," he replied as he stood.

"Please take me to Africa–or back to England," she pleaded.

He folded her into his arms and was surprised when she actually leaned into him slightly. Stroking her hair, he smiled, "We will not be taking you to Africa and I do not want to hear that request anymore. Africa is an untamed land; it is no place for a young woman alone."

"Neither is this place," she muttered, pushing away from him.

"We will not go back to England, either. That would be unwise," he replied.

"Why?" she squeaked.

"You will stay with me and that is final. The King would like nothing better than to stretch our necks and hang us all in the gibbet. We have spoken about all of this before," he replied as Aubrey flounced to the settee. A knock at the door broke the silence of the room.

"Entre," Black called as he reseated himself.

The door swung open and Jean Luc stood in the doorway, with a chart in his hand, "I thought that since we were unable to finish up on deck, you might want to work on the course now." His voice was quiet and calm as his blue eyes shifted from Black to Aubrey.

Black nodded and took out a bottle of wine and poured three glasses, "Bon. Mademoiselle Aubrey was just expressing her apprehensions about being left alone."

Aubrey started at the mention of her own name in the French conversation. Black handed Jean Luc two glasses of the wine, one of which he promptly took to Aubrey on the settee.

"Mademoiselle," Jean Luc smiled. Reaching out with a tentative hand, she took the offered libation. Their eyes met for an instant and that instant burned into his soul as he raised his glass to her and took a sip.

His personal moment was disturbed by Black's voice. "Put your charts out here."

Jean Luc turned from her and went to the table. As he spread the chart, he glanced up at his captain. "Would it not be polite for us to speak in English, Rene? She does not speak the language." The dark eye bore into him.

Black was not a man who liked to be told what to do or to even take gentle hints or suggestions. Jean Luc's own stare matched that of the captain's. His will was strong too and he thought nothing of his casual remarks and suggestions to the man. They had known one another for many years in friendship, in battle and, in times of sorrow. Black downed the contents of his glass and set it aside purposefully.

"She will learn."

"But until she does," Jean Luc countered.

Black chuckled, "Have you appointed yourself as her personal teacher? Am I to understand that you would take on the responsibility of taking care of her in my absence?" The questions came with underlying tones of suspicion. Many a man had been killed outright in the past for attempting to take a woman brought on board for the captain, or even becoming politely friendly with her. The men of the crew were expected by Black to respect the position of the captain's woman on the ship and protect her without return of favors. To come too close was a death sentence.

Jean Luc took up his glass and finished his wine, his blue eyes taking a fleeting glance at her. He would love to be her personal teacher and he would love to take care of her. Quite frankly, his feelings for her ran so deep that the threat of death from this man who stood before him, friend or captain, did not bother him in the least.

Leaning back over the charts without looking up, he drew a line and replied with a tone of unconcern in English, "If the captain orders it."

"The quartermaster does many tasks," Black chuckled in French as he patted Jean Luc on the shoulder.

"It does not include," Jean Luc began in French now as he shot another glance at Aubrey for effect, then finished, "Being a nursemaid."

Black laughed heartily at the comment and sat in his chair at the end of the table, propping his right foot up on another chair. Jean Luc glanced back at him and chuckled as well.

Aubrey sat on the settee trying to ignore them. The boy's clothing felt odd on her. She noticed the buttons from her dress strewn on the floor. Saddened over the loss of her first real womanly dress, she slipped easily to the floor on her hands and knees to retrieve the tiny treasures. Black and Jean Luc turned to watch her.

Repositioning himself over the table, Jean Luc had now afforded himself the opportunity to appear to be looking intently at the charts while stealing glances at her and taking in the curves of her body in the boy's clothing. She seemed lost in her own little world as she reclaimed a handful of the tiny buttons, then sat for a few moments. She sighed deeply for it was the only thing that she had of her own. Jean Luc saw her look around the room as if searching for something else.

"Captain Black?" she asked quietly.

"Oui?" Black asked from his chair.

"May I have a piece of that string?" she asked as she pointed tentatively to the desk to indicate a ball of twine amid the logbook and other items.

"Oui," he nodded as he poured more wine for himself before he stood and drew his dirk as he walked to the desk. Jean Luc watched her while the man cut a length of the twine for her.

"Merci," she said meekly as he handed it to her.

Appearing happy now, she moved to the quarter gallery and sat up on the sill. Looking at her in a stolen glance, Jean Luc saw the remorse on her countenance as she carefully strung the buttons on the twine. He noted also that she was drawing further into herself, separating herself from them and the world around her.

Later in the day, Black brought her up onto the deck. She stood at the nearby railing as he had moved to discuss ships business with Jean Luc. Finished with that task a moment later, Black approached her from behind, speaking to her as he drew near.

"You will get used to your new life," he told her. She shivered at the thought.

"Are you cold? Let me warm you," he said softly as he stepped in closer and put his arms around her from behind. She crimsoned in embarrassment as he pressed against her and laid his cheek against hers. He held her at the wrists as her arms were crossed over her chest, "There, is that warmer?" he asked close to her ear. She looked down, quite unsure how to react to this. Da had said that pirates would put people overboard if they did not cooperate. She watched the water as it coursed by, thinking about this. She could not swim.

"Yes, it is warmer, sir, but my feet are cold," she replied meekly.

He pulled her closer. "Je regrette, we do not have a pair of boots for your little feet. Perhaps later." He was enjoying this quiet reserve. Black closed his eye as the warm soft body against his and the feel of the ship under his feet brought back a flood of memories. Jean Luc stepped up, speaking in French, breaking into Black's thoughts.

"Rene, there is a ship ahead to our port; she flies the Union Jack."

"Are you certain to what she is this time?" Black asked in annoyance.

"Oui, Rene, I have seen it with my own eyes," Jean Luc growled.

"See, I told you that she was British," Black said arrogantly.

"Oui, Rene," Jean Luc nodded with a small look of annoyance.

"Warship or merchant?" Black asked, still holding Aubrey. She was trying gingerly, yet insistently now to release herself from his grip. It embarrassed her to be in this position in front of someone else.

She cast a nervous glance at Jean Luc who returned an indifferent look;

he answered with his own arrogance, "She is a frigate, Rene. One of the men has identified her as the *H.M.S. Bynum.*"

Black nuzzled Aubrey's hair and she shivered at the touch. He stood quietly in place for a time as if in deep thought.

"Fulford's ship. He carries thirty guns on board." Black finally said as he looked at Jean Luc with a gleam in his eye. Glancing up at the British flag that they flew from their own mast, he said, "Allow him to come closer. Man the guns, but do so quietly." He dropped one of Aubrey's wrists and brought his free hand up to the side of her face. Stroking her cheek with his thumb, he added in English, "Just as he is alongside, replace the Union Jack with our flag." He kissed Aubrey's cheek lightly.

Jean Luc turned from them to call the orders in a low tone of voice. The sight of her in Black's arms made him livid. Then turning back, he said, "Should she not be taken below, where it will be safer?"

"I will look to her safety, Monsieur. Tend to your orders," Black replied stiffly as Aubrey managed to twist free. The two Frenchmen seemed to be perturbed with one another.

"I am warm now, sir," she reported. With her back to Black, she did not see his look as he stared intently on her auburn hair. Not dark hair, not her, because of Fulford, he thought as his gaze shifted to the approaching British frigate.

"You must come below with me now," he began in English as he released her.

"Why? What have I done?" she asked alarmed, not understanding his abruptness.

"We are about to engage an old friend of mine who is a crafty fellow and I would prefer you were in the cabin."

She quickly scanned the deck around them; cannons were being rolled into place and arms were being passed out to the men. She looked up at the flag on the mast. "You fly the British flag. Why would the Captain of that ship fight with another British ship?"

"Because as he pulls alongside, we will change the flag so that he knows who we really are," Black smiled as he gently pulled her along.

"A trick?" she asked incredulously.

"Oui. That is what we do best," he nodded.

"Will you sink them, too?" she asked thinking back to the *Gull.*

He smiled broadly and with a twinkle in his eye he said, "Oh, most definitely, Mademoiselle. Captain Fulford imprisoned me over a year ago, which caused me to lose something very dear. He will pay for that loss." He seemed to have slipped into a reverie for a few moments. She frowned as he

71

sent her down the companionway ahead of him. Perhaps that man caused the unfortunate accident that had taken the sight of one of Captain Black's eyes, she thought to herself.

In the cabin, Black checked his weapons, then looking up, he told her firmly, "Stay in the cabin until I return."

"That is what the steward said to me when he left me in the closet on the *Gull*. He did not return," she said quietly.

"I will be back, and when I return, we will celebrate the death of an enemy." He smiled as he pulled the door closed behind him with a bang.

Aubrey looked out the quarter gallery window. The approaching British frigate was smaller than the *Widow Maker* and she could make out the uniformed sailors on board. When the *H.M.S. Bynum* was only halfway to the point of being parallel to the *Widow Maker*, she noted several of the sailors pointing frantically to the sky. She recognized the looks in their eyes all too well, having seen it on the faces of the men on the *Gull* the day they had come into the path of this ship.

There was a loud slamming sound of wood against wood as the port doors to the cannons were dropped almost in unison on the pirate ship. In the next instant, the cannons on that side of the ship erupted with deafening blasts, one right after the other. The force rocked the ship and Aubrey's feet went out from under her. She hit the floor on her bottom heavily but was back up in an instant, scrambling to the window ledge and rubbing the paining spot on her rump.

Men were running on the decks of the British ship. She saw a door drop open at the stern of the ship and the barrel of a cannon peeped out. Another blast from the rear of Black's ship went forth and Aubrey watched in horror as the newly exposed cannon of the *H.M.S. Bynum* was literally blasted from its place and it tumbled backward into the ship.

Aubrey slipped to the floor, covering her ears with her hands to try and shut out the awful noise. Huddled against the bulkhead under the windows, she squeezed her eyes tightly shut, remembering the *Gull*. Beneath her the ship shuddered with each barrage of reverberating cannon fire. The sound seemed to go on forever.

Black returned to the great cabin, unscathed and smiling triumphantly. Aubrey was still on the floor as Jean Luc entered behind him and shut the door. Slowly, she stood up and watched in disbelief as Black seemed to burst with excitement.

"That was excellent! He never saw it coming, never had time to react," Black chuckled as he poured drinks for himself and his quartermaster.

Jean Luc took the glass with a smile and a nod, "Retribution has been paid."

Aubrey watched the two men as they reveled in their excitement of the battle. Cautiously she commented, "But people died. Your attack has impacted on their lives both here and those of their loved ones."

Black graced her with a cold steely glare and the tone of his voice caused her blood to turn to ice water.

"Indeed, just as Fulford impacted on my life that fateful day." Then he quickly downed the contents of his glass and turned away from her. Jean Luc's blue eyes darted from his captain to Aubrey but he remained quiet. There was a knowing look on his face as Aubrey looked at Jean Luc now and frowned at him in question.

"You will get used to your new life," Black said suddenly and informatively as he poured more wine.

"Will I?" she asked thickly.

You will have to, Jean Luc thought as he watched her beautiful face trying to understand what was happening around her now. Blinking and frowning, Aubrey moved to lower herself onto the settee.

Chapter 12

A fortnight had passed since the sinking of the *H.M.S. Bynum* and the *Widow Maker* now drifted lazily on the currents. Occasionally Black would spend some time in the cabin with Aubrey, teaching her quick phrases and short commands in French. He seemed pleased when she caught on quickly and praised her for her accomplishments. But there were times Aubrey thought that he was lost in thought. Whatever it was on his mind, he seemed saddened enough that he abruptly stopped the lessons.

In her boredom, Aubrey had begun to devour all the books that she was able to read on the shelves of Black's cabin. Sitting tucked back into the corner of the settee with her bare feet flat on the cushions and the book propped on her raised knees, Aubrey was engrossed in a book about tropical islands and their inhabitants. The descriptive pages painted vivid pictures in her mind of places and peoples that were foreign and exciting to her.

Black came into the cabin, leaving the door open as he tossed his gloves on the table. He crossed to his desk and lay down his hat and pistols, then unbuckled his baldric and laid it down as well. He stood in the center of the room and looked at her in contemplation for a few moments. She glanced up at him from her reading, but the book was so interesting that she quickly went back into the depths of it, ignoring him. Suddenly, he was on the edge of the settee, trapping her. His advance was quick as he brushed his lips against the side of her face.

With smooth swiftness, he plucked the book from her hands saying easily in his deep voice, "Visit with me."

Aubrey squirmed nervously in his arm as he pulled her closer and down onto her back between him and the back of the settee. He pressed her mouth in a kiss and he felt her give in slightly to the embrace. It pleased him that she seemed to finally relax in the few encounters and he smiled down on her as he slowly broke from the kiss. The hazel eyes looked at him with uncertainty and he was mildly puzzled as he stared into the young face under him.

Like a dark shroud, a fog of uncertainty came over him as well. He took a deep breath and shook his head slightly to shake the feeling as he resettled the upper part of his lean frame a bit more to drape over her upper torso. Black could feel her trembling under him and he smiled down at her. "Why do you tremble so? There is nothing to be frightened of," he said as he began to kiss the side of her neck and untie the strings that closed her shirt. "I am not going to hurt you," he cooed against her skin as he worked his kisses down into the front of the shirt.

Aubrey pushed at his upper arms and pressed herself against the cushions of the settee. "Stop."

"Pourquoi?" he asked with a chuckle as he raised his head to look at her.

"Because I..." she muttered nervously as their eyes met.

That 'uncertain' sensation came over Black once more and he drew back a bit to look her over. The auburn hair caught his eye and he inhaled deeply. This was not what he wanted today. With determination to clear his head of the memories, he pushed aside the feeling again. What in the world was wrong with him? He had a beautiful young woman right here, very nearly in position for the taking–but he also had this nagging feeling of doubt.

"I enjoy your–company. You smell nice and you feel nice. If you would just relax, you would enjoy it, too," he purred to her in his deep voice. It was as if he was trying to talk himself into the encounter rather than her. Black dipped his face once more into the recesses of the front of her shirt and she emitted a small whimper of distress.

The quietness of the room was disrupted by the sound of someone clearing their throat. Aubrey jumped at the sound and let out a squeak of alarm. Black exhaled hard once more and dropped his forehead down upon her collarbone. Not looking toward the person who made the sound, he asked in a tone that denoted tiredness, "What is it?"

Aubrey's worried hazel eyes peered off to the side to see who had come like a guardian angel to disturb the captain in this, her stressful moment.

Jean Luc stood in the doorway with his hat in his hands as he reported in easy French, "There is a ship coming up on us from the starboard aft."

Aubrey looked now to the man over her for he had raised his head. She watched him roll his eye in annoyance as he said, "Do you recognize her?"

"Non, but she flies the Union Jack." Jean Luc reported further.

"Ame damne, they are like a plague drifting upon the seas," Black muttered. He straightened up from his semi-reclining position over Aubrey and pulled the strings of her shirt closed. He tied them into a neat bow as he replied, "I will be there directly."

"Aye, Captain," Jean Luc nodded, meeting eyes with Aubrey as she sat up slowly, then turning from the doorway to go back up on deck. Black looked back to her and Aubrey watched him worriedly. He was angry with her.

"You are very timid," he muttered as he stood to go to the desk and put on his baldric. She glanced out the windows of the quarter gallery and she could see the ship in the distance. Perhaps he would not be so angry if she

75

were to show him some degree of bravery somewhere.

"May I go with you?" she asked quickly. He chuckled at her as he tucked away his two pistols.

"Go where?"

"Topside, sir. I want to see the ship."

"Very well then, Mademoiselle, perhaps this will toughen you up." He nodded with the same smile as he picked up his hat and started out the door. He pointed to the table. "Bring my gloves."

"Oui, monsieur," she nodded as she grabbed them in her hand on the way to the door.

Jean Luc was surprised when Aubrey came out onto the deck behind Black, willingly.

"What is she doing out here, Rene?" he growled in French.

"She asked to come." The dark haired man shrugged as he took the long glass from Jean Luc's hands to look at the ship that came up upon them. He chuckled deep in his throat and handed the glass back to his quartermaster. With a slight turn of his body towards Aubrey he then said, "Well Precieux, you picked a good day to come up on deck for a lesson. This should be easy, this one looks a bit wet behind the ears."

"He is manning his guns," Jean Luc reported as he watched the ship through the glass.

"Oui, so he is," Black said chuckling. "Even though we fly his flag—he does not trust his own kind," Black added in an arrogant British accent to which Jean Luc chuckled in reply. Turning to his head gunner, Black said calmly, "Fire a warning shot across his bow. Let him think that we do not trust him either—even as kindred countrymen." With a quick glance at Aubrey, Black continued loudly, "I have some unexpended energy today. I think that we will engage him just for sport."

The men nearby laughed heartily at the joke. One of the deck guns reported loudly as the shot was fired. Aubrey's mouth dropped open as she watched the bow spirit of the British ship fall away by the blast. Perhaps this was not such a good test of her courage after all! Backing away, she turned to leave for the companionway steps. A firm hand caught her by the upper arm and she was suddenly facing Black again.

"Where are you going?" he purred with a smile as he plucked his gloves from her hands and pulled her up so that her back was against his chest.

"I–I want to go below," she stammered.

"Oh no, Precieux, you said that you wanted to be up here," he said matter-of-factly as he held her with his upper arms pressed into her shoulders and put on his gloves while she squirmed.

"The first shot has been fired, Mademoiselle, we are committed now. All who are on deck must stay and participate in the battle. N'est-ce pas, Monsieur Pierne?" he asked. Jean Luc made a face and pursed his lips as he looked at Aubrey pressed against Black.

"Oui, Captain."

Men in uniform were scrambling on the deck of the other ship. Jean Luc cast an angry eye to Black then down at Aubrey, saying tightly in French, "But she needs to be below, Rene. She has no part in this business."

The British ship returned fire from a small cannon. It fell short of its mark, but water sprayed up over the gunwale hitting Aubrey, Black and Jean Luc. Aubrey gasped and pressed herself tighter against Black's chest. He laughed heartily and cupped her chin in his hand, "Will you get in my pocket, Precieux?"

"I want to go below," she murmured.

"Non," he said firmly to her. Then he turned with the same firmness and shouted to his gunner, "Fire!"

Aubrey did not want to witness another sinking. Another shot crashed through the starboard gunwale of the British ship as she pulled up just off the port side of the *Widow Maker*.

"This little man is very brave. Look how close he gets," Black muttered to Jean Luc as he held a struggling Aubrey.

"Very brave or very stupid," Jean Luc growled.

"Well, let us think about whom we speak, mon ami." The two men shared a chuckle. Aubrey saw nothing funny in whatever it was they were saying. She continued to struggle against Black's grasp.

"Hold your fire a moment s'il vous plait, Monsieur Boulet," Black called down to the head gunner. "I think the little boy wants to say something to us," he added almost thoughtfully as he nodded toward the British ship.

"I am Captain Andrew Johnstone. By order of His Majesty the King, I order you to stand down and surrender your vessel," called the young British captain.

Black snorted, then, glancing at Jean Luc, muttered, "What an ass." Looking back at the British ship, Black called out, "Now why would you make such foolish demands on a ship flying your colors?" He made no pains to hide his accent even though Britain and France were not on the best of terms these days.

Johnstone rolled his eyes and looked at Black stoically, replying, "I do not believe that your ship is British, sir."

"She needs to go below," Jean Luc hissed referring to the still struggling

77

Aubrey.

"Chut, Jean Luc," Black growled. Looking to the sails, Black called, "He does not believe that we are British, monsieurs! Let him see who we really are. Show him our colors!" The young captain did not expect to see the black flag but he remained undaunted.

"Hmm, look how brave he is," Black cooed into Aubrey's ear.

"Set the woman free and you and your men will be spared," the captain called out.

"Do you suppose that he means to be your little knight in shining armor?" Black whispered.

"Spare the shot and bring out the rope? You go to hell, you British bastard!" Boulet yelled back from his position behind a cannon with a torch in his hand prepared to ignite the fuse at the command of his captain.

Aubrey struggled against Black's grip but he held her all the tighter, "Be still, Precieux, you are alarming the little sailor. He thinks that you do not want to stay with us."

The British captain looked pointedly at Aubrey and shouted over, "Let your prisoner go, or I will blast you out of the water and take her."

Black laughed heartily, "Blast me out of the water and then do what? Pluck her dead body from the wreckage?" Aubrey whimpered in fear and struggled all the more against his grip.

"Arrête!" Black hissed down to her, his tone making Aubrey still instantly.

"Rene," Jean Luc said tightly out of the corner of his mouth.

"Non, Monsieur, she stays with me," Black called back as he looked at the officer, then cut his eye to Jean Luc as if he were speaking to both of them.

"You will be tried for kidnapping as well as the demise of the merchant we saw wreckage from sometime back, sir," the man warned.

"Indeed? And how do you know that it was this ship that sunk that vessel? What proof do you have?" Black laughed.

"You have one of her passengers," the man called back condescendingly. Black laughed again.

"Vraiment? Why, my dear captain, you do not even know this young woman. Check if you make it back to England, her name is on no manifest."

Aubrey eyes dropped to the deck. She had been very stupid in running away that morning–especially the way she had accomplished it. As she had told Black and his quartermaster the first night aboard, no one knew where she was–and true, her name was on no manifest.

The British captain's voice drew her back and he questioned her, "Is this true?"

Aubrey hesitated in her reply and then she finally nodded her head in agreement to Black's claim.

"All of this is irrelevant; she is obviously your prisoner from wherever she comes. By the Crown, I order you to stand down, release her and surrender your ship," the young upstart said proudly.

Black rolled his eye and muttered, "This little man is annoying."

The British captain turned to call a command to his gunners and smoke belched from one of the cannons near him. The ball cut through the railing near the stern of the *Widow Maker*. Wood splinters showered the deck. Aubrey cried out and turned her face into Black's chest. He shielded her head with his gloved hand and made a face at the gaping hole in the railing of his ship.

"The little son of a bitch," he growled.

"What did you think he would do, Rene? Say 'Well please, forgive me sir, but I see that you have a prisoner there and she wants to stay with you. I guess I will just be sailing merrily along'?" Jean Luc spat in French. Black looked at him in disbelief, then chuckled. Raising his hand from Aubrey's head he waved it to Boulet.

Fire was touched to the fuse and the cannon belched smoke and fire. Aubrey watched as a large section of the British ship's railing was blown away. The men on that ship scrambled to the commands to tack away and make distance. Black's men jeered and laughed from their places on the ratlines and on the decks. Aubrey struggled frantically now and Black grunted at her sudden surge of energy to be free.

"Rene, she needs to go below. She is not," Jean Luc began but caught himself.

The dark eye turned on him with a scowl. Nearly shoving Aubrey to Jean Luc, Black growled, "Take her below, Jean Luc. I cannot fight properly with her in my pocket." Then he turned to Boulet and pointed to the British ship, saying with a great deal of annoyance, "Put him and his little ship on the bottom. He is boring me."

"I was hoping you would say that, Captain. Merde! I was bored a long time ago." Boulet smiled evilly as he touched fire to the fuse of another waiting cannon.

The percussion of the cannon made Aubrey feel as though her chest was going to explode as well. She screamed and broke away from the hold Jean Luc had on her. Taking off in a dead run, she headed for the companionway.

"Get her," Black ordered irritably. Jean Luc caught up with her in a few strides, then was pummeled with her fists as he took hold of her. Glancing from the British ship to his quartermaster struggling with the little fighting bundle, Black called out, "Jean Luc! Stop playing with her and get her below!"

"That is what I am trying to do, Rene," Jean Luc growled through clenched teeth. He finally scooped a fighting Aubrey up into his arms, scolding her, "Come along now. It is your own fault for being so foolish to want to come out in the first place." Then he chuckled and said closely in her ear, "Not that I am not enjoying it, of course." Aubrey stopped struggling and looked at him in alarm. With another chuckle, he set her firmly on her feet and gave her a little shove into the cabin.

Blast after blast reverberated from above. Jean Luc started to turn away but her voice stopped him.

"Please, do not leave me here alone, Monsieur Pierne," she gasped.

"I must go back on deck. You will be fine." Looking down into the frightened hazel eyes, he wanted to pull her up and kiss her. Would she tell Black if he did? Would he be able to stop himself with just one kiss?

"Go and sit down," he ordered instead, as he pushed her toward the settee. Aubrey frowned at him as he turned away to open the door which had swung shut with the rocking of the ship.

"I do not have to take orders from you."

A smile spread across his lips at her retort and said, "Everyone on board does."

"Not the captain," she reminded sharply.

"Corriger, Mademoiselle," he nodded, still not turning. The cannons reported from above and the ship rocked.

Aubrey stumbled a bit with the movement of the floor under her feet. Then she stepped forward bravely. "Not me."

Jean Luc chuckled towards the door and said in English, "You do, if the captain orders it." With that, he went out the door.

Black played with the British ship and her inexperienced captain until he finally became totally bored with it all and turned the battle over to a happy and willing Boulet. The master gunner made short work of the British ship and the men laughed and joked about the day's 'fun' as they cleaned up the cannon deck and reset the cannon with shot and powder.

Black returned to the cabin with a satisfied smile on his face as if he had been to port with a woman for the last few hours. His energy had been expelled and he was ready for a drink. Jean Luc came close on his heels and shut the door behind them.

"These British officers, they get younger and younger. Is the Crown so desperate for a Navy that they send farm boys out to do a seafaring man's job?" Black complained as he poured drinks for them.

"Well Rene, with the rapidity with which you blow them out of the water, I would imagine that England hardly has enough time to take the boys from mother's milk to the service!" Jean Luc chuckled as he accepted the drink.

In the melee outside of Black's crew overtaking the British ship and then sinking her, Aubrey had slumped to the settee, hugging her pillow. The stress was unbearable. She had tucked herself down into the corner of the settee with the pillow and blanket up over her head to try and shut out the terrible noise. Aubrey had lain so long in her hiding place, with her eyes shut tightly and her hands over her ears, that she fell asleep from the exhaustion of it all when the sea had finally fallen quiet again.

"Look here. You were worried about her," Black began as he sipped his drink and went to stand beside her. He reached out and stroked her hair that peeped out of the covers with his hand.

"The sounds of battle have rocked her to peaceful sleep." At the touch of his hand, Aubrey came up off the settee like a shot, wide-eyed and gasping in fear. Black was forced to move back with a slight start at her outburst.

Jean Luc sat perched with one hip up on the corner of the table, idly swinging a booted foot. "Oh, yes, Rene, I can see how very peaceful she is." His tone was condescending.

Black made a face at him and waved him off with his hand, asking of Aubrey, "Did you have a nice nap?"

"Nap?" Aubrey spat in alarm. She looked out the quarter gallery windows. The swirling water in the wake of the *Widow Maker* was littered with debris, some of which was still burning. There were bodies floating in the water as well. She crossed her arms over her chest, hugging herself, and muttered, "I will never get used to all of this. It is cruel and ugly."

Black chuckled at her soft spoken comment and he raised his glass, "Would you care for some wine, Precieux? It, like the victory today–is sweet." Aubrey merely glared at him. She had no idea how very cruel and ugly this new world would prove to be.

Chapter 13

The next morning, heavy clouds hung low over the dark water and it had been raining steadily since before dawn. Black had awakened early as usual. He looked across the room at the settee as he dressed. Aubrey was still asleep, with her back to him, nestled under the blanket. He wondered to himself why he was being so patient with this one. It was usually not his nature. He guessed it was because she was so innocent and apparently had been very sheltered in her younger years. Black smiled to himself sadly. That was not true. What he really wanted more than anything else was the woman he had on board before this one. He lowered himself into the chair at his desk and looked across the room, out the window at the pouring rain. His mind drifted back to another time, a little more than two years ago.

On their way to Martinique, a French occupied island in the group of the Windward Islands, the lookout had spied a slave ship flying the British flag on a Northward heading. She was recognized as the *Dodger* under the command of a Captain Troy. Black had ordered a change in flag on his own ship because they sometimes carried cargo other than slaves. With the British flag on her mast, the *Widow Maker* was mistaken as a merchant vessel from England and was able to come alongside very close to the slave ship.

After a confrontation with the captain, Black finally killed the man, then had ordered his men to board the slave ship and strip her of anything of value. After engaging in a fight and killing a man who was guarding slaves, Jean Luc had taken men and gone further into the hold where he discovered a beautiful island woman who was chained to the wall apart from the rest of the slaves. She was suffering from dehydration and had been severely beaten with a cat-o-nine. Jean Luc sent one of his men back to the *Widow Maker* to summon Black while he unchained the young woman.

The moment Rene Black stepped into the tiny prison and laid eyes on the semiconscious woman lying in the lap of his quartermaster, he was captivated. Taking her up into his arms, Black carried her to his quarters on the *Widow Maker*. The *Dodger* was stripped of all other valuables and promptly set on fire. The slaves, numbering only about twenty were put in the hold of the *Widow Maker* where they would have the choice of joining her crew or they would be put off safely at the next stop, thus giving them their freedom.

With the help of a Jamaican on his ship who knew of medicines and herbs, Black had taken great pains to see that the young woman was fed, provided decent clothing, and her wounds were tended to. At first she did not speak though he tried to engage her in conversation as Black himself spent long hours tending to her wounds.

When she regained enough strength to sit up, they shared dinner, wine and conversation in his cabin. By night, he would entertain her as if she were a queen. He told her all about his ship and about the prizes he had taken in his years at pirating. He would pour her wine and watch her eat with breathless fascination, sometimes not even eating his own meal. He was completely taken by her beauty.

On nights when he and Jean Luc would have ship's business to tend to, she would sit quietly and read from his library. Once Jean Luc had commented to him that either the young woman was a very slow reader or she was actually listening to them intently as they poured over charts. Jean Luc had also pointed out to Black how she watched the men as they worked on the deck.

When he realized that she could speak French, Black learned that the slave ship captain had taken her against her will from her home village on the island of St. Lucia in the Caribbean. Knowing the British and their fear of her culture, she had told Black how she had chanted incantations from her beliefs. She had hoped that it would frighten the captain of the *Dodger* into sending her back with the other slaves untouched. Unfortunately, she had only managed to frighten him into thinking that she was a witch and suffered under the lash. She was then chained in the deepest recesses of the ship with no food or water.

The captain told her that she would be executed when they reached the next port. However, when a hurricane had overtaken the *Dodger*, and nearly sunk her, the captain blamed the misfortune on her. He told his crew that she had put a curse on them. It was voted among them that she should be disposed of before any further misfortune befell the ship. They were prepared to hang her when Black's ship was sighted.

She was hidden from sight but Jean Luc had found her, nearly dead from her ordeal. Black had been glad that he had happened on the *Dodger* and he laughed at the stupidity of the British captain and his crew. He offered his bed to the beautiful young woman while he slept on the very settee that Aubrey now lay nestled in.

Every moment that she was apart from him on the deck, he would find himself watching her in extreme fascination. He treasured her company every moment of his free time and had schooled her on the workings of his ship. He and Jean Luc were surprised at her intelligence and her ability to learn quickly.

Then one night as he settled himself onto the settee, she came to him. Taking him by the hand, she led him to his bunk. The love they had made those days and nights had been overwhelming to him. Black had never felt so strongly for a woman before. But then, in the height of his bliss, he had to leave her behind. The parting had torn a deep wound in his heart because he could only blame himself for what happened next. Fulford imprisoned him and because he could not return for her, she had died.

Staring out the window and thinking of long sessions of lovemaking they had shared, Black's lips moved as he whispered her name. He closed his eye and there she was, smiling at him. Suddenly his reverie was broken as Aubrey stirred in her sleep. He watched her turn onto her back, stretch and inhale. He inhaled deeply himself to clear his mind of his memories. He knew Aubrey would never match the passion of his island beauty. Looking at her, Black knew she was only a diversion. No other woman had ever been able to satiate him in the same way as his dark haired island woman.

He could tell that Aubrey lingered in that abyss between deep sleep and waking. The covers were not tucked around her well anymore and he could see just the hint of bare leg peeping out. Her auburn hair was disheveled and his silk shirt that she wore as a nightgown molded to her body like a layer of second skin. Maybe some time with her would put his yearnings to rest for a while.

He rose from the chair and quietly approached the sofa kneeling easily beside her resting form. With the brush of his lips against her cheek, Aubrey opened sleepy eyes and looked at him. He was pleased that she did not seem startled and try to move away from him as she usually did.

He stroked her hair into place, speaking in a near whisper, "Bonjour, did you sleep well?"

"Oui, I–slept fine," she replied meekly attempting to pull the covers up over herself.

He easily caught her hand, "Leave them, it is not cold in here." He deliberately, yet slowly ducked his head into the recesses of her throat and kissed her neck. He slowly began to work his caresses downward. He trailed his fingers along the exposed part of her leg to her mid-thigh. She tensed and caught his hand.

"I should get dressed." Her voice was quiet. Black drew back and looked at her. He would gladly take her right now; the urge was strong today. He knew if he did it would probably have to be by force, and he did not want it that way. To lay Aubrey down gently and imagine for but a fleeting moment

84

that he was with his island beauty again might soothe his troubled mind.

"Very well," he said with a sigh as he stood and moved away from her. She sat up slowly, watching him all the while. He was disappointed in her, but this business of kissing and stroking was still very new to her. His caresses made her feel strange and it was quite unnerving. She had never experienced those types of feelings before and she had never been as close as this to a man before. She went behind the dressing screen and quickly changed her clothes.

When she emerged, he was sitting at his desk, writing in his logbook. She timidly approached the desk but he seemed to be ignoring her. It was a game for him that he did on purpose to see how close she would come on her own. She came all the way around the desk this time and stood beside his chair. To his great surprise, she lightly put her hand on his shoulder, "I am sorry if I angered you, sir, but..."

Let us see how far she will go today, he thought to himself as he continued to write and not look up at her. She pressed her hand a bit harder, "Captain, I said, I am sorry." He still ignored her, smiling inwardly. She exhaled in exasperation and removed her hand from his shoulder. As she turned to leave the desk, he reached out and caught her by the sleeve, holding her there.

"Je regrette. The words are je regrette," he said softly. Aubrey turned to look at him.

"Je regrette, Captain Black. I do not mean to anger you. I just..."

Still not looking up from his book he said quietly, "Sit down here with me. We will study your lessons for the day." She pulled up a chair and sat next to him to begin her French lesson for the day.

He would say a phrase and she would repeat it, then he would write it for her to read and copy. They had been working for about an hour when there was a knock at the door and Black called for the person to enter.

Aubrey looked up to find that it was the quartermaster. When his blue eyes met her gaze, she quickly looked down, blushing in embarrassment. He was very handsome and sometimes the way he looked at her made her feel strange inside. She tried to concentrate on the phrase she was writing.

"What can I do for you, Monsieur Pierne?" Black asked in their native tongue as he leaned closer to Aubrey and wrote two more phrases on her paper then nodded for her to continue her studies. Frowning at the paper, she proceeded to quietly mouth the words he had written.

Jean Luc watched her lips in fascination as she attempted to form the French words. To kiss those lips would be heaven. Shaking himself mentally from the sight, he said stiffly, "The weather has not hindered our progress on our course. We are making good time. Also, our fresh water supply has been increased with this rain," he reported, but Black was not looking at him.

Jean Luc glanced around the room to see that Black's bunk was unmade and his heart skipped a beat. Was Black bedding her now? But then he noticed that the covers were only disheveled on one side of the bunk. He cast a quick glance at the settee–blanket and pillows lay there, still ruffled from sleep. He released a slow sigh of relief. She was still sleeping on the settee.

Black looked up in time to see Jean Luc's perusal of the room. Smiling at Aubrey, he tapped at the lines he had written and instructed, "Say those phrases, Precieux."

In the best French she could manage she read the lines, her voice innocent, "My name is Aubrey, I am the Captain's lady. I am the Lady of the *Widow Maker*."

Jean Luc rolled his eyes to the heavens as Black looked up at him from the desk with a look of victory in his eye.

"Does she know what goes with the title, Rene?" Jean Luc quipped sarcastically in their language, knowing that she could not understand them.

"She will," Black smirked back as he ran his hand down over her back. Jean Luc saw her give a slight shudder at the touch as the man's hand neared her bottom.

"Will there be anything else, Monsieur Pierne?" he asked curtly.

"Non,"came the disgruntled reply. Jean Luc cast one last glance at Aubrey.

Turning to leave, he stopped when Black said in French, "I will be going off the ship tomorrow when we put in to port. As always, you will be in charge. I expect you to see to our guest's safety." Black was standing now and idly moving things around on the desk before him. He gently took the writing instrument from Aubrey's hand in the middle of her writing. She looked up at him in concern, his tone of voice sounded authoritative, had she done something wrong? She looked at the other man. Jean Luc was turned to face them, and he was looking from Black to her warily.

"So now I am to be the nursemaid after all, by your command," Jean Luc said with a smile.

Black returned the smile, "I told you, the quartermaster has many duties."

"As you wish, Rene," Jean Luc said respectfully. He turned on his heel and left the cabin. Once in the corridor, he put his hat and gloves on. Letting out a long exasperated breath, he then smiled. If only Rene knew how happy he had just made him with the task of watching over her.

After Jean Luc had left the cabin, Aubrey looked at Black in question, "Am I not doing well?"

"You are doing very well, but you really must relax," he began as he pulled her to her feet and wrapped his arms easily around her small waist. She quickly looked down and grasped his forearms, trying to hold herself at a distance from him.

"This is exactly what I mean. You are the Captain's lady, you said so yourself. You need to conduct yourself as such," he said firmly. He bent his head towards hers as she glanced up him nervously. Mustering all the courage she had, she turned her face up to his and accepted the kiss he gave her.

"Très bien." There was a smile in his tone. He heard the ship's bell toll twice for 9am.

"Well, it has just occurred to me that you and I have not had any breakfast yet. Why did you not say something?" He released her but she remained where she was.

"I was not hungry," she finally stammered.

"Nonsense, you barely ate at dinner last night. Come along, we will see what Cook has to offer. The galley should be empty and we will have it all to ourselves."

She closed her eyes slowly and then opened them. "I can eat in here."

"You will come with me," he said firmly as he took her by the hand and they left the cabin. Once in the corridor, he released her and she followed him toward the galley. The damp, yet fresh air, from above decks washed down the corridor. He strode on ahead of her and she was hard-pressed to keep up with him.

Two men passed them in the narrow passageway; each spoke to Black as they passed. The first to go by Aubrey recognized as the man who had brought her from the *Gull*. She thought that his name was Gibbs. The second man she recognized as well, Thomas Beaufort. There was something about him that did not set well with her. Not because he had been the one who had caught hold of her that day on the *Gull*, but there was something about him that sent chills down her spine every time she saw him. He scanned her with his gray eyes and clicked his tongue. She quickened her pace, nearly breaking into a trot to catch up with Black.

Looking back, she saw that Beaufort was standing in the corridor, watching her. She timidly reached her hand forward and caught Black by the sleeve. He turned slightly at the touch of her hand and he caught her hand in his as they continued to the galley. While the captain frightened her, Beaufort terrified her.

Gibbs stopped and looked back at Beaufort who was still watching her go toward the galley, "Thomas, what is it?" he asked.

"Fine bit of fluff, Beaufort said still watching her.

"Careful, Thomas, she is the Captain's woman," Gibbs warned.

"Well, I do not much care for the rules on this ship. Black expects us to do as he says and not as he does," Beaufort grumbled as they stepped out onto the main deck into the rain. Gibbs looked at him and thought that Beaufort was decidedly the cruelest man on board, next to the captain.

"I have seen a few men take an unsuspected pistol shot to the head from Captain Black for voicing their opinions to his rules," Gibbs said solemnly, trying to warn the other man into quietness.

Beaufort ignored the warning and grunted, "You are just a coward, Gibbs. Black does not scare me. I would like a piece of that little girl. She is fresh and would be very enjoyable." Gibbs watched as Beaufort walked off into the pouring rain. He wondered if he should warn Jean Luc of the other man's desires towards the girl. He had to admit, the girl was fine, and if it were only Jean Luc that he would have to go against, Gibbs might attempt to take her himself. But when she had been brought on board and Black had laid claim to her, that changed everything. He had no intentions of going against him no matter how 'fresh' the girl might be!

Chapter 14

In the empty galley, Black led Aubrey to his table and left her to go to see what Cook could prepare for them. She sat quietly, thinking about Beaufort and the way he looked at her. He made her feel very uneasy. Cook returned with Black and placed two plates on the table.

"Captain, I cannot possibly eat all of this food," she whispered, looking at the heaping plate.

"Eat what you can, but eat well," he advised as he began his own meal. She began to pick at the food on her own plate.

"That man, Thomas Beaufort," she began as she put some of the food into her mouth.

He looked up at her from his plate, "What about him?"

She bit her lip, wondering if she should speak her mind. Gathering the courage, she said, "I do not like him, sir."

"Why?" he asked in his deep voice as he took a drink from his mug.

"Because he is frightening."

Black chuckled low in his throat as he filled his fork with food, "Everyone on this ship is 'frightening,' they are supposed to be. Did your pere not tell you all the stories about pirates?"

"But he looks at me." She found herself complaining to him and ignoring his question. When he regarded her with his dark eye, she quickly looked down at her plate and began to push the food around with her fork. Why would he not talk to her about this? Was he not the least bit concerned that one of his crew made her feel very uncomfortable? Finally she put down her fork. "Can I go back to the cabin?"

He pulled off a piece of the hard loaf of bread they were sharing. "Are you finished eating?"

"I do not want anymore."

"You barely touched your food," he remarked.

"I am not hungry, I told you that before," she said tightly.

Black watched her tantrum as he continued to eat. She definitely had a temper in there somewhere, although she was not nearly as public with it as the other one had been. At any rate, her temper amused him. He sat back in his chair and said with a tone of disinterest as he waved his hand, "Then go back if you wish, but you go back alone and you will be hungry until dinner. There will be no more meals served until then. It is very likely that we may not eat then, depending on the weather today." He saw her shiver and he knew what she was thinking. Beaufort was out there somewhere, possibly between here and the cabin. Thinking that she would decide to stay until he left with her, it surprised Black when she stood up to leave. As she passed his chair, he reached out and caught her by the arm firmly.

"Are you forgetting something?" She looked at him in question. He pulled her closer and down toward him. She reluctantly, yet obediently, bent her head to his. His lips tasted like the wine he drank with his meal. Aubrey fought the urge to wipe her mouth, just as she had wanted to wipe her ear the night that nasty little friend of her uncle's had spoken so closely to her.

Aubrey looked down at the food on the table before him, remembering his warning. Black watched as she took a large chunk of the bread and clutched it to herself before she started for the door. Halfway across the room, she stopped to glance over her shoulder at Black. He had resumed eating and seemed to have already dismissed her from his mind. Suddenly she recalled the feel of Black's mouth on hers and she wiped her mouth with the cuff of her sleeve. Turning angrily, she stepped forward, letting out a small squeak as she ran against the quartermaster.

"Bonjour, Mademoiselle," he said, smiling. She looked at him then looked quickly back at the table where Black sat. Without a reply to Jean Luc, she quickly sidestepped past him and left the galley. Fear gripped her heart at the thought of running into Beaufort. Aubrey took off in a dead run to the great cabin and once inside, she slammed the wooden door and leaned against it, breathing heavily and clutching her bread against her breast.

Upon his entry to the galley, Jean Luc had seen Black detain Aubrey for the kiss and it angered him. But when he had seen her wipe off the kiss, it gave him new hope. Black would be gone from the ship tomorrow and not return until the next day. Perhaps he could get close to her and gain her trust.

"Why is it that every time I find myself alone with her today, you seem to show up?" Black said with a small smile as Jean Luc approached the table. The latter glanced toward the door.

"You are not with her, Rene. As a matter of fact, it looks to me like she does not appear to be pleased with your company today. I just saw her wipe off your kiss," he chided with a smile as he sat in the chair she had just vacated.

Black chuckled and finished the wine in his mug, "She is in the throes of a temper tantrum. She is very good at them."

"Like the other one?" Jean Luc asked.

"No, nothing like her," Black replied quietly as he stared at his plate.

"Well, what did you do to anger her, Rene? Did you ruin her appetite, too?" Jean Luc asked indicating the full plate of food she had left.

"I did nothing to anger her; she eats like a damned bird," Black grumbled, giving him a cold look. Jean Luc looked at him stoically but did not reply. Black rested his elbows on the table and waved his hands in a gesture of puzzlement. "She speaks of some foolishness about Beaufort," the captain said derisively.

Jean Luc snorted as he picked up a piece of meat from Aubrey's plate and put it into his mouth, "He probably frightens the hell out of her. The man is mad, Rene. Any woman of caliber would be able to sense that Beaufort is an animal when it comes to them."

"What do you want, Jean Luc?" Black asked tiredly.

Pushing Aubrey's plate away and leaning his own elbows on the table, he helped himself to a piece of bread. "I thought that you might be interested to know that we should be dropping anchor by midnight." Black sighed again, something was just not right with all of this. Aubrey did not seem to interest him enough. His thoughts drifted back again to the other young woman. Her many displays of anger and fits of temper had really stirred him, especially when she was angry with him for a real reason. It had made their lovemaking all the more pleasurable.

"It has stopped raining as well," Jean Luc was saying, bringing Black back to the present.

"Are the barrels of fresh water all stored?" the captain asked as he stood from the table.

Jean Luc followed suit and replied, "Not yet, that idiot Beaufort is seeing to it." He looked worriedly at Aubrey's plate. There was barely anything to the little thing now. She had better get an appetite, and soon.

Black returned to his cabin to find Aubrey sitting in the quarter gallery.

"Are you still angry with me?" he asked as he approached her.

"I am not angry with you, Captain. I am just bored," she replied glancing at him.

"Life at sea can be that way sometimes," he replied as he placed his hands on her shoulders.

"Well, what do you do then to occupy your time, when you are not overtaking and attacking ships? Do you never get off this ship any other time and see new places?" she asked in exasperation.

"Certainement," he replied looking past her to the sea beyond the windows.

This reply gave her new hope and she turned to him in excitement, "Then will you take me to shore sometime? Will I get to see things too?"

He merely nodded, still looking out to sea lost in deep thought. Finally he said abruptly, "It has stopped raining, let us go up on deck for some fresh air."

"Really?" she said gleefully and nearly leapt from her seat to follow him.

The deck was bustling with activity and Aubrey watched everything in wide-eyed fascination. The barrels of fresh water gathered from the rains were being sealed and stored in the hold. Jean Luc approached, noticing Aubrey watched with rapt interest.

"The water barrels serve two purposes," he began informatively as he leaned slightly toward her. She looked at him shyly and threw a fleeting glance at Black who merely regarded the two of them, somewhat disinterested. Aubrey thought that his was mind elsewhere, but said nothing.

"What is the less obvious purpose of drinking water?" she asked Jean Luc, wanting to learn.

"The weight of them acts as ballast for the ship. They help to weight the ship properly," he told her. She nodded, looking intently at Jean Luc. This man was interesting as well as handsome, but he was so bossy. She cut her gaze to Black and saw a grim look on his face as he directed his attention to the business on the deck.

Aubrey tentatively leaned out to look into the open hold where the water barrels were being loaded. Suddenly from far below, there was a tremendous crash and she backed away from the opening. Black and Jean Luc started in surprise and drew back at the sound as well. Beaufort, who was standing on the other side of the hold, and overseeing the task, leaned over the opening with a curse.

"What is wrong down there?" he called angrily in French. A stream of angry-sounding words in French rose from the decks below and Aubrey backed further away from the opening to the hold. Taking cover behind Black, she peered around him to look at Beaufort. To everyone's surprise, there was a second crash and the sound of frightened chickens could be heard. Four or five of the birds came up out of the hold and Aubrey clapped her hand over her mouth to squelch a startled shriek at the sight of the fluttering and clucking animals. Beaufort cursed again as a chicken came to light on his shoulder.

Peeking from behind Black, she stared at the sight of Thomas Beaufort standing with a chicken on his shoulder, then began to giggle. Jean Luc chuckled as well and cut his blue eyes down to look upon her. The giggle was a small delightfully delicious, childish sound amid the gruff curses, exclamations of anger and the sound of frightened chickens. Black looked around at her as she hung on his sleeve.

"Shh," he warned. He shot a warning look at his quartermaster, clearly not approving of Jean Luc's encouragement of her foolishness. Aubrey looked at Black quickly and saw that despite his attempt to be authoritative, a hint of a smile turned up the corner of his mouth. She looked at Jean Luc as he had stopped chuckling aloud but was stifling a laugh as well. Beaufort was now trying to shoo the chicken from his shoulder, and without thinking Aubrey burst into laughter.

Black rolled his eye as she buried her face in his sleeve, still laughing. He and Jean Luc were finally affected by her laughter and they both began to chuckle lightly.

"That is an interesting parrot," Jean Luc commented in French amid his controlled laughter. The comment was Black's undoing and he laughed aloud boisterously.

Aubrey tugged at his sleeve and asked, "Captain Black, what did Monsieur Pierne say?" Black leaned close to her ear and repeated the comment in English for her. She giggled all the more. It was the most fun Aubrey had since she was brought on board and she was reveling in it.

Ignoring everyone else on deck, Beaufort glared at her angrily for laughing at him. He again tried relieving himself of the chicken as the men on the deck began to make fun of him.

"Ah, see now Beaufort is truly the 'cock' on the ship. See how that hen clings to him?" LaVoie called out in French.

The other men on the deck erupted into uproarious laughter and Beaufort's face flushed with anger. With an animal-like growl, Beaufort snatched the chicken from his shoulder and it fell onto the deck with a squawk. Aubrey's delight turned to sudden horror as Beaufort brought a heavily booted foot down upon the hen, crushing its skull. With a shriek, Aubrey took cover behind Black once more. At seeing and hearing her reaction, Jean Luc drew a sharp breath. "Ame damne, Beaufort!"

Beaufort's gray eyes bore into Aubrey as she peered around Black's arm. "Thought that was funny, did you, you little..."

He caught the warning glare in Black's dark eye as Aubrey clutched at Black's sleeve again, whispering meekly, "I want to go to the cabin, Captain."

Black barked out orders to the men to capture the chickens and proceed with the storing of the water barrels. Taking her by the arm, he led her back to the cabin.

"You should not laugh at him," Black said stiffly as he pointed her toward the settee. "Beaufort does not have much of a sense of humor, by laughing at him, you will evoke him to be even more frightening to you than he already is," he went on.

Aubrey looked up at him with worried hazel eyes. Finally the man realized that Beaufort scared her, but what a terrible experience she had to go through to get the captain's attention on the matter.

"I did not mean to make him angry, but I was not the only one laughing at him," she said in a tone of pending tears. Black exhaled in defeat and drew his hand down over his face–she definitely did not have the courage of the other one.

That evening, Jean Luc joined them for dinner. As he and Black conversed in French, Aubrey looked disdainfully at her plate. She was hungry for a change, having left the bulk of her breakfast in a huff that morning. The bread had not filled her empty belly but when Black removed the cover of the main course and dished it out on her plate, she was sickened to see that it was cut up pieces of chicken. Jean Luc had been glad to see her smile and laugh today, but now he watched her in the dark mood.

"What are you doing? Eat your dinner," Black demanded when she pushed away her plate without touching the food.

Moving uncomfortably in her chair, she bent her head and said meekly, "I–I am still not hungry, Captain."

Black shook his head in mild annoyance. Cutting a piece of the chicken on his own plate he said gruffly, "Tomorrow I will be going off the ship until the next day. Jean Luc will be in charge. His word is law in my absence. If you misbehave, he will report to me."

Her head shot up in surprise. "I cannot go?" she asked suddenly.

"No, you will have to stay here on board this time," he replied firmly. She made a face, but did not reply back.

"See that she eats," Black said to Jean Luc in English, looking pointedly at Aubrey while placing a forkful of the meat into his mouth. The quartermaster nodded in reply and glanced at her, giving her a knowing look.

Aubrey did not seem to be happy with the announcement. Jean Luc, however, reveled in the idea and could not wait. Sitting silently, Aubrey thought that this was like being at the table with her uncle. Decisions were made for her and she had no say in the matter at all. She turned a hurtful look at Jean Luc. He will probably be bossy with me as well.

Chapter 15

In the pre-dawn of morning, Aubrey tossed and turned on the settee making Black sigh loudly. "What is troubling you?"

She suddenly stilled at the sound of his voice before saying quietly, "My stomach hurts."

"You are hungry. I can hear your stomach complaining all the way over here. It has kept me awake all night. You should have eaten your meals yesterday when they were offered. Get your clothes on and I will take you to the galley," he said as he sat up on the edge of his bed and ran his hand up the back of his neck. Soon, they were alone in the dimly lit galley.

"I am sorry," she said meekly as he set a plate in front of her and sat down heavily across from her.

He rubbed his hand over his face tiredly, and pointed to the plate as he mumbled in his deep voice, "Just eat."

She looked at the plate–cold chicken. The sight of Beaufort stomping on the poor unfortunate bird the day before came to mind. She was certain that this must be the remnant of it here on her plate and the thought sickened her. Glancing at the captain as she picked up her fork, she thought it wise to put aside the ill feeling and eat what he had given her. "Yes, sir."

Black sat watching her, his elbow resting on the table, cradling his chin in his hand. She ate relatively well and he reached out to steal a morsel of the chicken from her plate.

Speaking in quiet low tones that matched the mood of the darkened empty room, he began to carry on a conversation with her. Aubrey was full of questions and he smiled at her inquisitiveness. She asked about the places he had visited and he told her about his last trip ashore and most of what he had done, leaving out the more personal and intimate things. Seeing her smile frequently at his conversation, he saw it as a dropping of the barrier she had put up against him. Perhaps she did interest him a bit. After her breakfast, and with just a bit more relaxing conversation, he might be successful this morning. If he and his landing crew left for shore a bit later than he had previously planned, then so be it. The thought of taking her back to his bed this morning made him move a bit closer as he continued to engage her in quiet conversation. She appeared unaware of his change in position and he took it to be a good omen, punctuating his conversation with gentle caresses every now and again.

Cook was rattling pans, preparing the morning meal for the watch going off duty and the men who would replace them at daily duties. Some of the men who had seated themselves at a nearby table began to get loud, causing her to look up nervously.

" I am full now. May I go back to the cabin?" she asked quietly.

"If that is what you wish to do," he replied with a smile. He rose from his seat to accompany her, his eye wandering over her slim figure in the britches and shirt that she wore.

She stopped him with a hand on his arm and a small smile, "May I go alone? I will be fine; it is not that far. Please, Captain?"

Given his tendencies during their talk to touch her, she thought that to have him back in the cabin would surely mean a session of kissing and caressing her. What she wanted more than anything else now was to be left alone and sleep. With an easy, but disappointed smile, he pulled her to him and pressed his lips on hers. His kiss was searching and she pushed at him slightly to get him to stop. Aubrey did not want to anger him, but she knew that the men in the room were watching. Black finally obliged and gently pushed her away, saying in a low yet firm tone, "Go directly to the cabin."

She nodded, glad to be free of him. As she passed through the doorway and stepped just outside the galley she came face to face with the quartermaster. As she started past him, she stopped as he spoke, "Mademoiselle?"

"Oui?" She asked casting a glance into the galley towards Black's table. He was picking at the morsels she had left on her plate, his attention drawn to a conversation at the table beside him. Aubrey turned her gaze back up to Jean Luc who was speaking to her again.

"Do you have any idea what your station is on this ship?" Jean Luc asked. Puzzled, she looked at him.

"Those phrases that the captain had you say yesterday morn. Do you know what those titles include?" he went on, anticipating an innocent question. He had tossed and turned all night in his bunk, fretting over having heard her say the phrases roughly in French.

Aubrey made a face at him, yawned, rubbed her eyes sleepily and then asked, "I do not understand, Monsieur Pierne."

Black looked up to see his quartermaster and Aubrey in conversation. Jean Luc had a stern look on his face and Black watched with keen interest as he began to eat from the plate that Cook had set before him.

"I do not believe that you know exactly what those titles entail," Jean Luc was saying sternly but in a low tone of voice leaning closely to her. Their faces were just inches apart.

She was tired and her temper was short, causing her to snap at him. "Yes,

I do."

Jean Luc was hard pressed not to smile. She looked absolutely darling staring fiercely up at him with hands on her hips. He envisioned catching her face in his palms and pressing the angry pouting lips in a kiss.

"I think not," he replied firmly, hiding the smile in his tone.

"What then?" she asked raising her brows haughtily.

"Being the captain's lady means, that you take care of his needs," he replied, crossing his arms over his chest.

"I do take care of his needs. I get him things if he needs them, I keep his cabin neat and tidy, and I make his bed," she hissed in low tones. Jean Luc shook his head; this was going to be more difficult than he had figured.

"No," Jean Luc said evenly through clenched teeth. She looked at him and shook her head, still not understanding. Mon Dieu, was she actually that naive? But how beautiful she was this morning! he thought to himself. How in the world could he make her understand and not be crude, offensive, and embarrassing?

"What are you trying to tell me, Monsieur Pierne? Will you please finish this conversation? I want to go back to the cabin. I am tired and Captain Black expects me to go directly there, not stand in the corridor in idle conversation with you." She punctuated her reply with a stomp of her small foot.

The conversation was apparently becoming a heated argument as far as Black could tell. Sitting back in his chair, he continued to watch them. Aubrey seemed to be angry stomping her feet and standing with her arms akimbo. Black smiled at the scene, amused to see her this way. Perhaps there was some hope for her yet. Maybe with this newfound courage she would also find the courage to submit to his advances. Would she be as passionate in her intimacies as she was with her temper?

Jean Luc rolled his eyes, let out a long sigh before beginning again, "Surely you know what I mean,"

"Obviously I do not. You are very vague, Monsieur Pierne," she countered. Very well, clarity–she wanted clarity? Ame damne, he would give her clarity. He bent his head close to her face and she drew back on his advance slightly, some of the courage draining from her. Nevertheless, she stood her ground even when he had moved so close that his cheek lightly brushed against hers as he spoke into her ear.

Black arched a brow and sat a little straighter in his chair watching the scene as he reached for his mug.

"He would be making love to you instead of you making his bed. That is how you would be taking care of his needs," Jean Luc hissed tightly into her ear. He drew back, his blue eyes meeting her hazel ones. She was looking at him with a shocked expression on her pretty face, her mouth hanging open in surprise. His whole body ached at the sight of her. Those lips were so inviting.

Jean Luc was looking so intently into the beautiful face that her reaction caught him completely off guard. With a fierce and stinging slap, her small hand connected soundly with his left cheek. The strike changed his expression to one of complete and utter surprise. Aubrey turned quickly on her heel and hurried away toward the great cabin.

He put his hand to his face and rubbed at the paining spot. "La vache."

Black had raised his mug to his lips to take a drink when Aubrey launched her attack. He was coughing as Jean Luc strode up, rubbing his now reddened cheek. When he took down his hand, there was a neat small red handprint on his face. The touch of every small delicate finger was clearly visible. Black chuckled in delight at the sight of it.

"Oh, I am glad that you find that so amusing, Rene," Jean Luc complained as he slammed himself down upon the bench.

Black regained his composure, but with a smile he asked, "Are you accosting my woman, Jean Luc?"

"Hell no! She accosted me," Jean Luc retorted with a snort rubbing the stinging spot on his face again. Jean Luc's eyes suddenly narrowed despite himself. Your woman? She is my woman–or will be.

"She throws quite a nice little tantrum. What in the hell did you say to her to warrant that?" Black asked as he indicated the red mark on Jean Luc's face and chuckled again. Jean Luc shrugged and glanced at the doorway. "Well, you had best get back onto good terms with her. I will be leaving you on board to take care of the ship and you will have to take care of her welfare also," Black told him, sitting back in his seat.

"Oh merci Rene, you are truly my friend," Jean Luc grumbled.

Pointing to the weapons in Black's sash, Jean Luc added, "Please put your dirk in my chest now, Rene. Make sure you put it in my heart,"

"I will only be gone for a few days, Jean Luc," Black said through a hearty laugh.

"Mon Dieu, Rene, a few days?" Jean Luc groaned, pretending to be disgruntled at the prospect. Black laughed again and got up from his seat clapping Jean Luc on the shoulder.

Still seated, Jean Luc growled, "I do not know of any other ship that has the quartermaster taking on the responsibilities of a nursemaid."

As Black started away, he leaned down and said with a low deep rumble of laughter, "By order of the captain, mon ami."

When Black left, Jean Luc sat in quiet reflection. He would finally have her alone for a time. It was something that he had dreamed of since the first day that he had seen her. He smiled to himself, chuckling at her anger when she had slapped him. The flair of her temper delighted him, as it showed him that she had some bravery–an asset that could only benefit her in this new life.

Chapter 16

Black returned to the cabin and found Aubrey at the window, staring at the rising sun.

"Are you having a problem with Monsieur Pierne?" Black asked as he shut the door.

She turned toward him only slightly with her arms folded over her chest. "Non."

He raised an eyebrow at her and moved closer; her reply had come rather sharply.

"Really?" He cooed as he pulled her into his arms and brushed his lips against her cheek. "You dealt Monsieur Pierne a mighty slap awhile ago, would you care to tell me why?" he asked as his kisses wandered down her neck.

Out of his sight, she made a distressful face. "No sir. I am really very tired," she answered quietly.

He drew back and stroked her hair. "Very well then, Mademoiselle, let it be your little secret. Go lie down now. Sleep well." She easily extracted herself from his arms and nodded in reply. As she moved to the settee, he said, "Since you are so tired, and I know that the settee must be uncomfortable, would you care to sleep here?" He indicated the rumpled bunk with a thin smile.

"No," she replied quickly as she curled herself onto the settee and pulled up her blanket.

"I could punish him if you like," Black said as he poured water into the washbowl.

"What?" She asked in a startled voice.

"Monsieur Pierne—I could have him beaten for bothering you," he replied nonchalantly.

"No sir. We merely choose to disagree. It is nothing," she said easily.

Aubrey shivered at the thought of the man being beaten on her account. He had only embarrassed her, nothing more. She heard Black chuckle as she drifted off to sleep worrying about what the quartermaster had said.

Later that morning Black brought her up onto the deck before he left for the shore.

"Conduct yourself properly in front of the men, you are the captain's woman," he warned as he bent his head to kiss her goodbye.

100

"Jean Luc is in charge. If anyone should chastise you, you are to report them to him at once." As soon as Black got into the longboat, Aubrey returned to the great cabin.

Sometime later, Jean Luc went to the cabin to make sure that his 'charge' was all right. He tapped on the door. "Mademoiselle Aubrey?"

"Do you bring me my meal?" she asked tentatively from the other side of the door.

"No, but I can," he offered. Any reason to be with her. There was only silence as he waited patiently.

"Just a small amount, please, I am not very hungry," she replied. He quickly went to oblige her.

Within minutes he returned and knocked on the door. She slowly opened it and stepped back to allow him entry. He handed her the covered plate, offering her his most handsome smile. She turned and started to close the door and he put his hand against it.

"Perhaps you should leave it open."

He would rather had it closed, but for all intents and purposes, and to keep the pair of them out of trouble, he had made the suggestion. As she ate, Jean Luc sat at the desk and made an entry in the log.

"Can I go up on deck and sit in the sun?" she asked when she had finished.

"Well, certainement." Aubrey literally beamed at his reply.

"Really? You would let me do that?" He merely nodded and waved her ahead of him.

With the sun shining warmly on her face and the breeze blowing through her hair, Aubrey was happy to be on deck. She looked out at the tiny island beyond the surf and thought it looked like a green jewel on the ocean.

"What is this place?" She asked Jean Luc.

"Antigua," he replied, and then added, "we trade here."

"The things that you take from other ships?" she asked and he nodded.

"But you keep a lot of the things, the items that you need," she added and Jean Luc smiled. She was learning.

"Oui, that is correct. Stay right here where I can see you. Do you understand?"

With a nod, she replied, "Captain Black told me, I am to call on you if anyone bothers me."

"Bon, I will be on the quarterdeck," he told her.

Smiling at her and the excitement he saw in her hazel eyes, Jean Luc turned and headed back to his post on the quarterdeck, where he could watch her. Black's orders for her safety and well being were irrelevant. He was seriously concerned for her himself. Sitting on the edge of the cargo hold, she stared at the island and idly swung her legs back and forth.

Jean Luc found himself staring at her longingly as her auburn hair blew unruly in the wind and she fussed with it as she sat there. How he longed to run his fingers through the tresses. She was completely relaxed and quite a different Aubrey from the one he saw when Black was around. Jean Luc spoke with the helmsman about their departure course the next day. When he turned his attention back on her, what he saw caused a cold chill to run down his spine.

Beaufort had approached her, accompanied by Boulet and another man named LaVoie.

"Getting some air, little girlie?" Beaufort asked in English as he stepped in front of her, deliberately blocking her view of the island. Aubrey drew a sharp breath and her eyes darted from his face to the deck at his feet and gave him no verbal reply.

LaVoie moved closer to Beaufort, blocking Jean Luc's line of vision of Aubrey.

"Shall I ask you again in French? I know that the captain is teaching you the language," he said chuckling deep in his throat.

"He teaches her more than that I would wager," Boulet replied. The three men laughed and the sound chilled Aubrey to the core. Beaufort reached a gloved hand out and caught a wisp of her hair as it danced in the winds.

She leapt to her feet and without thinking, she swiped at his hand. "Kindly leave me alone, sir."

Beaufort backed away in feigned alarm, "Oh, she is on the attack." Laughter rippled among them again. Beaufort leaned closer to her and Aubrey found herself looking up into the cruel gray eyes.

"Attack me, s'il vous plait. I would enjoy that beaucoup! Jump up at me again and I will impale you, right here," he said as he dropped his gloved hand to clutch at his crotch. Aubrey bit her lip and her breath came in nervous gasps as he continued.

"Why not come with me and I can teach you some interesting things, too." He reached for her arm and she drew back from him.

Aubrey tried to move aside to go past him, but Boulet stepped in her path to effectively block her escape. Smiling down at her, he asked, "Where are you going?"

Now she was cornered between the three of them and the cargo hold.

"Please get out of my way, Monsieur," she said as bravely as she could, but a hint of fear escaped into her voice. Boulet's smile widened when he heard her fear and the sound of it aroused him.

"Non," he replied demonically.

She stood before them trembling in fear, not sure of what do next. Beaufort leaned closer to her face, his gray eyes cold. Glancing back to seek an escape route, she saw only the open latticed work cover that allowed light and air into the decks below. It was definitely not a place to stand on.

"You laughed at me. You owe me an apology."

She looked into his eyes and drew a deep breath. Looking down she whispered in fear, "I meant you no harm, sir."

"But still you laughed and you owe me," he said harshly. Aubrey's eyes darted around trying to find some way to escape them.

"Look at me, you little bitch," he growled at her. His companions gave a warning in French but he snapped back at them in reply.

"I said look at me!" he hissed leaning even closer to her face, his lips nearly touching her cheek. Aubrey looked up at him as he said through clenched teeth, "I ought to snatch you up right here, put you down on this deck and..."

Someone tapping him on the shoulder made Beaufort cut his sentence short. He wheeled around, and in his turning, his arm bumped against Aubrey. She stumbled back against the edge of the hold and lost her balance. She felt herself begin to fall backward but was stopped as a hand caught the front of her shirt and pulled her forward between Beaufort and Boulet. Now she was staring up into the face of Jean Luc and he was definitely angry. His blue eyes burned into Beaufort while still holding Aubrey in his grasp. Wide-eyed with fear, Aubrey listened as the men spoke angrily in French.

"You will put her on the deck and do what, Beaufort?" Jean Luc asked through clenched teeth.

"What in the hell do you think, Pierne?" Beaufort sneered.

"Over my dead body," Jean Luc growled back as he finally pushed Aubrey to the side and released his hold on her shirt.

"Anytime," Beaufort smiled as he fingered the butt of his pistol.

"Non, Thomas," Boulet warned as he put out a gloved hand.

Beaufort cast him an angry sideways glance as Jean Luc went on. "Monsieur Beaufort, do you realize that all she has to do is mention this incident to the captain in casual conversation. Who do you suppose would be laying on the deck then?" Beaufort looked past Jean Luc to Aubrey as she still stood stiffly behind the quartermaster with wide fearful eyes.

Beaufort turned back to Jean Luc and sneered, "You go to hell. She is just his sweet candy right now; soon he will turn her over to us and we will all have a taste."

"Believe what you like, Beaufort," Jean Luc said with an unfriendly smile.

"Thomas, Jean Luc is right. The captain would cut you to the quick if you touched her," LaVoie warned.

Jean Luc gave a gentle push to move Aubrey further from Beaufort but she took the opportunity to run to the companionway and below deck.

"Well, let us just see if the girl tells him," Beaufort snickered, then the three men strode casually away.

Jean Luc remained in place trying to control the insatiable urge to shoot Beaufort, but he knew Black used Beaufort's mean roughness to help keep the men in line. When he was sure Beaufort and his friends did not follow her, he went to the great cabin and tapped softly on the door. When he tried the door, he was surprised to find that it swung open easily.

"Aubrey? I am not here to hurt you. I am here to see if you are all right," he called to what appeared to be an empty room. Where the Devil was she? Please let her have come back here. He thought as he walked a few paces and looked around the room. Cupboards and closets lined the walls and she was small enough to fit in most any of them.

"I did nothing wrong. I stayed where you told me, just sitting there. Please do not punish me." There was a hint of sob in the tiny voice.

"I know that. You did what you were told. Thomas is a bully," he soothed. She stepped out into the waning light that shone in from the quarter gallery windows.

"I will never leave this cabin again," she said quietly. He looked at her sympathetically wishing he could take her up into his arms and comfort her.

"I want to go home, Monsieur Pierne," she said mournfully then mentally chided herself. Aubrey, you stupid little fool, home was just like this except this home floated on the ocean!

"Well, I am afraid that is not possible," he said breaking into her thoughts. Taking a step closer to her, he added, "I intend to report this to the captain."

A look of horror crossed her already troubled brow. "He will be very angry and blame me."

"No, he will not be angry nor will he blame you, but he really should hear of this incident from you," he told her sternly.

She looked at him pitifully. "I cannot."

He shook his head in a negative fashion. Was she that afraid of Black?

"Also be assured that as long as I am on this ship, Thomas Beaufort will not harm you," he told her. He approached her, pulling off his glove. Her eyes darted to the bare hand as he raised it and she stepped back almost in fear.

"Mademoiselle," he said as he easily outstretched his hand to her.

He saw the look in her hazel eyes as she finally recognized the outstretched hand as the gesture of trust and not some painful form of retribution for something done wrong. She stepped forward as well and put out her own hand as if to shake his. He gently took her hand and turned it to press his lips to the back of it. He was elated when he felt her fingers curl around his ever so slightly and he dropped his gaze to their hands to verify the touch. Realizing that he had noticed, she drew her hand back quickly and stepped back.

"Will you be needing anything else?" he asked straightening up.

"No, merci, Monsieur Pierne," she said in a near whisper. This was a far cry from the young woman who had argued with him in defiance and slapped him so soundly. He pulled on his glove and put on his hat. As he moved to the door and reached for the latch, her voice stopped him.

"Merci for saving me today, Monsieur Pierne."

He smiled easily and turned toward her. Saving her? Well yes, he supposed he was saving her.

"Call me Jean Luc, and you are quite welcome. I am at your service."

"Oh, I cannot call you by your first name, sir. That would not be proper," she said more formally now. He arched an eyebrow at her before he nodded and left the room. Aubrey moved forward quickly to lock the door and with a relieved sigh, she lowered herself on the settee.

Chapter 17

Aubrey had been sleeping when a knocking on the door awakened her.

"Mademoiselle Aubrey, I have your dinner here and I must put the day's entries into the log," came the voice of Jean Luc from the other side. Aubrey went to the door and opened it tentatively, peeping around it to make certain that it was the quartermaster on the other side. Coming into the cabin, he set down a steaming bowl then he moved to the desk.

"What is this, Monsieur Pierne?" she asked in a quiet sleepy voice.

"Venison stew. It is delicious," he replied not looking up from the book as he wrote.

"What time is it?" she questioned timidly.

"Nearly seven," he replied.

Silence fell between them again. With finality, he shut the book and stood. He walked toward the table to see that she had barely touched the bowl of stew.

"You had better eat."

"I am full," she replied.

"Are you certain?"

She nodded as she set down the spoon.

"Would you care to go up on deck? The air before a rain is quite refreshing, perhaps it will bring back your appetite," he suggested.

"Captain Black does not take me on deck after dark."

"Captain Black is a busy man. He has the ship to tend to," he replied.

"And you do not? Are your duties that different from his when you are in charge?" Aubrey asked curtly.

"It was an offer, Mademoiselle. You do not have to take it if you do not want to." He was standing closer and his tone was low. Aubrey swallowed hard and looked up at him.

"Good night, Monsieur Pierne," she said stiffly. Jean Luc smiled at her and shrugged.

"Not good night, bonsoir."

Aubrey hurriedly locked the door behind him. She then heard the sound of heavy rain up on the deck above.

"I could not have gone up on the deck, anyway," she said to the empty cabin.

On the other side of the door, Jean Luc heard the small complaint. He sighed deeply and pulled his hat on tightly, heading for the companionway.

After an hour or so, the moon came out from behind the clouds giving testimony to the fact that it had stopped raining. At the quarter gallery, Aubrey looked out longingly. Maybe a trip to the deck would not be so dangerous. If she were careful and crept up there, no one would even see her.

The doorway in the bulkhead would be a quicker way out to the deck, but with the position of it on the outer deck, she would surely be observed. Unbolting the inner door, she checked the corridor for a sign of anyone. The ship bell sounded twice for 9pm and all was quiet and still. It was time for lights out. Everyone would be in his respective bunk areas. Within seconds, Aubrey was stepping out into the fresh night air. The sky had spots of clear places where the stars shone through brightly. She stood in the shadows looking up at them in awe. The moon went behind the clouds again and the wind picked up a bit, ruffling her hair. For a time, she felt free and without worry. Turning her face up to the heavens, she smiled at the starry sky.

Suddenly her freedom and peace were cut short by a downpour of hard cold hard rain blowing sideways. She gasped and moved quickly to go back to the shelter of the below decks. Her feet slipped on the wet deck and she caught herself against the bulkhead. In the darkness, she ran headlong into someone. At that moment, the ship bucked on the sudden onslaught of wind-driven waves. With an alarmed cry, she found her feet slipping again, but a pair of strong hands caught hold of her.

Her first terrified thought was that she was in the clutches of Beaufort. Looking up through the rain that pounded into her face, she was relieved to see Jean Luc.

"What are you doing up here alone?" he asked sharply.

"I... I." she stammered.

"Look at you! Soaked to the skin!" he scolded. Holding her tightly by the arm, he guided her toward the companionway continuing in his reprimand, "Do you know how dangerous it is up here for you alone? I told you that I would bring you up here, but you must never come out alone, especially after dark."

"I do not have to take orders from you," she spat back as they went down the companionway steps.

"Indeed you do. Especially when I am in charge of this ship," he replied angrily as he gently pushed her toward the cabin door.

"Stop pushing me around!" she spat suddenly turning on him.

"Get in that cabin," he demanded in a low voice as he towered over her. In the light of the lantern that hung just above their heads, he looked down at the front of her wet shirt that left little to the imagination.

With embarrassed anger, she pushed at his chest to gain his attention to other places and hissed, "What are you looking at?"

A smile crossed his lips as he glanced back down again. Aubrey quickly folded her arms over her chest. Putting away the smile and putting on a much more stern face, he grasped her by the shoulders, and turned her toward the door of the cabin. Reaching past her with one hand as he clutched a handful of the shoulder of her shirt, he opened the door and pushed her inside the cabin growling, "Get in there with you."

Once inside, he shut the door rather firmly and turned on her. "Get out of those wet clothes before you catch your death of cold. Captain Black will hang me from the yardarm if you get sick from such an escapade."

"I am not going to change my clothes until you leave!" Aubrey spat.

"You will change now because I cannot trust you to do as I tell you when I leave. For all I know, you will sneak right back out of here and up onto the deck. You change when the captain is in here so get over there," he growled back.

Aubrey opened her mouth to protest and he raised the finger to her face. With a most unladylike snort and a stomp of her small foot, she turned from him to snatch up dry clothing and go behind the screen.

"You better stay far away out there," she spat from her place behind the dressing screen.

"Oh, you do not frighten me and I am not coming over there to look at you!" he spat back, hiding the chuckle at her threatening tone. He really did not need to be here as she dressed, but it gave him an excuse to be alone with her.

The rain had died down above them again and in the quiet cabin, he could hear the rustle of wet clothing in the quiet room. Thinking of her naked and so very close at hand, he inhaled deeply to control the desire that welled up within him.

She stepped from behind the screen and asked sharply, "There, are you happy?"

He wanted to tell her 'no', but instead he stepped toward her pointing his finger, "Never... I repeat never go on deck alone after dark again."

"Well, I am back in here now all dry and safe and now you may leave," she said firmly in reply. Jean Luc rolled his eyes in exasperation as he turned and left the cabin.

Aubrey awakened late the next morning, chilled from the night before. Looking at Black's bunk, she contemplated the thick warm quilt and the soft pillows. Captain Black was not here–he would never know.

Climbing up into the bunk, she pulled the quilt up over her and snuggled down into the recesses of its warmth. Just as she made herself comfortable, she was startled by a light tapping on the door and nearly bolted out of the bunk.

"You will eat now, Mademoiselle?" came Cook's plea in broken English.

"Non, merci," she called back in her meager French. She heard the man curse in his language and she made a face in reply. He shuffled away from the door and all was quiet save for the groan of the wooden hull of the ship as it rocked gently on the swells. Aubrey settled back down once more into the covers and she soon drifted off to sleep, feeling warm and safe for now.

In fitful dreams, she was in Uncle Jonathan's house and he was angry with her again. He raised his hand to strike her as he had so many times before, proclaiming his great dislike for her paternal heritage. As she flinched in her sleep against the heavy hand, she was suddenly conscious of a real hand touching her face.

Aubrey came up from the bunk with a gasp, her eyes wide with fear. Jean Luc sat on the edge of the bunk, his hand poised in the air, and a look of alarm was on his face at her violent awakening. She attempted to scramble away from him, managing only to entangle herself in the heavy quilt that he sat upon. The bulkhead of the ship further foiled her escape. Jean Luc caught her easily by the arm and pulled at the trapping bunk linens.

"Détendez-vous, Aubrey, I did not mean to alarm you." She calmed at once at the tone of his voice. "I heard you cry out, I thought that you were in trouble. Let me help you." Aubrey looked at him, blinking her eyes sleepily as he unwrapped the covers from her legs and pushed them back.

His voice was gentle and his eyes looked troubled. "I thought that perhaps one of the men was trying to accost you again." He freed her bare feet from the last of the entrapping covers.

"Here, let me help you," he purred.

"What do you want? How did you get in here?" Her voice was strained as she looked warily at his outstretched hand.

"Cook tells me that you did not take your meal this morning. I hope that you are not falling ill from getting wet last night." His voice was calm and quiet.

"I am fine. I was just– cold," she stammered continuing to look at the offered hand. The recollection of his touch flashed over her. It had actually been soft, gentle and comforting in her distress as he had awakened her. The urge to tell him about her dream was strong, but she pushed it aside. What care would a pirate have to a foolish young woman's nightmare?

Deciding that she probably would not take his hand, Jean Luc lowered it and got up from the side of the bunk, giving her some room.

"You need to take a meal. There is bad weather coming from the south and Cook has already told us that there will be no supper tonight," he said with an air of authority.

She smiled faintly as she got down out of the bunk. "I have survived without meals before, Monsieur Pierne."

Jean Luc frowned at her reply. Taking a deep breath and letting it out he said, "Please come to the galley and eat something."

She sighed as well with a hint of her brogue slipping out. "Well, all right then, if only to keep ya from going off on some tirade and proclaiming your authority again... like last night."

As Jean Luc bathed in his victory, he looked around the cabin. He frowned. The settee had the appearance of not being slept in and he had found her in the bunk this morning. The need to know burned deeply in him so as he followed her out the door he asked, "Have you given up your little bunk on the settee for the bigger one?"

Aubrey looked at him suddenly, noting the hint of disquiet in his tone. "No, I am using it in Captain Black's absence. It was–warmer. I do not know Captain well enough to sleep in the same bunk with him!" Her tone was flippant and a blush stole across her cheeks. Jean Luc smiled inwardly at the announcement. If Black knew she had told him, it would most certainly hurt the man's pride, especially if any of the rest of the crew knew that the young woman who was supposed to be the captain's woman was not sleeping with the captain.

Chapter 18

Jean Luc followed her to the galley and seated her at the captain's table. He took care to place her with her back to the galley, thinking that it might be less uncomfortable for her if she would not have to meet the stares of the men. This strategic positioning also afforded him a command view of her countenance as they spoke. Cook appeared immediately and set a plate before her. She looked down upon the mountain of ham and eggs in wide-eyed distress as the man moved away.

"Sweet Mary! I am not that hungry!" she breathed almost to herself. Jean Luc looked at his own plate, there was far much less on it than hers. Worried hazel eyes met his twinkling blue ones. He winked at her.

"Shh," he said as he easily exchanged his plate for hers. Then nodding to the plate, he asked, "Can you manage that?"

"I suppose," she replied.

"Then eat," he ordered with a small smile.

"Is ham, chicken, and eggs the only thing that you eat aboard this ship?" she asked.

Jean Luc laughed at the question "We get fish and turtle sometimes, and venison—but pork is more desirable for long voyages as it can be preserved and will last longer without spoiling. The venison we get if we are fortunate enough to go ashore and hunt. The chickens, well, we can keep them in the hold for a time, but they have to be fed, and keeping grain for them sometimes causes more trouble than they are worth," he said as he ate his meal. Aubrey listened to this information with rapt interest.

"What sort of trouble, Monsieur Pierne?" she asked.

"Well, the grain draws the rats," he began with an air of indifference.

"Rats?" she echoed with wide hazel eyes.

"Oui, have you not seen them aboard?" He nodded as he poured them some wine.

"No sir," she breathed.

Jean Luc was forced to hide a smile as he watched her look carefully under the table at their feet. A movement on the bench next to him caught his eye. Glancing under the table, he noted that she was straining to keep her toes on the edge of it, thus keeping her feet off the floor.

"They keep pretty much to the hold, near the bilge. But if there are food stores about, they are sure to get into them," he assured her. Suddenly the conversation did not interest her anymore as she continued to eat, but she

111

also continued to watch the floor for the horrendous little creatures.

"I am sorry that being on board gives you distressful dreams," Jean Luc began.

Aubrey put her mug of wine down slowly and looked at him. "I did not dream of this ship. It was a bad dream about another time–long ago."

He looked at her in concern, saying, "I am sorry to hear that."

After an extended quiet time of eating, she finally put her fork down. Jean Luc looked at her plate and saw that it was nearly empty. He smiled and winked at her.

"Cook will think that you ate that big pile of ham and eggs–he will be heureux."

"What is that?" she giggled lightly.

Jean Luc chuckled at the sweet sound and answered, "Happy."

"Why does he give me so much?" she frowned questioningly.

"He is used to feeding all these big men. It has been a long time since..." Jean Luc's voice trailed off and he wiped his mouth.

"If I ate all that he gave me every meal, I would be as big as them," she giggled, missing his abrupt ending.

Jean Luc surveyed her with his blue eyes. "Well, we could not have that now, could we?"

As Jean Luc escorted her from the galley, they were stopped by a man talking behind them. Jean Luc pushed her forward a bit and turned to look at the man who had turned now to his companion.

"See how he follows her?" The man said in French to his companion. With a grin that displayed yellowed teeth, the man said, "Monsieur Pierne, is she for us after the captain has had his fill? Have you had your time with her?"

"Is she good?" the other man chimed in. Jean Luc's blood ran cold at the mere thought of these two or any other man on board laying their hands upon Aubrey. The latter stood in hazel-eyed question as to the foreign conversation. Jean Luc merely looked at the man and tried to control his anger. Suddenly, the man's hand shot out past Jean Luc and caught Aubrey by the sleeve

"You are just a little peck," he said in thick accented English. Aubrey gasped and pried at the hand. Jean Luc stepped up.

"Take your hands off her, DeFoe." The man released her and took a defensive stance.

"You would do well to move along, DeFoe, and leave her be," Jean Luc warned. He wanted no more trouble while Black was away–it was bad enough to have to deal with Beaufort and his two idiot companions.

"Bonjour, Mademoiselle," DeFoe drawled over Jean Luc's shoulder.

Aubrey was too frightened to turn in reply even as the quartermaster gave her another small push to send her along toward the cabin ahead of him.

"Hmm, can you smell the fear in her?" DeFoe's companion said with a chuckle. At the sound of the man's laugh, Aubrey shot a glance up to Jean Luc and saw the muscles at his jaws rippling.

"I can smell more than the fear, mon ami. The bitch is in heat," DeFoe growled.

"You cannot smell that," his companion scoffed.

"That is why Pierne follows her so closely," De Foe put in with a guttural chuckle.

After the comments from Beaufort the day before, Jean Luc had enough of the derogatory remarks concerning Aubrey. Jean Luc threw out his left arm that pinned her against the bulkhead then with his right hand, he drew his double-barreled pistol smoothly and fired the first chamber point blank into DeFoe's chest. A surprised look replaced the smile on DeFoe's face as he was thrown backward, nearly knocking down his companion to the floor.

Aubrey screamed and threw her hands up over her face, thus locking Jean Luc's arm against her chest in the crook of her own arms. Jean Luc ignored her and swung the still smoking pistol toward the face of the second man growling, "The other chamber is loaded."

"I was only playing. I do not even want her. She is too petite, too young." The man stammered for reasons why he was suddenly not interested while looking cross-eyed into the barrel of the pistol.

"Get him out of here," Jean Luc growled as he kicked at the dead body at their feet, but not taking his eyes or his aim off the man.

The man nodded under the quartermaster's glare. Jean Luc tucked the pistol back into his sash and turned to Aubrey.

"Are you all right?"

Aubrey's ears still rang from the loud report of the pistol in the small space. She opened her eyes and dropped her arms. Looking both ways along the corridor, she saw that several men had come to the scene to see what was going on.

"Yes, I mean oui."

"Get out of this corridor! Get back to your posts!" Jean Luc yelled angrily to the men who had gathered. Aubrey started at his loud voice as he then gave her a gentle push once more toward the cabin.

Once inside and the door closed between her and the frightening event in the corridor, Aubrey found the courage to approach Jean Luc. He had seated himself heavily at the table.

"Why did you shoot that man, Monsieur Pierne?" she asked thickly.

Jean Luc regarded her with tired blue eyes. He did not think back in the beginning that having her aboard would be this much work. What had he been thinking? Lustful thoughts? No, he was just smitten by her beauty and he was in love–nothing else had mattered or even come into his mind when he had decided and planned to kidnap her and bring her with him.

"Monsieur DeFoe made a rude comment about you," he said as gently as his anger would allow.

"You would kill a man for a rude comment, Monsieur Pierne?" Aubrey asked quietly.

"His rude comments could escalate into more ugly things," Jean Luc shrugged as he pulled the pistol out of his sash. Aubrey stepped back so quickly that she nearly fell over one of the chairs at the table.

Jean Luc could not help but chuckle. "Do you think that I would shoot you?"

"Well," she began.

Jean Luc took out his powder horn and shot and proceeded to reload the pistol. Aubrey watched him in wide-eyed silence. When he was finished, he stood and tucked the pistol back into his sash and said, "Well, now that you are well-fed, and have had a bit of ship-board entertainment, I will leave you in the safe confines of this cabin and return to my duty. Should you need me,"

"I will be fine," she cut in quickly.

With a slight bow and a wink, Jean Luc left her alone. He smiled as he heard the lock bolt slide shut quickly. Aubrey was not smiling on the other side of the door. She stood with her back against the door and looked around the room in distress.

"Sweet Mary Mother of Jesus, what have I gotten myself into?" she muttered to the quiet cabin. Sliding down the door and coming to rest in a sitting position in the floor, Aubrey pulled her knees up to her chest and hugged them.

Chapter 19

Jean Luc met Black at the railing as he came aboard. Scanning the deck of his ship, Black pulled off his gloves and tucked them into his sash, asking, "No chickens on deck today, Jean Luc?"

"Non, Beaufort has all his parrots in order." Jean Luc managed to chuckle in reply, but a frown overshadowed his brow.

"What is it?" Black asked, noting the darkened look.

"Beaufort," came the curt reply.

"What about him?" Black asked as they stepped aside to allow members of the crew to bring on the supplies. Black's tone seemed tired and appeared to be bothered.

"Beaufort and his two idiot friends confronted Mademoiselle Aubrey yesterday morning after you left," Jean Luc reported. He saw the fire flash in the dark eye that regarded him. Raising a hand to silence the man before his outburst, Jean Luc said, "She is fine, untouched by any of them. Beaufort only frightened her."

"What was Beaufort doing in my quarters?" Black's tone was suspicious and hinted of anger.

Jean Luc cringed slightly, "She was not in your cabin at the time."

Black stopped in mid-stride and he looked pointedly at Jean Luc. "She was not in my quarters? Where did this happen?"

"Here on deck," Jean Luc said easily. Knowing the next question before it came, he said briskly, "Jesus Rene, she cannot stay locked up in your cabin all the time! She is not a prisoner, is she?" Black raised his eyebrows at the outburst. Undaunted, the quartermaster went on, "You used to let..."

Black raised a hand to halt the words and with a dark eyed glare, hissed, "You know better than to bring up that subject."

Jean Luc returned the glare with a cold blue-eyed stare of his own. "She asked, Rene. I put her where I could see her. My attention was drawn for only a moment."

"See to the supplies, and our departure," Black said curtly as he slipped down the companionway.

Aubrey was still in the floor just inside the doorway when the latch was jiggled from the outside. A small cry of alarm escaped her and she scrambled away from the door on her hands and knees.

"Aubrey! Open this door!" Black thundered from the corridor. The door swung open slowly and Black found himself facing her as she stood nervously, wringing her hands. In the next instant, and to the surprise of both she and Black, Aubrey flung herself into his arms exclaiming, "Oh Captain!"

He pushed her at arm's length, "I did not expect such a welcome from you, my dear." Looking up into his face, she noted that he appeared to be angry.

Guardedly she pushed away from him asking, "Why are you angry? Did something happen ashore?"

"No, Monsieur Pierne has told me about your incident with Monsieur Beaufort," he began as he moved to place his hat on his desk. "You had no business up on deck," he went on.

"I only wanted some sun and fresh air, sir," she muttered. She hoped that the quartermaster had not told him about her covert trip to the deck in the rain to the decks as well.

"Now you see what your wants will bring you, can you not?" he said curtly.

"Yes sir, but Monsieur Beaufort, he threatened me," she pouted, trying to steer his attention from the error in her ways to the frightening bully.

"He threatened you? How?" Black snorted.

"He threatened to..." she began, but was unable to finish the sentence for the ugliness of it. Black emitted a low chuckle and waved a hand dismissively as he untied the front of his shirt with the other.

"Idle threats."

Several long moments of silence passed and she asked nervously, "Did you have a good visit to shore, Captain?"

"I did," he nodded with a smile as he lowered himself into his desk chair.

She nodded, then with a sudden flash of bravery she stepped forward. "When can I go?"

"It is dangerous on shore." His tone was gruff as he picked up his quill to begin an entry into his log.

"No more dangerous than being left here," she spat back. Black looked up from the book and for a long moment, stared at her. Aubrey faced him with the continued air of bravery–the same she had mustered before Jean Luc in her confrontations with him. She watched Black's gaze moved about the room around them. A pang of fear struck her heart when she followed the stare and found that he was looking at the disheveled covers on his bunk. She mentally chastised herself for not having made the bunk when she got out of it.

"Hmm, been sleeping in my bunk have you?" he asked as he rose from the desk and came around it toward her. She backed up slightly but he reached out quickly and caught her by the wrist. "We will revisit the subject of your turn to go ashore after I have determined that you have earned a turn to go."

"Earned at turn?" she asked trying to twist her wrist free of his grip and backing away.

"Oui, earned a turn," he nodded as he pulled her toward the bunk.

"You see, my dear," he began as he scooped her up into his arms and put her down onto her back on the bunk and knelt over her. "On my ship, a person must perform certain duties within the scope of their position on the ship in order to earn the privilege to go on shore leave. Now, in seeing that you are the captain's lady, your duties would be to please the captain," he continued as he reached for the drawstring that closed the front of her shirt.

The memory of what Jean Luc had told her came to her mind. Her arms and legs flew into motion as she attempted to get out from under Black.

"What have you been doing in my bunk? Did you entertain the quartermaster to get the privilege to go up on deck?" he tormented.

"No! I was only sleeping!" she cried out in alarm at his accusation. Black managed to successfully place a long leg over both of hers to pin down the small but dangerously kicking limbs.

"Sleeping," he replied with a smug tone as his hands worked at the lacing again.

"Sleeping!" she repeated adamantly slapping and grabbing at his hands.

"You would not sleep here when I offered the bunk to you," he chided on as he pinned down her hands.

"Let me go!" she yelled.

"You seem to be getting angry. If you are angry, why do you not fight me?" he asked with a chuckle.

"I am angry! Captain Black, let me go!" She was screaming now. A deeper chuckle rumbled in his throat.

"You are not fighting me, you fight like a girl."

"I am a girl!" she spat. He laughed aloud and he glanced over the front of her.

"Vraiment? I do not believe you; I have never seen you undressed. Um, let me see." He pulled the shirt open a bit and she surprised him by managing to come up with the strength to free her hands to smack at his hands angrily.

"No!" With the viciousness of a wild cat, Aubrey struck out at him with her hands, laying scratches onto the exposed part of his upper chest with her nails.

Black drew back slightly and looked down at her with a grin. Through a deep chuckle he said, "Your little nails are quite sharp, Mademoiselle."

Black allowed her to wrestle with him for a few more moments, leaving her to think that she was actually being successful at her fight against him. Finally, he tired of the game and he pinned her down forcefully with a grunt. She was unable to move at all now, pinned hopelessly under the weight of him. She stared into his face, gasping for air as she pleaded desperately with him now for her freedom. "Captain, s'il vous plat, you cannot do this."

Black's dark eye wandered over her for a moment. The auburn colored hair caught his eye. She was not what he wanted. Drawing a deep breath, he said close to her face, "I can and if I were Beaufort, I would. I would not have wrestled with you this long." He paused and she dropped her eyes to look at the front of his shirt, she did not want to look at him. His deep voice droned on.

"If I were Beaufort, your clothing would be torn away and I would forcibly take from you what you protect so diligently."

He released her as quickly as he had snatched her up. He got up and straightened his clothing.

"Let this be a lesson to you, Aubrey. When I tell you that you cannot go out without me, I mean it."

Aubrey scrambled to her feet, "A lesson? You never take me out of here! You keep me prisoner in your own cruel way!"

Black turned toward her in her tirade, saying smugly, "I care for you."

In a flash her hand shot out to slap him soundly in his face, and she spat, "Liar! Pirates care for no one but themselves."

In the next instant, Aubrey realized what she had done. Black watched the color drain from her face but his thoughts drifted to another time. The memory of a dark haired island woman stood before him, face flushed with anger and he broke into a sad smile as he rubbed his cheek. Suddenly, he was back to the present and said, "Well done."

Aubrey erupted with new anger and shoved at him savagely with both hands. The force of it made him stumble back a bit. "I hate you!"

He laughed at her anger. "How many times have I heard that in my lifetime?"

"Why do you keep me here?" she ranted on.

"Because you amuse me," he chuckled, watching her as she huffed off to the quarter gallery with her arms folded.

Black watched her brooding for a minute. The posture and attitude brought back another time with the other woman. For a long moment, he stared at Aubrey's unyielding back but he saw another standing there. A knock at his door interrupted his thoughts and Black was seeing Aubrey once again as she refused to turn.

"Oui?" he called with a smile at her tantrum and laced the front of his shirt closed.

"Rene, we still need to talk," came the voice of Jean Luc.

"Entre," Black called.

The quartermaster stepped into the cabin, his hat in his hand. He glanced at Aubrey, noting her stance and recognized at once that she was not happy. He cast his glance back at Black as the man said with a sigh, "I am very tired, Jean Luc."

Recognizing the subtle suggestion to state his business, Jean Luc announced calmly, "DeFoe is dead, Rene."

"An accident I presume?" Black asked with a raised brow.

"No, it was deliberate," Jean Luc replied flatly.

"A murder? Has the perpetrator been put in irons? Murder is punishable by..." Black began angrily. The two were speaking in French, but Aubrey turned to listen and watch the angry confrontation with mild alarm.

"I know very well the punishment, Rene. I did not just come aboard yesterday," Jean Luc spat.

"Well then, Jean Luc, have you put the man in irons?" Black asked again.

"No, I have brought the man before the Captain to explain his motives," Jean Luc said smartly.

"You?" Black asked incredulously with a raised brow.

"Oui," the blue-eyed man nodded.

Black drew his hand down over his face tiredly, "What in the hell are you talking about, Jean Luc?"

"My orders were to protect Mademoiselle Aubrey in your absence. DeFoe presented himself as a threat," Jean Luc shrugged. Aubrey cast a startled look at the man, recognizing her name amid the French. She hoped that he was not reporting her impertinence to the Captain.

Black sat heavily in the chair at the end of the long table. "Let me see, I know that I am fatigued right now, but awhile ago you led me to believe that Thomas Beaufort had accosted Aubrey yesterday."

"Oui," Jean Luc nodded as he glanced at Aubrey. She was watching and listening intently now.

Black sighed, "Jean Luc, I know of your anger, though lately your reasoning behind it escapes me. These explosive episodes..." His voice trailed off as he shook his head. Jean Luc remained impassive save for the rippling of the muscles in his jaws. Aubrey looked from the quartermaster to the captain and could feel the tension between them. "I did not see Thomas, did you kill him as well?" Black asked tiredly.

119

"No, he still lives," Jean Luc replied with a hint of disappointment.

Black propped one booted foot up on the corner of the table. "Tell me what happened."

Jean Luc sighed this time. Perhaps Rene would not understand his logic in killing DeFoe, but he would take the chance and explain himself anyway. "While he generally travels in the company of Boulet and LaVoie, Thomas Beaufort is a 'solitary hunter'. He sights out his prey and then he attacks. He keeps the prey for himself alone, and depending on the prey, he generally attacks with no witnesses. The fortunate thing about Thomas' habits are that they make him relatively easy to control and predict."

Black watched and listened in interest. Jean Luc perched himself with one hip on the edge of the table, crossing his arms over his chest and regarding Aubrey with a glimmer in his eye.

She shot a glance at Black and found that he was looking at her as well. The stares of the two pirates and the foreign language they used in their conversation were making her nervous. She quickly turned to look back out the window.

Jean Luc began to speak again. "DeFoe, on the other hand, is a 'pack hunter'." Black turned his one-eyed stare back to his quartermaster as Jean Luc went on. "He will pursue his prey for himself of course, but he also delights in sharing his prey with the rest of his pack-mates. In fact, he gets more pleasure from the witnessing of the 'sharing' part than he does from his own take."

Black set his foot down on the floor heavily. The sound made Aubrey jump and she looked back at the two men in alarm.

"You seem to know a great deal about the habits of the men on my ship," Black said with a small smile as he stood up.

Jean Luc looked at him pointedly. "I make it my business, Rene, I am the quartermaster. That is how I keep the peace. That is how I keep them in control for you. They have to fear me and respect me as much as they do you."

Black chuckled at him and moved toward Aubrey who still stood at the window.

"Very well, leave us, Jean Luc. Set us a course for western waters," Black said as he reached out to touch Aubrey's hair.

"You will make a decision on a course without a vote?" Jean Luc ventured to question. Black raised an eyebrow and looked at him

"Do you question my orders? We are not at battle, there is no prize to take right now. Take the orders of the course change to the helmsman."

Jean Luc quite literally launched himself from his perch on the corner of the table with a huff. "By your order, Rene." The door to the cabin closed soundly with the pull of his hand. Jean Luc strode to the companionway, thinking about his auburn haired beauty in there with the captain.

When the door had closed, Black moved away from her in disinterest. He moved to his desk where he removed his weapons from his sash and put them down. Then he pulled off his shirt, making Aubrey drop her eyes in embarrassment. He smiled as he sat down on the edge of the bunk, smoothing the coverlet and pillow with his hand. Delighting in tormenting her, he said, "I am going to lay down here in my bunk where you have been sleeping. I am sure that your scent is on my pillow. Do you wish to add your presence here as well?"

"No, I do not," she spat at him.

Chuckling, he pulled off his boots and stretched his lean frame out on the bunk. He gathered the pillow up under his head as he rolled onto his side. Soon he was sleeping soundly, snoring lightly. Aubrey sat in the quarter gallery and watched as the island grew smaller and smaller in the distance.

Chapter 20

Sometime later, Black rolled over onto his back and emitted a deep sigh. Aubrey looked at him with an air of boredom. He stretched and then sat up.

"How would you like to go out on the deck for at time?" he asked.

"You scolded me earlier for just such a venture, then you played a terrible game with me," she said as she turned her head to look back out the window at the sky and water. Black came to his feet and moved to her. She slipped quickly from the sill and watched him warily.

"Well, perhaps I could arrange a sitter for you while you are out there and you would stay out of trouble," he chuckled as he pulled his shirt on.

"I did not get into trouble, sir. Your men," she began.

He raised a finger in warning to her. "Mind your tongue, Precieux. Do you want to go out on the deck or not?"

"Have I earned the privilege?" she spat in reply.

"You were as quiet as a church mouse during my nap. Oui, you have earned the privilege, come along," he said with a smile as he took her by the hand and led her out the door.

On the deck, Black looked up at Jean Luc who stood on the quarterdeck. Aubrey looked around the deck in mild dismay as men stopped their work to watch the captain tow her to the starboard railing. Jean Luc's blue eyes followed the pair, taking in Black's open shirt fluttering in the breeze. After spending a few moments with her in close and quiet conversation, Black walked away leaving her alone.

Aubrey's hazel eyes looked nervously about the deck. Some of the men were still watching her. Seeing the men's interest, Jean Luc strode forward deliberately and leaned with both hands on the railing of the quarterdeck, overlooking the main deck. Understanding the warning, and with mutterings in French about the untimely death of DeFoe, they went back to their duties. Jean Luc smiled to himself that he still commanded their fear. He now watched her himself as she turned her back to the deck and looked out to sea.

By now, the sun had begun its drop into the western horizon. Jean Luc stepped down the steps from the quarterdeck and continued to watch her covertly as he moved along the opposite deck. The sun shone through a break in the clouds of an approaching storm. The light on the water created the illusion of a pool of fire on the water in the distance. Jean Luc watched with a small smile as Aubrey fussed with an unruly lock of auburn hair. With a slight turn of her head, she finally captured the lock behind her ear.

The innocent movement made his heart skip a beat.

The ship bell chimed four times signaling that it was 6pm. Aubrey was still staring at the ocean as the sun peeked through the dark clouds and glinted off the water in a fiery alley. She seemed to be standing at the threshold of that alley. Jean Luc caught himself looking at her longingly, then quickly looked around to see if anyone else noticed his interest. To his great relief, most of the men were below to get the evening meal. Looking back at her, Jean Luc wondered what Black was doing, having left her here alone for so long.

Beaufort's voice calling orders to his watch crew drew Jean Luc's attention. The gray-eyed man had been on the deck all the while Aubrey had, but he had not approached her. He had barked commands to his crew and kept his distance. To have Beaufort on the day watch meant that he would be free to roam the ship after dark, making him a hungry lion on the prowl. Jean Luc clicked his tongue and knew he would have to remedy that situation. Looking back at Aubrey again, he saw that she had turned and was now facing the quarterdeck.

She was framed in the last rays of the sun as he stared at her face. As if she felt him watching her, she lowered her eyes from looking up into the sails to meet his gaze. He held her gaze for a few moments before she dropped her eyes to the deck. There was a small smile of embarrassment on her face as her eyes darted back up to look at him. The smile melted quickly as Black arrived seemingly out of nowhere. Stepping in Jean Luc's line of vision unknowingly, the captain approached her as she turned her back on him to stare out at the ocean.

"There is a storm brewing. It is time you went back to the cabin, Precieux," he told her.

"I want to stay out and see the stars," she said quietly.

"Non, it is very near dinnertime, and we will be having guests for dinner this evening in my cabin," he said firmly as he took her by the elbow to guide her to the companionway.

In the cabin, she stood in the quarter gallery and watched the water as Black went to the cupboard and took down a bottle of wine.

"Stop your pouting and come take your seat at the table," he told her.

Turning from the window, with arms folded over her chest she asked, "Who will be joining us for dinner?"

"Monsieur Beaufort and Monsieur Pierne." He replied as he poured himself a glass of the dark rich wine. At the mention of Beaufort, Aubrey shuddered violently. Her reaction went unnoticed by Black who had seated himself in his high-backed chair at the head of the long table.

"I am not hungry," she said tightly. It was a lie, she was actually famished, and the fresh air and sun had built her appetite to a degree that she had never experienced before. But to dine at the table with Beaufort made her stomach turn despite her hunger.

Black regarded her with his good eye and said with slight annoyance, "You will sit down here and eat, if I have to feed you myself."

Aubrey watched him with hurt in her eyes as he looked back at her passively and took a drink from his glass. A knocking at the door and the entrance of Cook and the cabin boy, Henri, silenced her and she turned back toward the window.

"Ah Beaufort, so good of you to join us," Black was saying from his chair. "Precieux," Black called to her. Aubrey turned to look at him as he remained seated, but used his foot to push out the chair in which he bid to her sit. She made a slight frown at the rudeness of the gesture but moved to the table to sit as not to anger him. Beaufort took up the seat right next to her and she felt her heart jump into her throat.

With blatant and deliberate movements, he reached across in front of her, brushing against her with his arm to take up the bottle of wine that sat on the table before his captain.

"Pardon, Mademoiselle," he said in throaty torment as he took up her glass in his other hand.

As he began to pour wine into it, Black chuckled deep in his throat, saying in pointed English, "Careful, Thomas, she is not an accomplished drinker yet. That wine is strong and she may not react well to it."

Beaufort cast her a sideways glance and replied in French, "She may react better than you suspect, Captain. It may relax her and take the prude from her demeanor." Aubrey stared blankly at the glass of wine that Beaufort had poured for her. He smiled at her, leaning closely, "Drink up, little one, and Thomas will pour you more."

She shot a glance at Black who looked at her with an air of a stern father. Turning her worried hazel eyes back to the man next to her she said quietly, "Merci, Monsieur Beaufort." Aubrey cast another quick glance to Black as he nodded with approval. His attention was drawn to the doorway and Aubrey followed his gaze. Jean Luc stood there with his hat in his hand.

"You are late," Black growled in English.

"I was seeing to tasks left undone by the first watch, Captain," Jean Luc replied tightly as he took a seat at the table and shot a look at Beaufort.

The latter snorted at him as he poured wine into his own glass. "My crew left nothing undone."

"Your crew did not secure the deck for the impending storm," Jean Luc growled in reply. Aubrey looked to the windows as she listened to the conversation. Hard rain was beginning to pelt the windowpanes of the quarter gallery.

"Jesu, all it does is rain here," Beaufort grumbled.

"It is the rainy season, you idiot," Jean Luc snapped back as he took up the wine bottle and poured his glass full.

"Who are you calling an idiot?" Beaufort roared back in French. The sudden loudness of his tone made Aubrey jump and she stared at him in alarm.

"Gentlemen," Black said quietly as he stood from his seat and picked up Aubrey's plate. The two men settled as they watched him begin to fill it with food.

She quickly laid a hand on his cuff, stopping him momentarily with her small plea, "I can do that, Captain."

He regarded her for a moment as he hovered over her at the table before he said reproachfully, "If I left it for you to do, you would eat nothing at all. Now, we will not discuss the issue of your nutrition anymore. Do you understand me?"

"Oui," she replied quietly.

"Did you eat so sparingly at home?" he went on to ask, as he set a plate full of potatoes and salted pork in front of her.

"Oui, I did, sir, when I was permitted a meal," she told him, making a face at the meal.

Beaufort looked at her in mild surprise and Jean Luc pursed his lips at the reply. Solemnly, Aubrey picked up her fork, stabbed at a small morsel of the meat and put it into her mouth. Jean Luc watched her lips tremble, for she was near tears with the captain's treatment of her.

"Well, eat your dinner. You have never been denied a meal on this ship," Black said curtly as he sat down in his chair.

"Her oncle was mean to her? What a very ugly man, this oncle of yours. Pauvre bebe—we will take better care of her than that," Beaufort cooed, making Jean Luc glare at him. We will take care of her? Did Beaufort have a mouse in his pocket? She would be better off left alone than to be taken care of by the likes of him!

"She is so tiny now, Captain. You would do well to fatten her up a bit. Why a strong wind would blow her overboard into the sea to be food to the sharks!" Beaufort laughed as he heaped his own plate full.

"Perhaps you should tie her to the mast the next time you let her out," he went on to say.

"You would enjoy that, n'est-ce pas?" Black asked as he dished food for himself.

"It would make me stand out like a flag in a stiff wind," was Beaufort's crude reply in French.

Aubrey listened to the foreign exchange and looked around the table at the other two men. Jean Luc was staring at Beaufort with the same enraged look he had shown when he had shot DeFoe. Black cut a piece of the meat on his plate, never looking up at any of them. As he brought the meat to his mouth, he said crisply in English, "Careful, Thomas."

Jean Luc looked to Aubrey now as he filled his fork. A tear slid painfully down her cheek that had been pinked by the sun today. She caught the tear daintily with her napkin and wiped her mouth.

"May I have some water, s'il vous plait?" Her voice was small and hinted of the distressed sob that she fought hard to suppress.

Black looked at her as if she were disturbing him with the request. He reached out and tapped her wine glass with the knife he held in his hand. "Drink your wine–do not waste it."

Jean Luc cleared his throat and wiped his mouth, tossing his napkin to the table and standing, said, "Eat your dinner, Captain, I will get her some water. I would like some as well. The meat is very salty tonight." Without waiting permission to do so, Jean Luc went to a side shelf and poured water for himself and Aubrey. Returning, he pushed aside the glass of wine that Beaufort had served her, and with a smile he said, "Your water, Mademoiselle."

"Merci, Monsieur Pierne." She nodded quietly, careful not to make prolonged eye contact with him in the presence of the captain.

As she took a sip from the mug to try and wash away the taste of the food as well as the large lump that had formed in her throat, Beaufort snorted beside her, "You spoil her, Pierne."

Jean Luc replied with a snort of his own and resumed his meal. He would love to spoil her, spoil her royally as she well deserved. He would do anything for her to make her happy, if she were his, when she was his.

Aubrey went back to working diligently on her dinner and listened to the men as they spoke in French and ate their meal. Her mind fell back to the times she had sat at the table of her uncle's table and yet was sequestered from the dinner conversation and company. She looked slowly to Black as he ate heartily and talked with much animation. Then she cast a glance to Beaufort as he began to speak. He stuffed food into his mouth and talked with his mouth full, sometimes food spilled back out. A small titter of laughter welled up in her for how foolish this grown man looked with such table manners. When the gray eyes shot up to look at her, she quickly dropped her gaze to her plate, still trying to suppress the giggle before it surfaced and caused her trouble.

Aubrey ventured to look at Jean Luc when Black rose from the table to get another bottle of wine from the cupboard. She sat as if hypnotized as she watched Jean Luc's profile. There was an arrogance about the man that infuriated her, yet there was also something deep and hidden in his countenance that denoted quite another aspect of the man. A strange feeling began to well up from deep within the core of her being as she watched him.

Beaufort shoved another mouthful of food into his already stuffed mouth, and with his free hand, he sopped up the liquid on his plate with a piece of bread. As he brought the bread to his mouth, his eye was caught by the stillness of the young woman next to him. Bent over his plate, he slowly put the bread into his mouth and watched her stare at the quartermaster. Beaufort looked to Jean Luc, who spoke to the captain, unaware of her stare. Looking back to Aubrey as he slowly chewed with his mouth open, Beaufort scanned her face and along the line of her body. His nostrils flared as he could just barely smell the freshness of the sea air on her.

Beaufort turned his attention back to the captain when Black spoke to him. Now Jean Luc's blue eyes drifted over to look at Aubrey. Meeting his gaze, she remained transfixed for a moment as Jean Luc picked up his now full glass. Darting his eyes to look at the other two men, he then looked pointedly back at her and winked. The young Irish woman's eyes batted ever so slowly and innocently back at him.

"Did you finish your meal?" Black asked, startling her.

"Oui," she nodded, fearful that he had seen the exchange.

Black did not appear the wiser as he looked over her plate. "See there, you were hungrier than you thought yourself to be."

"Yes sir," she nodded absentmindedly. There was a fluttering feeling in the well of her abdomen and she struggled to understand it.

"I would like to go to the window and sit now, sir," she said quietly as she turned her hazel eyes upon the dark-haired man.

"Go then," he said indifferently and impatiently waved his hand.

Chapter 21

Time passed slowly since she had left the men at the table. Plates and platters were pushed aside now and replaced by charts. With mugs of rum in hand, they worked and talked among themselves as Aubrey sat in the window ledge, watching the storm outside. Suddenly there was a blinding flash of light in the cabin and a deafening clap of thunder. Aubrey was knocked from the ledge and sent sprawling onto the floor amid a shower of glass and wood.

"Christ!" Beaufort exclaimed as the three men turned in unison toward the noise. Black moved forward quickly, dropping to his knees to pull Aubrey's limp body into his lap.

"She is unconscious," he reported, as he brushed her hair from her face.

Beaufort and Jean Luc looked from the unconscious young woman to the blown out window. Jean Luc was the first to speak, "That had to have caused more damage topside."

"Get up on deck, Beaufort. Make sure we are not on fire," Black ordered as he lifted Aubrey into his arms and stood.

"Aye sir," Beaufort nodded as he grabbed up his hat in his hurried exit from the cabin. Jean Luc followed Black to the bunk as he laid Aubrey down.

"She is injured," Jean Luc pointed out as he touched a slender finger to the side of her forehead at the hairline. Drawing his hand away, he smeared blood between his fingertips, showing it to the other man.

"Get me a napkin from the table and some water," Black said quietly as he brushed wood and glass splinters from her hair. Jean Luc held the mug of water as Black dipped it to clean the seeping cut on her forehead.

"Shall I call Pierre? Will it require stitches? He is no surgeon, but he is good with a needle and thread on the sails," Jean Luc suggested.

"Non, it is just a slight cut, it will stop bleeding directly. She is lucky to be alive, lucky that the lightening did not strike her as she sat there. We must have taken the hit somewhere above on the stern," Black said, his tone tender as he tended to the wound.

Jean Luc watched him and saw a man that he had not seen for at least two years. He was glad to see his old friend, despite the situation that had seemed to bring out the old Rene again. Another flash and clap of thunder broke the moment. Both men started at the flash and sound, then looked at the window.

"Go topside and see how we are. That idiot Beaufort could have gone below to hide like a bilge rat for all we know," Black growled as he pressed the napkin to the cut.

"Oui, Rene," Jean Luc replied with a nod.

Though he hated leaving her so vulnerable, Jean Luc noted that Black's attention seemed to be more concern over her injury than anything else. Given no other choice, Jean Luc hurriedly left the cabin while Black continued to keep the pressure on the wound as he picked wood and splinters of glass from her hair and clothing.

Memories began to fill his mind as Black fussed absentmindedly with the debris on her and checked the wound to see if it was still bleeding. Another injured young woman lay in this bunk, a long time ago. A deep sense of remorse came over him and for a few moments, he closed his eye against the pain. He spoke to Aubrey in quiet French, not seeing her but another lying before him.

With a start, Aubrey's eyes shot open, and she inhaled deeply. With her movement, he was immediately brought back to the present.

"Lie still now, you have been injured," he said easily.

"What happened?" she asked, blinking at him.

"Lightning hit the stern and you were blasted from the window," he informed her as he took down the napkin and inspected the wound closely, his face just inches from hers. In the glow of the lantern and the occasional flashes of lightning, Aubrey stared at his face. Black saw her frown and he smiled gently, thinking that her frown was a reaction to his administering to the wound.

"When this heals, you may have a very small scar but your hair will hide it," he said.

His smile faded as she reached up to touch her fingers to his cheek just below his right eye. Aubrey's eyes focused on the droplet on her fingertips as she drew back her hand. Was that a tear? Did her injury concern him that much?

She met his gaze and he straightened a bit, realizing her discovery. Black's mind flashed back to its previous wandering. It had been a long time since he had shed tears for her. What was happening to him?

A crash of thunder drew them both to the moment at hand. Black sat up from bending over her and cleared his throat as Aubrey squirmed uncomfortably when she realized that she was on his bunk.

"Where is everyone?" she asked quietly.

"I have sent them topside to check the ship, to make certain that we are not on fire," Black replied.

"Fire? That would be a bad thing," she said in mild alarm.

"Vraiment," he nodded as he dabbed at the spot once more. Authority crept over him like a dark shroud as did a growing desire sparked by memories. He looked down at her as she struggled to sit up.

"You must get out of these clothes, they are full of glass and wood splinters, and I do not want them to injure you more. To get any of that in your skin could cause a nasty infection. Let me get your little nightdress while you take these off. Then when you are changed, you can lie back down and you will sleep here." He put aside the napkin and leaned toward her.

Aubrey struggled under him as he succeeded in easily untying the laces of the shirt she wore. Her head was pounding furiously from the fall she had taken, but it did not stop her from continuing to try and fend off the advance he made. She was no match for him in her condition and as he untied the shirt, he pressed his lips firmly on hers.

Aubrey was surprised when the kiss ended as quickly as it began. "I will sleep where I always do."

"You will sleep here, and there will be no more discussion on the matter," he said firmly. Another clap of thunder reverberated around them and he stood up, muttering in a low growl, "Ame damne, I hate thunderstorms."

"I like them," she said softly.

"You would," Black grumbled as he looked at the mess of glass and wood in his cabin floor. She had loved thunderstorms, too. A knock upon the door broke the silence between them.

"What is it?" he called out, annoyed.

"You need to come topside, Captain. Monsieur Beaufort has called for you. We have been struck twice," came the voice of Boulet from the other side.

Black cursed again and pulled on his waistcoat. As he picked up his hat, he looked to see that Aubrey was inching her way off the bunk. Pointing a warning finger, he said sternly, "You stay right there." Then he was gone.

She dropped back down onto the bunk heavily. She felt light-headed and the cabin was spinning. Closing her eyes against the pain, Aubrey laid still, listening to the storm. After a short while, she opened her eyes, remembering where she was. Black's bunk was not where she wanted to be when he returned.

Black stepped out into the wind and rain and pulled his hat on a bit tighter. Jean Luc stepped up to him, nearly yelling over the tempest of the storm, "The first strike hit the stern, just as you said. Our only loss was the window of your quarter gallery. There was no fire fortunately."

Black nodded and asked in a shout over the din, "What of the second hit?"

"Some of the bow spirit was blown off, the rest of it was on fire, but the men put it out quickly," Jean Luc informed as the rain beat down on them.

"Where is Beaufort?" Black asked as he peered through the driving rain and the darkness. Jean Luc's keen blue eyes searched the deck for the man in question. He had a bad feeling in the pit of his stomach.

"I do not know, Rene. I have not seen him since you sent him out of your cabin to check the ship. Perhaps he is in the hold checking for leaks." Jean Luc gave himself no comfort with the suggestion and his worried blue eyes darted to the doorway to the companionway.

"Send the carpenter down to my cabin. That hole has got to be patched or we will drown in the bunk as we sleep tonight. We will make better repairs when we reach port," Black said loudly as he moved away.

A new concern grabbed at his stomach as Jean Luc watched the man go toward the companionway. 'We'? Jean Luc nodded in reply and searched the deck again, looking for Beaufort. As he made his way down along the deck against the wind, rain and waves, Jean Luc smiled despite the comment Black had made. She could sleep in my cabin, then she would be away from the rain blowing in the broken window. She would be warm.

Below in Black's quarters, Aubrey had finally decided to venture off the bunk. The ship rocked hindering her already unsteady gait. Halfway across the cabin, she heard the latch of the door. Worried hazel eyes watched as the door came open slowly. She would certainly be in trouble now. The Captain had returned and here she was doing just the opposite of what he had demanded.

The worry changed to unrestrained fear as Beaufort slipped quickly into the cabin and shut the door behind him.

"Bonjour, Mademoiselle," he smiled.

She did not reply at first but only stared at him. He looked around the room and she offered bravely, "Captain Black would not be pleased that you are here."

"He is busy with the ship," he said as he advanced a step.

"You must leave now, Monsieur Beaufort."

"I will leave when I am finished with you," he sneered as he stepped forward again. Her eyes darted to the table. She needed a weapon against him. Captain Black had told her what Beaufort would do, and that she would be no match for him.

"Your head is bleeding. Come, let Thomas take care of it for you," he purred as he extended his hands to her.

131

"Captain Black has taken care of me," she told him.

"I am sure he has, but he is greedy and should share you," Beaufort went on in feigned pout.

Aubrey's darting eyes caught sight of the long, ivory handle knife that Black had used to cut his meat at dinner. It would make a good weapon in the face of the man before her if she could just get hold of it. Beaufort lunged suddenly for her and she cried out in alarm, managing to slip out of his reach around to the other side of the table. Loud voices and heavy boot falls in the corridor outside caught his attention. As he looked to the door, she grabbed the knife and wielded it before her. He laughed at her stance of self-protection with the eating utensil.

Aubrey found herself wishing that the Captain would return. Beaufort was only a few feet away now. He rushed at her and she stumbled against Black's chair to avoid being caught by him.

"I cannot wait to taste you," Beaufort drawled as he continued to stalk her around the table.

Words and screams were frozen in her throat as she stared into the cruel gray eyes. He had slowly succeeded in getting her out into the open. With a growl, he lunged at her, reaching out to catch her by the wrist. Already, in his fast-working mind, he imagined her under him on the floor as he took his pleasure.

Aubrey found the voice to cry out and closing her eyes, she slashed out at him with the knife. She felt the hit and heard Beaufort roar in pain. Her eyes snapped open and she saw him step back from her. He held his right hand in his left one, looking at it in disbelief as blood ran freely from a large gash in the palm of his hand. Pure rage came over his already frightening countenance. "You little tease! Cut me, will you?" He made to lunge for her again but loud sounds of men in the corridor stopped him. Amid the voices, there was the distinctive tone of Black. Beaufort's gray eyes darted to the doorway of the bulkhead. He ran the risk of being seen going out onto the deck from that door, but he ran an even greater risk going out into the corridor. In a move that Aubrey thought he was rushing her, she readied but stared as he headed toward the bulkhead door instead. He was gone as quietly as he had come.

Chapter 22

"What is the status of the ship?" Black asked slapping at his wet clothing as he stood in the corridor with some men.

"We are fine. No water coming in anywhere except there," one man reported as he nodded his head to the companionway.

"Shut the damn doors, you fool," Black growled. He watched, shaking his head in disbelief as one of the men ran up and pulled the louvered doors shut, blocking out a great deal of the rain.

"Christ, do I have to think for all of you?" Black complained as the man came back down before asking, "How are things in the hold?"

"All is secure," another man reported.

A gust of wind and rain blasted down the companionway steps, as the doors were wrenched open amid cursing. Black turned to the sound and watched as Beaufort stepped down into the light of the lantern on the wall.

"Where in the hell have you been? I have been looking for you. You should have given me a report," Black spat at him.

"I was trying to take care of a little problem," Beaufort growled back as he wiped his face with the back of his arm.

Black's eye came to rest on a rag that was wrapped around the man's right hand. He grabbed Beaufort by the wrist. "What happened here?"

"I struck it against something sharp awhile ago," the man lied.

"When this storm dies down and the ship settles, go and find Pierre and have him stitch that. Be sure to put some sulfa on it in the meantime–before you lose it to infection. See Cook, he will have the medicine," Black told him.

"Oui," Beaufort nodded. He stomped away from the group growling in low tones, "Stitches! We will see who is going to need stitches when I am done with her, and I do not think Pierre has that much thread."

Aubrey felt weak in her knees that threatened to pitch her onto the floor assisted by the rocking of the ship. She moved as quickly as possible to the settee and sat down heavily. Her head was pounding and she looked at the knife in her hand. Lying back onto her pillow gingerly, she closed her eyes and held the knife tightly to her breast in case Beaufort should return. Captain Black would be angry for her having moved from where she was directed to stay, but she could not be concerned with that for now. Within minutes she slipped into the peaceful abyss of unconsciousness as result of the bump on her head.

"Damn that Beaufort. The next time we have a storm, I swear, I am going to send his ass up to the crow's nest. Called me out into the rain and he was not even there to give a report. Where the hell was Beaufort anyway? Thankfully, Jean Luc was about," Black was grumbling as he entered the cabin stripping off his wet hat and waistcoat and tossing them aside. His clothes ran with the water that pooled on the floor and ran in tiny rivers to meet with the pool forming from the blowing rain coming into the broken window.

He stopped short in his grumbling and looked at the bunk, thinking that Aubrey still lay there as he was speaking to her. But the bunk was empty. He looked around to the settee. With a deep sigh, he shut the door. He watched her sleeping as he peeled off his wet shirt. Had Beaufort not disturbed them, she would still be in his bunk, snuggled up against him. She would have had no other choice this night. Even though she was not quite up to a genuine session of lovemaking due to her injury, he would have at least been able to hold her. Or did he really want that tonight?

A knock on the door broke his thoughts and he opened it to the carpenter. He sat on the corner of the table sipping a glass of wine as he watched the man patch the hole in the window. He was surprised that the hammering did not disturb Aubrey as she continued to sleep, not moving a muscle and barely breathing. He nodded his thanks to the man as he left when his job was complete. With the door shut and the window boarded up slightly, the room fell relatively silent.

Shirtless, Black walked to the settee and looked down at the sleeping figure. He was surprised to see his table knife clutched in her hand and held across her chest. Frowning, he carefully extracted it from her hands, whispering, "Did you mean to use this against me, Precieux? You become more brave as the days go by."

Holding up the knife, he noted that the blade had blood on it. Frowning down at her, he watched as Aubrey inhaled deeply and turned to her side in silent reply, tucking her hands up under her chin. Her lips were parted slightly as if to invite the kiss of a lover. Touching her hair lightly, he whispered to the sleeping face once more, "You should be in the bunk. Monsieur Beaufort has spoiled our evening."

Reaching up to the back of the settee, he took down her blanket and covered her easily. With a shrug and rubbing his aching head, he went back to the task of undressing. He stripped off the remainder of his wet clothing, discarding it in the floor. He extinguished the fire of the lantern and eased his lean frame into his bunk.

Morning dawned brightly with no signs of the storm the previous night. The *Widow Maker* sailed along on full swells of the ocean as the sun beamed through the remaining windows of the quarter gallery. Black was awake, but rested against the pillows he had propped up against the headboard of the bunk. Aubrey began to stir from sleep as hammering on the deck above broke the morning silence. He remained silent watching her as she flinched at the bright light and pushed herself up into a sitting position. The memory of the knife in her hand was her first thought. She looked around for it frantically.

"Do you search for your weapon?" he chuckled.

She looked to the bunk in alarm and then quickly averted her eyes as she discovered that he was unclad and covered only to his waist with the sheets.

"No sir."

"Do not lie to me and do not be embarrassed. Have you never seen a naked man before?" he laughed again as he got up to dress. Her face flooded red again at the very thought of him standing there naked and so close.

"No sir, I have not."

"There, you lie again."

"I do not lie!" she retorted.

"Were you not here with me, you would be naked yourself and in the bed with some fortunate young man back in London," he went on in torment.

"I would not," she argued.

"You would. In fact, by now you would be fat-bellied with child," he chided on as he pulled on his shirt.

"Let me see this cut," he said changing the subject. She attempted to push his hands away, but he caught her face in them. "Be still now," he said quietly.

"My head hurts," she reported but calmed a bit under his gentle touch.

"Most certainly! I think that my head would hurt too had I taken such a fall. You were literally blasted out of the window last night," he said with a small chuckle as he inspected the wound.

Making a face and rolling her eyes to the ceiling, she asked, "What is that noise?"

"That is Jussac. He is repairing the ship where the fire was," he told her as he brushed her hair away from the crusted blood of the wound.

"There was a fire?" she asked in mild alarm as she pushed at his hands.

"It was not a big fire." Black shrugged.

"But a fire on board a ship is very serious, Captain," Aubrey said in all seriousness.

"Oui, that is true, but we are fine now. Do you see that Jussac has temporarily fixed the hole in your window? When we get to shore, he will find some panes of glass and repair it properly." he told her as he stood up and began to tuck his shirt into his britches.

"Why did you have a knife last night?" Black asked suddenly.

"Because," she began but faltered slightly while he waited for an answer. His stare was unnerving.

"I was alone and afraid." She replied quickly choosing not to bring up the subject of Beaufort any more than need be. He had scoffed at her the day before for whining about the man. What made her think that he would actually believe that Beaufort had paid her such a frightening visit! He would call her a liar again.

Black looked at her still wondering why the blade had been stained with blood. Shaking his head at his own wondering, he asked suddenly, "Are you hungry?"

"No sir, my stomach does not feel well this morning."

"How would you like to soak in a nice hot tub of water?"

Aubrey looked at him in mild alarm. "Do I smell badly?"

He chuckled low in his throat at the serious question. "No, I just thought that perhaps you might enjoy the comfort and relaxation of a bath."

He watched her ponder the offer and he added, "I will be topside, tending to the ship while you would have the whole cabin to yourself."

"May I lock the door?" she asked quickly, remembering once more the intrusion of Beaufort.

"Why certainement, Precieux, some things require the utmost of privacy."

"A hot bath would be nice, sir, merci," she said with a small smile.

"Bon," he nodded as he went to the door and opened it. Leaning out, he emitted a shrill whistle down the corridor and Henri appeared as if by magic. Black leaned close to him and gave his instructions in French; then the boy hurried off.

Chapter 23

She thoroughly enjoyed the bath. Her body ached from the fall she had taken the night before. After her bath, she dressed in a pair of black pants and a cream-colored gauze shirt that Henri once more had so graciously given her. She unlocked the door and then to occupy her time she began to tidy up the dishes still left on the table from the night before. She stacked them neatly and then moved to make up the Captain's bunk. She looked at the table of stacked dishes and giggled. Monsieur Beaufort had eaten like a pig last night, slopping and dripping food all about. He reminded her of old Mr. Adger that had come to Uncle Jonathan's house.

"You sound very happy now. Did the bath please you that much? If so, perhaps I will order hot water to be brought to you every other night to keep you in such a good mood," came the voice of Black from the doorway. It startled her and she let out a small gasp.

"You perform domestic duties very well; were you a chambermaid in London?" he asked as he moved into the room.

He watched her face darken, "No sir, I was made to do such chores," she answered curtly. Chores? Nay, more like punishment while in the home of her uncle, she thought to herself. When he was not verbally abusing her or physically abusing her with beatings, he would revel in dismissing all the staff and charging her with the monumental task of making the house in tiptop condition again after he would have guests over for dinner.

"Chores?" Black finally echoed as he sat behind his desk and waved for her to come near.

"You do not have any such chores on my ship, leave the dishes to Henri. Leave the bunk unmade, one never knows when one is inclined to crawl back into it for a nap, or for amour," he went on as she approached him warily. When she was within arms reach, he lunged forward and caught her about the waist, pulling her into his lap.

"I may want to go back in there right now. Hmm, you smell delicious, perhaps I will have some dessert on top of my breakfast," He buried his face into her neck, his overnight growth of whiskers poking into her skin.

"Captain!" she exclaimed in distress grabbing at him as one of his hands slipped up from her waist to her breast. Aubrey was greatly relieved when the small boyish voice of Henri broke his attention on her.

"Shall I take this away, sir?" The boy asked in French. Black easily pushed her out of his lap and grunted at the boy. Aubrey smoothed her clothing in embarrassment as Henri cast his brown eyes over her.

She cleared her throat and stepped closer to him. "Where are you from, Henri?" The boy continued to work and did not reply. His brown eyes looked at her and then shot to look at the captain as he sat writing at his desk.

"Answer her, boy," Black growled in English over his logbook.

Henri shot her another glance and as he picked up an armload of the dishes she had so carefully stacked, he said quietly, "I am Portuguese, Mademoiselle."

Aubrey's young face brightened as she stepped a bit closer, "Really? My Da went to Portugal. He told me that it was lovely there."

A frown replaced the brightness on her face as the boy merely nodded at her but gave no further reply as he quickly left with the dishes. Aubrey turned back to look at Black, the frown growing ever deeper. He glanced up at her and snorted, "Such an ugly little face. Did your mere not tell you that if you made such faces that some day your face would stay that way? Then you will look like the men on this ship!"

"Why are you so mean to him? I would like to talk to him, to have him be my friend," she said quietly.

"The boy is a pest, and he is just that, a boy. He has nothing for you. He still has a boy's body. He would piss in his pants if he were to see you unclothed. He would have no idea how to touch you," Black growled at her in reply. Her mouth shot open in horror at his comment.

"I do not want him to touch me! I do not want him to see me unclothed! I just want someone to talk to," Glaring at him, Aubrey saw that Black was looking past her.

"Do you see now what you are up against, Jojoba? She has a pout that demands all and a little bit of a temper to match that red hair. She wants someone to talk to. Can you do that as well? Do you think you can handle her?"

Aubrey spun around to see a muscular black man standing in the doorway dressed in light colored britches, a vest, and a bandana about his head. A thick gold hoop earring dangled from his left ear and there was a tattoo of a ship on his broad bare chest. He was well armed with cutlass and pistol in the red sash about his waist and was barefooted.

"Aye, Captain, she will be no problem," he replied in a heavy accent Aubrey had never heard before.

She stepped back a few paces, putting her right beside Black's chair, and asked timidly, "What do you mean, can he handle me?"

"Do not be alarmed, my dear. This is one of my best men, Jojoba," Black smiled.

"Mademoiselle, I am at your service." The black man smiled again as he offered her a deep sweeping bow. He moved forward, holding out his hand to her. She sidestepped instinctively toward Black, watching this newcomer warily.

"Give him your hand, Precieux. I know that your uncle taught you better manners than that," Black directed. Putting her hand out tentatively, she trembled as the man took her hand in his large one and pressed his lips to the back of it.

"Jojoba will see to your needs and your protection when I am off the ship," Black told her with a nod toward the man.

She looked at the captain in alarm, "But I thought that Monsieur..."

"He will not be on the ship all the time. Sometimes I require him to come ashore with me," Black interrupted.

"How many men will you assign to the task of watching me?" she asked.

Black chuckled and Jojoba followed suit as his captain said, "It is not the number of men that I assign to watch you that is the real concern here. It is the number of men on the ship who are watching you. I need a small army to protect you, Precieux. You are a tasty little fish on this floating sea of hungry sharks. Any one of these men would love to gobble you up. Therefore, I can trust only my best men for the job, because I know that they will protect you from the others and not be tempted themselves."

Jojoba ran his eyes over her and smiled at his captain, speaking to him in French.

"She is not at all like de other. Wid dat one, we needed an army to protect us!"

Aubrey looked to Black, not understanding the comment. Black's face darkened and gave the man a tight reply in French. Jojoba dropped his head at the apparent reprimand.

"Je regrette, mon Captaine, I speak out of line," he said thickly in English. With a sudden change in attitude, Jojoba looked at her, and pointed carefully. "Dat is a bad bruise on your head, Mademoiselle Aubrey."

She touched the small wound on her head gingerly, "Yes sir, I have a headache."

"Jojoba missed the storm last night. He came on board with me yesterday, but not of his own power. I found him in a tavern. So I had some of the men pick him up and bring him back with us. During the storm last night, he was still sleeping off a drunken stupor in the forward hold," Black chuckled. Jojoba smiled sheepishly in reply and shrugged his shoulders. Aubrey frowned at him.

"Perhaps I could fix her something for de pain? Such a pretty face should not be masked wid hurt," Jojoba suggested to his captain. Black nodded.

"Jojoba is well-versed in herbs and medicinal plants. He is from the islands."

Aubrey nodded slightly and looked to the man as Black continued, "He is my first mate."

"When de quartermaster is off de ship, I am in charge," Jojoba added with a grin.

"What of Monsieur Beaufort? I thought that he was next in line, at least that is what he is always bragging," she said with a bit more bravery and a flippant roll of her eyes. Jojoba laughed out loud at her comment.

"Not anymore. There has been a vote for a new First Mate. Jojoba is the winner of the vote. Monsieur Beaufort is the second mate now," Black said stiffly as he went back to his writing. Aubrey made a small face at the captain. She was certain that Monsieur Beaufort would not have taken that well at all.

Black put down his quill and slipped his arm about her waist once more, pulling her down into his lap. "Well then, I think that you will be a good girl for Monsieur Jojoba. Be careful of her, mon ami, as I have said, she sulks very effectively. She blushes at the drop of a hat and her pretty hazel eyes will play on your soft heart if you let them do so."

"We will get along just fine," Jojoba nodded with a friendly smile toward her.

"Leave us alone now, Jojoba. She has caught me up in her charm this morning. She has had a hot bath and smells like the fresh sea air. I must pay some attention to her now," Black chuckled as he kept her in place in his lap, despite her attempts to free herself.

Chapter 24

Jojoba exited the cabin, leaving the door open behind him to allow the cooler air from the corridor to enter the cabin. Black chuckled as he caught her in a kiss.

"Captain," she gasped as his hands began to roam once more.

He chuckled in her ear and caught the lobe with his teeth. A movement at the door caught Black's attention and he raised his head to look. Jean Luc stood in the doorway, looking down the corridor to his left, in the direction of the retreating Jojoba. Black clicked his tongue and pushed Aubrey out of his lap. She breathed a sigh of relief and brushed her clothing back into place once more as she directed her attention to Jean Luc.

"Now what in the hell do you want?" Black growled.

"When did he come aboard?" Jean Luc spat, waving his hat toward the door, referring to Jojoba.

"I brought him back yesterday. Where have you been that you have not seen him before now?" came Black's curt reply in French.

"I have been busy tending to your ship," Jean Luc replied in the same tone. Aubrey moved away from Black's reach now and watched the two men in their foreign conversation warily.

"What in the hell did you bring him on board for, Rene?" Jean Luc said, the anger rising in his voice.

"He is a good seaman and we need all that we can get," Black replied.

"Good seaman? Mon Dieu, Rene, are you serious? The son of a bitch left me for the British dogs!" Jean Luc spat. Aubrey moved herself further back from this angry conversation and took shelter near the quarter gallery window.

"It was not done in malice, Jean Luc. You are still alive and well, you need to forget that incident," Black scolded with anger still lacing his voice.

"Forget it? I cannot believe that remark from you, Rene. You who have held a grudge for over a year because of an incident that," Jean Luc began in rage. Black threw up his hand to halt the man.

"I have told you before not to mention that."

Jean Luc rolled his blue eyes. "That is just my point, Rene! You will not even talk about it. Yet you sit there and try to tell me that I have to forget? To face the very man who did that to me?" Jean Luc raged on.

"Jojoba will be helping to keep an eye on her when we are both off the ship. I cannot go ashore for business and pleasure all the time without taking you. You do still like to go ashore for pleasure, do you not, Jean Luc? You do still like the pleasure of a woman?" Black asked sarcastically.

Jean Luc drew back at the question that had suddenly changed the subject and came in English. Aubrey was looking at him in alarm and embarrassment at the comment.

"Well, of course I do," he replied in French. He could have shot Rene for the questions and he made sure not to look at her. Since he had seen her in London, the only woman in the world he wanted was the auburn haired beauty before him, but she was out of his reach for the present, and Black had just put another obstacle in his path to her, Jojoba. Glaring at Black in renewed anger, Jean Luc hissed, "Have you lost your mind, Rene? What would ever possess you to leave her in his charge? He cannot be trusted with the life of anyone!"

Black shot to his feet, pushing his chair backward in the process. "You dare to question my judgment?" he boomed.

The two men glared at one another while Black's mind went back to the incident Jean Luc spoke of. Nearly six months before, they had put into one of the bays in Jamaica. They had gone ashore to trade and sell stolen goods and relax after many long months at sea. Jean Luc, Jojoba and four other men were on their way back to the ship when some British soldiers had cornered them. A fight ensured and two men were killed from Black's crew while Jean Luc had been badly injured. Jojoba and the other two ran for the ship, leaving Jean Luc behind.

"They took you for dead, mon ami. It was a mistake," Black said quietly.

"A mistake that nearly cost me my life," Jean Luc said tightly.

Had it not been for a native woman, Jean Luc knew he would have died there in that alley. She and two other men with her had taken him from the alley to a hut on the outskirts of the city. He was nursed back to health within days and the two men took him back around the island to the small bay where the *Widow Maker* was moored. He had never seen the woman's face nor heard her voice. In his semi-consciousness and incoherent state, she was only a shadow to him.

Black felt a tugging at his sleeve and found that Aubrey had managed to move beside him but now her eyes were wide with fear as she gazed at Jean Luc. Looking back, he saw his quartermaster resting a hand on the butt of his pistol.

"Do you intend to use that on me, mon ami? If so, be careful of your shot that you hit your target and not some innocent bystander," Black said as he shifted his eye to look at Aubrey for effect.

Jean Luc looked down and slowly dropped his hand, saying tightly, "No

Rene, of course not. It was an involuntary move made in the heat of anger."

"I thought so. Your concern is a point well taken Jean Luc, but would you suggest that I leave her in the care of Beaufort in our absence?" Black droned on in French. He felt Aubrey clutching a bit tighter at his sleeve at the recognition of the man's name.

"Certainly not, Rene! How safe would she be then? The man is an idiot and you know his ways with women," Jean Luc began stiffly. With a great deal of inner struggle, he added, "And she is your woman. Would you wish that on her?"

"Precisely–she is mine and I will put her in the charge of whomever I please," Black replied in a firm tone.

Jean Luc calmed himself and looked around the room as Black sat back down in his chair and pulled it up to the desk. Aubrey still clutched at his sleeve and he gently pried her fingers from the material and kissed them.

"It is alright, Precieux. Monsieur Pierne is out of sorts today. He is just a bit cross."

Jean Luc's eyes came to rest on the still full tub of water in the corner. He imagined her there and a rush of heat swept over him as he turned his eyes back to her. She shot a glance at the tub and then back to him, a blush flashing over her cheeks as if she could read his mind. Looking at her for a few moments, a mind-numbing thought came over him. It was evident that Black had plans and the plans involved her.

"Why are you here?" Black asked, breaking him from his thoughts.

"To tell you that the repairs to the ship are completed with the exception of your quarter gallery. We are on good course for our next port as well." The conversation had calmed considerably and changed to English.

"Very well, merci. Shall we get back to the charts since you are here and have interrupted me?" Black asked. Jean Luc nodded and moved to the table, laying aside his hat.

"Jean Luc, do try and get along with the man, s'il vous plait. I cannot afford to have my best men fighting among themselves," Black said as he stood again.

"I will try, Rene."

Aubrey walked carefully around the long table, giving Jean Luc a wide berth and watching him warily. He smiled at her apologetically. Hoping to regain any shred of trust she may have had in him before his outburst, he asked easily, "Forgive me, Mademoiselle Aubrey. How is your head this morning?"

"She looks at you now like she does Beaufort," Black chuckled in French. Jean Luc cringed at the thought.

"My head hurts, Monsieur Pierne," she said stiffly as she lowered herself to the settee. Leaning back onto her pillow, she closed her eyes against the pain.

"Jojoba has promised to bring you something," Black reminded as he watched Jean Luc pin down the charts on the table. The latter rolled his eyes, asking in quiet French as not to alarm her.

"Are you certain that it will be helpful? Or will it be harmful?"

"Arguing again?" Black asked.

"Forgive me, Rene. Old habits are hard to break," Jean Luc said smartly in English this time.

"I have de medicine for Mademoiselle Aubrey, Captain," Jojoba informed him from the doorway.

Shifting his dark eyes to Jean Luc, the Jamaican made it known that he overheard some of their conversation. Black waved for him to approach her with the concoction.

"Drink dis, it will make your head feel très bien." The black man smiled at her as he went down on one knee to hand her a mug of steaming liquid. Aubrey looked at it hesitantly then took a small sip at the coaxing nod of the man. She made a face and looked at him.

"I am sorry, Monsieur Jojoba, but this tastes terrible. I could not possibly drink it."

"Ah! But wait!" He smiled again as he dug into a leather pouch that he had slung across this broad chest. She watched as he dropped two pellets into the mug and took it from her. He swirled the mug for a moment and then sniffed the contents. He handed the mug back, gesturing for her to take another sip.

She followed his direction and smiled. "It tastes like chocolate."

"See den? Jojoba will take care of you, ma petite!" he smiled in reply as he gently stroked a finger under her chin. Black chuckled at the exchange, but Jean Luc looked on with masked anger. No matter what Rene said, he would never trust the man again and it distressed him that now she was in his charge.

Jojoba left the scene after directing her to drink the entire contents of the mug, while Jean Luc and Black returned to the charts. After a time, Black looked at Aubrey as he stood with his arms folded over his chest and found that she had drifted off to sleep.

"She is not the epitome of the type of women that you usually favor, Rene. She is fair of skin, hair and eyes, she is très timide," Jean Luc remarked. Black looked at him quickly with a warning glance for him not to go further in his observations or comparisons.

"She amuses me. Would you rather I would have left her to die when the *Gull* went down?" Black asked tersely.

"Certainly not, Rene! That would have been a terrible waste. But how did you know she was on board?" Jean Luc scoffed.

"You knew she was on board. Would you not have gone to find her and take her off the ship given the circumstances? As a matter of fact, I am quite surprised that you were leaving such a treasure behind," Black countered cagily.

"Well, had I known where she was, but she was not on the deck when you pulled alongside," Jean Luc partially lied with a shrug.

"Now she is here, quite intact, too much so I might add. Just as pure as the day she left England," Black said with some disapproval. Jean Luc glanced up and met the dark eye.

"Are you confiding in me, Rene?" he asked. Black merely sniffed at him.

"But you have not answered my first question, Rene. How did you know she was on board?" Jean Luc said as he took a drink from his mug and looked across the room at the sleeping young woman.

Gibbs had gone to the steward's cabin to get her at the order of Jean Luc himself, having overheard the young man's plans to hide her. There had been no time for Gibbs to alert the Captain. Black smiled at him. "I may be blind in one eye, mon ami, but when it comes to beautiful women, my sight is extensive."

Jean Luc could do no more than nod to the reply as he drew a line from one point to another on the chart. To change the subject, he stood and pointed to the chart with a ruler. "There Rene, all charted for the next month, provided we do not run into any resistance or get caught and have our necks stretched before then! We are amid the thick of islands now and can moor at any number of them for whatever reason suits us."

"Bon, I will be going ashore when we reach Jamaica. She will be in your charge, I will be taking Jojoba with me to make use of his language skills and knowledge of the island," Black nodded as he looked toward Aubrey again.

"By your order," Jean Luc nodded, appearing unconcerned and disinterested. He would be alone with her and another chance to get closer. He gathered up his charts and left the cabin to go up on deck. Black returned to his desk to complete his entry from the day and night before.

Chapter 25

It was early afternoon when Aubrey finally stirred from her nap and looked around the room to find that Black was not in the cabin. She moved to the partially boarded window to look out at the ocean. The horizon was dotted with several small islands in the distance. Her heart leapt a bit. Perhaps this time he would take her ashore with him. Her thoughts were interrupted by the sound of the door coming open behind her. She turned quickly, ready to meet an unfriendly or frightening face. A sigh of relief escaped as Black stepped in removing his hat. He smiled at her as he tossed his hat aside, "Well, so you have finally awakened. Are you hungry? Surely you must be, you did not take a morning meal."

"I suppose I could eat a little," she nodded.

"Bon, I have already directed Cook to bring you a plate," he smiled. In the very next instant, there was a knock upon the door and Black opened it. Cook stood with a broad sparsely toothed grin and a bowl in his hand. Aubrey seated herself at the table and the man set the bowl before her.

She smiled up at him, "Merci."

The one tiny word threw the big man into an animated speech that she was at a loss to understand. Black chuckled at him and waved him away.

"What was he saying?" she asked as she stirred the contents of the bowl.

"You have made his day. He was concerned that you did not like his cooking and he was quite certain that you were starving to death and wasting away in here," Black said as he sat in his chair and propped his foot up on the corner of the table. Aubrey looked at the booted foot on the table and made a small face. Well, pirates did not have very good table manners.

"There are many small islands out there. Will we stopping at any of them?" she asked as she ate.

"Oui, this is the Caribbean and we make several stops among them," he replied with a nod.

"Will you go ashore?" she queried on.

"I will."

"Will you be taking me, too?" The question came as if from a child. Black looked at her thoughtfully and considered her age as opposed to his. He was a score and nine years old, well traveled since a young boy, and was a master of several languages. Compared to him, she was just a child.

"We will see," he finally replied, not wanting to commit himself and also not wanting to throw her into a tantrum. Aubrey passed the rest of her meal in silence, with him sitting in his chair just watching her.

Black stretched languidly in the chair and stood up. Looking down into the bowl, he noted that it was empty. He crossed behind her chair, sliding his hand along the back of her shoulders as he did so. When he reached the other side of her chair, he caught her by the upper arm and pulled her to her feet and up against his chest.

"We were interrupted this morning, just as we were last night."

"Interrupted?" she asked in feigned puzzlement.

"Hmm, oui," he said as he dipped his head toward her throat and one of his hands slipped up along her rib cage toward her breast. She caught the hand, but permitted him to kiss the side of her neck. He chuckled at her parry as he moved his kisses up the line of her jaw.

A distant thundering sound could be heard. He stopped with his kisses and frowned toward the partially boarded windows. Aubrey took the opportunity to try and push free of his clutches. He held onto her and lowered his head once more to press his lips on hers. She fretted through the advance as the thundering came again.

"There is another storm coming, Captain," she said as she pushed at him, trying to break his concentration on fondling her.

"That is a natural occurrence here," he murmured, undaunted.

"What if the ship should be struck again?" she asked on.

The thundering had built in succession and intensity. Black raised his head fully now and looked to the window once more. The sky was blue and there were no clouds for as far as the eye could see. He listened intently to the sound. She stood in his grasp, looking up at his puzzled face, "Captain? Is it a bad storm?"

"That is no storm," he said quietly as he pushed her easily from his grasp.

"What is it then?" she asked in growing alarm at his strange attitude.

A fierce pounding on his door made her let out a small cry of alarm.

"Captain! You must come to the deck right away! There are two ships in the distance to our port," came the excited call from the other side of the door.

Black cursed in French and swept up his hat and gloves in passing his desk. The door slammed loudly as he exited the cabin and Aubrey was left alone in the center of the room, wondering what was going on. She went to the windows to look out as best as she could. The ocean was empty, but the thundering sound continued.

"De lookout reports two ships to our port and dey are engaged," Jojoba reported as he handed Black a long glass upon his arrival on deck. He

147

scanned the ocean to the direction indicated, but the water was empty. He put down the glass and looked up at the man sixty feet above in the crow's nest.

"We cannot see them from down here! What do you see?"

"Two ships, one is a three mast galleon and the other is a twin-mast brigantine. They are both pirate vessels. One flies the skull and cross bones with another design that I cannot make out. The smaller ship flies a solid red flag," the lookout called down as he looked through his glass.

Black frowned to Jojoba and wondered aloud, "Who could they be?"

"I know many dat fly de Jolly Roger wid another design, but it does us no good unless we could see it for certain. De red flag, I have no clue." The man shrugged.

Black snapped the glass shut and looked back up the crow's nest as the man called down excitedly, "The smaller ship is pounding the hell out of the big one!" The thundering of what was now identified to be cannons came in rapid succession, confirming his report.

Beaufort muttered a curse from nearby as he looked at Black and they listened to the battle. Black looked around the decks at his men. All of them stood ready and waited in anticipation of his order.

Black exhaled deeply and put a hand on his hip, looking pointedly at his Jamaican first mate. "Make preparation for battle but keep the port doors shut and keep a close lookout on them. While I have no intention of intervening, I want us to be ready in case they should turn and come upon us. Apparently they have no idea we are here, although, if either one of their lookouts were to make a scan, they would most certainly see us as well as ours can see them. The fight is theirs, not ours; let it remain as such."

"Aye sir," Jojoba nodded then turned away to call out the orders to the crew as Beaufort relayed the orders to the gun crew. Black went to the quarterdeck and leaned on the railing, watching as his men made the ship ready for possible confrontation. He scanned the decks with his good eye and noted that Jean Luc was not in sight. He watched as Jojoba called orders to the crew and realized that it was late in the day now and the watch had changed. Jean Luc would no doubt be in his quarters.

Jean Luc had turned in his bunk and opened sleepy eyes to the pounding sound of the cannons in the distance. He ran his fingers through his light brown hair and exhaled tiredly. He wondered if he should get up and go on deck. It seemed rather quiet up there for as much noise as there was in the distance. Jojoba and Beaufort could be heard directly overhead now and Jean Luc listened to the commands. He lay listening as cannons were rolled into place above. Black was preparing them but he was apparently laying back right now from whatever it was. He sighed in relief and closed his eyes again.

A pristine vision of Aubrey drifted into his thoughts and he smiled to the semi-darkened room. A small frown crossed his brow for a fleeting moment. He wondered what she might be thinking right now with all this noise. Turning onto his side in his bunk and cradling his pillow against his chest he imagined holding her, whispering away her fears with words of comfort and terms of endearment. He drifted into twilight sleep, dreaming of carefully undressing her and making languid love to her.

Aubrey stared out the remaining windows of the quarter gallery. Then she stood up on the ledge and craned her neck to look to the horizon. She could see no reason for the sounds that filled the air. There was a rumbling from somewhere above on the wooden decks and she wondered what it was. Her heart was pounding nearly as hard and loud as the distant noise. She remained at the window, clutching at the boards that patched the broken panes and straining her eyes to see the origin of the sounds.

"Captain!" shouted the lookout. Black raised his head to look at the man high above.

"A British frigate has arrived on the scene," he reported.

"How goes the battle?" Black called up.

"The larger ship is crippling, but she remains afloat. She has turned her guns on the British frigate."

"What of the smaller ship?"

"She is tacking away with unbelievable speed," he informed with a tone of admiration as he watched in the glass.

"The captain of the smaller ship is no fool, hit and run, then leave the larger one to the prey of the British," Black muttered almost to himself. Standing next to the captain, Beaufort nodded in agreement.

"How is the big ship doing?" Black called up after a few moments of listening to the sounds of this new battle. As the man leaned over to call down the reply, there was a tremendous explosion in the distance and a ball of fire lit the sky.

"Jesu, who was that?" Beaufort exclaimed as his head shot up to look at the man above.

"The British frigate, she is in pieces," the man replied.

"Touched off her magazine," Black nodded with a grim smile.

"One well-placed grenade or ball will do it," Beaufort smiled evilly in

149

reply.

"De smaller ship?" Jojoba queried up as he came up the quarterdeck steps.

"Gone! Out of sight, as if she had never been there!" came the startled reply. The three men looked at one another with mixed emotions. A ship to move that fast had to have a captain with a cunning and calculating mind.

"I hope we do not come up against that one," Beaufort snorted.

Black cast him a disapproving glance and told him with an air of superiority, "That ship and her captain would do well to steer clear of me. I will gladly put her down if she crosses my path."

Chapter 26

That night, Black joined his men in the galley. They were all like a bunch of noisy ruffians. The battle that afternoon between the two ships of their own kind, although they had not really seen it, had sparked all their restless spirits. It had been a while since they had seen action of any kind.

In anticipation of their arrival to the big isle of Jamaica, Cook emptied all his stores and provided them with a grand buffet; copious amounts of rum were consumed. The larders and their libations would be restocked and filled to capacity with the visit to port and trading commenced. Wrapped up in the joviality of the evening as well, Black waived the normal curfew that he generally enforced on board. The men played dice, cards and the musicians played for them.

At four bells of the watch, Jean Luc wandered into the noisy galley. His hair was still ruffled from sleep and his shirt hung open.

"Join us!" Black invited with a smile and a laugh as he poured a mug of rum for his quartermaster and sat amid Beaufort, Boulet and Jojoba. Jean Luc cast his blue eyes around the group and let them come to rest on the Jamaican. The two stared at one another and it seemed that the air thickened between them.

"Sit down, damn you," Black finally growled drunkenly. Jean Luc lowered himself into a chair and picking up the mug; he downed half its contents before he set it back down heavily. Glancing at Jojoba again, he wiped his sleeve across his lips to dry them while the Jamaican stared at him through drink-glazed eyes.

Black poured Jean Luc's mug full again. "You missed it today, mon ami."

"I heard it," Jean Luc drawled.

"I wish I could have seen it," Beaufort said thickly.

"I wonder who the smaller ship belongs to," Black added with a nod as he drained his mug.

"Dey says de big ship may belong to Louis Savage. De lookout said tonight dat he taut dat de flag had a drawing of a man on a horse on it," Jojoba said in thoughtful reply.

"I thought he said he could not see it," Beaufort grumbled but Jojoba shrugged.

"Ah! That bastard Savage?" Black growled as he poured more rum.

"But who was the other one?" Beaufort still wondered aloud, echoing his

151

captain's words. Jean Luc listened to the conversation, but added nothing.

"Who flies a solid red flag?" Boulet asked pointedly after having sat so quietly himself for a time. Jean Luc's blue eyes flashed up to look at the man as he brought his mug to his lips.

"Perhaps dey will be moored in de bay when we get to Port Royale," Jojoba offered.

"I doubt it, whoever he was, he took off as soon as that frigate appeared. Must be a coward, to fight his own kind, but let those bastards have the sea," Beaufort snorted.

"No, not a coward Thomas, just careful. Obviously there was some argument between him and the larger ship, but it would have been unwise for the smaller one to break off battle with Savage, if that was whom the larger ship was, and to take up fighting with the British. Do you think that Savage would sit and wait while that battle was settled? Non, he would blast the pair of them out of the water. He is a deceitful bastard that give pirates a bad name," Black rumbled in his deep voice. The remark brought out a roar of drunken laughter.

"I have never seen anyone flying a red flag before. They must be from the Colonies," Beaufort muttered as he drained his mug. Jean Luc listened, pursing his lips, the muscles in his jaws rippling and his blue eyes looking from one man to the other as they spoke.

Cook approached the table with a plate in his hand.

"What have you there?" Black asked thickly.

"A plate for Mademoiselle Aubrey, sir. She has not taken a meal since earlier today," he said easily. Black stared at him as if he had no idea who the man was talking of for a few moments.

Beaufort grunted at Cook, "You spoil the hell out of her,"

"Stand up here and I will knock the hell out of you. I will put your arrogant ass through that bulkhead," Cook growled back at him as he set the plate down heavily.

Beaufort started to his feet. "Come on then, you bastard."

Cook drew back a large fist as Black's words commanded them both to stillness. "None of that. You take it ashore when we are moored."

The big man put his hand down slowly and took up the plate once more. "Can I take it to her?"

"I will take it, Captain," Jojoba volunteered thickly. Black looked at the man, as did Jean Luc. Black's eyes were glazed and he still seemed unsure of whom they spoke. The hair on the back of Jean Luc's neck bristled with anger at the thought of the Jamaican paying her a visit. Silence hung over the table like a shroud as the men looked from Cook to Black for the answer.

"I will take her something," Beaufort grinned.

"And we all know what that would be!" Cook spat at him.

"I will take it to her," Jojoba offered again.

Jean Luc sniffed at the man, "You are so drunk you would have it spilled all down the passageway before you even got to the great cabin. And besides, how does the captain know that you would not put some native poison in there to make her sick or kill her?" The Jamaican's dark eyes glared at Jean Luc for the accusation.

"Oui, you might put some mumbo jumbo curse on her and then she would not be able to open her legs to the captain," Beaufort laughed.

Jojoba snorted at the remark. Black smiled lightly, "I could still get in there."

"I will take it," Boulet offered.

"No, you would eat it, and she would still have nothing," Cook spat as he smacked the man's hands away from the plate.

"Send it with Henri," Beaufort offered.

"The boy is asleep back in the hold," Cook said.

Jean Luc emptied his mug and standing with an air of boredom and finality, he reached out to take up the plate and the utensils. "I will take it to her."

Black eyed him drunkenly, then snatched the knife from the utensils. "I will take this, mon ami. I would not want anything to happen to you on the way."

"Certainement, Rene. You do still keep a dirk on your desk, n'est-ce pas?" Jean Luc asked and smiled. Black chuckled at the reminder of his friend's play to be stabbed instead of playing nursemaid.

"Merci, Monsieur Pierne," Cook said quietly with a nod of his head.

Jean Luc left the table, casting a look of arrogant victory over all of them. Black stared at his mug for a few moments as the men around him continued to talk and laugh. Thoughts of another young woman drifted amid the hazy fog of the drink in his mind. Suddenly, Black fell quickly back into conversation as if nothing had occurred and nothing had been on his mind.

There was no light under the door of the great cabin. Jean Luc knocked easily and listened intently for a call to enter. He received only silence from the other side. Carefully and quietly he opened the door calling softly, "Mademoiselle Aubrey. I have brought you some late dinner." There was still no reply as he stepped all the way into the room.

In the light of the full moon that shone through the broken quarter gallery windows, he saw her on the settee. She was sleeping, curled on her side facing the room, and snuggled deep under her blanket with her auburn hair fanned out on the small pillow. He set the plate on the table, never taking his eyes off the peaceful scene. The urge to gather her up into his arms and carry her away to some secret place on the ship was strong, but he quickly put it aside. There would be another time, a better time in the future.

The noise of the galley drifted into the room and Aubrey stirred in her slumber, turning onto her back and pushing away the covers a bit. She sighed deeply and the sound sent waves of desire through Jean Luc. Would these be the sounds she would make during love? Almost as if it were a silent reply, a gentle smile crossed her sleeping countenance. He smiled back at her. With a sigh of his own, he turned from the room and left quietly, pulling the door shut behind him.

Black returned to his cabin nearly an hour later. He was not as quiet as Jean Luc and slammed the door behind him. The noisy entrance jolted Aubrey awake. Completely drunk, Black was bumping and grumbling around in the cabin, pulling off his boots, then dropping them unceremoniously onto the floor.

Fortunately for Aubrey, Black had no memory at the moment that he shared the cabin with her. Realizing that fact, Aubrey lay still amid her covers, barely breathing as she listened and watched him in the moonlight. He peeled out of his clothing, leaving the pieces where they dropped. Before she realized it, she was staring in mild fascination at his naked body on display before her in the moonlight. Her eyes were transfixed on him for a few moments. Suddenly she closed her eyes in embarrassment and felt the heat of a blush spread across her cheeks.

She prayed that he would stay on his own side of the room and leave her alone. Her prayers were answered, as he dropped down onto the bunk with a grunt and moved around restlessly until he finally settled down. Aubrey remained still and soon heard the familiar sound of his breathing as he fell into a deep sleep. With a relieved sigh, she closed her eyes and clutched the covers back up to her chin.

She had never seen a naked man before and the dim vision she had been afforded remained burned in her mind. Perhaps she had been sheltered too much. She knew nothing. Now here she was on a ship full of men who obviously knew a great deal about many things. Men who knew about women and had seen women. Her mind drifted back to what the quartermaster had said to her about pleasing the captain, and she shivered despite the covers she clutched so tightly against her. With the quartermaster on her mind, a strange thing happened to her as she finally began to drift back to sleep. She began to wonder in her mind what he might look like—unclothed.

Chapter 27

During the course of the night, Aubrey was awakened by an all too familiar cramping sensation in her lower abdomen. It was coming her time of the month and now she fretted over how she would deal with this situation on a ship full of men. How on earth could she possibly bring her needs to the attention of Captain Black? Never before had she discussed this delicate issue with a man. It was not proper. Mrs. Tanner always took care of her. Mrs. Tanner had told her that men absolutely abhorred this part of a woman's life. They looked upon the woman as 'soiled' and untouchable during this time. She had also told her that in some cultures, the woman was segregated from everyone else during this time.

Now in the pre-dawn hours, Aubrey sat up in the corner of her little makeshift bed and looked across the room at the man sleeping in the bed. What would he do with her? Would he lock her away somewhere out of sight and from any contact with everyone? Would he cease to feed her or even give her water?

A distressed frown crossed her brow as she eased out from under her covers. Standing, she saw the plate of food left on the table. Stealthily, she poured herself a cup of water and sat to pick over the food. It may be the last meal you get for a long time, Aubrey. These awful pains would bring the rest of the curse with them very soon. It would last about four or five days and she would be miserable during all of them. As she ate, she looked at the sleeping man. Should she wake him now? Should she wait until he woke up himself? She would have to tell the captain, even though the thought scared her to death.

The plate was very nearly empty when she heard him clear his throat. Looking up at him with wide startled eyes, she swallowed the food that she had been chewing.

"You are up early today but then, you slept a good deal yesterday. How do you feel?" he smiled as he stretched his lean frame and ran his fingers over his hair to put it into some semblance of place. She dropped her head and scanned the table before her nervously, trying to muster the courage to ask him for help. He got up from the bed and began to pull on his britches. Aubrey was careful not to look at him this morning, but the memory of last evening flashed through her already troubled mind. She drew a ragged breath as if she were in the throes of a sob. Black approached the table barefoot and shirtless.

"You ate all of that?" he asked as he pulled a chair up close to sit near her and indicated the plate. She nodded absentmindedly. The hangover that assaulted his head this morning was severe. Even with that, he did have a vague remembrance of the heaping plate of food that Cook had prepared for her. Putting aside the headache, he smiled at her and indicated the plate. "Would you like some more?"

Raising her eyes to meet his, and biting her lip she said thickly, "No sir, I am full but I need..."

"What do you need?" he cut in with another patronizing smile.

He watched her in keen interest as she inhaled deeply, "I need... I, well, sir, there is this... it comes sometimes..."

Black raised his eyebrows in question as she stammered along. He reached out to lay his hand on her arm and she found herself snatching her arm back.

"Please do not touch me, you would not want to."

He looked at her in question and she dropped her eyes to the table. "Well why would I not want to touch you?" He asked in a low tone and laughing lightly.

Aubrey's head dropped in pointed shame. "Captain Black, I..."

Suddenly it was as if a light went on in his paining head. He sat back in his chair and crossed his arms over his chest inhaling deeply. "So, it is your time of the month."

Aubrey thought that she might fall out of the chair at the so blatantly stated remark. Her mouth flew open and she looked at him in alarm. He chuckled deep in his throat.

"You are sometimes just too precious for words, so innocent, so demure. Do you think that I do not know about women? Do you think that I am ignorant and do not know of the nature of women and the course of their flow?"

"No sir, I did not say that, sir," she replied, biting her bottom lip nervously.

"Well, I do know and do you want to know something else?" he said confidently as he leaned toward her and caught her chin in his hand to raise her face to look at him.

"What?" she asked trying to back out of his touch.

He held her chin in a firm, yet gentle grasp, "I know that when I leave, if you go over to the drawer that is tucked under the frame of the bunk, you will find all that you need for your womanly purposes." She looked at him with a mixture of puzzlement and interest. Why would he keep such things in his cabin? Smiling and releasing her, he stood saying smugly as if he had heard her mental question, "You are not the first young woman to grace these quarters,"

As he moved away from the table to collect up his shirt and boots, his mind shot back for a moment. He had another young woman here, and Aubrey truly was not what he wanted.

"I am sorry to be such a bother, sir. Will you be locking me up somewhere?" she was saying as she stood behind him.

He turned with an audible laugh, "Lock you up? Why in the hell would I lock you up? Do you go crazy at this time? Do you froth at the mouth like a mad dog? Will you be running amuck and biting the men in my crew during your course?"

Aubrey giggled at the questions and then threw a hand up to cover the giggle. "No sir. But Mrs. Tanner says..."

"Who is Mrs. Tanner? Is she an old woman? Do not believe all that the old crones tell you, Precieux. Those things that she has apparently told you are old wives tales, beliefs and practices of the old days," he said, cutting her off as he sat to pull on his boots. She listened to him intently and watched as he took up his shirt.

"No, I will not lock you up," Black said as he slipped his long arms into his shirt. While he was neither abhorred nor distressed over her upcoming condition, Black found that he was simply not interested in pursuing his advances right now. He would not be here anyway. He would be going ashore today and take care of his needs. Perhaps a dark haired whore, he mused as he stood and turned to leave the cabin.

"Merci, Captain Black," she said timidly. She watched him leave and as soon as he was out the door, she rushed forward to slide the lock bolt on the door. On the other side of the door, he chuckled at the sound and put on his hat.

Aubrey dropped to her knees in front of the drawer and found a neat stack of soft cloths that she needed. She was still wondering why the man kept such things even though he had told her that she had not been the first woman he had ever had on board. As soon as she had finished taking care of her personal business, she unlocked the door so that he could return and take care of his own morning routine.

On deck, Black walked up the quarterdeck steps.

"You look mighty rough this morning, Captain," the man at the helm remarked.

Black stroked his hand down over his unshaven face and chuckled, "I got thrown out of my cabin early, Louie."

"Feisty is she? I hear tell them redheads are hot tempered and hard to handle," Louie chuckled back as he trained his keen blue eyes on the sea ahead.

Black nodded with a chuckle. As he passed to go to the railing, he grunted, "Oui." With a deep sigh, he propped one foot up on the gunwale and leaned his forearms on his thigh. The morning wind caught wisps of his long dark hair as he stared almost remorsefully out to sea. Lock her up? Because of her flow? Black smiled ruefully as he thought of another woman whose mean streak was worse during the course of her flow. Her fits of temper caused much entertainment as his men had kept a wide berth of her. Black sighed as he stared wistfully out at sea. After he thought he had given Aubrey ample time, he returned to the cabin.

She was folding her blanket as he entered and shut the door behind him.

"Better?" He asked as he moved to the washstand. She offered him no more than a small nod punctuated by a blush. Black began to lather his face and watched her in the mirror. She stood with her arms folded over her chest, hugging herself and watching him.

With his face half shaven, he turned to her with the razor in hand, "What is it now?"

She looked at him for an extended moment and then she said stiffly, "I do not mean to be such a problem for you, but I did not ask to come on this ship."

He chuckled at her and turned back to the mirror. "Have you heard any complaints out of me?"

"No, sir."

"Then, this is just a minor situation and it has been dealt with. How old are you now? Have you not learned how to deal with it yet?" He shrugged as he went back to his shaving. She did not reply and he went on.

"Someday you will have a time in your life when you will not be bothered with your 'visitor', then you will have a fat little baby at your breast and you will have to learn to deal with that," he said, wiping the excess soap from his face and tossing aside the towel. He waved to her to follow him.

"Come along now, I will take you to the galley so that Cook can see that you have not wasted away or starved to death."

"I am not hungry," she said guardedly, knowing that she used this excuse all the time whether it was true or not.

"I know, you had a nice plateful there that Jean Luc brought you last night, but come along anyway, and if you want more I am sure that Cook will pile a plate for you as high as you are tall!" He laughed as he took her gently by the hand and pulled her along.

Aubrey stared at the back of his head as he pulled her along. Monsieur

Pierne had brought her the plate?

They entered the galley and went to Black's table. Aubrey sat and wondered on this new piece of information about the quartermaster. Jean Luc appeared seconds later, as if her thoughts of him had conjured him up like magic. Her eyes quickly dropped to the table timidly as he smiled at her. He sat down heavily, rubbing his head.

"You, too?" Black asked as he stabbed his fork into the food on the plate that Cook had set before him.

"Hmm. Rene, you must get better rum. That stuff will kill a man," Jean Luc complained as he poured a mug of water and downed the contents.

"My mouth feels and tastes like I have been licking the bottom of the ship," Jean Luc went on to describe. Black chuckled and put a forkful of food into his mouth.

"Jesu, how in the hell can you eat after all that you drank?" the quartermaster grumbled as he watched Black enjoying his meal.

"You just do not have the stomach for rum, Jean Luc."

"Oh I have the stomach for it if it is good rum and not that swill we had here last night!"

Aubrey watched the two in quiet interest as they seemed to be actually conversing in a civil manner for a change. The conversation, though all in French, seemed relaxed and tormenting between them as they talked and chuckled.

Cook had stepped up and offered Jean Luc a plate, but the quartermaster waved it off, saying in English, "Give that to the Mademoiselle."

With a tormenting guttural laugh, Cook asked with a twinkle in his brown eyes, "Does your stomach disagree with you this morning, Monsieur Pierne? Are you with child? Which of these ugly bastards is the father?"

Black chuckled lightly as Cook stood grinning proudly over his own jest. Jean Luc rolled his blue eyes from one man to the other. Aubrey's face pinked at the remark made in English and she tried to hide a titter of laughter behind her hand.

"No Cook, I am not with child. But if I ever do have a baby, I will be certain to name it after you, just because you take such good care of me," Jean Luc countered as he slid the plate toward Aubrey. She quickly stopped its progress with her hand.

"No thank you, Monsieur Pierne, I am not hungry." Cook began to protest to the captain, but Black raised a hand in her defense.

"She is still trying to digest the mountain of food you sent to her last night. She ate it for breakfast. Besides she is a bit under the weather today as well." Aubrey looked at him in alarm at his announcement of her personal

159

condition that came in English.

Jean Luc looked at her. "You are not well? Was it the food perhaps?"

Cook's face broke into a mask of insult. "You do your share of packing away the food I bring to you. Do not blame her illness on my cooking."

"No sir, the food was very good. Merci Monsieur Cook and merci to you too, Monsieur Pierne, for having brought it to me," she stammered quickly. Cook seemed literally puffed up with pride at her compliment.

"Get your big ass back to the cook stove and feed my men," Black grumbled over his plate.

"Aye, Cap'n," the man nodded and sauntered away.

"And toss that lousy rum overboard!" Jean Luc added loudly. Then he winced and put his hands to his paining head. Black and Jean Luc fell back into easy conversation.

Aubrey sat for a time, listening again and poking idly at a deep indention in the top of the table. She gritted her teeth as the pain in her abdomen was intensifying with each passing second. Finally, she mustered the bravery to touch Black on the sleeve and whisper hoarsely, "I must go back, Captain, I do not feel well."

To her horror, he waved and called to the first mate as he had entered the galley, "Jojoba! Take Mademoiselle Aubrey to my cabin, she is not feeling well."

"Oui, Mon Capitaine," the black man smiled.

Chapter 28

Back at the great cabin, in a gentle and coaxing manner, Jojoba was able to find out what ailed her. He smiled gently and said, "Jojoba will take care of you, ma petite. I will fix you some tea, dat will make you feel better. Sit down dere, I will be right back."

Within minutes he had returned with a mug of steaming liquid in his hand, and smiled at her with a mocking British accent.

"Tea time."

She giggled at him despite the fact that she did not feel well. "Is tea your solution to every problem, Monsieur Jojoba?"

"De Capitaine does not know about 'tea time'. What would he know? He is French, dey drink de wine all de time." He smiled at her. His attitude was flippant as he set the mug before her with an air of a 'proper' Englishman. Aubrey giggled at his comical act and took up the mug.

"This does not look like any tea that I have had in my uncle's house," she said as she swirled the contents.

"It is not. Dis is a tea made from a flower dat grows on my island. It will soothe your belly ache and make you feel better," he smiled back as he sat across from her at the table.

Jojoba continued to dote over her until mid-morning. After settling her with the tea, he opened the pouch that hung about his broad chest.

"I have here some perfumed oil for you to use pour le bain," he said as he produced a small ornate bottle.

"And I have dis." He gave her a small wooden box.

"Capitaine Black, he told me dat you are a very proper young lady, so Jojoba bets dat you keep your free time in sewing." Aubrey's eyes lit up as she took the gifts. The box contained colored yarns and needles and a thimble. The oil in the bottle was some exotic fragrance she had never smelled before.

"Jojoba will have to get you some fabrics, ma petite. Maybe I can steal some scraps of canvas from de men as dey get done with dem," he smiled at her.

"Merci, Jojoba," she said with a yawn.

Then he proceeded to entertain her more by telling her of his island. He described it in such vivid detail that she could see it in her mind as she sat with her chin resting in her hands and with her eyes closed. When she yawned again, she looked at him sleepily as he playfully scolded, "Look at you den, ma petite, falling asleep at de table you are. Did you get no rest last night?"

"I was up very early," she said with another yawn.

"De tea has relaxed you? Do you have de pain now?"

"No, I do not. Merci, Monsieur Jojoba."

"You call me just Jojoba. No 'Monsieur' is necessary," he smiled at her as he took her gently by the arm and pulled her up from the table.

"Where are you taking me?" she asked sleepily.

"To lay down in de bunk where you can get some rest, ma petite," he said as he pushed her gently onto the side of Black's still unmade bunk. She balked a bit, but with his soothing attitude and her relaxed state, she finally lay back amid the covers. He pulled the quilt up over her and tucked it in. "Dere, tight as a cork in a keg."

"Merci, Jojoba," she smiled at him sleepily.

"Go to sleep now, ma petite. I will just put your little treasures over dere under de settee. Every pirate should hide der treasures in a place where only dey know. When you wake up, you take care of dem better," he smiled at her. His attitude with her was like one of a caring father as he tucked her presents away under the settee.

"De bath oil, you put a few drops of dat in your water and I guarantee ma petite dat it will put de Capitaine in de mood pour amour," Jojoba said with a grin as he tucked at the quilt again. Aubrey's eyes closed slowly and she nodded to his comment, not truly understanding what he was saying to her. As he left the cabin, she turned her back to the door with a sigh and snuggled her head deeply into the pillow.

Jojoba joined Black and Jean Luc on the deck.

"Well, how is Mademoiselle Aubrey?" Black asked as he scanned the horizon with his long glass.

"She is feeling much better now and is sleeping," the first mate replied.

"Bon. Merci, Jojoba," Black nodded.

"Also, Capitaine, I was going tru some of de chests of clothing dat was taken from a recent plunder. I found a little pair of boots dat I tink would fit her quite nicely. She should not have to run about de ship in her stocking or bare feet. She is a lady," Jojoba added. Black nodded his thanks as Jean Luc watched the Jamaican move away from them. He fretted about the fact that Black allowed the man to be so free with his administration of herbal remedies with her.

"What is wrong with her? Is she fretting over slapping me the other day?" he asked with a hint of torment in his tone. Black just snorted at him and raised the glass to his eye.

"Seasick perhaps?" Jean Luc queried on.

Black put down the glass. "Seasick? For as long as she has been on board? If she were going to suffer from that, she would have done so and been over it by now."

Jean Luc shrugged and pursed his lips. "Oui, one would think so."

"Seasickness." Black snorted again. As he raised the glass once more, he added, "If she was seasick, this would be the first case that I know of where someone suffered from it once a month! God forbid we should all have the same type of seasickness! She is ailing with the course of her flow, you fool."

"Oh, I see now," Jean Luc nodded in new understanding.

"So now, mon ami, your charge is slightly under the weather and you will have to deal with her temper while I am ashore," Black went on to say, lowering the glass and turning to him.

Jean Luc faked a sarcastic smile. "Merci, Rene, you are far too kind in your tasks to which you assign me."

"I have nothing to do with the timing of the course of nature. You are just lucky I suppose, because just think of how much more difficult she will be to handle. Her tantrums will increase ten-fold, and now she will throw in buckets of tears and she will whine like a baby," Black tormented on.

"That would be refreshing, Rene, considering the temper from the other one," Jean Luc said as he looked out at sea. He missed the warning look from Black as he went on.

"How many times did you have to put have your cabin back in order, Rene?" Jean Luc asked then looked pointedly into his captain's eye and added, "A day?"

Despite his warnings about past memories, the comment was Black's undoing. The captain had tried to hold down the smile at the memories of her fits of temper, but Jean Luc's stare caused Black to burst into laughter.

"True, mon ami. We do not know yet how the mood will be for our newest guest," Black said amid his chuckles. He clapped Jean Luc on the shoulder, "The best part of all is that I will be ashore, missing all of it!"

Heavy clouds had been building to the south and large hard drops of rain were soon pelting them.

"Every day at the same time," Black growled to the thunder and lightening overhead as he and Jean Luc retreated to the great cabin with the charts.

When they entered the cabin, Jean Luc was mildly distressed to see her sleeping among the covers of Black's bunk. He missed the surprise in

Black's eye at finding her there as well. Their entrance did not affect her in the least. Black leaned over her sleeping form; "She is sleeping very soundly."

"As she was last night when I brought in the plate of food from Cook," Jean Luc nodded, trying to maintain an air of unconcern. He knew that Black would leave her alone for the course of her condition and he knew also that Black would be gone off the ship long before that would come to pass. Black moved to his desk and sat down to take quill in hand.

"We should be at the island by nightfall," Jean Luc reported as he leaned over the charts.

Black nodded from his desk, "Bon."

Jean Luc looked back down at the charts and cut a quick glance to the sleeping young woman across the cabin. It was good that they would soon be there. It shortened the time that Black will be in the way and I can get closer to my auburn-haired beauty.

At two bells that night, Black stood looking down at the still deeply sleeping Aubrey nestled in the bed linens and pillows of his bunk. Choosing not to disturb her and with a low groan, he turned out the lantern and pulled off his shirt before wandering to the settee. The last time I slept on the settee, no, it is best not to have that memory. Black literally threw himself onto the cushions and turned his back to the room.

At sunrise Black was dressed and cast one last glance at Aubrey sleeping in the bunk. She gave barely the appearance of breathing. He leaned closer over her and finally, in the brightening hues of the new day, he noted the gentle rise and fall of her chest. He reached tentatively out and lifted up one of her eyelids with his thumb. The hazel eye beneath rolled lazily and he drew back his hand. Pulling the quilt up to cover her, he muttered, "How much of that concoction did Jojoba give you?" As he pulled on his gloves and put on his hat, he chuckled to the sleeping figure and said in a low voice, "You should be no trouble for your 'nursemaid' at all." Then he turned to the door and left the cabin quietly to join his shore party on the boat trip to the island.

Chapter 29

A British warship had sailed into the harbor a few hours after Black had gone ashore. Though the *Widow Maker* was flying the Union Jack, Gibbs had been sent by Black to advise that the officers of the warship were inquiring around the town about the unknown British ship in the harbor. He had sent word back to Jean Luc that he was indisposed and would not be able to return to the ship without fear of being recognized. It was his order that at the first sight of trouble, Jean Luc should weigh anchor and take the ship around the island to some cove and hide. A message would then be sent to Black and the rest of the shore party.

It was late that same afternoon when Cook approached Jean Luc. The big man had come to him complaining that Aubrey had refused food. Cook had been very adamant, stating that she made no sound on the other side of the door at all. Although he knew that she was well enough when Jussac had made the repairs to the quarter gallery window, Jean Luc decided that even though he was in the midst of a possible crisis on deck, he would have to check on her. Knocking soundly on the door to Black's cabin, Jean Luc could not help but think about how he did not have time for this right now.

Having gotten no response from his knocking, Jean Luc pounded the door once more. Tilting his head to listen, he called impatiently, "Mademoiselle!"

The bolt slid back and the door came open slightly. She stood looking up at him through the crack of just a few inches. "What do you want?" Her tone was thick with guarded anger.

"Cook says you will not answer the door. He came to bring your meal and you would not respond," he said in reply. Her aversion to eating was beginning to play on his nerves.

"Well, I have answered the door to you and I do not have to let any of you in. Tell Cook that I am not hungry," she said curtly as she began to push the door shut.

His hand shot up to keep the door from closing and he growled low in his throat in impending anger, "Do not shut this door in my face."

With a grunt, she threw up both her hands and pushed the door harder. He put up his other hand and was surprised to feel her use her entire body against the door, "Go away!" Her demand came as a shout laced with a sob.

Decidedly, she was no match for him in strength and he easily pried his way into the cabin growling, "No."

Aubrey backed away from the door in horror as he slammed the door

165

behind him with a reverberating bang. The situation in the harbor and her stubbornness had pushed him to the edge.

"You listen here," he began pointing a finger at her.

"I am in command of this ship and you will obey my orders now. When that man comes here with food for you, I do not care if you let it pile up to the ceiling, you will let him in with it. Do you understand me?" he roared angrily. Her mouth dropped open at the sight of his six-foot frame towering over her. She had never seen him direct such anger at her. Before she could respond, he was scolding her again.

"Furthermore, when I come to this cabin, it is for a purpose and you will open this door to me. Do I make myself clear?"

As he spoke to her, his eyes drifted to the window. Since the *Widow Maker* was moored at an angle to conceal her name emblazoned over the quarter gallery windows, he could see the warship beyond and her decks seemed to be very active for this late in the day. Looking back at Aubrey, he was just in time to see her rushing him. She planted her palms firmly into his chest and, with a grunt, shoved at him with all her might.

"Get out of my cabin!" she spat at him. Jean Luc stumbled against the table in the center of the room. In love with her or not, this was the last straw of the day. Gritting his teeth and trying to keep in mind that he was fighting with a young woman and not with a man, he advanced on her angrily. She squealed in alarm and retreated behind Black's desk. Jean Luc pursued her.

"This is not your cabin," he sneered at her as he continued to give chase.

"It may as well be! I am here all the time! Alone! He brought me on board this awful ship and then he leaves me alone! He lies! He tells me that he cares but he does not! He promises to take me ashore and he never does!" She was shouting at him now as she successfully evaded him. The cat and mouse chase angered him all the more. Finally he caught her by the arm and as he pulled her towards him, she fought him like a little wild animal.

With gloved hands, he caught the little hands with the scratching nails, then he pinned her against the bulkhead just to the right of the quarter gallery windows with a grunt. He held her there for a few moments and they glared at one another. Although he knew she was referring to Black, her words burned in Jean Luc's mind. 'He brought me on board this awful ship and then he leaves me alone! He lies!'

The strong urge to tell her the real truth pressed him. I brought you on this ship actually, by setting you up on the *Gull*. You would have been on this ship no matter had you come to the docks that day or not. Looking into the hazel eyes that were filled with hurt and fear, he clenched his teeth because he did care.

"Now you will listen to me," he began breathlessly.

"No, that is all I do is listen. I am to be seen and not heard. I sit here for hours alone everyday. Even when he is here, I am alone most of that time as well, he will not even talk to me, to engage me in conversation," she said through tears that now fell freely as she pushed against Jean Luc's arms. Finding no freedom in using her arms and hands against him, she kicked at his legs with her booted feet.

"Let me go!"

"Stop it. You are going to hurt someone!" Jean Luc said as he managed to avoid the sharp little dangerous knees that came up swiftly in their attack against his crotch.

"That is the idea, you idiot!" she screamed back as she continued to fight him.

"Arrête!" he spat in French.

"Let me go," she growled vehemently as she connected her foot with his shin successfully.

He winced and in an exhaled breath he spat, "Ouch!"

"Let me go then! I am going to tell Captain Black that you came in here and tried to assault me!" she continued to threaten. Jean Luc rolled his eyes at her.

"Oh, I do not give a damn if you tell him. That is the least of my worries at the moment. In fact, if we live through this day, I will tell him myself! But not before I have turned you over my knee and paddled your britches," he said smugly into her face.

She stopped immediately, glaring up at him in alarm. He was hard-pressed not to laugh as she breathed, "You would not dare."

"Do not tempt me," he replied thickly. "I would wager that it has been a long time since you have had a paddling," he added with an amused smile.

Her rage was quickly replaced by fear. Aubrey suddenly realized that she was now pinned tightly between the bulkhead and this angry pirate as she gasped for air from the struggle.

Jean Luc exhaled forcefully as sweat glistened on his face and droplets made their slow trip from his temples and down the line of his cheek. Aubrey was staring up at him and then she looked worriedly down at the front of her body taking in the closeness of him. He followed the gaze, lingering on the gentle swell of her breasts outlined by the shirt she wore. With a small distressed whine, she looked down at her hands that he held against the wall. He slackened his grip on her hands just a bit, realizing that he held them with near-crushing pressure.

Aubrey's mind raced. The battle was over and he, decidedly had been the victor. Perhaps it was time to apply the charm, "Monsieur Pierne, I am sorry, ah, je regrette. I was angry and hurt with the Captain," she began haltingly in a mixture of the French she was learning and English.

He raised his brows in amusement. "Vraiment?"

"Yes, well, let me go. You can let me go now," she nodded as she looked up at him with fawn-like hazel eyes, and a little apologetic smile fleeted over her lips. He chuckled at her, drinking in the sweetness of her tone and eyes.

His chuckle rekindled the temper in her and she lashed out again, kicking him soundly in his shin and nearly pulling her hands free of his. "Let me go!"

Jean Luc caught her tightly once more with a curse in French for the hit. He pushed his body against hers once more to pin her writhing body against the bulkhead.

"Listen to me," he hissed close to her ear as he cut his eyes to look out the window. There was even more activity on the deck of the warship. In the struggle, it had nearly slipped his mind.

"This port is an incredibly dangerous place, especially for a young lady of your caliber. It is crawling with cutthroats, scoundrels, thieves, and murderers," he began.

With raised her brows, she countered angrily, "And this ship is not?"

"A point well taken, to be sure," he nodded and then continued, "Nevertheless, you are here, and not over there."

Aubrey looked to the window as he nodded to the port. After a fleeting moment, and thinking that she was finally going to behave, he slackened his grip on her hands once more. She immediately flew into action and he pressed his body against hers again saying thickly, "Do not fight me anymore. You would be wise to settle down and listen to me."

"Let me go and I will," she whispered dryly.

"Not yet, I cannot trust you to be still and not attempt to seriously damage those parts of my body that I care very much to keep safe and intact," he replied just as dryly as his eyes darted to the nether regions of his body for effect. Her head turned away in pointed embarrassment.

"I know that you are upset, but as I have said, this port is very dangerous. That is why, I am certain, that Captain Black has chosen not to take you this time," he said softly to the turned head as he still continued to hold her pinned to the wall. Looking back at the window he watched the activity on the warship for a few seconds. With an exasperated sigh he said gently, "Look, look out the window."

Aubrey turned her head slightly, cutting her eyes to look in the direction he indicated with an air of a spoiled child. "Look at what?"

"Do you see that big ship out there? The one that flies the Union Jack?" he asked quietly.

"The one with all the men running all about on it?" she asked as she shot him a glance.

"That very one," he nodded. Aubrey shrugged with an air of indifference.

"That is a warship carrying fifty cannons and has a crew of well over one hundred and fifty men. Those men live to fight, they sniff the air for it," he told her as the hazel eyes turned up to look at him fully.

"So what does that have to do with me? I am no threat to them. I am not a pirate," she spat, another tantrum rising in her tone.

"That much is true, but we are, and you are with us. At any moment, I may have to order us out of the harbor. The warship captain has been inquiring about us all morning. If he discovers who we really are, there will be hell to pay," he went on. Aubrey seemed to hang on his every word.

"Do you see those little doors on the side of her hull?" He asked as he nodded at the ship again and pulled her gently toward the window a bit so that she could see more clearly. She inclined her head in subtle acknowledgement.

"Those are her cannon ports. If her captain finds out our true identity, all those little doors will fall open and we will be staring down the barrels of half his cannons. If we– if I do not keep alert, one broadside blast from those twenty-five cannons will put us on the bottom of this harbor in minutes. We will all be in the water, that is, those of us who are not killed outright by the blasts or the explosion if he touches off our magazine," he went on to explain. Aubrey raised hazel eyes wide with alarm to look into his blue ones.

"I do not want to go in the water, Monsieur Pierne. I cannot swim." He looked down into the hazel eyes and Jean Luc felt his heart melting for her.

"I can swim, but I do not want to go into the water, either!" he finally said with a grim smile. He felt her relax in final defeat against his hold on her.

"But I wanted to go ashore."

He let go of her hands and she remained in place. Unconsciously, he stroked a gloved finger along the line of her jaw. "I know, but it is impossible."

Aubrey caught his hand quickly and he felt her shudder against him. A warming sensation began to rise in his loins as he still held her pressed against the wall with his body, but a movement out the window drew his attention. The warship was lowering a longboat.

"Ame damne," he cursed quietly.

"I must go to the deck now. Stay here, please and be good," he said quickly as he released her and left the cabin in a hurry.

Chapter 30

Aubrey remained standing against the bulkhead, her whole body tingling. She could still feel the touch of his body against hers, as she stood rooted. Certain intimate parts of her felt as though they were actually swelling with heat and she gasped at the sensation. She pushed away from the wall and went to the window.

A boat carrying about six men in the familiar red, white and blue uniforms of the British Navy was rowing swiftly toward the *Widow Maker*.

"Sweet Mary!" she breathed. Her head shot up to look at the ceiling as she heard the heavy footfalls of several men. Then she heard the now familiar sound of the capstan as it ground on the deck at the hands of many to hoist the heavy anchor from the water. She could even discern now, the sound of the heavy canvas sails cascading down into place to catch the winds. Looking back at the port, she stared. The quartermaster was doing just as he had predicted. He was leaving the port.

"But what about Captain Black?" she asked of the empty room. Carefully and quietly, Aubrey slipped out of the cabin.

Once on deck, Jean Luc had merely given a subtle head nod to set the remainder of the crew into action, dropping the sails and raising the anchor. He strolled on the quarterdeck with an air of boredom with his hands clasped behind his back and watched both the progresses of the crew as well as the longboat that approached. He glanced up at the flag, it snapped briskly in a breeze that blew from the island toward the mouth of the harbor. Even the wind seemed to be to their advantage.

Turning toward the port in his meandering stroll, he saw heavy black clouds building on the other side of the island. He exhaled forcefully. It looked like they were in for a hell of a storm.

"What heading, Monsieur Pierne?" the helmsman asked quietly.

"Take us to the other side of the island. Captain Black has instructed that if we came up against trouble to go there and then send someone on foot for him and the rest of the crew," Jean Luc replied in the same quiet tone. The man nodded his head and glanced to see the progress of the anchor. Normally it took a very long time to release them from the clutches of land, but today the men had really put their backs into the capstan and the anchor was just clearing the water dripping with sea grass.

"Take us out, Monsieur Ballet," Jean Luc said easily as he continued to watch the longboat.

"Aye sir," the man nodded as he gave the wheel a mighty heave. The *Widow Maker* tacked slowly and Jean Luc watched as the sails caught the first gusts of the wind. The little noise on deck as the men set the sails was broken by a crisp British accented voice calling from the approaching longboat.

"You, there!"

Jean Luc cleared his throat and ignoring the call, muttered to the helmsman, "Keep us steady as she goes. Make no cause for alarm; we are merely finished with our trade here and we are leaving the harbor before the storm," the man nodded and winked.

"I say! You there! Are you the captain of this vessel?" The voice called out again. Jean Luc stepped undaunted to the railing and looked down.

"Aye," he called, mimicking the British accent.

"What is your business here? You are not familiar to us," the man called up.

Jean Luc shrugged, "We are new, sir."

"Let us come aboard."

"Alas, but we are underway, sir. We must stay on schedule to our appointed trade in Africa," Jean Luc shrugged with a face of remorse.

From the companionway, Aubrey crouched in the shadows, listening and watching. Her heart leapt as she heard Jean Luc's response. They were finally going to Africa? Had Monsieur Pierne decided to take her there after all?

"State your business here," the man called again.

"We are but simple merchants, Lieutenant, trading in spices and cloth goods." Jean Luc shrugged again.

"Let us come aboard, lower your anchor," the man demanded.

"We have done nothing wrong, sir. I cannot stay longer or my employer will not pay us if we are delayed," Jean Luc went on. He glanced up at the sails, they had fallen slack for the moment and he cursed under his breath, where was that damned wind? Looking back down, one of the sailors had drawn his pistol.

"They are not merchants, sir. I recognize that ship now. She is the *Widow Maker* and they are pirates," one of the oarsmen spat.

"Stop now in the name of the King," the Lieutenant bellowed. A shot rang out from the sailor's weapon and hit the railing near Jean Luc.

"Je regrette, Monsieur Lieutenant, but I have other plans," Jean Luc smirked, no longer concealing his accent as he drew his own pistol and fired at the man.

A small cry of alarm leapt from Aubrey as the ball hit the railing and wood splintered around Jean Luc. She suddenly found herself in the arms of a large man as she was snatched abruptly from the top step and pulled down into the darkness of the corridor. She attempted to cry out in alarm again and a heavy hand clamped down over her mouth.

"Chut, Mademoiselle, you will get us all killed!" came the voice of Cook close to her ear. She ceased to struggle against him and he dropped his hand from her mouth.

"Why are they shooting at Monsieur Pierne?"

"They have recognized us. Our ruse did not work," he said tightly.

Aubrey's eyes widened as she remembered Jean Luc's words in the great cabin.

"Will they fire the cannons at us?"

"Without a doubt. Get back to the great cabin now and hide. If they manage to board us and they find you out and about, they will take you for a pirate as well and kill you, if you are lucky," he commanded as he pushed her through a gang of men running for the companionway.

Jean Luc pulled off the shot as the Lieutenant fumbled with his own weapon. The ball hit its mark and the man was thrown backward into the water, blood spreading quickly from the wound in his chest.

"Are we ready?" Jean Luc bellowed.

"Aye!" the gunner yelled back from the gun deck.

"Drop the doors and show her what we have," Jean Luc ordered as he quickly reloaded his pistol. Glancing down at the longboat, the men left seemed to be at a loss of what to do in light of the death of their leader.

"Get rid of them," Jean Luc growled to one of the crew pointing at the longboat with his pistol. The man produced a grenade and lit the fuse. Running to the side, he tossed the hand-sized bomb into the floor of the boat. The occupants scrambled to get away from it but before they could jump overboard, the grenade went off. Pieces of longboat leapt out of the water with the explosion and some landed on the deck of the *Widow Maker*. Stamping out several pieces of burning embers, Jean Luc cursed, then growled at the man, "Ame damne! Do not set us on fire as well, you idiot!" The pirate merely shrugged and smiled at him sheepishly.

"Michele!" Jean Luc yelled to the helmsman as he looked up at the sails to see them slack. A glance to the warship revealed that cannons were being moved into place.

"Here is the wind now!" Michele yelled back as he gave the wheel another mighty turn.

"Good thing then, because I think that we have drawn their serious attention," Jean Luc replied as he leaned over the quarterdeck railing.

"Give them a volley!"

The cannons on the port side of the ship fired in succession and balls screamed toward the warship. Jean Luc raised his glass to look upon her decks. The captain was red-faced and screaming orders to his crew to return fire and get under sail.

On shore, Black stood in the second floor window of a bordello. His open shirt fluttered in the breeze that had whipped up on the island port. He watched as his ship was leaving the harbor, then looked to the progress of the warship. Several balls from the *Widow Maker* crashed into the decks of the other ship. Its captain had been caught off guard, and as always, Jean Luc had been right on the mark. The wind caught in the sails of the warship, but with her extra weight from the greater number of cannons she carried, she was too slow.

It was as he predicted; they were found out. Jean Luc was taking the *Widow Maker* around the island to hide and call for them later. Lightning cracked the sky overhead as Black turned from the window, muttering, "I hate this time of year."

"Come back down here, lovey, the weather is fine." The woman in the sheets cooed at him. Black looked at her with a thin smile. She was not what he really wanted but she would do. He pulled off his shirt and leaned down to press his lips to her throat.

Jean Luc watched the warship lumbering around to make for the mouth of the harbor. "She will never catch up. Take a course straight out until we cannot be seen by her, then head north to come back around the island. Find a quiet cove, this one will do," he ordered of the helmsman as he pointed to the cove on a chart of Jamaica. They turned their attention from the map as they heard the unmistakable whistling of cannonballs. Several of them hit the water to their stern, just short of their mark.

In the great cabin, Aubrey had been standing at the window until the cannonballs flew. Yelping in alarm, she dashed to the door. Cook's words echoed in her ears, 'Hide, if they find you about, they will kill you, if you are lucky.'

"If I am lucky? Why would the British Navy kill me? What would they possibly do to me, especially once I have made them to understand that I am not a pirate, but a prisoner of them," she said aloud to the warship that pursued them.

She looked around the room, her eyes coming to rest on the cabinets and closets that lined the walls. Those hiding places were far too obvious for anyone. Aubrey pondered the situation as cannonballs continued to splash behind the *Widow Maker* and the port grew smaller and smaller in the distance. I must be more inventive in my choice of hiding places. She thought as she scanned the room.

Chapter 31

With the full wind of the storm in her sails, the *Widow Maker* plowed through the water to the open sea.

"Stand ready, in case she gets a burst of speed on us," Jean Luc ordered to the man in charge of the gun deck.

"Aye, sir," he nodded and turned to relay the order.

It was not until they were well out of sight of the warship that Jean Luc called for them to stand down. By then, the storm was beating down upon them and darkness had fallen quickly with it. The cover of the rain had aided their getaway, but now the rain, the high seas and winds threatened them as quite another type of enemy–Mother Nature. The helmsman fought the wheel as the men on the lines fought the sails.

Lying in her hiding place, Aubrey could not see what was going on outside and the sounds were a bit muffled. She knew that it was storming, but she did not know that they were no longer being chased. The ship pitched and rocked violently. Her heart pounded with fear and anxiety. Over the tempest of the raging storm, she did not hear the door of the great cabin open nor did she hear the opening of closets and cupboards then the slamming of the door again.

"I cannot find Mademoiselle Aubrey." Cook reported, shouting into Jean Luc's face over the storm.

"What do you mean you cannot find her?" Jean Luc yelled back.

"I caught her lurking at the top of the companionway when you were talking to the Lieutenant of the warship a couple of hours ago," Cook began. Jean Luc made a face–why does she not listen to him?

"I made her go back to the great cabin. I told her to hide. I told her that if they caught her they would accuse her of being a pirate too and she would be killed by them," Cook replied. Jean Luc rolled his eyes.

"Why would you tell her something like that?"

"Because I was afraid that they would do far worse to her if they caught her. You know how they are, Monsieur Pierne. They are worse than us and they get away with it, while we do the dead-man's jig." His narrative ended in an ominous tone. Jean Luc looked at the big man for a moment, then he nodded.

"Merci, Cook, you did well. Help the men here on deck as best you can."

175

Jean Luc moved quickly toward the companionway. Waves were crashing over the railing and the ship continued to be tossed about on the sea like a toy. Vivid recollections of atrocities that he had witnessed of British sailors flashed through his mind as he hurried below. Water cascaded down the steps. If they took on water and sunk, she would be lost down here. He had to get her topside with him. He thought to himself as he threw open the door to the cabin.

'I cannot swim, Monsieur Pierne,' her voice echoed to him as his blue eyes searched the darkened cabin. He looked at the cabinets and cupboards; she was tiny enough to fit in most any of them, but surely Cook would have already looked there. He moved to the desk to look under it, then looked under the settee.

"Mademoiselle Aubrey!" he called out. Just as he did so, there was a deafening clap of thunder covering his voice. Standing in the room near the bunk, with his hands akimbo, he looked around.

"Where are you?" he muttered half to himself. Lightning flashed as he opened his mouth to call out again, "Aubrey!" Perhaps the use of her given name would bring her out, if she were even in here. The crash of a wave overhead and sound of cascading water down the companionway, coupled with another clap of thunder covered the call again. Lightning flashed as he scanned the room again. Something on the bunk made him frown in confusion. The thunder rolled long and deep as he approached the bunk, looking closer. As lightning struck again, his hands shot under the pillows and he clasped them around something soft and firm.

With a heave, he pulled her out from under the pillows and onto the floor before him. She screamed in unbridled fear and hit the floor fighting for dear life. As he caught the flying arms and legs he muttered, "I have thought long about getting you into bed, but this was not what I had in mind."

With the room dark, she had no clue who held her and shrieked in terror.

"Aubrey, Aubrey, be still, you are alright, it is only me," he soothed as he held her against his chest, still holding the arms and legs that threatened to assault anything in their path. She settled immediately upon hearing his voice.

"Monsieur Pierne?"

"Oui, Jean Luc," he nodded.

"I thought you were,"

"I know. Come now, you must come up on deck with me. It is not safe here," he said pulling her to her feet.

"Why?"

"The storm threatens to take us down and to be here in the great cabin if

176

that happens would mean that you would be trapped. On deck we may run the risk of being whisked overboard, but we may have a better chance of survival," he explained as he led her along. When they reached the steps, another wave came down them like a waterfall. She pulled back in fear, her hand slipping from his. She made to run in the opposite direction, toward the bowels of the hold, anywhere away from the water that faced them.

His booted feet slipped on the wet boards as he scrambled after her and caught her about the waist with one arm. He lifted her off her feet and, carrying her on his hip like a sack of flour, he started up the steps.

"Keep hold of me," he ordered as they came out onto the deck and he set her on her feet. The sight of the storm-pounded decks brought new fear to her face.

"No! I do not want to be up here!" she squealed as she made an attempt to run off again. He kept his arm firmly around her.

"Hold me!" he ordered again as a wave crashed over them. He pulled her tighter against his body to brace them against the onslaught of water. The deck pitched violently, each man on deck fought his own battle with nature to stay afoot and not be washed over. Jean Luc moved toward the bulkhead beneath the quarterdeck with Aubrey in tow. Another wave pounded them as he lost his grip and she went down on her knees to the deck. Jean Luc turned to watch in horror as she tumbled along with the wave to the opposite side of the ship.

The *Widow Maker* tipped high in the water on his side, causing the side where Aubrey had been swept to dip low in the water. Another wave washed her along a few more feet as she struggled, spitting and gasping, while trying to come to her knees against the pressure of it. This wave slammed her into the gunwale. Jean Luc saw that she had been deposited very near an open cannon port by the last wave. She was stunned, but was trying to get up against the pull of the tipped ship that seemed determined to keep her pinned there. She will be washed out the port door. He thought to himself in an instant. As another wave hit him from behind, he rode it to the railing. It slammed him into the gunwale on the other side of the port, throwing him halfway over it.

He righted himself and reached out to her, yelling over the noise, "Come here! Give me your hand!" She tried to blink the tears and seawater from her eyes to see him. Getting to her knees successfully this time, she reached for him in desperation. He caught her wrists, but as he dragged her past the port, another wave hit. It swept her off her feet and the demon water began to suck her out the port door.

"No!" he yelled as he pulled on her with all his might against it.

"Kick with your feet, try to get a foothold on the side!" he shouted to her. She was coughing violently, having taken in large quantities of water with each onslaught, but she did as he bade with all the strength left in her.

Finally, he pulled her up to him again and held her in a near crushing embrace against yet another wave. She lay in his arms, exhausted and still coughing water. He moved toward the bulkhead and tucked them into the corner. He wanted to be on the other side of the ship, the side that was taking the hits, but the ship pitched and rocked so that there was no way for him to drag them both across. Water pooled and swirled around them as he pulled them wearily to the deck. Another wave washed over them, covering their heads for a moment. She panicked in his arms, fighting against him and the water.

"I have you, you are all right," he soothed close to her ear.

"I am going to drown!" she choked as she clawed at his shirt and tried to climb over him to some unknown safer place.

Jean Luc pulled her back into his lap and threw a long leg over her to keep her still.

"Non, ma chérie, I have you," he said reassuringly.

Aubrey turned her upper body toward him and threw her arms about his neck. She sobbed in fear as yet another wave assaulted them. He held her tightly against the pull of the water and braced them in the corner with his other leg and foot pressed into the gunwale.

Chapter 32

The storm had pounded the ship for hours, but the *Widow Maker* had held her own against it. Dawn was breaking over the horizon as the seas finally fell into gentle swells. Jean Luc had fallen into exhausted and twilight sleep, still holding tight to Aubrey as the tempest began to die down and the waves had stopped pounding the two of them.

His eyes opened slowly to the brightness. Aubrey was still draped over him, her arms about his waist now as she lay partially in his lap with her head resting against his chest. Jean Luc brushed her wet auburn hair from her face as her breath came in gurgled gasps. Moving his leg from hers, he pulled her up into a straighter sitting position and patted her back forcefully. "Aubrey!"

She replied with a strangled cough and a violent vomiting of seawater onto the deck. She pulled herself from his grasp and crawled away a few feet on her hands and knees, still coughing and spitting water. He moved to kneel beside her, holding her hair out of the way with one hand and resting the other on her thin waist as he looked her over. There were no injuries that he could see. In the search, his eyes came to rest on the front of the shirt she wore.

It hung open with the weight of the water that still soaked it. He was afforded a full view down into it. Her breasts were small, but well rounded with delicate light brown nipples that stood like little peaks as she continued to empty her stomach and lungs of the seawater. Patting her back, he drew his attention away from the delicious sight.

"There, are you all right? Talk to me now."

"I am..." she began and a session of coughing came on again. She took a deep ragged breath and finally finished with, "I am all right but cold."

He smiled at her, noting the exposure once more.

"Indeed."

Jean Luc helped her to her feet but her legs were shaky. Looking up at the helmsman as he supported her, he called, "Michele! Where are we?"

"I do not know! I can see no land! We were blown off course," the man called back with a shrug.

Jean Luc muttered a curse. Aubrey slipped from his arms slightly and he turned his attention back on her. Sweeping her up into his arms he called, "Check for damage! I will be up directly to see if I can tell where we are."

"Aye sir. Monsieur Pierne?" Michele called down.

"Oui?"

179

"Is she all right?" he asked, nodding his head to Aubrey as she hung limply in his arms.

"She will be fine, swallowed too much salt water but I think her lungs are clear now," Jean Luc replied.

"Good thing then. Captain Black would be a might upset if something happened to her," the man nodded as he looked to the horizon.

Jean Luc looked down into the pale face of the young woman he held in his arms and muttered, "Not nearly as upset as I would be."

Jean Luc pushed her down in a chair in the great cabin. She had stopped coughing, but her breathing still hinted of some water in her lungs. He picked up her small blanket and draped it about her shoulders. Patting her shoulders and arms, he said easily, "You will need to get out of these wet clothes." He crouched before her to use the blanket to pat at her thighs to try and absorb some of the water.

"You left the captain," she said in a voice strained from coughing.

"We will go back for him," he said firmly as his blue eyes darted up to look into her hazel ones.

"I thought that you were angry with him?" he asked as he rubbed her upper arms briskly to bring some heat back to them.

She looked at him for a moment, her lips were blue and her teeth were chattering. "I was. I am."

"Well, which is it? Was or am?" he queried in mild anger at her concern over Black. She frowned at him for a moment.

"You left them back there. What if those men find them out? Cook says that men from this ship would be killed for being pirates. I do not understand, I thought that they were your friends?" Her voice now hinted of rising anger.

Jean Luc looked at her in surprise as he stood up, "I was obeying orders, for your information,"

"Just like you were obeying orders when you chose the course to bring the *Gull* into the path of this awful ship?" she asked, her voice lowered to a mutter.

"What?" he spat.

"I could be in Africa now—in a new life were it not for you. Instead I am here, a prisoner, all alone. Then I nearly drowned last night," she replied in the same fashion as she came to her feet, throwing off the blanket. He glared at her. She set her jaw and lunged at him, shoving her hands into his chest. Was this action the extent of her forms of attack? he wondered to himself as he stumbled back slightly at the hit.

"I saved your life last night and you thank me by attacking me?" he asked with brows raised.

"Oh, and then what should I do to thank you, Monsieur Pierne? Should I be givin' ya a kiss instead?" Aubrey blurted out. His mouth dropped open for a second. When she was truly angry, all the 'proper teaching' she apparently had been given was lost and the thick Irish drawl came out of her in all its Celtic glory.

With a smug smile and placing his hands on his hips, he said, "Well, I think that a kiss would fill the bill, for the moment." Now it was her turn to stand, mouth agape, then her hazel eyes flashed.

"Not bloody likely!" she spat as she threw up the stinging little hand to slap him. With lightning swiftness, he caught the hand with just enough pressure to make her wince.

"Never raise your hand to strike me again," he told her close to her face as he spoke with clenched teeth.

"Or you will do what, Monsieur Pierne?" she growled back.

"I already told you what I was going to do to you for your little tantrums," he said in smug reply. To emphasize his point, he squeezed her hand until she winced again. She tried to free the trapped hand with her other one and when that proved to be fruitless, she raised her free hand to slap him. He rolled his eyes at her determination and he caught that hand as well, "I will turn you over my knee, Mademoiselle," he threatened.

"You let me go, you arrogant bastard!" she squealed angrily in her drawl.

"You have certainly duped Rene with your little act of being 'precious'. How proper is it for a young lady to make rude accusations about my parents when you do not even know them?" he chuckled at her.

A long silence fell between them before she huffed, "What about Captain Black?"

"I told you, we will go back for them," he shrugged and released her.

"What if he is dead?" she asked.

"Then this ship is mine," he said flatly.

"You would be captain of the *Widow Maker*?"

"Oui," he nodded. He was having a grand time now with this and he was not about to tell her that it was not that simple. There would have to be a vote for the position of captain.

"And what would become of me, Monsieur Pierne?"

"You would still be the captain's lady. So now that I know your true nature, I will be well prepared for you. Prepared to paddle your seat every time you become unruly."

She reacted to the comment just as he had expected. With a very unladylike snort, she flew into him again. Jean Luc caught her hands, laughing. She was like a little wild animal again. He scooped her up into his arms and amid squeals and words that were foreign to him, he carried her to the bunk. He held her over the center and just let her drop. Aubrey hit the bunk with a distressed squeak.

"Now," he began as he dusted his hands over her. "I would love to stay and play with you, but I have a ship to run and a course to set."

Stepping out into the corridor, he slammed the door behind him. Jean Luc went up to the deck both enraged and aroused after the argument. The cool winds fanned his troubled brow as he looked over the charts to try and determine where the storm had pushed them. With his mind locked into the task of setting them to rights, the passion for her died in him as well, for now.

Finally, in exhausted exasperation he threw up his hands and turned to the helmsman. "This is impossible, I have no points of reference out here. I will have to wait until tonight when the stars come out then I can better judge where we are. We can only hope that between now and then, another storm does not blow up. As best as I can determine, the storm was coming across the island from the north, thus pushing us at least in a southern direction."

"But the winds seemed to be coming in circles." the helmsman offered with a shrug.

Jean Luc looked up at the sky and squinted at the sun. With a disgruntled click of his tongue, he noted that it stood directly overhead. Sighing deeply he said, "Follow the path of the sun, take us to the south from that point. I am going below to my cabin for some sleep,"

"Aye sir," The man nodded from his station.

After stripping out of his clothing and washing up, Jean Luc literally threw himself upon his bunk. He sighed deeply and closed his eyes. After a few moments he began to chuckle. The vision of Aubrey's face after he had dumped her onto the bunk had been precious to say the least. She was a gem, a pretty little Irish gem. As he drifted off to sleep, his thoughts were on Aubrey Malone.

Chapter 33

It was well past sunset when he awakened and dressed to go on deck. The stars shone brightly in the sky overhead.

"Now I can tell where we are," he said to the helmsman. After taking a few sightings, he gathered up his charts. With a brief list of commands to the watch and the helmsman, he went down the companionway steps and toward the great cabin. It was the only place that would be well lit enough and had enough space to spread his things out to set their course. But then, it would mean the opportunity to be with her as well. He knocked on the door, then stood waiting for the answer, wondering what sort of mood she was in now.

"Who is it?" came the soft feminine voice from the other side.

"Jean Luc Pierne. I have ship's business to tend to."

"Do you not normally carry out your duties on deck, Monsieur Pierne?" she parried, keeping the door closed. He rolled his eyes and sighed, she was still in a mood.

"I must use the table, the lamps and the log book," he replied to the door. After an extended moment, the door bolt slid back and the door came open.

She backed away from him as he nodded to her and moved directly to the table to set out his charts. He noted a plate on the table with very few leftovers on it. A goblet of wine sat beside it, nearly empty as well. As he pinned down the charts, he picked up her goblet and turned slightly toward her to hand it to her. "Mademoiselle."

She nodded and took the goblet tentatively from his hand, then moved away toward the window.

"It is good to see that you are eating. How are you feeling this evening?" he asked as he continued to busy himself. She watched him move to the desk, pick up the logbook, then return with it to the table.

"I am fine," she nodded again, speaking quietly.

"Bon," he nodded in reply.

Jean Luc worked silently for several minutes as she watched him. Suddenly, he left the cabin, leaving her standing alone in the cabin and looking at the table nearly covered by the charts. Glancing out the door that he had left standing open, she wandered to the table and looked at the papers that were laid out there. The numbers, dots, lines, drawings of ragged-edged, and odd shaped circles on the papers seemed to be gibberish. She leaned closer and saw some words there as well. Turning her attention upon the logbook that lay open beside the papers, she ran her finger along the words written in French.

The sound of a throat clearing came from the doorway caused her to jump back from the table in alarm. Jean Luc came into the room, laid a navigational instrument on the table beside the charts and took up the quill.

"Interested in learning the art of navigation, Mademoiselle?" he asked not looking at her as he jotted some writing down in the log.

"No sir, it looks too hard. I cannot understand the writing," she replied.

"It is not difficult. Ce n'est pas malin," he shrugged.

Aubrey frowned at him. "What?"

"I said, 'it is easy'. I thought that the captain was teaching you how to write and speak the language?" he said as he drew some lines on the chart before him.

"Yes, well, I am having a difficult time," Aubrey stammered as she dropped her head regretfully.

"Hmm, perhaps you do not have the right teacher," he said as he wrote in the logbook again. Aubrey's head shot up as he cut his eyes to look at her.

"You would teach me?" she asked in disbelief.

"I would, I can." he said as he charted some more. Waving to her, he said, "Come here. Can you read this?"

She approached him warily as Jean Luc turned the logbook so that she was at a better angle to see the written pages. With an unsure look at him, she leaned over a bit to see the book in the light of the lantern.

"These are amounts of money, it is denoted in francs," she began as she pointed at the mark for the currency and the numbers.

He nodded, then pointed at a column of words. "Can you read these?"

She leaned closer. The movement made her brush up against his arm with her shoulder gently. She frowned at the words for a moment. "These are items," she began.

"Read them," he nodded as he made another series of markings on his charts.

"Le sel, salt, le poivre, pepper, le riz, rice, le vin, wine, sucre, sugar," she said as she ran her finger down the list.

"Bon," he nodded.

"Poudre, powder?" she went on and then looked up at him for clarification.

"Black powder, for the guns," he nodded as he moved to the cupboard. She mumbled over the book as he took down a bottle of wine and poured himself a goblet, then watched her out of the corner of his eye.

"Are they what we have taken, or are they things that the captain has listed that we need?" he quizzed.

"He says here, that they are things needed," she answered.

"Say the word," he said as he approached the table taking a sip from his goblet.

"Besoin." Aubrey said hesitantly. He nodded again and held up the wine bottle to her in a gesture asking if she wanted him to fill her goblet. She licked her lips gently. Before she made a decision on her own, he stepped forward and filled her goblet for her.

"See then, it is not so hard," he commended as he set the bottle aside and took up the quill once more. He watched her from the corner of his eye as she literally puffed up with pride at her success. With a small smile, he reached to take the book from her, "Pardon."

She backed up a step and watched as he wrote in the book.

"I thought that only the captain could write in that book?" she asked after her long silence.

"Whoever is in charge of the ship is responsible for making the entries in the log," he informed her, not looking up at her.

Jean Luc moved from the book and back to his charts. She took a sip of her wine and set the goblet aside, looking at him covertly. As he wrote on his papers and drew lines, she inched closer to the logbook and craned her head to look at the words there. With a decisive sigh, Jean Luc straightened and smiled at her. She smiled back nervously. He picked up his sextant from the table and went out the door once more. Aubrey did not hesitate to go to the table now to look at the book that was becoming so interesting and intriguing.

When Jean Luc returned, he found her leaning over the table with her chin resting in her hand. She was bent over, her upper torso was laying on the tabletop, and her small booted feet stood on tiptoe as she balanced herself there. Jean Luc's blue eyes scanned the line of her lithe body. He lingered over the delicate curve of her back, her little round bottom, and her shapely thighs and calves in the britches. A fire began to build in him once more as he approached the table. Aubrey ignored him as he emptied his wine goblet. His eyes still lingered on her and she continued to ponder over the words in the book laid out before her.

He quietly laid aside the sextant as she idly reached up and tucked a lock of unruly auburn hair behind one ear. Jean Luc's eyes devoured the sight of the little exposed lobe. He set the goblet down, asking in interest as he neared her, "What are you reading?"

Aubrey glanced up at him quickly, as if she had forgotten he was there. "Ah, I can make out only some of the words still, but I have found my name here," she reported with a fleeting blush.

185

"Did you?" he queried on in interest as if he did not know it was there. Leaning next to her in the same fashion as she nodded he asked in English, "Where?"

"Here," she replied pointing.

"Ah! Voici!" he smiled as he glanced back at her, pointing as well. She giggled slightly at his play.

"Hmm, and what does it say here about Aubrey?" he asked as he leaned beside her on the table and rested his chin in his hand.

She frowned at the words around her name and then with a small defeated sigh she said, "I do not know, Monsieur Pierne."

"Let me see," he said as he pulled the logbook toward himself and ran a long finger along the lines of words quickly.

"It says here that Aubrey Malone is a very unruly little charge who is prone to fits of temper and insubordination. And that Monsieur Pierne will be engaged in two very angry and physical quarrels with her while Captain Black is away."

Jean Luc cut his blue eyes to look at her. Her mouth dropped open a bit as she frowned at the book. When she looked at him, a small smile of mischief turned up the corner of his lips.

She giggled deliciously, "It does not say that!"

"Oui, it does. Look," he said pushing the book back and running his finger along the lines.

"Aubrey Malone," he began with a smile directed at her.

She giggled again, "You jest, Monsieur Pierne!"

He chuckled in affirmation as their eyes met for a moment. In a near whisper she said, "When I was a little girl, my Da told me stories about pirates."

Jean Luc remembered her tale about her father on the first night she had been on board the *Widow Maker*. He deduced that she had been so nervous that night that she did not recall telling him and Black.

"And what did your pere say?" he asked quietly. It delighted him when she remained in place beside him and continued with her confession, lowering her lashes slightly.

"He told me that pirates were mean men. He said that they were ugly and dirty—that they had missing teeth and smelled foul of breath and body," she said with the innocence of a child. Jean Luc snorted in amusement at the description—it would fit most of the men on board.

"Did you share your pere's teachings with Captain Black?" he asked inquisitively.

Another giggle erupted from her and she squelched it with her hand.

"No!"

"Hmm, but you choose to share this information with me," he said as he reached up to remove her hand from the sweet-looking mouth.

"I am a pirate, Aubrey. Do I fit the picture that your pere has painted for you?" His tone was low.

Her face crimsoned as he held her hand and stroked the back of it with his fingers.

"Non."

"And what of the captain, does he fit your pere's description?"

"No, but he frightens me."

"Perhaps it is because he is the captain," he said easily.

Aubrey shook her head slowly and then replied thoughtfully, "My Da told me that pirates do bad things to people they capture. Especially women."

Jean Luc sighed and then said firmly to Aubrey as if he were speaking to a child, "Some pirates are that way, but not all of us."

Aubrey looked at him with such innocent eyes that he had to add, "It is not my way." Then he took her hand to his lips and pressed it with a soft kiss. "Tu es très jolie, Aubrey," he said softly. The hazel eyes looked at him in question.

"You are very pretty, Aubrey," he repeated in English as he dropped his gaze to her lips. She was biting them nervously. He leaned toward her ever so slowly, pulling her hand closer to his chest as he did so. She drew back a bit and he cooed, "You are all right, trust me."

She remained still as he lightly touched his lips to hers then drew his head back. The parting of their lips made a soft smacking noise in the quiet room. Aubrey licked at her lips quickly and bit them again as he straightened, pulling her up with him by the hand that he held. With a smooth yet deliberate move, he caught her about the waist with his other arm, pulling her up against his body.

Aubrey did not resist, but she dropped her head and said in a small voice, "No man has ever told me that, except my Da. I always thought that other men found me ugly."

He frowned down upon her while still holding her hand. With his fingertips of his free hand, he tilted her head to face him.

"You are more than pretty, you are beautiful. Any man who has seen you and not told you so is either blind or a fool," he purred as he lowered his head to press his lips full upon hers with a bit more purpose.

Recalling the experiences Black bestowed on her, she was surprised that somehow this seemed much more comfortable. Jean Luc gently prodded her lips with his tongue and she willingly parted them. She tasted of the wine she had been drinking, mingled with her own sweetness. Jean Luc relished the kiss and she began to relax. Finally breaking from it, he brushed his lips over her cheek and down the side of her face to the ear she had exposed earlier. She remained calm and obliging as he caught the succulent lobe in his lips for a second then proceeded with feathery kisses to the side of her throat. The scent of her was intoxicating.

Fearful that he would frighten her, he suddenly drew back and released her. Looking over his papers he cleared his throat. "I need to finish with this and give the course to the helmsman."

She merely nodded, touching her fingers to her lips nervously. Her heart was pounding—never before, when Captain Black had embraced her had she felt this way.` A tingling and warming sensation coursed through her. She watched him silently as he finished up and rolled the charts into tubes. Picking up his sextant he turned to her.

"Bonsoir, Mademoiselle."

"Bonsoir, Monsieur Pierne," she said quietly. He smiled at her use of French and turned to leave the cabin.

"Monsieur Pierne?" she called, stopping him in his tracks and his heart for a moment with her sweet voice.

"Merci for helping me with my French." She smiled gently.

His eyes twinkled, "Avec plaisir." Then he turned toward the door again and just before he exited he turned back saying thickly, "Please call me Jean Luc." Aubrey looked at him for a long moment and then he said, "Je suis satisfait de ton travail l'école." With that, he turned and left the cabin, pulling the door closed behind him. She moved to the door to slide the lock bolt into place and leaned against the door with a frown, repeating the words in a whisper to herself and wondering what they meant.

Jean Luc mounted the companionway steps chuckling to himself.

'I am satisfied with your performance in school?' Why did I say that? As he came out onto the deck and the gentle winds caught in his hair he smiled, because I have assumed the position as her teacher! In more ways than one!

Chapter 34

Morning dawned and Aubrey opened her eyes, stretching languidly under the heavy large quilt that was on Black's bunk. He was gone and she felt safer using the better sleeping accommodations in his absence. Her muscles ached from the ordeal of the storm two nights before and the softness of the bunk helped to make her more comfortable. She lay still, listening to the morning noises amid the groan of the wood hull.

In the sleepy haze of her morning, her mind drifted like the ship. It went back to the day Captain Black had left her alone again. Monsieur Pierne had been there, even though they had argued. He had been there for the storm, too. As much as she loved thunderstorms, it had been truly frightening. Aubrey made a face as she remembered how evil she had been with him yesterday, even in light of how well he had taken care of her. Those thoughts lead to the memory of the previous evening.

She remembered his touch, his gentle hands and caressing fingers–and the kiss. The warming sensation washed over her again and it pooled in the bottom of her abdomen. She moved in the bunk, pulling the pillow closer to her chest as she lay on her side for a few quiet moments. Something had happened between them last night. It was clear to her that her feelings for him were far different than her feelings for Captain Black.

By midday, she was bored. The encounter with Monsieur Pierne the night before was intriguing to say the least. She knew that if Captain Black were to find out, he would be very angry with the pair of them. Sighing deeply, she wondered why Monsieur Pierne had not come to check on her today. She looked out the quarter gallery window. Perhaps he was too busy with running the ship and setting them back on a new course.

Thoughtfully, she turned her eyes to the logbook that still lay on the table. Sitting in a chair nearest the book, she pulled it before her and opened it. Black's neat and ornate handwriting began in the center of the first page. 1 Janvier 1720

How long had Captain Black told her that he had been at sea as Captain of the *Widow Maker*? She tried to recall as she thumbed through the pages.

A knock upon the door drew her attention and made her heart flutter in hopes that it was Monsieur Pierne. "Who is there?" she called.

"Henri. I bring your dinner," came the boyish voice.

"Oh," she muttered almost dejectedly as she got up to let the boy in. She was still quite fond of him and still considered him friendly and enjoyed his company. But Captain Black was right—he was just a boy.

As Henri set a bowl of steaming liquid on the table, she surveyed him objectively. He was tall and lanky, much taller than she was. His hair fell to his shoulders in brown curly locks. She raised a brow and thought, it was a wonder the men did not take him for a girl. His shirt hung loosely on him, just like those he had given her. His young chest was not muscular. Not like Monsieur Pierne. His young face had not the slightest hint of facial hair to be shaved, not like Monsieur Pierne. She became suddenly aware that Henri was staring at her.

"Is something the matter, Mademoiselle Aubrey?" he asked in his boyish voice that squeaked sometimes when he spoke. Monsieur Pierne's voice was deep, though not nearly as deep as Captain Black's, but it was also caressing. Her heart leapt in fright as if the boy could know what she was thinking.

"No, Henri," Aubrey said, then hesitated slightly before asking sweetly, "I would like to take a bath. Could you bring me some water, s'il vous plait?"

"I will ask," he said warily then left the cabin.

When Henri returned, Cook was with him. The man looked at her sternly and said in his thick, accented voice, "A bath? We do not have enough water on this ship for such things. We have a shortage of water on board as it is."

"Oh, well merci, Cook. Then that is quite alright, I will forego the bath," Aubrey replied, again disappointed.

Cook nodded then left. Henri stayed behind and asked sheepishly, "Will there be anything else, Mademoiselle?"

"No Henri, merci for the dinner," she managed to say stiffly.

He smiled at her, "It is my pleasure to serve you, Mademoiselle." With a curt bow, he exited the cabin, leaving her alone.

Turning her attention to the bowl, she noticed the odd-looking arrangement of food there. She recognized pieces of turtle meat, fish and shellfish. There was another meat there that appeared to be chicken. Mixed in with this medley of meats were pieces of hard-boiled eggs, pickled onions, cabbage, grapes and olives. She made a face and took out the olives. Picking up a piece of the chicken, she popped it into her mouth. Pungent spices assaulted her taste buds and she ran for the water pitcher. As she poured a goblet of water to take back to the table, she looked up and noticed some books tucked in behind the bottles of wine.

Aubrey pulled out the last two books in the row and opened the cover of each. With a triumphant smile she said, "1716 and 1717." Taking the books back to the table with her, she picked at the morsels in the bowl with her

190

fingers while she scanned through the books. Her limited command of the language left her at a loss to actually read the contents, but she was able to decipher names of ships taken, places visited and various prizes.

As darkness fell, she lit a lantern beside the bunk and sprawled out on her stomach to continue her reading. In the book dated, "1717", she noticed one particular word in Black's hand that came repeatedly during the late months of the year. When it first appeared, it was in conjunction with a ship called the *Dodger*. She did not understand the repeated word. Frowning, she decided that she would ask Monsieur Pierne what the word was.

The ship bell tolled and she glanced up to see that it was very dark outside. The stars seemed to float over the black ocean. Frowning again, she got up from the bunk and stretched to her full height, her hands high above her head. Monsieur Pierne had not been here all day–even to put an entry down in the log, she mused.

A loud rapping from the other side of the door caused her to jump and squeak in alarm.

"Lights out!" came the booming voice of Boulet. The knob began to turn and she dashed to the door to stand against it as Boulet laughed, "Monsieur Beaufort said that I should tuck you in since he is ashore and cannot do it himself."

"You lie, Monsieur Boulet!" she yelled as she slid the lock bolt home. Sliding to the floor against the door, she could not believe that she had been in here preoccupied with the books so long that she had left the door unlocked.

"Put out your lantern, Mademoiselle. You are no more special than the rest of us. But then perhaps the captain affords you those types of rewards in return for his visits between your legs," he chided on. Aubrey felt a rush of heat wash over her face at the comment. It seemed to her that Beaufort and Boulet were one in the same, where one left off the other would take up in the torment of her.

"Leave me alone, Monsieur Boulet," she called back as bravely as she could.

Boulet turned from the door with a guttural chuckle. A movement in the shadows caught his eye and he laid his hand upon his pistol.

Jean Luc stepped into the light of the lantern that Boulet held.

"Is there a problem, Monsieur Boulet?"

"Non, I was just tucking the lady in," Boulet sneered. Jean Luc's eyes met Boulet's with a cold icy stare.

"Get to your watch," Jean Luc finally said in a snarl.

On the other side of the door, Aubrey heard Jean Luc's voice. She stood

191

from the floor and listened intently. Boulet could be heard grumbling, then, after an extended silence, a light tapping on the door gave her a start.

"Mademoiselle, are you all right?" Jean Luc called gently.

"Oui," she replied.

"Put out your lamp now, s'il vous plait. Our lamp oil supply is running low until we reach port," he said kindly.

"I will," she said in a small voice from her side of the door. Then after a few moments of silence the door came open and she asked, "Monsieur Pierne?"

"Oui?" he replied as he turned to look at her framed in the doorway, backed by the light of the cabin within.

"Will you be making entries into the log tonight?" Her question surprised her nearly as much as it surprised him.

"Je regrette, Mademoiselle, but it is too late. As I have said before the oil supply grows small and we must conserve. We still have another whole day and night before we reach the other side of the island to pick up the captain and the crew," he replied with a small sad smile that she could not see in the darkness of the corridor. He saw her shoulders drop in apparent disappointment.

"It has been lonely today," she said in sad quiet tones.

"Did you eat your dinner?"

"Oui, all of it. Even though it burned my mouth," she nodded, grateful for the small conversation.

"Bon," he nodded.

"I wanted, I had hoped that you would help me some more with my French," Aubrey said easily.

"I was very busy." His tone dropped and she cocked her head to listen intently.

"Perhaps I will have more time tomorrow to put down the log and work on it with you," he replied.

"Bonsoir, Monsieur Pierne," she said as she backed up and shut the door.

Jean Luc pursed his lips and rolled his eyes upward. He had stayed away deliberately, thinking that he had frightened her. Now here she was right before him, practically begging for attention of any sort from him. Sighing deeply, he went to his own small, dark, and lonely cabin. As he undressed for bed, he ran the events of the night before over in his mind.

Chapter 35

Another morning dawned and Aubrey ate her breakfast alone at the big table in the middle of the cabin. How she would love to go up and sit in the sun, and the fresh air. With her mind made up to do just that, she quietly left the cabin. She got just outside the companionway entrance before he caught her.

"Please tell me that I do not see you up here alone," Jean Luc scolded as he caught her by the sleeve of the billowy shirt she wore.

She pulled insistently from his gloved hand. "I am suffocating down there."

"Very well then. You sit right here and do not move," he said as he pointed to the lip of the hold opening. Moving away from her, he went up to the quarterdeck to converse with the helmsman. She looked around the deck, some of the men were looking at her and she dropped her gaze. They looked like Da's pirates.

"Do not fall asleep here, and fall backward down into the hold," Jean Luc warned as he sat beside her.

"I was not falling asleep." she shot back.

"Well then, did you come up here to bask in the sun, or did you come up here to learn something?" he asked.

"Learn something?" she asked in puzzlement.

"Ah oui! Learn a trade, help out," he nodded as he waved his hand out to indicate the men working on the deck about them.

"I cannot do any of that. I am too small, too weak," she stammered.

He smiled at her and muttered out of the corner of his mouth, "You were not too small or weak to set me back twice when you shoved at me!"

Aubrey dropped her head sheepishly and smiled.

"Raoul, s'il vous plait," he called as he waved a hand at one of the men to draw near. Aubrey suppressed the urge to make a face as the man came closer. His clothing was in shambles. His bare feet were blackened with filth. Jean Luc noted the look in her eye and felt her lean slightly closer to him making distance between her and the man approaching. Jean Luc stifled the urge to chuckle.

"What are you doing, Monsieur Pierne?" she whispered as the man stopped before them.

"I understand that you like to sew. Raoul here is a tailor of sorts. He mends the sails. Perhaps he could use your help on the ones that were damaged in the storm the other night," Jean Luc began, tormenting her.

"I can leave you with him then you could be out in the sun and air and no longer bored," he went on. Aubrey looked at him in alarm. He spoke quickly and with much animation to the man.

The man talked back, spitting and drawling his words from a mouth sparse with teeth. Jean Luc heard a little whine of distress escape from her as she pressed a bit closer when the man extended his hand to her.

"I think I have had enough sun. May I go back to the cabin now?" she asked Jean Luc, distress written all over her face.

"You do not wish to learn a trade?" he asked with a chuckle.

"Non."

"Merci, Raoul," he told him with a laugh. The man chuckled as well and moved away. Jean Luc stood up and motioned for her to go before him.

"We will have dinner, then we will work on your French and I will update the log," he nodded as they went down the companionway.

Jean Luc was delighted to find that suddenly the friendship and trust between them was growing by leaps and bounds. They sat at the captain's table in the galley for the evening meal, but he still remained distant in the presence of the men. Aubrey picked at her plate, taking only a bite now and then. Black would be returning to the ship soon and the distress of it was evident in her demeanor.

He made a face at her and pointed at her with his fork. "Do you know what I can get for you? Something that I know you will like very much. Beaucoup!"

"What?" she asked in disinterest as she poked at the food on her plate and raised her eyes to look at him. He motioned for her to lean closer to him over the table. She made a small face, but did as he bade. The shirt she wore allowed him a small view of the tops of her breasts and his eyes fixed there.

"I can get you some water, pour le bain. Would you like that?"

"Really? But Cook says there is a shortage of water. I asked for bath water yesterday and he told me no," she told him.

Jean Luc snorted in reply and pulled off a chunk of the hard loaf of bread they shared. "Cook thinks that water is only for cooking and drinking. He does not take a bath. We have had more than our fair share of rains these past weeks and our stores of water are more plentiful than our stores of powder!"

"May I have it now?" she asked.

"Well, after you have finished your dinner," he said. Aubrey made a face, but offered no argument as she went back to work on her food. There were hard-boiled eggs that she had cut into pieces and some small potatoes to which she had done the same. The main course was a fish. After a few moments of picking at it with her fork and trying to pick out the bones, she waved her hand in surrender and pushed the fish aside on the plate.

"Here. Watch," he said firmly as he reached across the table with his fork and grasped the tail of the fish with the fingers of his other hand.

"These were caught by your friend Henri," he told her as he worked on de-boning the fish. Aubrey watched in interest but at the mention of Henri, her eyes shot up to look at him and a mild look of distress crossed her brow. Aubrey recalled how she had been thinking of Henri the day before, and comparing him with the captain and the quartermaster.

"There," he said as he presented the fish to her. She looked over chunks of fish and the neat pile of bones beside it.

"Merci."

"You know, I think that Henri has his eye on you," Jean Luc told her conversationally as he resumed his meal.

"Captain Black says he is too young. Besides he is just my friend," she said in defense.

She was relaxed until Boulet entered the galley. Striding past them, he seated his tall gaunt frame at a nearby table and looked over at her. Jean Luc looked at her as well and saw that her demeanor changed immediately. She put down her fork and it appeared that she might choke on the food she was trying to swallow before she finally got it down. She took up her wine glass with a shaking hand to drink, apparently attempting to wash it down further.

Jean Luc tried to get her attention. She was staring at Boulet, her hazel eyes locked on his blue ones. "Mademoiselle Aubrey," Jean Luc called easily.

She continued to stare at Boulet.

He cast his eye to Boulet and saw him lick his lips as he held her in his hypnotic stare. Jean Luc fought the urge to get up and punch him soundly for the lewd gesture.

"Aubrey," he finally hissed quietly and tapped her foot with his under the table.

Aubrey finally broke from the trance and looked down at her plate, picking up the fork and looking at Jean Luc apologetically, "What were you saying, Monsieur Pierne? I am sorry." Her eyes rose from looking at her meal to meet his timidly as if she had been caught doing something dreadfully wrong. He held her now for a time with his blue eyes, but in a far gentler stare.

"Eat your dinner or no water," he reminded her with a nod. She went back to work on her plate, a great deal slower now. They ate in silence again.

195

Finally, in a very tiny voice she breathed, "Monsieur Beaufort." He frowned at her for her having brought the man's name up.

"Monsieur Beaufort and Monsieur Boulet are," she stammered.

"Are asses." Jean Luc remarked quickly in annoyance as he raised his glass to his lips and looked at her. She exhaled and cast a quick glance at Boulet, who now was engaged in conversation with LaVoie.

"He is very frightening," Aubrey said in a whisper as she leaned across the table toward him.

Jean Luc drained his glass and set it down. He leaned toward her and said in a confidential tone, raising a finger, "Perhaps so, but whenever you see him, just think of this."

"What?" she asked.

Jean Luc smiled at her mischievously and looked at the man out of the corner of his eyes. She followed his glance and then looked back into Jean Luc's blue eyes as he said in a near whisper, "Monsieur Boulet sucks his thumb like a baby when he sleeps."

Aubrey burst into a nervous giggle that caught the attention of a few men nearby, including Boulet and LaVoie. Jean Luc smiled and she quickly squelched her own humor by clapping a hand over her mouth.

Boulet leaned back in his chair, eyeing the pair of them. Seeing that Boulet was trying to intimidate her again, Jean Luc whispered, "Remember what I said."

In spite of the situation, she let another small giggle escape as she thought about Jean Luc's ridiculous comment.

"He does not," she breathed.

Jean Luc shrugged his shoulders, "Perhaps not, but does that thought make him less frightening?"

She looked once more at Boulet who was speaking to LaVoie again. "Oui, Monsieur Pierne."

"Hmm, you see," Jean Luc said putting his hand down on the table firmly. Then he raised a finger in warning, "Do not let them see that you are afraid of them, nor should you provoke them in any way."

She nodded in reply, "I will try not to."

A silence fell over them again. Boulet's voice could be heard as he spoke to his comrades. The galley was beginning to make her nervous now.

"Can I have my water now, Monsieur Pierne?" she whispered as she indicated her plate. He cast his eye over it to see that plate was empty save for the fish bones.

Knowing by now that wine would calm her to a certain degree, he tapped her glass with his fork. "Finish your wine." She did and wiped her mouth with her napkin.

Jean Luc stood and indicated for her to go before him.

As they entered the great cabin, she turned on him in sudden excitement. He stepped back in mild alarm, thinking that she was going to shove at him for some unknown reason again.

"You would be very proud, Monsieur Pierne," she began.

"Vraiment?" he said as he shut the door to the cabin and lay aside his hat.

"I have been reading the logs, or trying to, and I can understand some of what I read now," she said proudly.

"What logs?" he asked, mildly concerned.

"The ones up there," she said pointing dutifully at the wine cupboard.

"Oh really?" he asked slowly in English.

"Oui." She beamed at him then added with a frown, "But I have one small perplexity."

"That is?" he queried on.

"What is 'Mala'? It does not look like a French word. Is it an island or a ship?"

Jean Luc had recognized the word and also noted that she had mispronounced it as 'ma la'. Squelching the urge to correct her, he replied, "Do not worry yourself with it. It is nothing to concern you," he said stiffly. The air of jubilation over her accomplishments dropped quickly and she looked at him speechless for a moment.

"What have I done wrong?"

"You have done nothing wrong, Aubrey," he began gently.

"Ne te mets pas en colère," she said slowly, but still trying to prove her accomplishments. He smiled easily and approached her.

"I am not angry with you. Your French is coming along very nicely. Just do not use Captain Black's log anymore to practice. I should not have used that for the lesson. It is my fault," he said. He took her hands in his and bent his head down to catch her eyes with his. "Do me a favor, s'il vous plait."

"Qu'est-ce que c'est?" she asked slowly.

He smiled in approval, and then said more seriously, "Put that word out of your mind. Do not let the captain know that you have been reading the logs. He is very protective of his logbooks and his privacy," he began.

With a click of her tongue she muttered, "Some aspects of his privacy." Her mind recalled how he blatantly undressed down to the skin right there before her as if it was supposed to be all right with her.

Jean Luc merely frowned and went on, "Will you keep your knowledge of the books a secret for Jean Luc?"

"Oui," she said quietly.

He smiled again, "Très bien." Jean Luc said as he sat at the desk and made the entry into the log. Aubrey waited anxiously for her bath water to arrive. She smiled nervously at him as he easily stood and came around the desk, moving closely toward her.

She stood in her place, watching him. There was a knock on the door and he looked toward it. Jean Luc had hoped for a few more minutes between them. Aubrey looked at him wondering why her heart was pounding so. She exhaled nervously, "You take very good care of me, Monsieur Pierne. I appreciate your kindness and I would like to thank you for that. Merci."

He shrugged, moving a bit closer. "I have told you before, it is my duty, and these are my orders from the captain."

There was a second knock. She cast a quick glance at the door and then looked back to him.

"I am sorry that we did not get along so well in the beginning. I am sorry that I was so–difficult." Her voice was small and apologetic.

The rapping sound came a third time. He made a face at the intrusion, finally saying in an informative manner, "Your bath water is here."

"Come in please," she called as she backed away, making distance between them.

Jean Luc retreated to the desk quickly pretending to write again as Henri entered with two buckets of steaming water.

"There are two more out there," the boy smiled. She smiled back at him, casting a nervous glance at Jean Luc. He was still watching her even though he appeared to be engrossed in the logbook.

"Thank you, Henri," she said easily.

"Carry on, Henri," Jean Luc said as he turned the page in the log and dipped the quill into the inkpot.

"Aye, sir," the boy nodded as he poured the water into the tub and then went to retrieve the other buckets.

"I hope four is enough, Mademoiselle. Cook said there will not be anymore to give for such frivolous things as baths. He made such a fuss the whole time for these," the boy apologized.

"It is not necessary to bother the Mademoiselle with all of that information, Henri," Jean Luc said in even firmness.

"Sorry, sir. Sorry, Mademoiselle," the boy said quietly.

Casting a frown at Jean Luc, Aubrey turned a pleasant smile on the young man. "Four is fine, Henri. Please tell Cook that I am sorry to be such a bother to him."

With the task done, the boy politely excused himself from the cabin, shutting the door behind him.

Aubrey advanced on the man at the desk, placing her hands on her hips. "Do not be cross with him like the captain is. I like Henri, he is a fine young man."

Jean Luc looked at her for a few moments and chuckled at her as he continued to write. Dropping her hands from her hips, she placed them palms down on the desk and leaned there for a few moments. Jean Luc continued to write and pay her no mind. Finally she exhaled loudly to draw his attention, tapping her fingers on the desk and looking at him.

"Will you be finished there soon?" she finally asked in quiet firmness. He stood from behind the desk, shrugging.

"I am not finished with the log, but I can take it with me." Aubrey watched him as he drew nearer and an odd sensation coursed through her again and she shivered despite herself.

Biting her lip, she asked quietly, "Did you call me by my first name in the galley earlier?" He was close and her heart had begun to race a bit.

"Why, yes, I did. And there is something else that I would like to say," he smiled.

"What?"

Jean Luc stood before her. They would not have much more time alone. Black would be back on board by the next evening. He wanted to let her know how he felt about her right now, hoping that it would not frighten her. He caught her gently in his arms and lowered his head towards hers. She remained in place, turning her face up to his as he said, "Je rêve de toi toutes les nuits. Je t'aime."

He pressed her lips in a deep kiss, searching her willing mouth and he stroked one of his hands down the line of her back to her bottom. She gasped against his mouth and he broke from the kiss saying, "Détendez-vous, relax yourself. You are fine. Trust me." She did relax and his hand went on the gentle path again as he kissed her mouth. He was surprised and pleased that she remained in place.

"What did you say?" she whispered as he trailed his kisses down the side of her throat.

"I said that I dream of you every night and that I love you," he said quietly against her ear.

Aubrey drew a deep breath. "Really?"

"Vraiment," he nodded, his blue eyes sincere. She smiled nervously and he smiled back reassuringly as he pulled her in for another kiss. Moments later, he put on his hat and with a gentlemanly tip of it, he left her alone in the cabin. She did not notice that he had forgotten to take the logbook with him.

Chapter 36

Using a dressing robe that Black had given her from one of the recent plunders of a merchant ship. Aubrey slipped out of her britches and shirt, but just as she started to step into the tub, she pulled on the dressing robe and went to the settee. Kneeling on the floor she reached far back under the piece of furniture to retrieve the small wooden box that Jojoba had given her. She took out the small bottle of perfumed oil that he had given her. It was not the captain she wanted to please as Jojoba had said.

Aubrey sat on the floor pondering her feelings. Why was she acting like this? Why had she suddenly been overcome with these feelings for the quartermaster? It was most certainly not proper of her to want to make herself pleasing to a man like this. She had no ties to this man, she barely knew him. As she sat in the floor with the bottle in her hand, she recalled his gentle kisses and the sensation coursed through her again. She got up and crossed to the tub and let a few drops of the heavy oil fall into the steaming water. The air in the room was suddenly permeated with the fragrance.

A short time later as she was curled up on the settee, sewing, there was a light tapping at the door to the great cabin.

"Who is it?" she called as she came slowly to her bare feet.

"Jean Luc. I, ah, forgot the logbook," he said from the other side of the door.

After she let him in, he started for the desk, then he turned toward her, casting his eyes over her. She was wearing the robe over the silk shirt that Black had given her for a night shift. Jean Luc slowly approached her and she watched him warily.

"I thought that you had to finish in the log?" she asked, as he was just a couple of feet from her.

"Alas, I told a small lie. I was finished with the log before Henri brought your water," he said easily with a small smile. He stopped and rolling his eyes around with a look of wonder on his face, he inhaled deeply, "What is that smell?"

"It is some perfumed oil that I put in my bath. I am sorry that it displeases you," she said in a small voice.

His heart leapt with joy. She was attempting to please him? He stepped closer, "It is very intriguing. May I have a closer sample of this exotic fragrance?"

She graced him with a shy smile. Jean Luc was further elated when she allowed him to pull her gently into his muscular arms. With slow hesitant moves so he would not alarm her, he lowered his face into her neck to breathe in the fragrance. He felt her shiver slightly in his arms as his nose touched the side of her throat. He then ventured to kiss the scented and soft skin ever so gently.

Jean Luc caught her easily under the chin and raising her head, he moved in to cover her mouth gently with his. Giving into the kiss, it surprised her that kissing Jean Luc seemed so much more natural and pleasant than kissing the captain. Aubrey suddenly tried to push away after a moment, her voice was a whisper as she looked down at the front of his shirt then back up into his face, "This is very improper of me. Please forgive me, Monsieur. I do not know what has come over me. Please do not report me to the captain."

Holding her gently, yet firmly closer to him, he whispered back, "Please call me, Jean Luc. There is nothing improper about it and I would never dream of reporting this to him. Trust me, just give in to your feelings if you choose to, Aubrey," he whispered again as he pressed his lips on hers once more. She sighed as he trailed kisses across her cheek then buried his face into her perfumed neck again. Her hands clutched at the back of his shirt as she relished the sensation of his lips on her skin and she relaxed in his arms. His hand slipped easily up along her side, and in over her rib cage. With gentle ease, his hand cupped her left breast. Aubrey gasped and caught his hand.

Jean Luc dropped his hand and smiled in apology at her, "I push you too quickly."

She trembled in his arms and he recognized it as sexual excitement coursing through a woman's body. He took a step back from her before he lost himself in the desire that was building.

"Forgive me if I have frightened you. But you must know, I fell in love with you the first time I saw you. I know that Captain Black has claimed you, and were he to find out that we have had any contact,"

"He would be angry," she nodded. He gently enveloped her into his arms once more and his lips came close to barely touch hers.

"Will you play a game with me?" he whispered against her lips.

"What game, Jean Luc?" she asked quietly. His name coming from her lips was like sweet strains of angelic music.

"Not so much a game but would you keep our secret?" he said as he bestowed little kisses to her lips. Aubrey looked into the gentle blue eyes. She began to feel the strange sensations once more and she also felt a dread that their time would soon be at end and the captain would be back.

Pushing gently from his grasp, she whispered, "Oui, Jean Luc, I would take it to my grave." Pulling her back, he pressed her sweet mouth in another deep kiss.

The ship bell tolled above them, signaling the hour of midnight. She pushed from him easily. "You should go now,"

"Not yet," he whispered.

"I will be in trouble with the night watch for having the lantern lit so late," she said.

"Put it out then, and you will stay out of trouble," he shrugged as he released her. Once the flame was out, the room was thrown into sudden darkness. Both of them remained in their respective places as their eyes adjusted to the dark. The stern lights outside the quarter gallery window reflected off the calm waters, adding some light to the darkened room.

Jean Luc came toward her slowly and she seemed rooted in place.

"Merci for using the lovely perfume, it compliments you." His tone was easy and quiet.

She moved uneasily as he caught her in his arms again, "Jojoba gave it to me. He said that it would please the captain. He said that it would make him in the mood for..." She struggled with the word, trying to remember it. He watched the frown on her face, and an uneasy feeling lay in the pit of his stomach as he wondered what the Jamaican might have told her.

"Was it a French word?" he finally asked. She nodded, still making a face at the fact that she could not remember it. Pursing his lips he asked carefully, "Was it 'amour'?"

Her eyes lit up, "That was the word, what does it mean?"

He sighed deeply at her innocent question. "It means love. He told you that the perfumed oil would please the captain and put him in the mood for love."

Aubrey looked up at him suddenly, and he felt her body stiffen slightly in his arms. She was suddenly reminded of Jean Luc's comment to her about her duty to take care of the captain's needs.

"Oh."

Jean Luc watched now as her eyes darted back and forth.

"That is not what you want with him, is it?" he asked.

She dropped her head again, and her voice was soft in her reply, "Non."

"And that is not how it has been, has it?" he asked, wanting her to confirm Black's confession.

"No," came her reply in English this time.

He gently enfolded her in his arms against his chest and rested his chin on the top of her head. "I am sorry that you are so unhappy with your life on

202

board. I would do anything to make it different for you, better for you."

After a few moments of silence, she pushed away from his embrace and went to the quarter gallery. He followed her slowly, standing close behind her as she folded her arms over her chest and looked out the window at the light on the water and the port in the distance beyond. Then he watched as she climbed up into the window ledge and folded her legs under her, tucking them up under the dressing gown.

"I like the fragrance of the oil," he reiterated quietly from behind her trying to bring back the intimate moment.

She turned her head slightly toward him as she replied with a shy tone of voice, "I had hoped that you would."

Jean Luc eased closer, carefully slipping his hands about her small waist. Again he was delighted that she did not move away or protest.

"All aboard will be sleeping now, except the night watch," he informed her in a whisper. She nodded her head, still staring out the windows. With great delight, he felt her timidly lean back against him and she put her hands nervously over his. Then raising a pointed finger, she asked, "What is that star there?"

"That is the North Star. We use it to steer by. It is the brightest star in the heavens," he told her as he laid his cheek gently against hers. It was like a dream come true for him to be this close to her. In all the days that he had watched her in London, he had prayed for such a time as this. In his musing and enjoyment of having her close, he suddenly realized that she was speaking quietly again.

"You cannot see the stars too well in London but out here, they are so bright and there are so many."

"The stars make pictures in the sky. Different star formations are used in navigation as well as the North Star," he instructed.

"Sometimes, late at night, when the captain is sleeping, I creep over here and sit and look at them, until nearly dawn. The captain gets up very early, so I creep back to my bed before he awakens. I hate to leave from looking at the stars most mornings, they are beautiful," she told him.

"As are you," he whispered in her ear. She turned to look at him again, a hint of question on her face. Turning her toward him, he took the side of her face in his hand and pressed his lips on hers once more.

Aubrey accepted the kiss and then she gently pushed at him, "You should be going now."

He sighed in agreement and leaned his forehead against hers.

"I wish I did not have to, I would rather stand here all night and look at the stars with you. But you are correct."

"If you were the captain of the ship, then..." Her voice had trailed off and she put a small hand over her mouth as if she had said something wrong. He smiled down at her gently for the comment had given him a feeling of hope.

"Someday, ma chérie," he whispered as he kissed her again. His tone and the embrace made her shiver again.

"You must go," she said breathlessly and reluctantly pushed him away. She dropped her eyes to the floor and not wanting to submit them to any further distress over the situation as it was, Jean Luc left the cabin.

Aubrey sat huddled in the window. Feelings were building in her that she was unfamiliar with, and the more she thought about Jean Luc, the stronger those feelings became. With a small gasp of wonder at herself, she put a hand to her mouth. She realized that she wanted someone to hold her and caress her and kiss her, but Captain Rene Black was not the one. It was becoming painfully clear to her that she was trapped.

As Jean Luc moved to the galley, he wondered if he was pushing her too quickly. He prayed that he had not frightened her. He wanted her to trust him. When he had held her, it had felt so natural. Something had to occur--she had to be with him and not Black.

Chapter 37

By the next afternoon, they had dropped anchor in a tiny cove on the other side of the island. A great deal of Jean Luc's day had been taken up by safely navigating them around the reefs. A longboat had been sent to shore with a party headed by Boulet to find the captain and the others and bring them back to the ship.

In the quietness of the morning, Aubrey was sitting on the bunk, having occupied her time most of the day with the items Jojoba had brought her for sewing. The cabin was immaculate. She had taken great pains to make certain of that. The tub of water had been emptied and the door to the corridor stood open allowing the breeze to flow through freely.

As she sewed, Aubrey's mind had been lost in thoughts of the night before. Mingled with those thoughts, she could hear her father's flute playing an old Celtic tune. Jean Luc announced his presence by clearing his throat. She looked up in alarm and stuck her finger. With a small painful moan, she stuck the sore digit into her mouth.

"Did I cause that?" he asked as he stepped into the room and shut the door.

"Non, I am just clumsy," she said, taking the responsibility.

"Let me see," he said with a small smile as he reached to take her hand. Aubrey watched him in wide-eyed silence as he pressed his lips to the injured finger. Then he rubbed it lightly, saying, "Je regrette."

"Have you been very busy today?" she asked trying to break the silence.

Jean Luc sat down beside her. "We are moored as you can well see. And we have sent a boat to fetch the captain and the men."

"Oh," she replied. Jean Luc noted a distinct tone of disappointment in her voice.

"You do not sound very happy."

"Should I be?" she asked almost flippantly. He dropped his eyes to the floor.

"I hoped that you are as unhappy as I am."

"Then why do you not just leave them?" Aubrey asked. Her own suggestion startled her and she dropped her head in shame.

"Rene is my friend," he said quietly.

"I should not have suggested such a thing. I am sorry," she said quietly.

"Besides, even if he were not my friend and I left them, there would be a mutiny. There are many men on board who are loyal to Rene; they would kill me and then where would you be?" he told her.

"You said that you would be captain," she argued back. He smiled slightly.

"I was being arrogant that day in our argument. To be captain, one must be voted in. Such in the event of the death of the captain during battle, illness or a storm but to deliberately leave or maroon a man and assume his place is not wise, especially if the man is liked among the crew," he explained. She frowned at him. Black was liked?

"Now do you want to learn today?" he asked with a bright smile, trying to change the subject.

"What would you propose to teach me to say today?" she asked with a shy smile.

"I never proposed that I was going to teach you to say anything." He moved his face closer to hers.

When their lips were just inches apart, she said quietly, "I think that I have already learned this." He chuckled in reply. She remained still as he touched his lips to hers. He easily passed his arms around her and pulled her into a reclining position under him as he continued to kiss her. She leapt into defensive action, pushing at him.

"You are all right, I will not hurt you," he soothed. Aubrey relaxed slowly as he bestowed feathery kisses to her face. Smiling against her cheek, he said, "There, see. I would never hurt you."

He brushed his lips down over her throat and proceeded downward with his kisses, easily untying the black shirt that she wore. He frowned a bit noting that it was obviously the captain's shirt that she wore. The skin beneath was soft and pristine. He began to easily inch the tail of her shirt up out of its neatly tucked place in her britches as his mouth sought hers once more.

"Rene frightens me," she said in quiet confession as he kissed her throat. He ceased his caresses to her throat and pulling on the shirt.

"I know," he said almost apologetically.

She turned on her side away from him. "Do you think that he may find someone else?"

"What?" he asked stroking her hair, not quite understanding what she was trying to say.

She toyed with the edge of a pillow. "Someone else? Another woman, and then he would not want me any more."

"I do not know." He shrugged, running his fingertips along the exposed skin on her back where he had pulled out the shirt. She shivered at the touch, but remained in place.

206

"If he did, if someone else came along," she turned back to Jean Luc; her voice was almost a whisper. "What would he do with me?"

He looked at her for a long time, hesitating to answer her. The look in her eye was sincere and questioning. Finally he said easily, "Well, as crude as it may sound, he may release you to another man."

"I am no more than a piece of property, his property." Her voice was bitter.

He reached out to stroke her hair. "Some men might think that way."

She lay there quietly looking at him as he leaned up on one elbow. He toyed with a lock of her hair and stared at it with a faraway look in his eyes, recalling the first day that he had seen the beautiful mane.

"Jean Luc, do you believe that a dream can be a premonition of the future?" she asked suddenly.

"I have never really thought on it. Why do you ask such a question?" he shrugged.

"A few nights ago, as I slept here..." She looked around the cabin.

"I dreamed that Captain Black came back from the island, but he was not alone."

"Jojoba and the men returned with him of course," Jean Luc said.

She nodded and then said almost too quietly for him to hear, "There was someone else too."

"Who?" he asked, intrigued by this dream of hers.

"A beautiful woman. A native woman from the islands, with long black flowing hair and almond shaped eyes as black as coal and her skin was the loveliest shade of light brown." Aubrey's voice was almost like a song as she described the woman. Looking down at her, he was glad that she looked at the ceiling and not at him. At the mention of the island woman, Jean Luc's face had changed. Aubrey did not see the light of recognition in his eye for a fleeting moment.

"What happened?" Jean Luc asked and moved his hand to toy with the bottom of her shirt.

There was a long pause from Aubrey and she said, "He brought her on board. He seemed so incredibly intrigued by this woman." Her voice trailed off.

Jean Luc began to kiss her neck, and between gentle kisses he asked, "What of you? Were you in this dream?"

"I was there, but he did not want me around anymore. He was very mean to me," she replied quietly.

"You do not want to be with him anyway, why should this dream distress you?" he asked.

207

"It was not the fact of him not wanting me that distressed me. It was that I was alone and I was frightened."

"Was anyone else in this dream of yours? Did anyone else care that Rene no longer wanted you?" he asked as he slowly moved his hand up under her shirt.

She remained still and calm, but she looked him straight in the eye and said, "There was someone."

She allowed him to continue kissing her and to inch his hand even higher.

"What did I tell you a few days ago?" he asked as his long fingers stroked the velvety skin.

"I told you that I loved you," he said before she could answer. Aubrey's hazel eyes were riveted to his blue ones. Jean Luc's hand easily moved over her bare breast beneath the shirt. She reacted with a slight gasp and caught him by the forearm. He looked down at her for an extended moment as he kept his hand in place. Then in a soft voice he said, "Let me touch you, Aubrey. You are so beautiful." She slowly dropped her hand from his arm and allowed him to gently knead the soft mound. Jean Luc covered her mouth with his and kissed her deeply. Breaking from the kiss, he raised his head to look into her eyes.

"I am sorry I caused you such a fuss these past few days. I wish you..." she began in almost a whisper. A shrill whistle from above interrupted her and Jean Luc sat bolt upright. She leaned up on her elbows and asked confused, "What is it?"

"The captain is coming aboard." he replied in a strained voice. He looked down at her, adding, "We cannot be found here. Put yourself together for he will come right to his cabin the moment he boards. Please, for your own sake as well as mine, be delighted to see him. As much as it pains me to order this of you, greet him well. That is if you choose to care about me at all."

She was hurt by his last comment. As he turned to leave, she quickly leapt up and grabbed his arm. "Jean Luc, I do care." He looked down at her hand on his arm, then pulled her to him and kissed her hard before he dashed out the door. Staring at the closed portal, she tucked in the shirt and brushed her hair into place.

Chapter 38

The quiet ship was suddenly thrown into a bustle of activity. Black would return to the cabin soon and Aubrey sighed at the thought. She also found herself wondering how long it would be before he would leave the ship again, and leave her in the care of Jean Luc. She shook her head at her own thoughts. Not long ago, she had been angry because he had left her on board while he went to shore. Now she did not care.

It seemed all too soon when she heard his deep voice clearly as he spoke to the men on his way to the cabin from the companionway. Acting almost as a buffer, Jojoba preceded him to the great cabin and met her with a smile.

"Oh ma petite! Look at how pretty you are dis morning!" She smiled back at him from her seat at the table. He set down a small ornate casket on the table before them and pulled up a chair next to her. She glanced at it in interest and then went back to her sewing.

Black seemed to be in a dark mood when he entered the cabin. Aubrey remained quiet as he stepped up to the table and flipped the lid on the box open. Jojoba whistled through his teeth as he beheld the treasures within. Aubrey put down her sewing and peered at a mound of jewels in the box.

Jojoba glanced at her and then smiled at his captain. "Ah dis has caught her eye, mon Capitaine." Jojoba chuckled. Embarrassed, Aubrey sat back in her chair and pulled up her needle from her sewing again, trying to appear undaunted by the little treasure chest that Black had brought in.

"You may pick something if you like," Black said indifferently as he poured himself a mug of rum. She continued to appear entirely engrossed in her sewing.

"Ah ma petite, look at dese pretty earrings," Jojoba said as he withdrew a pair of dangling earrings. They had small ornate crosses on them with black onyx middles in each one. Black had come closer to the table with his mug in hand when Jojoba pulled out the earrings and laid them on the table.

Aubrey barely had a chance to see them before Black scooped them up quickly in his free hand, saying curtly, "Not those." He clutched them in his fist and turned from the table. Aubrey and Jojoba looked at him bewildered. Black turned to glance back at them. "They do not compliment her. The style is not good for her."

Black moved to his desk as Aubrey and Jojoba looked at one another. A small frown crossed her face as Aubrey watched him open his fist and finger the earrings in silence for a moment. Then he laid them gently on the table as if they would break. He settled himself into the chair behind his desk and took another drink from his mug.

Jojoba smiled at Aubrey, patting her arm.

"No matter, ma petite. We will find something else pretty for you. More pretty dan dose."

Black cast him a dark glance at the condescending tone in Jojoba's voice at the end of his sentence. He set down his mug to pick up his quill. Aubrey continued to watch him as he pulled out a piece of paper and began to write.

"I cannot wear earrings anyway, Jojoba." She said with an air of defiance. Black glanced up at her comment then his eye shifted to look upon Jean Luc as he stepped into the cabin. Jean Luc was glaring at the Jamaican who sat so closely to Aubrey.

"You called for me?" he asked tightly in French to Black. The latter nodded and waved him to the desk.

At the sight of Jean Luc, Aubrey felt a flutter in the base of her stomach and goosebumps broke out on her arms. She was glad that the long sleeves of her shirt hid them.

"How about dis?" Jojoba asked, pulling her attention away from the two men. "Here is a nice gold medallion," the Jamaican was saying with a smile as he pulled it out of the box.

"No! No medallion!" Black snapped over his mug as he prepared to take another drink. Three pair of eyes looked in alarm at him now. Jojoba dropped the item back into the casket, clicking his tongue.

"Never mind, Jojoba. I think that the captain has changed his mind about me picking something," Aubrey said in quiet firmness as she waved her hand at the jewels. Picking up her sewing, she retreated to the settee and sat down.

"I have not changed my mind, Mademoiselle. You just cannot have those earrings or a medallion," Black said as he rose from the desk and went to the table.

"It does not matter, Captain, I picked neither of the items in question anyway. I do not want anything," she said in a small pouting voice. Black ignored her and the three of them watched as he poked a slender finger into the casket, searching.

Finally he plucked out a pair of plain gold stud earrings and tossed them on the table. "There."

Jean Luc frowned at his abruptness over such a trifling subject. He looked down at the ornate earrings on the desk where Black had laid them, and then he cast an eye to the plain ones Black had chosen for her.

Jojoba picked them up and carried them to her. "Here, des are pretty."

Aubrey looked into the brown hand that held them, and then she looked up at him in apology. "Merci anyway, but as I have already said I cannot wear earrings. I do not want anything from there."

"I will pierce your ears, ma petite," he offered as he caught her chin in one hand and he gently pinched at her earlobe with the hand that held the earrings. Jean Luc looked at them, wanting to lash out at the man for putting his hands upon her. Black seemed undaunted as he went back to the desk and began to write.

"No, I do not want you to do that. It will hurt," Aubrey was heard to whine.

"No mon petite, I will do it so dat you will not feel it, I promise," Jojoba tried to coax her. Then he looked at her closely, his tone dropping to a barely audible level. "Hmm, what is dat I smell? You have used de oil I gave you?"

Black was so engrossed in whatever he was writing on the paper, the noise from the corridor and above decks of the men at work to stock the ship that he missed the comment. But Jean Luc, in his intent sideways observation of her, caught the comment very clearly. It peaked his interest even more as he turned to watch them. Aubrey was blushing and she shot a nervous glance in the direction of Jean Luc and Black.

"Did he like it?" Jojoba asked with a knowing smile and in a near whisper. Aubrey's eyes dropped to Black and then she slowly raised them to meet those of Jean Luc. He held her in his gaze and then winked at her.

She smiled shyly, "Yes Jojoba, he did."

The Jamaican had missed the exchange, but he chuckled at her reply, thinking that she meant the captain. He patted her hand. "Ah see, Jojoba knows."

For once, Jean Luc realized that he was pleased with something that the Jamaican had done. He looked quickly back as Black began to speak.

"There, when the men are all on the deck, these items need to be voted on before we leave port."

"Aye sir," Jean Luc nodded as he looked over the paper that Black had handed him.

"Jojoba, go call the men to the deck," Black said as he stood with his mug.

"Aye sir, but first, might I please give a little trinket to de Mademoiselle?" The black man asked.

"Be quick with it," Black spat.

"See, I have brought you a gift from my island. I wish dat de captain would have brought you along, you would love de island, ma petite. I was so frightened for you de night of de storm." He spoke almost too quickly for her to understand with his accent. As he spoke, he dug in his pouch.

"I was fine, Jojoba. Monsieur Pierne took good care that I was safe during the storm, just as he was ordered to do by the captain," she assured him as she patted his arm.

"Here," he said as he handed her a string of tiny shells.

"Dese are from my island."

"Merci!" she replied delightedly as he put the necklace around her neck.

Captain Black cleared his throat and Jojoba made a hasty exit, shutting the door behind him.

Jean Luc noted the attitude of his friend. He frowned at the excessive drink that Black was putting away so early in the day. Up until now the conversation had been in English, but suddenly Jean Luc asked in French, "Is something troubling you, Rene?"

Black poured himself more of the rum and he offered the bottle to his quartermaster, who politely declined. Aubrey had resumed her sewing.

"Did you," Black began in French, but then his brow wrinkled in puzzlement and he looked around the cabin.

"Do you smell something, Jean Luc? An unusual aroma?" he asked in English.

Aubrey let out a small yelp from her place on the settee. The two men looked pointedly at her as she stuck her forefinger into her mouth, "Stuck myself with the needle," she said quietly with the digit still in her mouth. The look on her face was one of pure innocence and Jean Luc squelched a chuckle. Black was still looking around the room, searching for the origin of the aroma.

Jean Luc shot a glance at Aubrey. The soft fragrance of the oil she had used the night before in her bath lingered lightly in the air and it provoked mild stirrings in him. Seemingly undaunted as he sniffed the air, Jean Luc shrugged and lied, "I do not smell anything, Rene."

Black shook his head and began again in French, "Anyway, did you see a woman at port the last time you and I left the ship?"

Jean Luc lifted a brow and looked taken aback. "Ah, Rene, one could take that question one of two ways. Besides it is a question that is rather personal."

"I meant did you observe one, one that was familiar to you? One that you have recognized by sight?"

"No Rene, I did not. I did not see any woman in any fashion, except perhaps the one who served me my dinner and drink at the tavern," Jean Luc replied as he shot a glance at Aubrey as if she could understand what they were saying.

"Hmm, is that all she did for you, mon ami? Then your trip to shore must

212

have been very frustrating," Black chided.

Jean Luc pursed his lips. "I saw nothing of interest there. Why do you ask?"

Black's countenance turned solemn as he stared across the room at Aubrey who sewed quietly, disinterested in their foreign conversation. The dark eye was upon her, but it appeared to Jean Luc that Black did not truly see her.

"I heard a rumor that there is a young woman pirate..." he began, his voice sounding distant.

Jean Luc's eyes widened and he moved uncomfortably, "So? Rene, there are many women who take to our profession, openly and covertly. Calico Jack sails with two of them as we speak."

Black's gaze settled on his quartermaster and with a click of his tongue, he growled, "they are part of his crew and his mistresses. It is rumored that this woman sails with no man as her captain—but that she is the captain of her own ship. It is a fast ship too, they say."

Jean Luc's expression mirrored Black's. "Vraiment?"

"Oui. It is said that she goes about blatantly picking fights with the British Navy," Black nodded as he moved toward the quarter gallery windows. Giving Jean Luc an intense look, he added, "I hear she flies a solid red flag." Jean Luc returned Black's look with one of surprised interest.

"The one that followed us?"

"Perhaps," Black answered with a shrug.

The room fell silent between them. In the stillness of the room, Black said almost to himself, "In town this morning, I thought I saw... but that would be impossible." Black shook his head to rid himself of what had happened. But his mind's eye took him back for a fleeting moment. A woman with long dark hair had disappeared quickly around the corner of a building. As he reached the corner, he had found only an empty alley. But for an instant, the woman looked like...

Aubrey brought her sewing up to her mouth to cut the thread with her teeth. She looked at the two men who had suddenly stopped talking. Black looked as if he were in another time and place while Jean Luc had a stolid expression on his face.

"Captain, is there to be a meeting of the men?" came the monotone voice of Thomas Beaufort from the open doorway. Black and Jean Luc looked quickly toward him, their thoughts broken by his intrusion.

"Oui," Black nodded as he put his mug on the table.

Beaufort advanced into the room. He leered at Aubrey as he came between her and the other two men. It took ever fiber of her being to remain calm.

"They are very nearly all gathered, with the exception of the ones returning in the longboat. They should be on board within the hour," Beaufort reported. Jean Luc looked over the paper that Black had given him again. His attention was caught by the sound of someone sniffing the air loudly. He looked toward the sound and found that it was coming from Beaufort. The latter had his eyes closed and was sniffing the air in an animated fashion like some kind of an animal. Beaufort turned his head toward where Aubrey was seated with her sewing and Jean Luc saw a thin smile spread over the man's lips. Black was pouring himself more rum, not paying Beaufort any attention until the man asked in English, "Captain, what is that smell here in your cabin?"

Beaufort's eyes were still closed so he did not see Aubrey and Jean Luc meet worried gazes. Her eyes were glazed with terror and Jean Luc tried to mentally will her to calmness. Black had his back to them and was putting the rum bottle away, thereby missing it as well.

"You have been down in the hold with the rancid water too long Beaufort, it has made a home in your nostrils. There is no smell in the captain's cabin." Jean Luc scoffed quickly. Black chuckled at the comment, but Beaufort shook his head with a sly smile with his eyes still closed.

"No Jean Luc, it is not a bad smell. But it is not a familiar smell either. It is sensual and intriguing."

Aubrey thought that she might faint as he opened his eyes and looked deliberately at her. He moved closer to her and this finally drew Black's attention. Jean Luc glanced at the captain and saw the look of suspicion in his dark eye.

"Thomas, what is your business here?" Black asked as he came forward slowly. Beaufort ignored him and continued his slow advance on Aubrey. Black had a look of disbelief on his face. Jean Luc was surprised that Beaufort chose to be so brave in his advance on Aubrey in front of the captain.

Beaufort continued his advance and just as he came to stand directly in front of her, Aubrey found she could contain herself no longer. Jean Luc had directed her not to let the man see her fear but she gave in easily to the emotion now. Leaping up from the settee with a frightened yelp, she dropped her sewing on the floor. In her retreat, she pushed past Beaufort, shoving at him with both hands and ran to hide behind Black.

Beaufort grunted as she passed, then turned to follow her and look upon her as she hid behind the captain clutching at the back of his jacket. Black glanced around at her then glared at Beaufort.

"The smell, or rather, aroma comes from her, Captain." He began looking at her as she peered around Black.

With a leering smile, he cooed at her, "Why do you run and hide from me, little one? Thomas will not hurt you." Black's face was a mask of anger as he stepped toward Beaufort. Aubrey still clung to his jacket with both hands fisted in the folds of material at the tail. Jean Luc put out his arm between her and Black in warning for her to separate herself from him physically. Black's hand lay on his pistol and Jean Luc fingered his pistol as well. It was evident that Black was on the verge of an impending explosion of violence. Aubrey released her grip and dropped her hands to her sides, fearfully watching the three men face off as she stepped backward, making space between herself and the angry pirates.

"Do not concern yourself with the 'aroma', Monsieur Beaufort. Remember that she is the woman of the captain. Find yourself a whore at port. Now get out of my cabin and on deck with the rest of the men," Black grumbled angrily.

Chapter 39

Jean Luc was glad to see Black take a stand against Beaufort's continued pestering of Aubrey. Looking down at his bandaged hand before his gray eyes met with her frightened hazel eyes, Beaufort finally chuckled and offered her a sweeping and mocking bow then he left. The hush lingered over the room for a few more moments before Jean Luc finally broke the silence, speaking in English.

"I think that I will have that drink now, Rene."

Black was glaring at the doorway where Beaufort had exited. "Ass," he growled.

"He does that all the time, Rene," Jean Luc informed the captain, as Black poured him a mug of rum and another for himself.

"He does what?" Black asked over his mug as he looked at Aubrey. She carefully went back to the settee, giving the two men a wide berth.

"Torments her. I am forever calling him down for it. He gets bolder by the day and if I were you, I would be very worried about his intentions. You know Thomas and how he is," Jean Luc finished in French.

"What is that aroma?" Black asked in puzzlement.

Aubrey's gaze dropped to the floor, her voice was nearly a whisper as she replied, "It is some bath oil."

Jean Luc's heart sank for it would not be their secret anymore.

"Really? Where did you get this–bath oil?" Black asked.

Her hazel eyes rose to meet his stare, "Jojoba gave it to me."

Black glanced at Jean Luc. "Go topside, the men should be gathered by now. I will be up directly, I have some personal business to tend to." Black set down his mug and walked toward Aubrey, who had resumed her seat.

"Aye sir," Jean Luc replied in a less than happy tone. Casting a glance at her as he left the cabin, he saw a new worry and fear in her eyes as Black had strode toward her.

With the door closed behind Jean Luc, Black said, "Jojoba gave you this oil? Let me see it."

"I did nothing wrong, I only put a few drops into my bath last night," she explained.

"Bring it to me," he said firmly. Sighing with dejection, she dropped to her knees on the floor and took out her personal possession box. He sat down on the settee, holding out his hand to receive the bottle. She placed it into his hand and remained on her knees as he opened the cork. Passing the bottle under his nose he looked at her saying, "This is a very extravagant and expensive gift that my first mate has bestowed upon you. What did you do for him to deserve such a gift?"

"I did nothing! He just gave it to me," she nearly shouted at him in retort. His brows rose at the volume and tone of her voice.

"You will give it back," he said flatly as he re-corked the bottle with a slap of the palm of his hand.

"But why? I did nothing wrong. I took a gift offered by a friend. That is not fair!" she argued.

Black's mind was in turmoil from the effects of the rum he had drank, the intriguing information of the elusive female pirate captain, the woman he glimpsed, the blatant actions of Beaufort against the captain's woman, and now the knowledge of Jojoba bestowing personal and expensive gifts to her. Aubrey's retort was ill taken and he struck out in a flash of anger before he could stop himself. He dealt her a quick backhand to her mouth.

Aubrey never moved from her kneeling position on the floor but her head jerked from the blow. She slowly put her hand to her mouth and he watched her remove her hand to look at the blood on her fingertips from the cut he had made at the corner of her lip. Tears welled in her eyes, but she suppressed the sob that built in her chest.

"Monsieur Jojoba gave it to me," she began thickly.

Black looked at her as she continued to struggle with the emotion. She wondered if she should tell him the truth as to why Jojoba had given her the oil. Looking at the blood again, she decided that it would be wise, hoping that it would prevent him from further anger and perhaps a more severe beating. It distressed her to think that she had escaped one abusive man only to fall victim to another. Drawing a deep breath she said, "He gave it to me–to please you."

Black's dark eye stared at her for a long moment, then he pulled a handkerchief from his pocket and handed it to her.

"Wipe your mouth and hand, I have business to tend to on deck. You will accompany me." She took the handkerchief and did as he instructed. When he handed her the bottle of oil, she looked from it to him. Anger built in her towards his attitude as though he had no recollection of having struck her. Snatching the small bottle from his hand, she faced the quarter gallery window and drew back her arm.

Black saw that she meant to throw the bottle and he caught her wrist with one hand as he took the bottle in his other.

"Would you throw away such an expensive gift then?" he asked quietly.

"Yes, I would. I would throw away any gift no matter how expensive or extravagant if the thought behind it were not genuine or it could be misconstrued to mean something other than what it did," she replied easily.

Smiling almost cruelly, he let go of her wrist. Then he caught her by the back of her neck and pulled her upper body down across his knees, "Let me smell this oil a bit closer."

She struggled to free herself as he buried his face in the back of her neck. Her cheek was pressed hard against his knee and she managed to turn her face toward his knee in an attempt to bite him to make him release her. He was surprised to feel her teeth against his leg.

"That would be unwise, Aubrey," he warned as he let her up before she actually bit him. Still holding her in his grasp, he smiled at her.

"I am most certain that Jojoba's intentions were entirely honorable, given his reasoning. By all means, keep you little bottle of perfumed oil."

She stared at him blankly as he put the bottle on the table by the settee and ordered her to come with him to the quarterdeck. She followed closely on his heels, especially when she saw the sea of men on the deck. She had heard both he and Jean Luc mention the number of crewmembers on board but until now, she could never have fathomed their mass. Men were everywhere, on the deck, up in the ratlines, and even up on the yardarms.

Standing on the quarterdeck with Black was frightening today, with all eyes seemingly on her because she stood so close to him and he demanded their attention. She cast a quick look to Jean Luc and found that he was looking at her with a frown on his handsome face. Remembering the cut on her lip, she glanced nervously at the crew and ducked back behind Black in an effort to hide from them and Jean Luc. She did not want him to see her with a swollen and cut lip. The change in location worked well as she put her fingers to the sore place on her mouth to check her fingers for blood. From where Black stood and from where she hid, she looked down the quarterdeck steps to see Beaufort standing at the bottom, watching her.

This new location did not hide her from him. At the sight of Beaufort, she unconsciously grasped the back of Black's jacket, crushing the fabric in her hands. He glanced back at her and growled, "Relax, you are fine."

"I want to go below," she said quietly.

"Non," he spat as he turned back to put his attention on Jean Luc as the quartermaster read from the paper in hand. Aubrey peeped around Black at the sea of men and shuddered visibly. Keen gray eyes caught the reaction from the bottom of the steps and Beaufort came up three steps to say to her, with a smile, "Ugly lot, are they not?"

Black cast him a warning glance and Beaufort stopped in his tracks, offering him a thin smile and folding his arms over his chest, appearing to be interested in the meeting.

Jean Luc had finished his duty, as the crew's representative, having announced the decision of the crew's votes to Black. The latter leaned on the railing to address them, leaving Aubrey in the open again. He spoke in French, which she could not understand so she stared at the back of his head in puzzlement and fear. After a time, she became aware that Jean Luc was staring at her. She had dropped her hand from her mouth in her security of hiding behind Black. She put her hand back to cover the cut but it was too late. By the look in his eye as he shifted his gaze to the captain, she knew that he had spied the wound. She saw the familiar sight of his jaw muscles clenching in anger.

Aubrey dropped her head, looking back at him with pleading eyes in silent communication. He had to remain silent over the incident or she would suffer all the more and he would most certainly be punished as well. The thought of his own punishment meant nothing to Jean Luc, but the thought of more punishment dealt to her was unthinkable.

"Weigh the anchor, drop the sails. The next port of call will be Bimini," Black said to Jean Luc as he turned away from the railing.

"Aye sir. To your places, men! Weigh the anchor and drop the sails!" Jean Luc called out to the men below.

The men disbursed quickly and Aubrey looked up to see the sails drop almost simultaneously at the command. Men ran along the yardarms as if they were as broad and as flat as the decks of the ship. Several men on the main deck turned the capstan as the chain and rope holding the massive anchor came up out of the water dripping, clanking and groaning. The ship was now free of the land's hold on her and with the wind filling the sails with loud buffeting noises, the *Widow Maker* began her slow tack away from the island.

She had never been afforded the opportunity to be on deck during a departure and the sights and sounds together fascinated her. Black ignored her as she stood against the railing watching quietly. He stood at the navigation station going over the charts with Jean Luc.

Finally, Black turned from Jean Luc and approached Aubrey. He took her gently yet firmly by the arm and led her toward the quarterdeck steps. Beaufort still stood at the bottom of the steps as Black gestured for her to go down them ahead of him. Aubrey looked down into the gray leering eyes as he smiled at her and she hesitated in her descent.

"Move, damn you," Black growled from behind. Aubrey cast a startled glance over her shoulder at him, thinking that he was fussing with her.

"I–I cannot go down, Captain," he stammered.

"I can see that. Damn it, Beaufort. Move," he replied curtly.

Beaufort stepped aside and gave Aubrey a mocking bow. "By all means, pass, Mademoiselle."

Black pushed her gently from behind and Aubrey went down the steps. As she passed Beaufort, he leered down at her again. Black stepped up close to the man, his face only inches from Beaufort's.

"I grow tired of your antics today, Monsieur Beaufort. Take care you do not anger me further," he warned. On the quarterdeck, Jean Luc smiled slightly.

Chapter 40

As Black escorted Aubrey back to the cabin, he let out a deep sigh. He felt as though he was losing control of his ship and his men, perhaps even his mind. There was something about the sight of the woman this morning, had she even been real? He could not shake the unnerving thought that maybe, just maybe... but that was impossible. To make matters worse, Beaufort had twice today made advances toward Aubrey within his very sight!

Black opened the cabin door allowing her to precede him then closed the door behind them. He took off his hat and laid it on the table.

"Are you quite over your little tantrum?"

She wondered that if she did not answer him, would it ignite his anger and cause him to strike her again. Aubrey touched her hand to her smarting lip.

"I am very tired, I think that I will lie down."

"Are you not glad that I am back?"

"I am glad," she lied.

He seemed to ignore her as he reached and picked up the string of shells, brushing his hand against her breasts, causing her to shiver uncontrollably. Snickering, he said, "How very native."

She gave him an annoyed look. "I think that it was a lovely thought."

He chuckled again and said in his deep voice as he cupped her chin in his hand, "Perhaps, but how do they compare to my gift? You did not choose from the baubles in the casket. But what about this?" He reached into a pocket and produced a fine gold chain. Her mouth dropped open in surprise. It was only an uncontrollable reaction. This was the finest piece of jewelry she had ever seen or possessed. He took her hand in his and dropped the chain into it.

"Merci," she found herself gasping.

"Is that all for poor Rene?" he asked in feigned sadness then finished with, "A polite merci?"

He passed his arms easily around her waist. "Such a small thank you for such a grand present? Can you do no better than that? In the future there will be more added to this." Then he crushed her against him and kissed her. She winced at the pressure of his lips but was fearful that if she resisted, he might become angry. Instead she suffered through the embrace. After a few seconds that seemed like an eternity to her, he broke away from the kiss. Still holding her tightly, he proceeded to wander down her throat with his kisses.

Aubrey shrugged to try and get him to stop, but he continued on, his hand wandering up to the very breast that Jean Luc had caressed earlier. She began to panic as the kisses went lower into the front of her shirt and he held her tighter. Her breath came in gasps. "Rene, please," she whined.

Suddenly and without warning, his hand shot up to grasp her by the chin, his long fingers digging into her flesh. With his face inches from hers, he hissed, "You do not seem to understand, Precieux. I am prepared to take what I want from you. You fail to remember that I saved you and had you brought on board the *Widow Maker*. I could have left you there to drown with the others on that garbage heap the *Gull*. I am your protection, and you owe me."

Her mind was in turmoil. He still held her face in a vice-like grip and she closed her eyes tightly against the pain. Tears squeezed out of the corners of her eyes as he tightened the grip on her face until she opened her eyes to look back up at him. She shook uncontrollably with anger and fear. It appeared that the dream was beginning to take life as she stood here locked in his clutches.

He stared at her angrily, still holding her face tightly and she felt powerless to break free from him. Black's mind reeled as a face appeared into his thoughts. She was not like... Merde, but she is gone now! In the next instant she was being pushed forcefully away from him. She found herself falling as she put her hands out to try and catch herself. Aubrey hit the floor with a thud and she quickly scrambled away from him fearfully as he stepped after her. He reached for her and caught her by the shirt that she wore.

"Get up," he hissed as he pulled her to her feet. Then with a sigh, he reached down for the chain that had fallen from her hand in the struggle.

"Will you not even wear my gift? Is it not good enough for you?"

She backed up a half step, brushing the tears from her face. The chain dangled from his outstretched palm.

"Shall I fasten it on?" Swallowing hard and looking at him, she stood riveted to the spot, trembling violently. He appeared no longer angry and even his countenance had changed. The look in his eye was gentle and he smiled lightly. His quick change in demeanor further frightened her. Aubrey stood still as he walked behind her and put the chain around her neck and fastened it. He laid his hands on her shoulders gently again and kissed the side of her throat. She stood petrified and silent. He laid his cheek against hers and said, "You have been sleeping in my bunk during my absence?"

Cold chills ran down her spine and she shivered again, "Yes," she replied faintly.

"Pardon?" he asked sharply. She cringed, waiting for the devil in him to come back out.

"Oui," she replied a bit louder, speaking in the French she knew he was waiting to hear.

"I am certain that you found it comfortable."

"Oui." The answer came meekly, she was afraid to lie to him now.

"What did I try to tell you before? Well then, since you are accustomed to the comfort now, imagine how comfortable and warm it will be tonight, when you do so with me. There will be no more of your sleeping on the settee. You are the Captain's lady and in his bunk is where you belong," he replied curtly as he stepped away from her. She cringed as she remembered Jean Luc's words outside the galley.

But then the comment angered her and she took a step forward. "I do not," she began, but was cut short as he turned on his heel, a look of fire in his eye.

"You do not what, Aubrey?"

She looked at him for a moment and then said, "I do not mind sleeping on the settee, I do not want to disturb you. Sometimes I have bad dreams and I might cry out in my sleep and wake you. You should not have your rest disturbed."

"It disturbs me that you do not sleep in my bunk with me. I would hold you in comfort if you were awakened or frightened by a bad dream." He pulled on his gloves and put on his hat. He straightened his waistcoat and said, "Please remember that while you do have free roam of the ship now, lights out is still at two bells. You will be expected here long before then. It is not wise for you to roam the ship after dark. Someone could take you far below in the hold. It is not a pleasant place there my dear, I assure you." He seemed to be thoroughly enjoying this episode of frightening her. With a grunting laugh he said, "Now if you will excuse me, I have business to tend to while we depart from the bay."

She watched him leave and wished she could make herself disappear before the bells tolled twice tonight.

Black went up on deck with an attitude that revealed nothing of the incident with Aubrey. He approached Jean Luc. "I see that everything is in order, Monsieur Pierne."

"Oui Rene," the navigator replied. Something was awry; Jean Luc felt it in his bones. He quickly scanned the deck between them and the door to the lower level of the ship. There was no sign of Aubrey. The cut that he had seen on her lip still angered him. Putting the anger aside to protect her, Jean Luc decided to attempt some small talk to try and get information.

223

"I am sure Mademoiselle Aubrey was happy that you have returned," he said in casual conversation.

Black pulled on his gloves a little tighter. "Hmm, oui," he replied as he looked around the ship. "Did the *Widow Maker* sustain any damages from the storm?"

"Only a few tears in the sails, the men finished patching them up yesterday," Jean Luc reported.

"Bon," the dark haired man nodded. There was extended silence between them. Suddenly Black asked, "How did you and Mademoiselle Aubrey get along during my absence?"

Quite unwilling to expose himself or Aubrey he shrugged and replied, "Well, she locked herself in your cabin. She did permit me entrance to keep up the log. The night we ran into the storm and in order to maintain her safety in the event that we had taken on water, I had to force her out of there. That is after we actually got in and I found her."

"Found her?" Black echoed.

"Oui, well, she is very imaginative with her hiding places," Jean Luc nodded, remembering the night well. Black seemed lost in thought, so Jean Luc waited quietly.

"She is a very difficult young woman to deal with. She is not very cooperative, despite her timid nature. We fought most of the time," Jean Luc added.

"Indeed, I have discovered this myself," Black nodded. Then with a chuckle he added, "Perhaps we should have let her go down with the *Gull* and saved one of those old cronies instead."

Jean Luc looked at Black incredulously and shuddered visibly and replied, "Mon Dieu, Rene, that does not even sound tempting. I saw those women; one would have had to be at sea a very long time to bed that!"

The two of them shared the laugh and then Black said, "Please join us in my cabin this evening for dinner. I promise she will be no less than the perfect hostess. You and I have business to discuss. Bring your charts and materials. Plot a course for Bimini and then the mainland."

"France?" Jean Luc asked with a hopeful tone. Black chuckled as he strode away.

"Non, the Colonies," came the captain's reply over his shoulder.

"The Colonies?" he echoed in a quiet voice, then called out, "As you wish, Rene."

Aubrey was sitting at the table when Black came back to the cabin and went to his desk. He gave her a sideways glance and said indifferently, "We will

224

have company for dinner."

"Who will be our dinner company?"

"Jean Luc. He and I have business to discuss," he replied as he opened his logbook and seemed to search for something. With a nod, he left the cabin just as abruptly as he entered.

Aubrey just stared at the closed door in disbelief. He acted as though she had not been in the room. She walked over to the mirror and looking at herself, smiling ever so slightly at her reflection. She noticed that her face was bruised where he had held her so tightly earlier in the day. This discovery dismayed her, for the handsome quartermaster would certainly not be happy with the sight of the bruise on her face.

"Sweet Mary, how did I get myself into this?" Aubrey asked aloud to the empty room.

"Why did I not stay in England? Perhaps a fixed marriage would not have been quite so bad after all. If only one of them had been half as handsome and dashing as these two here." Her state of self-pity was interrupted by a heavy knock on the door and she jumped with a start.

"Mademoiselle, Cap'n says we should bring you this. Says you might like a hot bath after such a long day." It was the voice of the young cabin boy, Henri. She opened the door so that Henri and Cook could carry in buckets of steaming water and poured them into the large tub.

"A bath two nights in a row? I thought that there was no water for such frivolity?" she asked.

"If Captain Black says there is enough water, then there is enough water," Cook grunted, in obvious disapproval.

"Well, I am not to be blamed for this. I never asked for it again after you told me no," she spat back.

Henri could be heard to giggle boyishly at the exchange. Cook cuffed him in the ear. "Get back to your chores, damn you."

As the two began to leave, the boy turned to her. "Cap'n says dinner will be at six o'clock." She nodded in reply and, at the same time, noticed Beaufort and Boulet passing the opened doorway.

Boulet looked into the cabin and caught sight of the steaming tub of water, and said in English for her benefit, "Hmm... preparing the captain's supper in his cabin tonight, Cook?" The big man flew off into a tangent of foul language in French as Beaufort and Boulet burst into hearty laughter. Aubrey slammed the door to all of them and slapped the lock bolt into place.

"Animals," she growled to herself as she began to slip out of her clothing.

She had one hour to prepare herself. The hot water felt wonderful and she wished that she had more time to relish it.

Chapter 41

After her bath, Aubrey unbolted the door and sat in the quarter gallery to await Black's return. Entering the cabin a few moments later, Black cast a cursory glance at her before giving his attention to pouring himself some rum.

"Would you care for some rum, Aubrey?" It was the first time he had used her real name in a long time.

"Non, merci," she replied calmly.

She watched him pour a mug of rum for himself, "How unfortunate, you might enjoy the relaxation of it," he smiled, then downed the entire mug and brushed at his mustache.

"I hope you will not be too bored with the conversation this evening."

"Then perhaps after dinner, I should go elsewhere," she commented evenly.

He laughed at her and waved his arms to indicate the ship, "You are one woman on a ship of ruthless pirates, in the middle of the Caribbean. Where would you go?"

She looked him in the eye for several seconds and then replied bluntly, "Overboard."

He began to chuckle again and poured himself another drink as she regarded him with her hazel eyes. At that moment, there was a light knock upon the door to the cabin. Black raised the mug to his lips. "Entre."

The door swung open and Jean Luc stepped in. Aubrey looked from Black to Jean Luc as the captain downed the second mug of rum. Jean Luc made a polite bow and extended his hand to her, "Mademoiselle."

She stepped forward and put her hand in his. He bent his head to lightly kiss the back of her small hand. His eyes shifted to Black who was pouring yet another mug of the drink, paying no attention to them. Looking back into her face, she saw Jean Luc frown slightly as he spied the bruise. She easily put her hand up to cover the spot as he dropped her hand from the welcome gesture. Jean Luc's blue eyes wandered over her and his throat went suddenly dry. It took a moment to realize that Black was speaking.

"Jean Luc, I know that you will enjoy some drink with me."

Jean Luc's eyes were still on Aubrey, but he replied, trying to keep from croaking out the words, "Oui, merci."

Black handed a mug of rum to his quartermaster and motioned to Aubrey "She will not drink with us. No matter, sit down, Mademoiselle." His voice was somewhat harsh and hinted of too much alcohol already. Jean Luc looked at him and then at Aubrey again as he seated himself across from her. She did not look back at him but merely looked down at the table. His keen eyes noted the bruises again on her chin and cheeks as well as cut at the corner of her mouth. He shot an angry glance at the captain. Black was crossing behind Aubrey on his way to his own seat at the table. As he past her, he deliberately trailed a slender finger across the back of her shoulders. Jean Luc saw her clench her teeth and shudder, but she still did not look up or make a sound.

"Jean Luc tells me that the two of you had some problems during my absence," Black stated as he sat down at the head of table. Before she could respond, there was a knock upon the door. "Entre," the captain called.

Cook entered, followed again by the cabin boy carrying the food for the meal. As the boy laid silverware for Aubrey, he smiled shyly at her.

Fire flashed in the eye of Black and he snapped a remark to the boy in French that she did not understand, and the boy's face paled.

Aubrey shot an angry look at the captain, in Henri's defense she said, "There is no need to be rude with him. He means no harm." Jean Luc smiled at her defiant air.

Black looked from the boy who was now leaving, to her. "The little brat needs to learn his place. You, Mademoiselle, would do well to keep your tongue in the presence of my crew, also." Jean Luc saw trouble brewing. He gently tapped her leg under the table with his foot, trying to warn her to mind her temper with the captain. She shot an angry look at Jean Luc who ever so slightly shook his head in warning against opposing Black.

The captain was not paying attention as he began to eat calmly. "Now what about you and Monsieur Pierne?" he asked.

"I beg your pardon?" she asked curtly.

"Did you argue with Monsieur Pierne?" he questioned.

"Monsieur Pierne and I chose to disagree most of the time, Captain, as always," she replied flippantly. Jean Luc rolled his eyes at her continued attitude.

"I understand that Monsieur Pierne saved you from being washed overboard during the storm," Black told her, ignoring her demeanor. Jean Luc listened and watched guardedly.

"I have no real recollection of the incident other than I was scared out of my wits. I know only what I have been told," she said, going back to her own meal. Jean Luc wondered who had informed Black of the incident. Silence fell over the three of them for a brief time, and then Black started again.

"Did you thank Monsieur Pierne for saving your life?"

227

"Yes," she answered in irritation.

"What?" he snapped.

"Oui," she repeated in French.

"How did you thank him?" he pressed. She looked at him incredulously. Even Jean Luc was looking at him in question. Black touched his napkin to his lips. "Well?"

"I said 'thank you'. What would you expect? Or shall I ask, what would be your order?" she replied flatly. Jean Luc tapped her again under the table with his booted foot. Damn it, but she was playing with fire. Black picked up his mug and drained it as he looked at her. She glared at him from her seat at the table.

"You know, Mademoiselle, I have promised Monsieur Pierne that you would be no less than the ideal hostess this night at dinner. You are making me look bad. Do you think that you could find some ounce of charm somewhere beneath your hot Irish temper and eat your dinner, smiling gracefully as we finish our meal?" Black asked as he wiped at his mustache with long slender fingers. She looked at Jean Luc who watched the two of them silently with a fork in one hand and a knife in the other, poised over his plate.

"Je regrette, Monsieur Pierne, please forgive my manners. I have brought ugliness to the captain's table."

Jean Luc merely nodded. His true desire was to tell her that her very presence brought a beauty that was beyond words.

With a glance at Black to catch his response to the apology, Aubrey's eyes dropped to look at her own plate and she took up her fork. Black chuckled in his throat and set about eating his meal as if he had never started anything in the first place. The rest of the meal was spent in silence.

After they were finished, Black stood and went to a nearby table.

"Could I interest you in a brandy, Jean Luc?" The quartermaster accepted the offer. Then Black looked at Aubrey.

"Will you have some?" Jean Luc caught her eye and motioned for her to accept one small drink to appease him.

"Only a small one," she replied to Black as Jean Luc winked at her.

Black handed her the drink, then he motioned for Jean Luc to join him at his desk. Aubrey tasted the thick liquid. She gasped and was thrown into a coughing spell. Black glanced at her and chuckled as he tipped his own small glass back and drained it of the brandy. Finally suppressing the cough, she chose not to finish her share and she set the small glass aside, out of sight.

During the French spoken conversation, she noticed that Jean Luc appeared concerned, while Black was very adamant. They moved about the room deep in conversation. Occasionally she picked out a name of a place or ship and there was much discussion about the British. All the while, Black was drinking, and he was growing more intoxicated by the moment. Aubrey stared at him, having never seen him consume so much alcohol at one time.

As she rose to go to the quarter gallery, Black caught her by the arm on her way past his chair. He held her there while he was still talking to Jean Luc. She stood as his captive, waiting patiently for him to let her go. Jean Luc could only look on at her in quiet pity as the half-drunken man brushed his lips along the outline of her bruised jaw. Black muttered something in his native tongue that she did not understand, then, smiling at her, he patted her backside and released her arm. Moving quickly to the window seat, she tucked herself into the shadows.

For sometime, the two men continued to talk when suddenly and without provocation, Jean Luc's fist shot out and connected soundly with Black's jaw. The latter dropped to the floor with a thud. Jean Luc leaned over Black's prone body and said, "Sleep well, Rene."

Chapter 42

Aubrey moved forward slowly from the shadowed recesses of the cabin.

"What are you doing?"

"Protecting your virtue, Mademoiselle," he said in a strained voice as he lifted Black's limp body from the floor, put him over his shoulder and carried him to the bunk.

"Pull down the covers," he instructed. She looked at him questionably but did as he asked. He dropped Black onto the bunk with a grunt.

"Pull off his boots," he ordered and again she did so without question. Jean Luc then proceeded to undress Black.

"Help me, quickly. Unfasten his belt," Jean Luc told her. She backed away from the bunk in slack-jawed surprise.

"I think not," she nearly squeaked.

He stopped and looked at her sternly. Taking her by the wrist, he forcefully pulled her back toward the bunk. His voice came in a hiss

"Aubrey, you must trust me. Now help me." Then he released her. Aubrey stood motionless as he went back to his task.

"Trust me. Surely you have seen him undressed before now, you do share a cabin with him. Now is not the time for discreteness," he stated firmly as he pulled off Black's britches. In the shadowed recesses of the bunk, she finally began to assist him. Within minutes, they had him in the bunk as if he had gotten there himself.

Jean Luc then turned to Aubrey. "Now, take off your clothes."

"What?" She asked sharply as she stepped back from the bunk once more.

"Just take off you clothes. Trust me," he said gently but insistently as he stepped toward her and pushed her toward the dressing screen. She looked over her shoulder at him.

"You keep saying that," she remarked. She went behind the screen and removed her clothing.

Jean Luc's arm shot behind the screen and he demanded, "Give them to me." Aubrey stood far back in the shadows, covering herself as she tossed the britches and shirt over his arm.

"Put on your night clothes," he told her.

"Hand me that shirt on the chair by the bunk," she demanded back.

He picked up the shirt and handed it behind the screen, asking, "This is what you wear at night?"

"Yes, well, it was all I was given," she said and snatched it from his hand. After a few moments, she came from behind the screen and reminded him, "You will recall, I was taken forcefully to the *Widow Maker*, and my small personal bag went down with the *Gull*."

He raised a finger in warning and said, "Not now, we do not have time to argue. We have to work together on this task."

She shrugged at him with an air of indifference. He eyed her in the shirt. The silk material clung to her small frame and only covered her to mid thigh. Becoming aroused at the sight of her, Jean Luc had to remind himself of what he had planned. Taking her by the arms and pushing her toward one of the chairs, "Sit here," he said quietly.

"Why?" she asked pulling back slightly.

"Sit," he repeated sternly. She did as he directed and watched him as he knelt on the floor before her. He sighed and looked at the unconscious man in the bunk. He smoothed back his longish brown hair and leaned closer to her, placing his hands gently on her waist. "You must follow my directions perfectly if you are to be safe from him this night and tomorrow."

"What about after that?" she asked looking at him as if she were hanging on his every word.

"One step at a time," he replied easily. She sat watching him as he moved closer, lowering his eyes to look at her lips.

"You must trust me, Aubrey," he said quietly as he touched his lips to hers and then pressed the kiss a bit harder. She pushed him away.

"How is this going to protect me? Should I be protecting myself from you then? Captain Black is going to wake up and catch you, then both of us will be in trouble," she retorted in a quiet hiss.

"Aubrey," he cautioned.

He pulled her back into the kiss, thankful that she was receptive as she kissed him back. Closing his eyes, he moved downward with his kisses. She pushed at him again.

"This is all rather interesting, Jean Luc, but I still fail to see how this will protect me. It appears that you have just knocked him out so that you can have your way with me." He sighed in exasperation, ignoring her comment and kissed her on the lips again. She relaxed in his arms once more and he began to trail his kisses downward for the second time. She remained still.

Jean Luc easily slipped one arm around the small of her back as she sat before him. Then he pressed his kisses down the front of her throat and began to cross diagonally downward toward her left breast. He was elated to feel her relax in his caresses and she sighed easily. He gently pushed the front of the shirt open allowing him to progress slowly.

231

Black began to move around in the bunk in his drunken unconsciousness. Aubrey's head snapped around to look in his direction and her body tensed under Jean Luc's caresses.

"Relax, he will not awaken," he murmured against her skin. She began to relax once more because what he was doing felt rather nice, even considering the circumstances. Black began to mumble and move again, which was a bonus distraction for Jean Luc's plan. His wandering kisses stopped at the top of her partially exposed breast. At this point he began to press his kisses harder. She turned her attention back to him and she tried to push him away, "Stop it, Jean Luc!" she scolded in a whisper.

"Trust me," he murmured unmoving.

Black thrashed again and mumbled louder in French, quickly drawing her attention to him again.

"Merci for your help, Rene," he whispered in French against her skin. At that moment, Jean Luc bit her in the very spot he had been kissing.

Aubrey emitted a yelp of pain and there was the resounding smacking sound in the room as she caught the side of his face with her open hand. Pressing his body forward onto hers to keep her in the chair as she tried to rise from it, he winced and caught her hand as she drew back again.

"Merde! Do not do that! It hurts!" he hissed at her.

"So did that, you animal!" she hissed back as she pushed at him with her knees and laid her free hand over the quickly appearing bruise on her left breast. He held her there and she struggled for a few seconds.

"Let me up!" she fussed as she pushed one leg out straight to try and shove at him with her bare foot.

"Be still now. Forgive me if I was not as romantic about the bite as Rene may have been had he succeeded."

Aubrey ceased to struggle immediately, "What?"

He looked at the man on the bunk. Black had calmed too, still deep in his drunken slumber. Jean Luc looked back at her and he was met with tears of anger in her eyes.

"Why did you bite me? You told me that I could trust you." Her voice was low. He glanced at the exposed place on her breast and noticed that it was turning a deep shade of purple. Following his gaze, she pushed against him again.

"How dare you? Let me go. Is this what I get for trusting you?" she hissed.

"I told you," he began as he continued to hold her. "All of this is to help you tomorrow," he told her. She rubbed the place where he had bitten her.

"Help me? How on earth could something like this help me?" she asked, her voice going up a few octaves.

"Captain Black has this ritual that he does to his women," he began. She listened with a puzzled look in her eyes.

"You see, it is his habit, his way. On the first night of his having a woman, he places his mark upon her." He reached out and gently brushed the purple and red mark still revealed by the open shirt.

She slapped at his hand and hissed, "Stop it."

"I am sorry, I really did not want to hurt you like that," he told her as he caught her hand and pressed it to his lips.

"His mark?" She echoed his earlier remark as she pulled the shirt tighter and looked at the unconscious man on the bunk.

"It is to show others that he has had you and you are his alone."

"How do you know this?" she asked.

"I have sailed with Rene Black for many years," he told her.

"You mean he does this, every time?" she asked with worried eyes.

"Only once, just the first time," he assured her.

"Well, that is–barbaric," she grumbled. Jean Luc watched her as she continued to look upon the man on the bunk.

"But it will fade, this will fade," he said gently.

"So how would anyone know then?" she asked.

"Before it fades, a more permanent mark will be made," he continued quietly.

"More permanent? How more permanent?" she asked with the fear rising.

"A tattoo, a design of his own that he has created for just this purpose," Jean Luc informed her.

"You lie," she retorted as she stood to face him and shoved at him angrily. He took the hit and did not answer, but the look on his face revealed that he was not telling her a lie. Jean Luc saw the panic rise in her eyes.

"I do not wish to be tattooed. Why have you done this for him? I trusted you. You told me that I could trust you and I was foolish enough to believe you," she said accusingly.

"It was not for him. This is at best some protection from having to deal with him for the first time. Your first time," he said quietly. Her face flushed and she looked at him, pulling herself to her full height.

"You are very presumptuous, Jean Luc. What are you saying? How is it that you assume that it would be my 'first time' as you call it?" His gaze made her look to the floor.

"I do not have to presume, Aubrey. Our own encounters here in this cabin alone tell me the tale of a young woman who has never been with a man before. I doubt seriously if you had ever been really kissed before he did so."

Her face crimsoned deeper but she still did not look at him. He shrugged.

"Not that it is a terrible thing, you understand, that you have not experienced your first time. You just do not need to experience it in the manner that he would choose."

She finally looked at him in surprise. "I think that you need to stop, Monsieur." She looked at Black and then back at Jean Luc, "How long do you think this ruse will work? Did you stop to think that I have to be in here with him at night alone, every night?" Her voice came in a hushed, but angry low tone.

"I promise that I will protect you as much as I can, Aubrey. Now, you must go to the bunk," he said as he gently but insistently pushed her toward the bunk.

"You are trying to protect me, yet you tell me to get in the bunk with him?" she asked.

"He ordered that you were to sleep in the bunk beginning tonight, with him." Jean Luc said.

She looked at him, "How do you know this?"

"He told you when he held you there earlier, but you did not understand him," he replied. He slowly approached her and she did not move away from him. He smoothed her hair on either side of her face with his hands and looked into her eyes.

"I am sorry for hurting you but he would hurt you more. He will sleep the night because he is drunk, dead drunk. In the morning he will have too much of a headache to accost you. As soon as you awaken you must leave this cabin and come on deck. Do not seek me out but stay topside as long as you are able." She looked around the room; Jean Luc had placed Black's and her clothes in a strategic arrangement around the room to give the illusion of a consented joining between the two of them. With easy movements, he pulled her into his arms and he kissed her on the forehead. "Please tell me that you are not angry with me."

She stood there for a long time, and then looked at the deeply sleeping captain. He did order that earlier today.

"I am not angry with you, Jean Luc, but I do wish that you would have let me in on your plans before you carried them out."

"There was no time. I had to take the opportunity as it arose," he told her. She sighed deeply and looked at the empty side of the bunk with a worried expression. Jean Luc turned her face to look at him and gently kissed the bruises on her chin.

"Sleep well, ma chérie, I will see you tomorrow." With that, he released her and left the cabin quietly. She stood for a time, still looking at Black, and rubbing the smarting bruise on her breast. Finally, she climbed up onto the bunk and settled herself down on top of the covers. She pulled up an extra blanket and curled herself on her side facing him. She had not realized how exhausted she was and soon she had drifted off listening to the soft snoring of Rene Black as he slept soundly next to her.

Chapter 43

Aubrey awakened in the early pre-dawn hours. Forgetting that she was not alone in the big bunk, she stretched her small frame out to its full length in a slow languid motion and then she was still and completely relaxed. She inhaled deeply and exhaled slowly. For a few moments she remained stretched out, feeling the distinct rocking motion of the big ship. The sea must have large swells today. She mused to herself as she stretched again. What if Jean Luc was the Captain, and I was his lady? A small smile stole across her lips as she yielded to her fantasy. She pushed away the covers and breathed deeply again, her eyes still closed.

"Hmm. Will you not offer up your best defense?" came the low rumbling voice of Captain Black from extremely close beside her. The sound snapped her out of her fantasy and turned her blood to ice. Her eyes snapped open wide.

The room was still and semi-dark. A setting three-quarter moon lit the room through the quarter gallery windows. Aubrey was on her back, covers half pushed down her body. Her heart pounded and her breath came in quick nervous gasps. The big ship rocked rhythmically as she turned her head slowly. Next to her, Rene Black laid on his back as well snoring quietly. It had been a dream. She rose quickly and quietly as not to awaken him. Maybe it was all a dream, last night included, she thought as she went behind the screen to dress. She pulled on the britches and then slipped out of the silk shirt. She was distressed to see that the purple mark was still on her breast. That part had not been a dream. She pulled the black shirt over her head and tucked it into the britches. She picked up her boots on her way past the bunk.

Quietly, she let herself out of the cabin and went up the steps to the deck. Captain Black had told her that she could roam about the ship now. She wondered why he had suddenly changed his mind. Had things so drastically changed so quickly? What about the men? Was she suddenly safe from them now? Although she was happy for the freedom, she was still mindful that Monsieur Beaufort was still on board and he alone would be the deterrent for her wandering too far.

The wind was blowing stiffly and whistled in the lines as the big ship creaked and groaned while it rocked along the large swells blown up by the wind. She looked up at the sails as they were billowed out with the wind in them. She could see the stars as they faded into the light pinks and blues of the morning sky. She pulled on her stockings and boots as she sat on the steps to the quarterdeck. Tucking herself into a corner by the stairs, she crossed her arms over her chest against the chill of the morning. The deck was deserted and she enjoyed the peace of the ocean.

The sea swells, some almost fifteen feet high, were white capped. Occasionally the spray from one of them would pepper her face, stinging her and taking her breath away. Even though she was now damp and cold, the experience was exhilarating. She thought about the conversation between Jean Luc and Black the night before. She wondered if it had anything to do with their present course. Her peaceful reverie was disrupted by the jovial voice of Jojoba.

"Mademoiselle Aubrey, you are awake so early! Why are you not cuddled up in de warm bunk?"

"I could not sleep, and I did not want to wake the captain," she replied. It was not a lie, but absolute truth because she definitely did not want to wake Black.

"Come wid me, little one, I know you have not eaten yet. You need to eat and we got to get some meat on dem bones. I cannot have you getting sick on me. Captain Black would hang me from de yardarm." He took her by the hand and pulled her along behind him.

"I am not very hungry, Jojoba," she smiled.

"You come with Jojoba anyway, before de wind blows you off de deck. I have to make sure Cook has de meal for de men. Dey be a hungry lot when dey wake up." He led her down into the galley and seated her at a table.

"You wait here, little one. When I come back maybe you would like Jojoba to braid your hair to keep it out of your face. It looks like it is going to be a windy one today." The galley was warm and smelled of food. She began to get sleepy and was resting her head in her arms on the table when Jojoba returned.

"Here now, sleepy one, let me see." He proceeded to brush her hair into place with his hands, using his long fingers as a comb. She remained still and allowed him to braid her hair tightly against her head. As he braided her hair, a few of the men passed by and made remarks to him in French. He replied back curtly and they silently moved on. She thought about this for a moment and remembered Black's anger over the perfumed oil.

"Jojoba, would the captain be angry with you because you are with me?" she asked.

"Oh no, ma petite." When Jojoba was finished braiding her hair, he tied it with a thick piece of black ribbon he had produced from his pouch.

"Dere now, it will stay out of your beautiful face now," he smiled.

"Merci," she replied.

Aubrey left the warmth of the galley as more men began to come in for the morning meal. She was surprised at the courtesy and respect with which they treated her. In their passing conversations, she picked out a few French words she understood. They referred to her as the Captain's lady. She touched the mark on her chest and her thoughts went to the events of the night before and Jean Luc's narrative.

She looked around the deck for Jean Luc but he was nowhere to be found. She made her way to the bow of the *Widow Maker*, wondering what she would do today to pass the time. She found a place to sit and just enjoy the ride. The sea was dark blue with white caps. With the wind blowing around her, she could hear nothing and was in a place of her own. Sometime later Jean Luc appeared on deck and went to his post. He scanned the deck for her, and seeing that she was safe, he set to his work for the day.

Below in his cabin, Black was coming out of his drunken sleep. He felt around with one hand, but it was empty. He rolled over and looked at the place where Aubrey should have been laying. He saw the blanket, the rumpled pillow and covers. He smiled to himself. "She must have been cold." He sat up and smoothed his long dark hair as he looked around the room. His clothes were strewn everywhere. He exhaled deeply and chuckled aloud to the empty room.

"I should not have drank so much, I guess I missed the full effect of the evening." He cleaned up, dressed and left the cabin to go to the galley for breakfast. He found himself practically alone in the room. He called to Jojoba and asked him about the whereabouts of Aubrey.

"I saw her go topside, sir," was the shrugging reply.

"Has she eaten yet?" Black asked.

"Non, mon Captaine, I do not tink so. She was in here earlier, but not to take a meal."

"Find her and bring her to me, then," he ordered.

Slowly making his way to her, Jean Luc saw Jojoba first. By the way the man acted, he knew who the Jamaican was looking for and quickened his steps. Fortunately he reached her first and as though he was looking over the railing of the ship at the water below, he spoke to Aubrey, "Remain still and pay me no mind. Are you all right?" he asked.

"Yes, I left the cabin before dawn while he was still asleep."

"Bon. Now here comes Jojoba. You and I both know why he is coming for you."

"To take me to him," she grumbled.

"Please, play his game reasonably and safely. Only you know what you will allow and not allow," he warned.

"Ma petite," Jojoba called to her as he got closer.

With a glance at Jean Luc, she stood to meet the first mate. The Jamaican cast a glance past her at the quartermaster who appeared busy watching the water flow past the bow.

For effect, Jean Luc cupped his hands and shouted to the helmsman, "Steady as she goes!" Then he acted as if he had just seen Aubrey and Jojoba. He ignored Aubrey and gave the Jamaican a curt nod, which was returned.

"Ma petite, the captain asked dat I bring you to de galley for breakfast," Jojoba said to Aubrey with a smile.

Black sat at his table in the back, alone with an impressive meal lay before him. He smiled without parting his lips and he wiped the corners of his mouth as he stood holding out his hand when she approached.

"Bonjour." She waited nervously as he kissed the back of her hand. Pulling her closer, he brushed his lips against her cheek and she did not resist.

"Sit down," he said as he pulled a chair close to his. Cook appeared on the scene and set down a plate and utensils.

He stroked her cheek idly before moving his hand down her neck and over her left shoulder. His thumb hooked in the open front of the shirt and he pulled the shirt open to reveal the mark on her chest. Aubrey wanted to stop him but she remained still, watching him. Black's face wrinkled into a slight frown at the mark. There was the distinct imprint of teeth marks there. Was he so drunk last evening that he left teeth marks this time?

Aubrey fretted over the fact that the open shirt exposed her far more than she wanted. She finally caught his hand with a blush. Looking up into his face, she now saw that he had a gleam in his eye as he beheld the bruise that he obviously thought he had placed on the pristine skin.

"I am really not very hungry, Captain," she finally replied.

He resumed his meal and countered, "Nonsense, this not eating for days must stop."

"What have you done here?" he asked with a wave of his hand to her hair.

"This is to keep my hair from blowing around in the wind today."

"Who has done this? You?" he asked conversationally.

She sighed and carefully replied, "Jojoba braided it."

"How very native," he said, echoing his remark of the day before. She shot him a sideways glance and leaned up to pick up a banana from the pile of fruit.

"I like it. Do you have something against natives?"

He glanced at her as he cut the meat on his plate, but made no remark. No, he did not really have any qualms against natives. As a matter of fact, he was wishing that he could hold a certain native woman against his body this very moment.

Feeling sure of herself now, she leaned back in the chair and peeled the banana in silence.

"I trust you slept well last night," he began as he continued to eat his breakfast. She merely nodded in reply. He reached over to lightly touch her chest and gently stroked the back of his long fingers directly against the mark.

She nearly pushed his hand away, but decided that it may not be wise to do so, "I slept well," she replied sharply. His hand slipped to her lap and he squeezed her upper thigh.

"Très bien."

She looked him over. It was frightening how very handsome he actually was despite the loss of one eye. As his hand began to inch further up her leg, she scooped it up in her free hand and held it.

"What can I do today, Rene? I am getting bored with nothing to do."

He chuckled again and intertwined his long fingers in hers. "Well, we could return to my cabin."

She tried to hide a panic-stricken look and tone in her voice. "I need fresh air, too, and the fresh air might give me back my appetite. I want to go on deck and enjoy the day, I do not want to be in the dark cabin all day." She allowed him to pull her close for kisses on her face and neck. Black closed his eye and his mind swam with the memory of another woman as he caressed Aubrey.

"It appears that it may rain, you may have no other choice," he murmured against her skin.

At that moment, Jean Luc appeared in the doorway. Seeing them at the table, he groaned to himself, "Ma foi, he is trying to make love to her even here."

Aubrey caught sight of Jean Luc before Black did. She cleared her throat and easily pulled herself free from the captain's embraces.

"Here comes my nemesis," she whispered.

Jean Luc seated himself across from his captain and nodded to Cook as the man set a plate before him, then shot a glance from Black to Aubrey. The captain had resumed his meal and Aubrey was graced with a look of blatant jealousy. She frowned slightly at Jean Luc. How did he expect her to act at this game?

"Monsieur Pierne, I trust we are on good course?" Black said as he finished up his meal. Jean Luc had been watching Aubrey in mild fascination as she quietly ate the fruits, when Black's remark brought him out of his musings.

"Ah, yes, we are sailing along at good speed." Black was not looking at him, but at Aubrey as well.

"Bon," he replied as he toyed with a loose lock of hair that had escaped from the braids.

Jean Luc sat there for a time, his fork suspended over his plate. She continued to eat with an air of indifference. Black, in a sense of showing off for his crew that were still present, cupped her chin in his hand.

"Do you see my prize, Jean Luc? She is the best of the treasures from the *Gull*. I am glad that we saved her after all." Aubrey blushed but remained still and calm as she met eyes with Jean Luc, who had the irresistible desire to kill Black on the spot, friend or no friend.

"Oui, Rene," he answered in a strained voice.

"Well, my dear, I must tend to my duties as captain," the dark haired man said as he stood. He leaned over and grasping her by the shoulders, he kissed her full on the mouth before he released her and said, "You have full run of the ship. Do be careful and you know what time curfew is." She bit her lip, but did not reply.

"I will be with you directly, Rene," Jean Luc said then took a bite of his breakfast.

Black merely nodded, then left the galley. With a few more quick mouthfuls, then washing it down with his wine, Jean Luc stood up.

"You are permitted free run of the ship, now do be careful," he repeated quietly.

"I do not intend to go any further than the deck. But I must return to the great cabin some time. You said that I would be safe," she replied, his comment sending a chill through her.

As he turned to leave, she called his attention. "Jean Luc?"

"Oui?"

"What about what you told me the other night?" she whispered as she stood.

He looked at the floor and sighed. "We will have time together again. He will go ashore in Bimini and perhaps he will find something there that interests him more than you." She nodded. The remark should have been cause for insult, but Aubrey was not insulted–she was hopeful.

241

Chapter 44

Later Jean Luc noticed her on deck, looking into the sails as if in a trance. Then she crossed over to the side rail. She held onto the lines and watched the swells go by as they coursed along. He noticed how she watched the men as they went about their duties, as if she were trying to learn everything around her. He found himself looking at her too often, so he forced himself to take extra strides to busy himself with his work, assuring himself that as long as she was up on deck, she was relatively safe.

A few hours later, he looked around and she was sitting nearby at the stern of the ship on the quarterdeck. He could see that she was exhausted. It began to sprinkle rain just as he managed to get close enough to speak to her without arousing suspicion.

"You need some rest. Did you sleep at all last night?" he questioned in English.

"Some. I wish I could go below and take a nap," she replied.

He looked around. "Black may be in the galley. You need to get out of this rain, it looks like we are in for a good one."

She sighed, "I cannot take this wind any longer, either. I will just have to take a chance that I can be left alone and can get some rest."

"When you go into the cabin, if he is present, implore to him of your fatigue. Perhaps he will honor your request for a reprieve from his advances for a time. I will try and make myself present when the rains come. That should allow you more time." With a dutiful nod, she left the deck to go below. He looked after her with a worried expression. He would not be able to keep her from Black forever.

Aubrey went below and stepped into the cabin. She shut the door then leaned against it in exhaustion. She pulled off her boots and turned to move further into the room. It was then that she saw Black sitting at his desk watching her intently. The sight of him there made her gasp in alarm.

"Forgive me if I frightened you," he droned in his deep voice.

She calmed herself and replied, "I did not mean to disturb your work. I did not know that you were here. I am tired and it is beginning to rain."

"Nonsense, you are not disturbing me, do as you may," Black said as he went back to his books.

She set aside her boots and wandered quietly around in the cabin. She stood in the quarter gallery for a time, but watching the waves and rain made her even more drowsy.

"This weather has made me so tired," she said, as she looked at him for a reaction.

He merely looked up at her and then his dark eye drifted to look at the still unmade bunk. Carefully, Aubrey went to the bunk and sat on the edge letting out a tired deep sigh. Soon, she was lying back on the bunk, with her legs dangling over the side. Black looked up to notice that her chest rose and fell in a deep rhythmic motion.

Black stood up and quietly stepped to the bunk. He stared down at the auburn hair for a long moment. She was not what he wanted, so why had he taken her for himself? He had not bothered with the women from their raids of other ships for nearly two years. His interest was with someone else who could never be here in this cabin or with him again. Mon Dieu, how he missed that one!

Slowly he released a long and tired sigh. Disinterested in the woman sleeping in his bunk, Black turned and went back to his desk. About half an hour later, there was a light knock on the door.

"Entre," he called in a low tone of voice, not looking up from his work.

The door opened and Jean Luc stepped in. The first thing he saw was Aubrey deeply asleep on the bunk. She was on her side with her back to Black as he sat at the desk. Her hands were curled up under her chin, her face peacefully relaxed. He breathed a silent sigh of relief that she was so peaceful.

"I will go," he began.

"No, stay. We have paperwork to tend to."

"I do not wish to intrude, or disturb," he began as he gestured to Aubrey with his hat.

"You will not disturb her. She has been sleeping like that for about half the hour. She seems very tired," Black replied.

Jean Luc pulled the chair up to the desk. "We should be in Bimini by dusk tomorrow. The winds are good, but the high seas slow our progress today," he reported, keeping his voice low.

"I have business on shore there. Do you wish to go this time?"

"Perhaps with the second rotation, Rene," Jean Luc replied.

Black nodded and informed him, "In that case, you will have the ship in my absence. I will not be taking Aubrey ashore, which means she is in your charge again." Black looked up at her sleeping form as he spoke.

"Aye sir," Jean Luc replied feigning a tone of annoyance at the thought of having her in his charge again.

Chapter 45

Aubrey awakened to an empty cabin. She put her boots on and went up on deck. The day was still balmy, but the sky had cleared and the sea swells were not as high or tumultuous as earlier in the day.

She noticed that Black was standing on the quarterdeck with a long glass to his eye. Jean Luc was standing on the main deck not far from where Aubrey stood and he had a glass as well. They seemed intent on something behind the ship. The crew on the *Widow Maker* were moving about with an air of urgency.

Aubrey turned to look, but she saw nothing.

She looked harder, straining her eyes against the brightness of the sun and water. Then in the distance, she began to make out the shape of a ship. She looked up at Black and saw that he and the others appeared concerned about the swift approach of this ship. Time dragged on as they watched this ship approach.

"Perhaps their destination is Bimini. That would explain their route," Jean Luc suggested. Black made no comment as he glanced at his quartermaster then turned to the men on the deck.

"Be ready, Monsieur Boulet."

"Ready and awaiting your order, Captain," Boulet called up from the cannon deck. The port doors remained closed to show nonchalance while the men continued to watch this ship's approach.

As the ship neared, Aubrey saw that it flew a different flag, one she had never seen before. It was not British or from any other country she knew. Her eyes followed down the mast to the ship deck. It was a finely built brigantine with two masts and as many guns as the *Widow Maker*, and it was coming up on them at an incredible speed.

All too soon it was closer, and Aubrey was now able to see the men scurrying about on her deck. Black called to his own men, telling them to turn the *Widow Maker* about to catch more wind in the sails. The big ship tacked and when the wind caught, it nearly shot through the water.

Moving to Jean Luc, Aubrey could hear him speaking to Black.

"Oui, Rene, and she seems to be a fast one. She is closing the distance at a tremendous speed," Jean Luc replied tightly.

The two men lowered their glasses and watched the ship approach. Aubrey had been watching the ship in fascination, for it had cleared a great deal of distance in a short time. All the sails seemed to burst with the wind and the ship seemed to fly over the water.

"It is the ship with the red flag," Beaufort reported in a loud voice from the forecastle.

Aubrey looked to Black in surprise when she heard him ask in English, "The ship with a woman as her captain?"

"Oui, if the rumors you heard were correct," Jean Luc answered with a nod. The two men raised their glasses to their eyes once again.

"Perhaps the stories we have heard are true about her. Interesting," Black said almost to himself. Jean Luc dared to cast a quick glance at Black, but the latter was preoccupied with the approaching ship. Aubrey went to the side to get a better look while watching the other ship close fast on their port side.

It was a magnificent ship, although slightly smaller than the *Widow Maker* was. The bow spirit was carved into the figure of a young woman, with a shapely body and bared breasts. The head rails of the ship were painted gold and the ship was trimmed in red. A solid red flag snapped briskly in the wind high above her decks.

"It is the ship we have seen twice before," came the voice of the man in the crow's nest from high above. There was excitement in his voice.

Black glanced back up to the crow's nest with a disgusted growl in his throat.

"It is the same one," Jean Luc nodded guardedly.

"Watch for any strange activity, Jean Luc. A woman is never to be trusted. When they get in the realm of a man, they are uncontrollable and unpredictable," Black said easily in his deep voice as he raised his glass and watched the oncoming ship.

The men on the decks of the *Widow Maker* were moving about quickly in preparation for battle. Aubrey watched the men nervously for she had been witness to enough battles in her time on the ship to last her a lifetime. Black lowered his glass slowly and looked at Jean Luc. The other man lowered his glass also and returned the gaze.

The pirate ship was running parallel with the *Widow Maker* now. The close proximity of the other pirate ship made Aubrey very nervous, as well as the way Black was acting. She tucked herself away as not to be seen by the men on the other ship, but so that she could still see what was going on.

The two ships raced along beside one another for a time, spray flying from the bows of both of them. Looking at Jean Luc, then to Black, Aubrey saw that something on board the other ship caught Black's attention. She looked from him to the other ship, following his gaze. What she saw both stunned and shocked her. Her mouth dropped open in shocked surprise as she drew a startled breath. Backing slowly away from the gunwale, she ran against Jean Luc who stood behind her with the long glass back up to his eye. Aubrey looked up at Jean Luc and then at the ship across the way.

Halfway up the starboard ratlines of the other ship, Aubrey saw a young woman clad in black britches, a red shirt and a gold sash about her slim waist. She had long black hair that flowed in the wind and her skin was almost the color of bronze. The woman on the other ship had sighted Black out also, as she clung to the lines with a long glass to her eye. Aubrey saw the woman call down to someone on deck. She then slipped the long glass into her belt and drew her rapier in her right hand. As the ship passed the *Widow Maker*, the woman saluted Black with the weapon almost mockingly.

Aubrey looked up at Black. He just stood there, but there was a look of recognition in his eye. He set his jaw and merely watched her as they passed. At the last moment, the ship turned to starboard sharply and cut across the bow of the *Widow Maker*. Black stepped forward as if to try and stop the move as Jean Luc cursed in French from behind Aubrey. Catching himself, Black looked back to the woman on the ratlines. He was graced with a slow smile from the beautiful woman. Seeing her smile, he realized that she knew his every move even before he did it. Although the knowledge made him furious, he was also furious that the dark haired woman would knowingly make such a dangerous maneuver.

It appeared to Aubrey that the *Widow Maker* might run head on into the other ship. She watched in fascination as the ship came across to the starboard bow of the *Widow Maker*, then sailed on, leaving Black's ship in her wake. As she sailed away, they could read the name on her stern. Above the quarter gallery, emblazoned in gold letters, was the name *Enchantress*.

Aubrey looked up at Jean Luc questioningly but neither spoke. Jean Luc merely nodded at her; both of them were recalling her dream of a few nights before. Black came down from the quarterdeck toward them, his jaw still set. Aubrey could see the muscles bulging, and cringed.

"Who is she?" she whispered to Jean Luc.

"Her name is Mala," Jean Luc replied quickly, pronouncing the name as 'may lay'.

"The word in the logbook," Aubrey stated.

As she looked up to Jean Luc with her next question, she found that he was watching her closely, with a knowing look in his blue eyes.

"What is she to him?" Aubrey asked, nodding toward Black as he approached them, the muscles in his jaws working feverishly.

"She was once the Lady of the *Widow Maker*, and his lover," Jean Luc began. Before Black reached where they were standing, Jean Luc added,

"Now she is the Captain of the *Enchantress*."

Aubrey turned to watch the other ship as it plowed on in the distance ahead.

"Captain?" she questioned under her breath.

She was drawn viciously out of her fascination when Black grasped her by the arm tightly and began to pull her along behind him as he strode along the deck. She looked back at Jean Luc anxiously and he stepped forward.

"Captain."

The man in black stopped suddenly, so suddenly that Aubrey ran into him. He glanced down at her, and for a moment she thought that he had no idea who she was or why she was in his hand. Then the look changed and he stared at her in a most frightening manner. He turned his attention to his quartermaster.

"What are you orders, sir?" Jean Luc questioned, undaunted by the menacing glare. Aubrey looked at him in surprise. What was he doing? Was he not going to try and stop him? Black was obviously angry and it appeared that she would be the recipient of that anger. Would he beat her? She had hoped Jean Luc would get her out of whatever was about to happen. She looked at him incredulously. He was asking the man what were his orders!

"You have your orders, Monsieur Pierne. Steady as she goes on our course to Bimini. Remain prepared for engagement. She is not finished playing with us yet," Black said firmly as he looked to his starboard bow. The other ship was nearly gone from sight. Then just as suddenly as he had stopped, he started again with Aubrey in tow.

She found herself being taken down the companionway steps at a rapid pace, nearly falling once as he pulled her along. As they reached the bottom step, she pulled back from him. "Captain, where are we going?"

He regarded her with his good eye but did not answer. He began walking again, pulling her roughly along. Her heart was pounding as they neared the doorway to his cabin. She knew that this was the end of her innocence. He would surely have his way this time and in addition, he was demonstrating all the habits that Uncle Jonathan used before he would deal her a sound beating for no reason at all. With a deep breath, she began to prepare herself mentally for what was about to take place. To her surprise, he passed the doorway of the great cabin and went farther back into the recesses of the big ship. Aubrey now found herself looking back toward the cabin with longing, for she would rather Black take out his anger on her there than where he dragged her along to now.

Looking forward into the darkness of the hold, she got a bad feeling. This was a place she had never been before and she pulled back again, with a little more force, successfully freeing herself from his grip and backing away a few steps. He growled and turned.

"Captain, where are we going?" she asked again, a hint of hysteria rising in her voice as she stared at him in the near darkness of the hold. Still he did not answer her, but lunged at her. When he caught hold of her again, his hold was tighter, causing her to wince.

Black continued on his way pulling her along. Finally he stopped and she saw that there were two men sitting on kegs in an area lit by two lanterns swinging from the ceiling beams. Black spoke in French to them and a third man stepped out of the shadows. He was dark-skinned with decorative markings all over his bare chest, arms, and legs. Aubrey stared at the man in unmasked fear. She had never seen this person before. His lack of clothing and native markings on his body gave him a fierce look.

As Black spoke to the three, he pushed Aubrey down onto a stack of sacks and stood behind her with his hands on her shoulders, holding her down. She watched as the tattooed man nodded while Black spoke to them in rapid French. Aubrey watched in mind-numbing terror as the native advanced closer and eyed her. He reached out toward her with a dark hand, reaching for the front of her shirt. She drew back against Black and looked up at him.

"Rene!" she screamed in fear. He glanced down at her but held her in place as she tried again to get up.

Finally he spoke but the low, deep tone in his voice and his response sent chills down her spine. "I am going to leave you here for a time, Precieux. You will go to sleep for awhile and when you wake, you will be back in the cabin."

One of the other men came forward with a cup of liquid. At this point she fought desperately to get away, her legs and arms flew into motion as she tried to claw her way out from under Black's grip. He held her steadfast and the other man advanced to help hold her, dropping to his knees to grab her by the legs.

"Aye, she is a feisty one, Cap'n," the man grunted in English with a thick accent that she did not recognize. She tried to kick at him again.

"Did not have this much trouble with the last one," he added as he finally caught the furiously kicking appendages.

"Never mind that," Black growled back in English. She struggled desperately, but her strength was no match for the two of them. The man with the cup advanced again, and, clamping her nose with his fingers, he forced her to drink from the cup. Aubrey sputtered and gagged at the foul-tasting liquid but her desperate struggle was in vain. The man succeeded in pouring most of the drink into her and she was forced to swallow it in order to breathe.

"Just have him get the job done, and remember, if any of you touch her otherwise, I will know and then I will have your hands and balls run up with the flag as you stand on the deck and watch them," Black growled in his deep voice as he ceased to hold her on the sacs and stepped back. Aubrey became aware that she was no longer being held down, but there was a heavy sensation settling over her body. Arms and legs would not respond to her brain's commands to move from the chair. There was a dull hum in her ears, reducing the conversation of the men to hushed whispers. Even though her eyes were wide with terror, she found that she was slowly losing sight of her surroundings.

Chapter 46

Sometime later, Aubrey was back in the captain's cabin. The *Widow Maker* had sailed into and dropped anchor in a cove on the northern shore of Bimini. Black had given his men permission to go ashore if their duties were finished and he busied himself with preparations to go ashore as well. Aubrey stood in the quarter gallery facing the windows watching the water. Her head hurt and she gingerly touched a bandage on her left breast, in just the spot that Jean Luc had marked in his ruse.

Black had taken her down to be tattooed, just as Jean Luc had described. She looked at the dark haired man with eyes red from crying. Aubrey wanted to scream at him and tell him that he had not made the conquest that he thought, but it did not matter anymore. It sickened her when she thought of the tattoo that Black had so blatantly ordered the man to put on her. It was a violation in the worst form as far as she was concerned. She hated him now more than she feared him for what he had done.

"I am sorry that you cannot come ashore with me, my dear, but it would be too dangerous," he said as he came toward her.

She ignored him, making him chuckle. He brushed at her hair with his hand, but she easily moved his hand away. He sat next to her in the seat and she moved to avoid his touch, but he reached out and laid his hand on her thigh. Aubrey looked away from him.

"You see, if any other man should try and lay hands upon you he will see the mark and he will know that you are not to be touched, lest he answer to me."

She turned to look at him, saying, "No man wants a branded woman."

"The men of our lot are not concerned much about markings and brands, my dear. The only time such a mark concerns one of our kind would be if they recognized my mark. My mark promises them punishment or death," he replied arrogantly. A wave of nausea coursed over her and she moved away from him quickly. She could not tolerate his presence or his arrogance any longer. There was an abrupt knock at the door before she could say the scathing remark burning to be said.

"What is it?" Black snapped.

"The longboats are ready, sir," came Beaufort's voice from the other side of the door. Black looked at Aubrey and she looked at him.

"Entre Beaufort, I will be with you in a moment." The door snapped open and Aubrey turned her head in alarm toward the sound. Beaufort had entered

250

looking at the floor but as he crossed the threshold, he raised his head to see her clutching her shirt against her.

A lewd smile stole over his face, exposing his yellowed teeth. "Forgive me Captain, I did not mean to disturb your–pleasure." Her eyes lowered, as Beaufort looked her over wantonly. Black was looking at her as well as he strapped on his baldric.

Shaking his head with a feigned sorrowful expression, he said, "I guess I must leave you now, there is some place that I must be at a certain time today and I cannot be late. I will be gone for several days." Aubrey merely looked at him. Black picked up his hat and gloves and tucked his pistol into the sash about his waist. Catching the back of her head with his free hand, he pressed his mouth upon hers. He forced her lips apart with his tongue. As he withdrew from the kiss, he caught her bottom lip in his teeth for a moment then he straightened and put his hat on.

"Adieu, my dear." With that, he left the room behind Beaufort. In his haste to get to his appointed meeting, he did not secure the door all the way and it swung back open slightly.

As they exited the room, Aubrey heard Beaufort ask in English, "She is giving you trouble, Captain?"

Black was heard to chuckle, "Non Beaufort, sometimes she just likes to argue."

Aubrey was oblivious to the oversight on his part to pull the door securely as she moved across the cabin to lie wearily down on the bunk and rolled over onto her right side with a sob. She was beginning to feel very sick now. The sobs increased until she finally fell into an exhausted sleep. The last thought on her mind was that for several days she would have peace from him, but what then?

When she awakened, darkness had fallen and she had no idea what time it was. Getting up, she felt weak and thirsty. Her clothing was soaked with perspiration. Aubrey went to the table and, with a shaky hand, struck the flint and lit the lantern in the center of the table. Pouring a cup of water as she sat down, she frowned at the tabletop before her. She wondered if all that had passed had been a nightmare. She drank down the water quickly, but it did not satisfy her thirst so she poured a second cup of water, asking of the empty room in a weak whisper, "Did he really take me below to those men? Did they really..."

Aubrey raised a shaking hand to touch her left breast. Pain and the sensation of searing heat flashed into the area and she emitted a small yelp of pain. That had really happened. The urge to look at the area came to mind, but a thought of disgust put it quickly out of her mind.

"With whom are you talking? The captain is ashore," came the voice of Jean Luc from the doorway. Startled, she looked quickly to the door and the motion made her dizzy. Jean Luc was standing on the threshold of the door that was now open all the way and with Henri beside him. A look of concern crossed Jean Luc's handsome features. Her face was flushed and she appeared to be disoriented.

"Aubrey?" he asked as he stepped further into the room.

"The Captain is gone?" she stammered.

"Oui, he has gone ashore several hours ago," Jean Luc answered with a nod as he approached her slowly. Henri followed tentatively.

"Cook came by to see if you wanted any dinner. He found the door open and you were in the bunk. He sent Henri to find me and tell me that you appeared ill," Jean Luc went on as he watched her raise her cup to her lips with a shaky hand.

"Cook was in here? While I was sleeping? I, ah," she stammered. They watched her shakily pour another cup of water.

"Is the captain gone now?" she asked, repeating herself.

"Oui, he will be gone for sometime. We have men rotating shore leave, so, that..." Jean Luc was saying. He trailed off as he watched her and did not like how she was acting. She seemed to be having a hard time concentrating on the conversation, retaining the information.

She drank more water but it spilled from the corners of her mouth. She tried to wipe the water away, but her arms felt too heavy to move. There was that same loud ringing sound in her ears as when Black had left her below. She moved to set the cup down but Jean Luc reached to take it from her. She let it go before it was on the table or before he could take hold of it. The cup hit the table with a metallic clang and the water spilled out. Aubrey slumped on the table in front of him and he scrambled to her side. Henri was at his side just as quickly.

Jean Luc eased Aubrey back up into an upright position in the chair, brushing the sweat-dampened hair from her face, calling softly, "Aubrey?"

Her eyes rolled back in her head, her jaw hung slack and she gave him no reply.

"Mon Dieu!" he cursed quietly as he slipped an arm under the back of her knees and stood with her. She was like a limp rag in his arms as he picked her up, and he could not believe how hot her skin was.

"Monsieur Pierne, what is the matter with her?" Henri asked in alarm as he moved closer to Jean Luc's side.

"I am not sure, Henri," Jean Luc said stiffly as he carried her to the bunk and laid her down.

"Ame damne, she is burning up with a fever," Jean Luc said as he brushed sweat-dampened hair from her face once more.

Henri stepped back in alarm. "The fever? My mamma and papa died of the fever."

"Chut! I did not say, the fever, I said a fever. Shut the door before someone in the crew hears you. Mon Dieu! If the men were to hear you say 'the fever', they would think that we have the plague aboard and they would all jump ship. Do you want Captain Black to find out that everyone left the ship because of what you said?" Jean Luc scolded.

Henri went to the door quickly and shut it. "Je regrette, Monsieur Pierne."

"Bring me that pitcher of water and a rag," Jean Luc ordered. Taking the rag from the boy, he dipped it into the pitcher to wet it. Then he ran the damp cool rag over her face, forehead and neck. Aubrey moved restlessly under the rag, mumbling incoherently. As he passed the rag over her collarbone, he noticed a corner of the bandage sticking up from the open front of her shirt. A pang of alarm struck his heart.

"Henri, we have no doctor on board and Jojoba has gone ashore. Mademoiselle Aubrey is obviously very ill. I must tend to her as Captain Black has put her in my charge, but I need your help."

"I will help you, Monsieur. I like Mademoiselle Aubrey," he said quietly. Jean Luc cast him a glance and smiled easily as he lifted Aubrey into his arms from the bunk

"Pull down the covers there. Then I want you to go get me some fresh water and some long strips of clean cloth. Make certain that they are clean."

"What do you need with the long cloths?" The boy asked as he pulled down the covers. Jean Luc laid Aubrey gently back down onto the bunk.

"To lay across her fevered brow and I will drape a cool cloth across the back of her neck. This fever must be broken." This part of his idea was true, but when the boy left, he was sure that upon further investigation, he would find that he was going to have to replace a bandage as well.

With Henri out of the cabin, and the door tightly closed, Jean Luc opened the shirt Aubrey wore exposing her chest. He made a face as he saw that a filthy strip of cloth was bound around her upper chest, covering the tops of her breasts. Taking his dirk, he easily cut away the crude bandage. An audible hiss escaped him as he peeled it back from the top of her left breast. Just above the nipple of her left breast, there it was. The mark was the size of a piece-of-eight coin with small ornate letters, RB. Jean Luc looked at the mark for a time. Although he had never actually seen Black's mark on a woman, he had known of it.

He got up and brought a bottle of rum to the bunk. With the water and the rum, he carefully cleaned and disinfected the fresh scar on her chest. Looking down at the dirty bandage, he shook his head. A light tapping at the door announced the boy's return and Jean Luc pulled Aubrey's shirt closed to cover her.

Once the boy was admitted in and the door was closed again, Jean Luc said, "Bring me that silk shirt over there on the settee."

As Henri went to retrieve the shirt, Jean Luc picked Aubrey's upper body up into his arms and slipped her arms out of the shirt easily. Henri watched intently as Jean Luc worked. Interested eyes took in the bare skin of her back as Jean Luc held her against his chest. The boy craned his neck slightly, trying to see more of the young woman and Jean Luc could not help but smile at the adolescent urges in the boy. It was decidedly the first time Henri had ever seen so much of a woman undressed–even though Jean Luc was careful that he could only see her back. Jean Luc did not hide his own observance of the beauty in his arms. His blue eyes wandered down over the front of her, then pulling her closer to his chest, he tossed the shirt aside.

"Henri," he began easily.

"Oui, Monsieur Pierne?" the boy asked in embarrassment, knowing that he had been caught doing something wrong and his young face flushed. Jean Luc managed to slip Aubrey's arms into the sleeves of the silk shirt and pull it up over her bare back.

"I do not think that Mademoiselle Aubrey would be happy if she knew that you were looking at her in such a state of undress. Turn around while I finish putting her nightshirt on."

Henri obliged quickly. While the boy had his back turned, Jean Luc quickly wrapped a clean strip of bandaging around her to cover the wound.

"Monsieur Pierne?" Henri asked quietly, as he fidgeted in his spot.

"Oui?" Jean Luc answered, tucking in the loose ends of the bandage.

"Would Mademoiselle Aubrey not be upset if she knew you were looking at her?" The boy's question was blatant, especially for a cabin boy to his superior. Jean Luc had to suppress a chuckle for the question was honest.

"Well Henri," he began as he lowered Aubrey back down onto the bunk. Casting his eyes over her, he began to button the ornate buttons on the shirt.

"Women are generally apt to be less upset over a man seeing them as they would a boy. Your time will come someday, lad. You will enjoy the sight and feel of a woman," Jean Luc said, glancing at Henri. The boy's face had crimsoned even deeper and he dropped his head to look at the floor.

"What about the captain? Would he not be upset with this undressing of his woman?" Henri ventured to query on.

Jean Luc set his jaw, "The captain's business is not your concern, boy. You would be wise to keep your tongue and mind your place."

"Aye sir," Henri nodded quickly, unwilling to make the quartermaster more angry.

"There now, there is but one more thing to do so that she will rest comfortably," Jean Luc said. Henri turned back to the bunk tentatively as Jean Luc quickly pulled the shirttails down.

"What is that, Monsieur Pierne? May I do it?" Henri asked innocently. Jean Luc smiled easily again.

The young fellow's caring was sincere. Jean Luc looked around the room.

"Well, you can pour me a cup of water for her and bring that blanket that is on the settee. She will be chilled with this fever and it will make her warm."

Henri stepped to the task with a smile and Jean Luc watched in mild amusement as Henri nodded to the bed covers.

"Pull those up on her, Monsieur Pierne, they will help keep her warm too, and then I will put this one on top."

"Of course, how could I not have thought of that?" Jean Luc nodded as he pulled off her boots and pulled up the covers. Then he leaned out of the way so that Henri could add the blanket to the pile.

"Is there anything else, Monsieur?" Henri asked anxiously.

"No, you can return to your duties now. We would not want Monsieur Beaufort to be angry with you. Merci for your help, I am certain that Mademoiselle Aubrey thanks you as well," Jean Luc said with a small smile. Henri nodded and moved to the door, stopping only at the sound of his superior's voice.

"Do not mention any of this to anyone. As I said before, at the mere mention of the word fever in whatever content, the men might panic. If the word should get out, you could be severely punished."

"Aye sir, I will not mention a word of this. Mademoiselle Aubrey never leaves the cabin anyway unless she is with the captain, so no one will miss her."

Jean Luc dampened the long cloths and draped one across the back of her neck and shoulders then one on her forehead. Black had taken a good part of the crew away to shore with him again, and Jean Luc was glad for that. He pulled a chair over from the table and lowered his lean frame into it with a deep sigh while he stretched his long legs out, propping his booted feet on the foot of the bunk. Aubrey moved restlessly in her fevered state, mumbling incoherently.

He dozed for a time and awakened to the tolling of the ship bell, sounding the next watch. It was 4pm Leaning over her, he touched a gentle hand to her feverish brow. Jean Luc peeled back the covers and opened the silk shirt to check her bandage. By the light of the lantern that he had lit, he noted that the wound did not look quite as bad anymore. He cleaned it again and applied the sulfur that Henri had brought in earlier. Cradling her in his arms, he applied a water soaked cloth to her mouth, managing to get a few drops of water between the dry and parted lips. Tucking her back in neatly, he settled back down in his chair.

Chapter 47

Sometime just after dawn, he was awakened to a light tapping at the door. Henri stood in the corridor and Jean Luc stepped out of the room, shutting the door behind him.

"How is she, Monsieur?" the boy asked.

"She rested quite well last night, Henri."

"I came to tell you that a longboat has returned. They have supplies on board and have come with orders to unload and return to port," the boy reported. Jean Luc looked toward the companionway as Thomas Beaufort came stomping down the steps. The gray-eyed man stopped abruptly when he saw Jean Luc in the corridor and exchanged looks with him.

Jean Luc looked back to the boy. "Has the captain returned as well?"

"No sir," Henri said in a low voice as he shot a glance at Beaufort, who was approaching them.

"Merci, Henri, you may go back to your duties now," Jean Luc said as he patted the boy on the shoulder. Turning as if to give the illusion that he had been traveling the opposite direction along the corridor when the boy had come to him. Jean Luc turned to look at the man as Beaufort shot a glance at the door to the captain's cabin.

"Bonjour Pierne," Beaufort drawled. With a bad feeling in the pit of his stomach, Jean Luc was sure that Beaufort had apparently had some hidden agenda on his mind when he came down the companionway, and yet the presence of the quartermaster had foiled it.

"Beaufort," Jean Luc nodded.

"We have supplies to bring aboard," Beaufort offered.

"Indeed, Henri has told me so. Where is the captain?" Jean Luc asked as he started to walk toward the galley, wanting to draw Beaufort away from Black's cabin and the defenseless Aubrey. Beaufort followed, although with much reluctance.

"I have not seen him. I suppose he has found himself a whore in the port and is in bed with her right now," Beaufort replied as they entered the galley that was now slowly being inhabited by the remnants of the crew that had not gone ashore.

Jean Luc looked around at the tired-looking men. In an attempt to change the subject to business he said, "Have the men who went ashore yesterday returned today so that this lot may have their turn."

"Aye sir," Beaufort said arrogantly.

They sat together at the captain's table and the cook brought them plates of food and mugs of drink. Jean Luc covertly watched Beaufort eating and finally said, "When you return to shore, tell the Captain that all is well here. We spent a quiet night."

Beaufort nodded and took a drink from his mug. Wiping his sleeve across his mouth he said, "When I find him and if he has not killed himself over some whore." Beaufort stabbed at the food on his plate, not looking up at the quartermaster and continued, "He had to leave in a state of frustration yesterday. That little redhead bitch he has was not very accommodating before he left, and he had his sheets to the wind when he got to shore."

Jean Luc had to maintain an air of unconcern as he nodded in apparent understanding.

"You should go ashore, Jean Luc. There is a wealth of fine whores in the town. Jesu, they will do anything you want in that town. Man of your rank should have plenty of money to get one. I had this woman last night who..." Beaufort began.

Jean Luc raised his hand. "Thomas, I do not care to hear about your personal business. Perhaps I will go to shore next time, I am not interested this trip."

"Could be a long time," Beaufort warned.

"I will manage," Jean Luc nodded with a small smile.

After the meal, Jean Luc was forced to go to the main deck with Beaufort to see to the loading of supplies and the unloading of more trade goods from the hold. As he watched the proceedings of the loading of stores into the hold, he worried about Aubrey who was alone below. The fever had broken, but he wanted to be there when she awakened.

Beaufort stepped up, breaking him out of his thoughts. "You stare at shore like you got a woman on your mind. Are you sure you do not want to go back in my place? I will tend to the ship." Jean Luc paused for a moment, looking at the man. At least he knew where Beaufort was when he was ashore.

"No, I was just contemplating our next course. We have been very fortunate so far with our takes. I wonder if there is something grander in our future. Captain Black has suggested a vote to cruise the Windwards," Jean Luc said, feigning him off.

Beaufort shrugged, "Suit yourself, stand here in your foolish musings of treasure in the future. I think of the present and I think that I will go find that whore I had last night and take some treasure from her."

"Happy hunting," Jean Luc replied tightly as Beaufort threw a leg over the gunwale to climb down the ladder into the awaiting longboat.

With the bothersome and dangerous Beaufort gone again, Jean Luc slipped down the companionway to the great cabin. Opening the door quietly, he stepped in. He was surprised to see Aubrey dressed and sitting on the ledge of the quarter gallery, her head bent in pointed remorse.

"Aubrey," he said delighted that she was up and about. Her head shot up in alarm. Apparently she had not even noticed his entrance. He was distressed to see her spin around in the ledge to face the windows, drawing her legs up against her chest and putting her back to him.

"Aubrey, please do not be angry with me," he said as he approached. He recalled all too well the expression on her face as she had looked to him when Black was dragging her away to the hold.

"I am not angry with you, Jean Luc. What could you have done? You are not the one who," she began quietly to the windows, her voice breaking. He waited as she contained herself and continued, "You are not the one who defiled me."

"Defiled you?" he echoed.

"How else would you describe placing a permanent mark in such an intimate place? He has made me ugly beyond reproach, Jean Luc. He has branded me like they brand common thieves." Her voice broke again and she dropped her head into her hands. Jean Luc stepped closer, watching her with pain in his heart at her remorse.

"I will be alone forever. No man will ever want me, not once they see this. They will either be afraid to touch me or be abhorred by the ugliness. No man will ever desire me."

Jean Luc put his hands gently on her shoulders, and leaned his head close to her ear. "I desire you. I have always desired you, ever since the first day that I lay my eyes upon you. I have seen you and this has not made you ugly in my eyes." Jean Luc was turning her now toward him.

"It does not change my feelings toward you, ma chérie. I have loved you since the first day I saw you and I always shall." Dropping his head for a moment, he said in quiet tightness, "I should have challenged Black for you long ago, to prevent this."

"He would have killed you for doing so," she told him. Then her face went ashen as she realized what he had confessed to.

"You saw the mark on me?" Her voice was strained as she glared at him. Jean Luc merely returned it with a calm stare.

"How dare you? You took off my clothes?" she spat angrily as she made to get out of the window ledge, but Jean Luc blocked her escape.

"You had a raging fever yesterday evening. The wound was becoming dangerously infected. Who do you think cared for you? Who do you think dressed the wound with clean bandages? Who do you think put you to bed? I was as discrete as possible, but there was no avoiding seeing that part of you. Would you have rather that I left you? Would you rather that I had given the task to Cook?" He found himself arguing.

A frown crossed her angry brow and she settled a bit. "Cook?"

"Oui, he is the one who generally tends to the medical needs of the crew in the absence of Jojoba since we have no doctor or surgeon on board," he nodded firmly. Aubrey made a face, thinking about how she may have been exposed to the big man had Jean Luc decided not to take responsibility.

"And so now you are not quite so upset with my decision?" He was looking deeply into her eyes. Long moments of silence hung between them now and she finally squeezed his hand.

"Thank you for taking care of me, Jean Luc."

He reached up to brush his hand along the curve of her jaw. "You are most welcome. I am sorry that I was not here when you awakened. I meant to be, but I was called away to see to the loading of the ship. How do you feel today?" Then he chuckled at his own question and said, "You are arguing with me today, this is a good sign. It means that you are feeling much better! Last night you only muttered to my conversation and I could not understand a word of what you said. I have never heard such a language. I think that perhaps you were making it up in your fever."

"It was Gaelic, no doubt, my Da taught me. Uncle Jonathan punished me whenever I spoke it in front of him. So when I was alone, confined to my room, or in bed at night, I would speak it to myself so that I would never forget."

"Could you eat something if I had Cook or Henri bring it?" he asked with a nod, as he stroked back her hair.

"I will try," she nodded.

"Come back to the bed now, ma chérie, and rest," he coaxed as he gently led her to the bunk and tucked her back in neatly.

"I will send Henri with some food and he can keep you company. He knows that you have been ill. He thinks that it was just a fever," he added.

She nodded in reply, but he could see that she was not really paying attention to him. She stared out the quarter gallery windows at the clouds and water beyond. He sighed deeply at her despondency and he stood to go to the door.

"Jean Luc," she said in a whisper.

"Oui?"

"Did he mark her too? Mala?"

Jean Luc pursed his lips and lifted his blue eyes to look at her, "Oui."

Aubrey made a disgusted face and turned her head to look at the wall beside the bunk, "He is an animal. I hate him."

Chapter 48

Aubrey had supped on broth and water for the evening meal then fell asleep in her weakened state. At the sounding of the third watch, Jean Luc came into the cabin quietly. He gathered up the medicines and bandages, and poured a basin of fresh water. He moved to the bunk and gently awakened her.

"Aubrey, ma chérie, I must change your bandage–it needs to be clean and fresh to keep the healing process moving along," he said softly when she stirred.

"Can I not do it myself?" she asked.

"What do you know of wounds and medication?" he asked with a cocked brow.

"Nothing," she said quietly.

"Well, what can you do?" he said flippantly as he took hold of the covers and she reluctantly allowed him to pull them down. She endured the procedure with much embarrassment and shyness as he completed the task as quickly as he could.

"It is healing nicely and looks very good," he said easily.

Aubrey shot him a glance. "You are referring to what, Monsieur?"

He smiled sheepishly at the end of his remark. "The wound looks good–and I cannot tell a lie, your breast is very nice too, Mademoiselle." He leaned toward her easily and she blushed as his remark. Aubrey remained still as he pressed his lips on hers passionately. The kiss lasted for several long moments. When he finally drew back he asked softly, "Does my kiss reflect how I still feel for you?"

"Oui," she nodded.

"Hmm, then what is your pleasure tonight, ma chérie?" he asked as he brushed his fingertips over her cheek.

"Stay with me awhile until I fall asleep, please. We have so little time together and now that I have this." She indicated the mark then added, "I think that he will not be so polite anymore when he returns."

Jean Luc smoothed her hair and smiled gently as he took her hand in his. "I will stay with you."

Aubrey closed her weary eyes and held his hand tightly. He remained by her side until her hold on him relaxed.

The next day, Aubrey kept to herself in the great cabin and that evening she refused to let Jean Luc check or dress the healing scar. She had insisted that she had taken care of it herself. He honored her refusal with an air of disgruntlement and left her alone. Lying in his bunk that night, he fretted over her sudden change in attitude toward him.

On the third day after Black had ordered the mark placed upon her, Aubrey ventured up on the deck late in the afternoon. She stood near the companionway, watching Jean Luc from a distance as he went about his daily tasks on the quarterdeck. He looked up after a while, and noting her observance of him, he gave her a gentle smile.

Aubrey went to the starboard railing and stood staring down at the water. A shiny object dangling from her hand caught his eye. Moving to see a bit better, Jean Luc saw that it was the gold chain he had noticed that she had been wearing about her neck since Black's return from Jamaica. He clenched his teeth now as he had then. It was an extravagant gift bestowed upon her by the captain as part of his 'possession' routine. It would be augmented later with more gifts–this much Jean Luc knew. He could offer her no such finery–his only gift could be his undaunted love.

He watched as she fingered the fine object and seemed to be contemplating it. Then with a mixture of disbelief and relief, he watched as Aubrey turned her hand palm downward and allowed the fine treasure to fall into the lapping water below. He approached her carefully, with an air of authority for the benefit of the men around them.

"Take care, Mademoiselle, that you do not fall overboard or at the very least–lose something valuable." The face she made told him that she knew that he had seen her let the chain slip into the water.

"Merci for your concern," she muttered.

"I do not think that you realize just how much I do care," he answered in low tones.

"You are mistaken, Monsieur Pierne, you have made it quite clear," she said quietly as she leaned to look down at the water.

"I would like the opportunity to explain myself a bit more clearly," he said barely moving his lips. There was extended silence between them for a few moments.

"Why are you on this ship, Jean Luc?" she whispered suddenly.

He drew a deep breath and clasped his hands behind his back. "Because it is the ship that I choose to be upon."

"You are nothing like them," she said as her eyes darted to look at the crew around them. Then with a viciousness that surprised him, she hissed, "You are nothing like him."

"He is my friend," Jean Luc replied.

Hazel eyes flashed at him angrily. "You can stand there now and say that in the same conversation where you say that you care for me? Knowing what he has done?"

"Aubrey, I..." Jean Luc started but she was not listening to him anymore. She threw herself away from the railing with an attitude that he knew all too well now. Her boots clicked on the deck as she strode angrily away and down the companionway. Jean Luc set his jaw as he watched her go.

In the great cabin, Aubrey stood looking out the windows at the sun setting on the horizon. She turned with a gasp as the door latch clicked and the door snapped open. Jean Luc was standing in the doorway, a stern look on his face. His blue eyes bored into her hazel ones as he shut the door soundly behind him. Aubrey rolled her eyes and turned away from him. In a few short strides, Jean Luc was upon her and taking her arm, whirled her to face him.

"What has happened to you is something that I know you will never forgive Rene Black for and I hold myself just as responsible. To be quite truthful with you, I did not think that he would do it–not to you. But something happened to press him to do so." Aubrey looked at him and knew that there was something on his mind that he was not sharing regarding Black and the incident.

She snapped her arm from his grasp. "Let me go and get out of here."

"Chut! You must listen to me." He argued back as he caught her by the arms again.

"Will you manhandle me now?" She spat.

"Be still and listen. Of course I will not do that," he said evenly. Aubrey dropped her head as he pulled her closer and touched his lips to her ear.

"You bear a mark, this much is true. But when I look upon you, I do not see it. I see only you and that part of a beautiful young body that I have been privileged to see. Do you not understand, Aubrey? I love you, no matter what." His voice came in hushed yet serious tones as she continued to stare at the floor. He raised her face to look at him in the now darkened room. "Do you understand?"

Aubrey looked up at him and said quietly, "Jean Luc, I hope that you get your own ship someday and I would very much like to be the woman of that captain. But I also hope that you never get this ship because it is full of the devil and is doomed to Hell. I hope that he goes with it." Jean Luc understood her anger and he held her close to him.

"We will speak no more of him," Jean Luc said easily as he bent his head towards hers.

"Repeat after me," he began in English and then he finished in French, "Give me a kiss."

Aubrey did as he bade, giggling through tears at his game. He smiled at her giggle.

"I will give you as many kisses as you can stand and more."

Jean Luc pressed his lips upon hers, grateful that he had pulled her out of the depression. Long impassioned kisses followed as he held her pressed gently against the wall. Jean Luc opened his eyes and rolled them to look toward the ceiling as music and men having a good time could be heard from the deck above. With her head pressed back against the wall in another deep kiss, Jean Luc's fingers stroked down her throat and he began to open the front of the shirt that she wore. Breaking from the kiss, she caught his hand.

"I have already put on a new bandage."

"Who said that I was about to do that?" he asked as he gently shook his hand free of hers and proceeded to unbutton her shirt. She looked down at his hand then up into his face. He pressed her in another kiss as he pulled her shirttails free of her britches. His hands slipped up along her bare back beneath the shirt and he kissed her throat.

"Take this off and let me see you," he whispered against her ear. He felt her shiver slightly.

"You are beautiful, ma chérie—let me see you," he coaxed. She looked up at him for several long moments. The feel of his hands on the bare skin of her back gave her chills in some regions of her body and yet heat seared through others. Finally, to his delight, she slowly slipped off the shirt and let it fall to the floor at their feet. Jean Luc dipped his head to engage her in yet another kiss as his hands gently searched the front of her body. She remained timid, yet receptive to his caresses in the fading light.

His searching hand stroked her belly. Very easily now, he unfastened the top button of the britches she wore. As he worked the next button, he gently kissed her throat. When his fingers moved further into the partially opened britches, Aubrey caught his hand with a sharp gasp.

Jean Luc was on fire and would not be contented this night with kisses alone. Her young girl behavior must be replaced now. It was time for her to learn the ways between a woman and a man. Jean Luc could feel the need in her body that she was too inexperienced to express.

"I have told you time and time again that I love you. Let me show you," he whispered thickly as the music and men grew louder above them.

Aubrey knew what he was suggesting as she watched him remove his own shirt. Casting her eyes over his bare chest, she confessed, "Jean Luc, I know nothing. No one has ever spoken to me of the intimate affairs between men and women. You will think that I am simpleton."

"Have I not taught you to speak a new language?" Jean Luc asked as he stroked her cheek.

"Oui," she nodded with the same unsure look.

Smoothing her hair, he whispered against her lips, "Then let me teach you this as well."

Before she could reply, he scooped her up into his arms and carried her to the bunk. In slow gentle movements he coaxed her into removing her boots and britches. She now lay naked beside him as Jean Luc soothed her apprehension with whispers in both French and English. His fingers gently explored and caressed silken places that he had longed to touch since he had first seen her in England. Only when he could feel that she was relaxed and her body responded to his touch, did he rise to remove his own boots and britches.

He smiled gently down at her in the light offered by the stern lamps shining in the quarter gallery windows. Aubrey laid on the bunk, struggling between looking at him in all of his naked glory and looking away in shy embarrassment. He eased his body over hers, gently pressing his knee between hers to part her silken thighs. She suddenly tensed and caught at his arms. Her voice came in a frightened gasp. "You will hurt me."

"Non, ma chérie, never," he purred. He stroked expert fingers into the mat of curls between her legs until he could feel the tenseness of her body ebb away and she clung to him in wonder at the new sensations he was introducing to her.

"Je t'aime," he whispered against her neck. He moved his body over hers slowly and Aubrey felt the strange hardness against her thigh. As he gently entered her, he felt her tense over the strangeness of their bodies joining. With a swift movement, Jean Luc thrust deeply into her. Aubrey felt a searing pain through her body as Jean Luc covered her mouth with his. The scream went no further than his kiss.

"Je regrette, ma chérie. But it will not happen again. I promise." Jean Luc whispered close to her ear as he pressed gentle kisses about her face. Feeling her relax once again from his kisses, he began to move.

With gentle urgings, Jean Luc coaxed her to move in a way that he knew they both would enjoy. Soon Jean Luc's movements quickened, then, with a deep and final thrust, he released himself into her. Aubrey moaned quietly in her own passion. Jean Luc's climax was earth shattering. Never before had he known such pleasure with a woman, and most certainly never before had Aubrey experienced such pleasure. He held her as they lay resting. She began to cry and he raised his head to look at her. Taking her face into his hands, and reaffirming his pledge to her, he kissed her deeply. When he drew back from the kiss, Aubrey was still crying.

"Ma chérie, what is it? I am sorry I hurt you but you must trust me, it will not hurt again," he cooed.

"No Jean Luc–this was–wonderful," she whispered with a tearful smile.

"Then why do you cry?"

"Because it cannot be real, not for me. I could never be so happy. I want this to be forever, and it cannot. I love you, and you say that you love me–but I am the prisoner of a monster," she continued to cry.

"Ma chérie, some day you will see, there will be no one between us," he soothed.

"What will I do when he comes back?" she asked forlornly.

"We have another whole day and night yet. Let us not worry about that until the time comes. Let us enjoy one another for now," he soothed as he kissed her again.

Chapter 49

Dawn was beginning to light the morning sky when Jean Luc slipped out of the bunk. He looked down upon her sleeping visage. She was still naked, nestled among the bed linens on her side, with her hands tucked under her chin. Jean Luc smiled as he remembered their night together. She did not sleep much during the night as his need to make love and touch her happened several times. The sadness was gone from her beautiful face and had been replaced with a peaceful dreaming mask. Slipping on his shirt, he watched a small smile turn up the corner of her mouth as she dreamed and he smiled in return.

Ever since the first day that he had seen her in the market place, he had dreamed of this time. But in his dreams, they did not have the worry of another man between them. With a sad smile now, he leaned over her and touched his lips lightly to hers, not wanting to disturb or wake her. She sighed deeply and turned onto her back, the movement exposing her chest. He cast his eyes over her soft inviting breasts and the need for her began to rise again. With much reluctance, he knew that he had leave to prevent them from being discovered, so he finished dressing. Jean Luc pulled the covers up over her and left the cabin quietly, undetected by anyone.

Jean Luc went to his own cabin to prepare himself for the day. Once on deck he looked across the waters to the docks at Bimini. Black was there somewhere, probably in the bed with some wench. Jean Luc smiled to himself. She had quenched his fire for her, for the time being anyway. He sighed. What would he do when Black came back on board? His time with her would surely be ended then. He went about his daily routine, reveling in the memory of the previous night.

Aubrey awakened several hours later. She sighed deeply and rolled onto her side. She cradled the pillow he had laid his head on against her naked body. She inhaled deeply, closing her eyes remembering with a small smile how he had felt against her. She was just beginning to relax in the memory when her eyes shot open. She buried her face in the pillow and then pushed it away in disdain. It had the scent of Rene Black on it.

She rolled onto her back and looked at the ceiling. Nothing in here would remind her of Jean Luc. Why should it? This was Black's cabin, Black's bunk. She sat up, pulling the sheet off the bunk and wrapping it around her. She got out of the bunk and went to the washstand to prepare herself for the day. She looked at the bunk and then at Black's desk, as if he were there. She slipped her shirt on over her head and promised herself defiantly as she looked at Black's desk. Tonight she would go to Jean Luc's bunk. She wanted to be with him, not with the captain.

Jean Luc did not see her all day. He was afforded little time to go down to the main cabin to see her himself, and she had not come up on deck by herself. Once, during the course of the day, he ventured to knock at the cabin door. There was no reply from within, even to answer his calls of her name and the door was locked. Fearful that he would draw attention, he had moved away, disgruntled and worried. He hoped that he had not frightened her the night before, although she had seemed willing, even in her inexperience.

"Have you seen Mademoiselle Aubrey? Has she eaten today?" Jean Luc asked of Cook in an authoritative manner as he sat in the galley at dinnertime.

"Non, monsieur," he replied as he handed Jean Luc his plate of food.

"Mon Dieu," Jean Luc exhaled silently as he struggled with whether he should sit here and eat his meal or go check on her. He glanced around the galley as it filled with men for the evening meal. Most everyone was on shore, so the few men left could all come to dinner at one time if they chose to and there was not impending business with the ship's operations. He noticed that Beaufort had returned to the ship. Too bad, it would have been nice if he had gotten into an argument and gotten himself killed, Jean Luc mused to himself. Beaufort was sitting across the room with his two friends. The man could not be trusted and Jean Luc would have to be very careful with his contacts with Aubrey. He found himself wondering whether he had seen Beaufort the night before up on the deck with the other men in their revelry. Not remembering worried him.

As he poked at his plate and pondered the situation, a movement from the doorway caught his eye. His heart skipped a beat as he noted that Aubrey had entered the galley. She had stepped timidly into the galley and was looking around the room. One of the men had come behind her with the intent of coming into the galley. Jean Luc watched tensely as the man gained her attention respectfully and discretely. She was the captain's woman and they all knew it.

She looked at him in surprise and then moved out of the way. She turned her attention to look back around the room before her. Knowing that Black's table was situated in the back of the room, she looked over the men in that direction. Aubrey's face lit with delight when she saw Jean Luc there. He had stood up to gain her attention as well.

Beaufort saw him stand, then he turned to see Aubrey approaching the table and he watched her with hungry eyes. Just as she was about to pass him, Beaufort deliberately put one long leg into the aisle. Aubrey stopped short and looked down at his leg across her path.

Jean Luc sat down slowly, watching to see what would happen next. She did not appear to be quite so frightened this evening. Would she assert herself with this arrogant bastard now? Aubrey turned her head purposefully to look at Beaufort. In his seated position, she was just above eye level to him, "Excuse moi," she said evenly in French. Looking at Boulet beside him, she thought back to the silly remark that Jean Luc had made about the man and she struggled to keep a giggle in check.

Beaufort merely looked at her with his gray eyes and smiled without parting his lips. She took a deep breath and started to step over his leg. As she did so, his grin broadened into a toothy smile and he raised his leg ever so slightly. He pulled his leg up between her knees as she tried to step across. He intended to trip her giving him a reason to put his hands on her. A feigned attempt to help her up, but that was not to say where on her he would put his hands. She disappointed him though by catching herself and grabbing the edge of a nearby table. The two men with him watched intently and laughed at her foiling of his plan. Beaufort cast them an angry glance.

Aubrey looked away, standing there for a few moments. Her face displayed an exquisite control of seething anger. Beaufort put his leg back down and took a draught from his mug, taking his eyes from her for a second. Aubrey turned her attention back to Beaufort and presented him with the sweetest smile she could muster considering the circumstances. He looked at her in question and at that very instant he got the surprise of his life. Aubrey drew back her booted foot and kicked him squarely on the side of his knee. He immediately withdrew his leg and roared in pain as he cursed her in French. His friends laughed all the louder and he cursed them as well. She strode past him, tossing her head with an air of triumph, the movement making the auburn tresses dance lightly. Jean Luc covered his mouth with his napkin to hide the laugh that threatened to escape. Her demeanor changed the moment she came to the table where he sat.

"May I sit here for dinner?"

He stood immediately. "Certainement, this is the captain's table, your place is here." It pained him to say the words for others to hear. She looked at him knowingly. They both knew whose woman she had chosen to be.

"Here, this is for you," he said pushing his plate to her.

"This was your plate sir, not mine," she retorted, pushing it back toward him.

270

"Eat," he persisted, pushing the plate back in front of her again.

"Cook can bring me another," she said as she pushed the plate back.

"Eat," he said firmly, pushing it to her again. Lifting the fork and picking morsels from the plate to put them into her mouth, she rolled her eyes at him.

"You conducted yourself well with Beaufort just now," he commended quietly in English as he poured her some wine. To set the conversation, he raised the bottle. "You probably drank much finer wine in your rich uncle's big house," he stated.

She looked at him in surprise. "What do you know of my rich uncle?"

He sat forward in his chair, taking a piece of bread and said, pointing a finger at her. "I knew where you lived, that you lived with your uncle who is wealthy and I know that you like the marketplace."

She put the fork down slowly and looked at him stunned. "How do you know these things?" He sat back, looking around as one of the men passed them. She sat staring at him, waiting for an answer.

"Eat. The night could be long," he said with a mild air of authority.

She made a face at him. "Will you bully me now?"

"Eat your dinner," he said again.

"Can I have some water, too?" she asked angrily. He got up from the table and soon returned with a cup of water.

"There, now eat."

She sat quietly eating as he watched her. Finally she looked around the room and then at him and whispered, "Why are you being so mean to me? Why do you bring all of this up now? After last night." Her voice sounded confused. He sighed for it was not his intent to be indifferent with her. It was a necessary show for the men around them.

He leaned forward as nonchalantly as possible and whispered, "I will come to your cabin later and we will talk. Eat your dinner now, you have not eaten all day."

She looked down and picking at the food, she whispered back,

"Thank you for the water. I was rarely allowed wine at my uncle's home because he said I was too young. I suppose I am still acquiring a taste for it. I cannot imagine how you would know, but my uncle is wealthy and he does have a big house. And for your information, I do not like the marketplace, I love the marketplace." She looked back up at him and saw a twinkle in his eye.

"I know." His tone sent odd sensations through her body and she shivered. Then waving at her plate, he said firmly, "Finish your dinner now, it is getting cold." He went to the cook stove and came back with a plate of food for himself. At his bequest, she ate nearly all the food on the plate. As she ate, she wondered how he could know so much about her. As he ate, he looked forward with great anticipation to their meeting after the meal. He would go on the pretext of making entries into the logbooks again, and he would leave the door to the cabin open. After he had finished the entries, he would close the door, if she were willing.

She finished her meal and, with a mild air of feigned defiance, she stood and said, as she pushed the empty plate toward him, "There Monsieur Pierne, I have eaten my dinner. May I go back to the cabin now?"

"Go straight back and speak to no one," he replied over his plate with a measured degree of authority.

As a parting shot, and because Beaufort and his friends were still nearby she said curtly, "I intend to tell Captain Black how mean you spoke to me." He saw her cut her eyes over her shoulder at the table where Beaufort sat still rubbing his knee. Jean Luc chuckled lightly in understanding and went back to his meal. Black had at one time called her a treasure. Well, she was a treasure. There was no doubt about that!

Chapter 50

Aubrey was sitting on the settee when there was a knock at the door. She laid aside the book she had been reading and let Jean Luc in.

"I need to make entries into the log, Mademoiselle," he said politely as he removed his hat. She stepped back into the room and returned to the settee and her book as he went to the desk. Several men went by the doorway on their way to the deck or hold area for the evening. They glanced in and saw him at the desk, while she was on the settee reading, apparently ignoring him.

Aubrey's heart was actually racing at the thought of him there. Her mind drifted back to the night before. She stole a glance at him every now and then, but he did not look up to her. She began to worry whether the night before had just been a terrible trick to have his way with her and she had been naive enough to fall for it. She really did want to be with him. The more she thought about the night before, the more she began to feel frustrated at him sitting there ignoring her. She sighed in her frustration and slouched further down in the corner of the settee, trying to concentrate on the words in the book before her. It was getting dark and she was now having trouble seeing the print. She sighed again and went to light the lantern.

As she stood, she noticed that he had gotten up from the desk and was going to the door. He was leaving? He said that they would talk. She thought to herself incredulously. It was all a trick last night. He did not mean any of the things that he had said to her. She mused to herself as she lit the lantern. Aubrey replaced the globe on the lantern and turned to go back to the book as she heard the door shut. He was leaving, he had tricked her last night into giving the most intimate part of herself willingly to him and now he was leaving. But when she turned around, she saw that he was standing against the closed door looking at her. She returned the gaze and remained where she was. Is he going to trick me again? She wondered.

Jean Luc reached in his pocket and took something small out of it as she watched him. He held out his hand, his fist closed tightly around the object. "I have something that I think belongs to you," he said in a quiet voice.

She looked at him suspiciously. "What is it?"

"Why not come and see what it is?" he replied with a small smile. His tone made her feel strange inside. She stepped closer to him and put out her hand. As she held her palm out under his fist, he easily opened his hand and the object dropped from it.

She pulled her hand back and looked at it in genuine surprise. "My bracelet, I dropped it," she stammered.

"It dropped from your arm the night you went to your window. The night the nasty little man came for dinner to your uncle's home," he finished in a quiet voice. Aubrey looked at the bracelet and then at him, he cocked his head sideways. "Was he meant to be a potential husband?"

"Yes." She shivered and made a face that brought a chuckle from him. Then she looked at him seriously. "How do you know so much about me? How did you get this bracelet? Why do you wait until now to bring all that you know into the open?" He smiled at her but did not reply. Their eyes met for an extended moment and she slowly came closer. He easily pulled her into his arms and pressed his lips on hers, gently at first, then more hungrily. She yielded at once to his embrace. He was not playing tricks on her, she could tell.

He broke from the kiss and hugged her tightly, "I am sorry for my attitude at dinner, but we have to maintain a distant relationship in front of the men. If any of them were to find out about us and tell Black, we would both be doomed."

She looked up at him. "But what do we do when he comes back?"

"Then we cannot be together. We must make the best of it while we can," he said sadly as he kissed her again.

She pushed at him. "I would rather not be in here with him."

"I know, but there is nothing we can do."

"No? Tell him that you... want me." she stammered.

He smiled at her. "I wish it was that easy, Aubrey. I have wanted you with me since the first time I saw you in the marketplace in London. I followed you everywhere, even to your home."

She made a face at him. "Not my home."

He pulled her to the settee. "You know what I mean."

"You were following me? Why?" she asked surprised.

"Because it was my intent to kidnap you and bring you to sea with me," he confessed. She looked at him for a time, unable to believe what she was hearing.

"Really?"

"Oui. I was very unhappy when the captain took you for himself," he replied as he pulled her into his arms for another kiss. He caressed her for a time and she willingly allowed him to do so. He could feel the heated passion rising in her body as he held her and felt the same happening to him. He stood and pulled her up with him and started toward the bunk. He was surprised when she resisted.

She looked at the bunk and then at him. "Not here, not there."

He looked at her in puzzlement. "Where then?"

She bit her lip nervously, and said with a small shy smile, "Your cabin, your bunk."

He pulled her close to him and nuzzled her ear. "Are you sure?"

She replied with a nod of her head. Excitement coursed through him at the thought.

"We cannot go together. I will go first and then you will have to come on your own. It is getting late so there should be no one in the corridors. Stay here for a time and put out the lantern for lights out," he instructed. She agreed to do as he directed, he told her where she would find him and he sent her to the settee, putting the book back into her hands.

"I will be waiting for you, ma chérie," he whispered as he kissed her. He put on his hat and went out the door saying, "Thank you, Mademoiselle, for allowing me to enter the day's information into the logbook. Make sure that you put out your lantern when it is time. Breakfast will be at the regular time should you care to partake." A couple of men passed through the corridor as he carried on his act of authority. She nodded at him with a feigned air of indifference.

After waiting the instructed time, Aubrey put out the lantern and went quietly out the door into the corridor. Jean Luc had told her that Beaufort had been assigned duties above deck. Had Jean Luc planned this meeting all along? Was that his reason for getting Beaufort out of the way? She wondered as she quietly made her way to the cabin he had directed her to. Stopping in front of the cabin door, she looked up and down the corridor to make certain she was alone before she knocked every so lightly. The door came open to reveal a dark room within. A gentle, yet insistent hand grasped her by the wrist and she was pulled into the room as the door shut quickly behind her. She was alarmed that she had knocked on the wrong door and would find herself in the presence of one of the other men. Fear rose up as she heard the bolt slide into place behind her. She heard movement in the room and held her breath, peering into the darkness, hoping her eyes would adjust to it soon. She stood still as a violent trembling began to rack her body and, taking a chance, she whispered, "Jean Luc?"

There was no reply, but the sound of a match striking in the silence made her jump. She watched the light of the match touch to the wick of a lantern. Relief flooded her as she saw his face in the light above as he lit the lantern. She emitted a nervous sigh as he put the globe back on the lantern and came toward her. Aubrey remained where she was, looking nervously about the room as he advanced. She finally looked back at him and only then did she notice that he was without a shirt. Her breath came in short gasps as he took her into his arms and pressed his lips on hers. Once more she yielded to his embrace.

"Why do you tremble?" he asked as he kissed her throat.

"I thought that I was in the wrong cabin," she replied quietly. Her breath came in small gasps again as he pulled the shirt over her head and gently ran his hands down over the front of her, his lips following the same path. The heat of passion was rising in him quickly as he easily picked her up into his arms and carried her to his bunk. His hands wandered over her as he lay next to her, kissing her.

In a short while, they were both naked and under the sheets. He eased his body over her, still kissing her. She accepted him willingly and he thrust into her gently, but insistently. She trembled under him, gasping. His movements quickened and she accepted each thrust.

When he awakened, he looked at Aubrey sleeping peacefully beside him. Jean Luc smiled as he thought of how often he made love to her throughout the night and she had accepted him each time.

Glancing over his shoulder to the small window in his cabin, Jean Luc could see the early light of day peering in and he groaned. Rene would return today and his time with Aubrey would be over. Jesu, but this felt so natural for her to lying beside him like this. He hated to wake her, but she would need to leave his cabin soon so they would not be detected by anyone. Slipping out the bunk, Jean Luc let her sleep while he dressed. He watched her from the mirror as he shaved. Finally he leaned over her and kissed her awake.

"You must get up now, ma chérie, and dress. The sooner you get back to the great cabin, the less likely it will be that you are discovered."

"I will," she replied sleepily. Keeping with his regular regime, Jean Luc left the cabin and went up on deck, satisfied in the thought that she would be away and unnoticed.

Chapter 51

The small island of Bimini was a virtual fountain of activity for storekeepers and merchants. For the first two days, it was business as usual. Black was able to sell the stolen goods for a very good price. He then took care of the provisions and ensured that everything would make it to the ship. He ordered a couple of his men to see to the task of loading the provisions in the galley or in the cargo hold.

On the morning of the third day, Black made his way through the town. His mind was so preoccupied on business details that he did not notice the man leaning against a post on the porch of a building idly watching the happenings on the street. As Black walked past him, the man took a step back and bumped into him. The move knocked Black towards the door. Before he could react, the door flew open and Black was seized by strong arms and dragged inside. The man outside on the porch closed the door and resumed his stance on the post as if nothing had happened.

Black was dragged and shoved unceremoniously into a chair. The place used to be a tavern but now it was dusty and full of cobwebs. He jumped to his feet and started to fight his way out, punching two of the men closest to him. Behind him, he heard the cocking of a pistol and whirled around to face his assassin. Then he froze.

Leaning with the chair on its two back legs, booted feet crossed at the ankles and propped up on the table sat the Captain of the *Enchantress*. A sword lay on the table near her legs and she held a pistol pointed at him. She was dressed in a red silk shirt, gold sash about a slim waist, and black britches that molded to her legs like second skin. Her long dark hair hung loosely behind her.

The first thing Black noticed were the dark eyes, cold and cruel. Mala sat unsmiling, yet more beautiful than he could remember. Had he not just seen her up in the ratlines as her ship cut across the bow of his? Remembering the closeness and danger of such a move, his anger flared as it had then.

"Bonjour, Mala," he said as calmly as he could although he seethed inside. Mon Dieu, you are so beautiful and I thought you were dead! his mind screamed.

"I trust your last two evenings with Yvette were most satisfying," she said dispassionately in French.

"But of course. Any evening with a luscious and willing wench is most satisfying," he replied in the same language with a smile. He added a deep bow in her direction to augment the insult.

Still unsmiling and appearing unperturbed by his comment and gesture, Mala stated in English, "Let us hope she did not leave anything more on you than, shall we say, the fragrance of her, ah, perfume."

A couple of the men chuckled at their captain's quip. Black glanced at them before returning Mala's unfriendly gaze. With an overly exaggerated sigh, Black asked, "What do you want, Mala?"

"You, dead," she answered quietly.

Black knew that the first rule of knowing one's adversary was to know certain signs either spoken or silent. In Mala's case, her tone of voice spoke volumes. He knew that if she yelled and shouted at you, you could almost guarantee walking away alive. If she spoke to you as if you were a child or if she spoke so softly that it was almost a whisper, you were dead. The softer the whisper, the deeper in your grave you would be.

Remembering this, Black stared at her uneasily. She had spoken those two words too softly and still no emotion showed on her beautiful face. Her men also caught the deadly tone of her voice. A wave of unrest passed through the men in the room. The silence in the room had become almost deafening, so it was no wonder that every man nearly jumped out of his skin when Mala's boots scraped the table as she moved to stand, the chair landing on all fours with a loud thud.

Mala strode toward Black, who noticed the pistol was still in her hand. She stopped so close to him that he could smell the sweet fragrance of her. At that moment, his mind was assaulted with countless memories of the two of them on his ship. It seemed so long ago. She had been his lady, the Lady of the *Widow Maker*. He had to mentally shake himself back to the present.

Looking into Mala's unsmiling visage, Black was reminded of a time that he had seen Mala's deadly side. It was on a raid of a merchant ship on the seas. Black was dealing with the first mate while a couple of his men held the captain. The first mate was not answering questions even under the threat of killing his captain. Suddenly Mala walked up to the first mate and without smiling she had said quietly,

"Tell us where it is kept or I will kill everyone on board while you watch, starting with your captain." Black had not wanted to kill the captain. The man was the leverage they needed. But before Black could say a word, Mala raised her pistol and shot the captain without taking aim, her dark eyes trained on the frightened first mate. The first mate jumped and stared unbelieving at this heartless woman, who then raised a second pistol and turned it to the second mate, again never taking her eyes from the first mate. Mala pulled off the second shot and the second mate had fallen backward onto the deck.

Still the first mate said nothing, frightened to silence by her actions. Mala dropped both pistols and lifted her empty hand. With a chuckle, one of Black's men gave her another loaded pistol and she turned it on the helmsman. The frightened and decidedly soon-to-be unfortunate man crossed himself and loudly began to pray. Without further ado the first mate blurted out the whereabouts of the chest containing the jewels and coins.

Black and his men let out a whoop but Mala did not move nor did her eyes leave those of the first mate. When the chest was up on deck, the men looked to Black for the permission to open it. Black looked to Mala wanting to share this moment together but all that were present were surprised to see Mala step closer to the first mate. Black did not like the closeness but again before he could say a word, Mala had lifted her pistol to the first mate's temple and said, "Bang!"

The first mate fainted dead away. Everyone from the *Widow Maker* laughed uproariously. Smiling at her as she approached him, Black only shook his head and gave a nod to open the chest, knowing that his men would probably tell that tale for years to come.

Back to the present, Black was beginning to understand how the first mate felt when Mala held the pistol to his head. He knew that if it took every ounce of his strength, he would not faint like that first mate had. When Mala made no other move but remained standing close to him, looking at him, Black stated calmly as he spread his arms slowly, "You want me dead, Mala? Then here I am for you to do as you will."

For a long moment, she made no move. Then suddenly, she wrapped her arms around his neck and pulled him to her for a kiss that he definitely remembered of long ago. The kiss was deep and full of passion. Black did not want it to end as he enveloped her into in his arms. He tasted the rum she must have had already this morning and the kiss became deeper.

All too soon the kiss ended. Mala lowered her arms and as Black released her, she stepped a few paces back from him. Black frowned slightly as he realized that even now, and throughout her closeness, she had still not smiled. Then her gaze left his as her dark eyes darted to look to one side. Before Black could turn to see what she saw, he was hit on the back of his head.

While she gazed down at the unconscious man, two more men came out of the shadows where they had been hiding. One man retrieved Mala's sword from the table and handed it to her. When Mala made no move except to take the sword, he stated in an impatient tone of voice accentuated by a thick Scottish brogue, "Let us be done with this so we can finish our business."

Silence greeted his statement. He looked at Mala and did not like what he saw. Her eyes seemed to softly caress Black. The Scotsman wanted this done and he fidgeted in his place hissing, "Kill him, Mala, and let us be gone."

Still not looking away from the unconscious man on the floor, Mala said, "Make it look like a robbery and leave him in the alley where he can be found."

When she turned away sheathing her sword, the Scotsman asked incredulously, "Ye no' gonna kill him?"

One of the crew went to place a hand on the Scotsman to remind him to whom he was speaking but the other shadowed man was shaking his head in warning, thus stopping the crewman from touching the Scotsman. Confused, the man followed the silent command. The shadowed man also saw and understood the caressing look that Mala gave Black. There was a smile on his face as he hoped that Mala would do something to the Scotsman for questioning her orders, anything!

"I changed my mind, Mr. Deats," she finally replied, looking pointedly at the Scotsman.

"But 'twas your plan, Mala," he pressed on.

Mala whirled around to face him angrily that he would continue to question her actions.

"Yes, it was my plan. Now my plans have changed. Do you have a problem with that, Mr. Deats?" she replied coldly. The Scotsman did not reply and the two of them stared angrily at each other.

The shadowed figure stepped further out into the soft light of the room. He was about a score and five years of age with sandy-colored hair and knowing blue eyes. The ruggedness of his face only enhanced his handsomeness, as did his tall and lean stature. Deciding that the tension needed to broken, he told the gaping crew members with a hint of levity in his voice, "Well, you heard the captain. We make it look like a robbery, mates."

Mala left with the men to supervise the 'dumping' of Black in the alley. It was Deats who had planted the idea of killing Captain Black in Mala's mind. He knew of her past association with him and wanted nothing less than to see the man dead. It would have been all the sweeter to see the deed done by her hand. Nearly six feet tall with dark hair and intense brown eyes, Deats harbored the idea of having this woman captain grace his bed. Damn! He thought to himself. He was sure the embellished story of Black with Yvette would be the final straw. What woman would want a man who finds pleasure with another woman?

"Damn!" This time Deats spoke aloud. He turned to find the sandy-haired man still there and staring at him thoughtfully.

"When it comes to you or Rene Black, you know you will always come out the loser," the man said quietly to Deats. The Scotsman glared at him.

"He could still turn up dead."

With a shrug, the sandy-haired man replied as he turned to leave, "It just better not be by your hand, Mr. Deats. I swear Mala has a sixth sense, and you can guarantee that she will find out how, why, and who did it."

Deats was now furious as he glared at the other man. He had never liked this one and he only put up with this upstart because Mala had practically ordered it since the day that she had saved him. Grabbing the sandy-haired man by the arm and turning him so he would face him, Deats growled, "Are ye in the business of tellin' on yer fellow crew members, laddie?"

Knowing it would infuriate the Scotsman more, the sandy-haired man smiled at him. With a nonchalant shrug, he told Deats calmly, "I am only telling you what I know, Mr. Deats."

They heard footsteps approaching and Deats released the younger man. Mala entered and quickly noted the close proximity of the two men. She knew they did not like each other and was constantly hearing from one about the misdeeds of the other.

"That will be enough. We do not have time for this squabbling. Deats, head back to the ship and make sure we are ready to leave in the next few days. I am getting that uneasy feeling again."

Deats made no move to leave only continued to stare at the other man. How he would love to throttle the little...

"Deats!" Mala stated firmly.

He glanced at Mala then left without a word or backward glance as she called the attention of the younger man, "Morgan?"

The sandy-haired man turned his attention to his captain. "Aye, Captain?"

"Shall we see that the doctor is around to care for a wounded man?"

"Aye, Captain," Morgan smiled and followed after her.

His smile grew bigger when he heard her say as they left the building, "Then we will have a nice talk with this Mademoiselle Yvette."

When Black came to, it was dark outside the window. He realized he was in a bed but as he moved to gaze about the room, he was stabbed with a sharp pain in his head. He winced and raised his hand to find it bandaged. A sound was heard and soon a man appeared at Black's side.

"Oh, good. You are back among the living. How do you feel?"

"I feel like I have been hit from behind," Black answered testily. The man chuckled as he stepped closer.

"Where am I?" Black asked. His gaze taking in what he could without moving anything else.

"You are in my home. I am Doctor Reed. You were found in an alley by a couple of boys. Looks like you were robbed. Your pockets were turned inside out and such. Do you remember anything?"

Black remembered every bit of what happened, especially Mala's kiss. He remembered that when she stepped away, he wanted her right then and there. Unfortunately, he also remembered that throughout his entire meeting with Mala, she never smiled and she had said that she wanted him dead. Why? He shook his head slowly trying to make sense of a relationship that had once been so dear to his heart but had somehow turned sour.

The doctor, who had been watching Black's every move, misread the gesture.

"Oh well, that is to be expected. But perhaps you can remember more later." The doctor helped Black get comfortable. "You rest now and we will see about getting you someplace to recuperate."

Black realized he was very tired but he also needed to get back to his ship. What would Mala do with his ship? Black closed his eyes to ease the pain in his head. When he opened them again, there was sunlight coming through the window. Mon Dieu, did I sleep all night? Black thought to himself.

Carefully, he got up. He sat at the edge of the bed willing his head to stop spinning. He noticed his clothes draped over a chair and carefully he made his way to them. His rapier was missing along with his pistol. Mala was always thorough, he thought in disgust.

Quietly, he went to the door and listened. Even though he heard nothing, he went to the window and saw that the window faced an alley. Black stealthily opened it and climbed out. His head ached and he made to rub his temples but felt the bandage. Quickly, he removed it so as not to attract attention and made his way back to the main thoroughfare. The street was busy for what seemed like mid-morning as Black made his way to the tavern and Yvette. Suddenly he stopped and realized that Mala had mentioned Yvette!

A young woman dressed in lavender and escorted by an elegantly dressed man walked by him. The man took his arm and Black was led across the street. When he turned to the couple, Black realized that they had moved him out of the way of a wagon drawn by two horses.

Nodding his thanks, Black moved on but had only moved a few feet when he turned to look at the couple again. They had disappeared from sight. Had the woman resembled Mala? The man reminded him of, Morgan?

Black resumed his slow journey to Yvette. Black entered the tavern and made his way up the stairs. Stopping at Yvette's door, he knocked and entered when he heard her bid for him to come in. Standing before him was the woman in lavender and next to her was Yvette.

"Well, you look a sight. One would be given the impression that you were robbed," Mala said condescendingly.

"Damn it, Mala. Did you have to leave me defenseless?" Black growled.

"That is the usual remnant of a robbery, Rene. Though, I am sure you did not come here to discuss your defenses or rather the lack of them. Yvette, I leave him in your very capable hands." Black caught the deadly look in Mala's eyes as her dark eyed gaze turned to Yvette. Glancing at Yvette, he saw the whore watching Mala warily.

"Morgan, let us leave Rene's things on his favorite playground, the bed."

"Mala, I need to talk with you," Black said suddenly.

"No Rene, we have had our talk," Mala hissed as she watched Morgan place the rapier and pistol on the bed.

"Mala, give me a few minutes," Black insisted.

Mala turned on him barely concealing her contempt. He flinched and felt a cold chill race down his spine at her cold reply, "You could be dead in a few minutes."

Morgan and Yvette looked from Black to Mala and back to Black again as the two captains stared at one another. Morgan interrupted by saying, "Captain, we should be going if we are to catch the tide."

Chapter 52

"The captain is returning." A crewmember reported to Jean Luc, nodding toward the shoreline. Jean Luc turned to watch Black as he strode angrily along the dock. The quartermaster stood with his foot propped up on a cannon carriage as he watched the longboat being rowed toward the ship. He sighed deeply. His time with Aubrey was at an end–at least until the next time Black left the ship... provided that the man did not insist on his coming ashore as well.

Meeting Black as he stepped onto the deck, Jean Luc started to speak but thought better of it as he noticed the man's dark mood. Something had happened on the island. Jean Luc looked over at the island and saw nothing out of the ordinary. He looked back at Black just as the latter disappeared towards his cabin. Within seconds, the slamming of a door below decks could be heard.

Black threw himself onto his bunk and stared into space. He had no idea how long he had laid there as his mind tumbled over the events of the last few days. The knock at the door broke into his thoughts and with a grunt he called for the person to enter. Jean Luc entered the room and glanced around. His heart skipped a beat when he did not see Aubrey in the cabin. Mild panic coursed through him and he prayed that she had gone to the galley. Beaufort was back on board, and given the man's proclivities toward her, Jean Luc hoped that she had sought out Jojoba for safety. The Jamaican was the lesser of the two evils. "Is all well, Captain?" he asked carefully.

Black swung his booted feet over the side of the bunk and sat up. Rolling his head from side to side to relieve the tension he felt, he let out a deep sigh. Straightening up, Black looked to Jean Luc and said, "Mala is here."

Jean Luc looked perplexed. "But her ship..."

"Is on the other side of the island," Black finished irritably. Jean Luc moved to take down a bottle of rum and two tankards. He set them on the table and Black joined him. Downing a large portion of what Jean Luc poured for him, Black began his story of the last five days. When Black had finished, Jean Luc asked, "So this was yesterday?" Black nodded in reply.

"And Yvette?" Jean Luc queried on as Black looked into his tankard.

Black snorted and said in controlled anger, "Mala had told Yvette before I arrived, that she was to take care of my head only. Anything else and she, Mala, would kill Yvette for touching me again!" As hard as Jean Luc tried, he could barely suppress the smile. Black saw it and let out a growl.

Quickly, Jean Luc told him, "Excuse moi, mon ami, but it sounds to me like Mala was jealous."

"She wanted me dead, Jean Luc! Why should she care about Yvette?"

"Well Rene, if you will recall, Mala's first words to you were about Yvette. Does that not reek of jealousy to you?"

Black sat still and stared at Jean Luc. Then two men gave in to easy laughter as they drank.

Jean Luc did not know how long they had sat there drinking, or how long it had taken Black to tell his tale of his visit to Bimini and his meeting with Mala. He worried about Aubrey, hoping that she would not come into the cabin while they were there. Jean Luc wondered what had happened to her. Why had she not been here before Black's return as he had instructed her to do? He had to find a way to get the man out of here and up on deck. He also hoped that she would not or had not been seen leaving his cabin. On the other hand, Black did not even seem to notice that she was missing. Perhaps he was so wrapped up in his time spent with Mala that he had momentarily forgotten Aubrey, Jean Luc thought.

"We should go topside and see to the storing of supplies, Rene," Jean Luc said easily. The dark haired man looked at him thoughtfully for a moment and then looked around the room. Jean Luc's heart skipped a beat when Black's gaze came to rest on the bunk. There was an odd look in his eye.

Black stared at the bunk but did not see it. Instead he thought about Mala and how she had felt against him, just before he lost consciousness. Why was she so angry with him? He rubbed the back of his head and felt the slight knot there. Damn, what did they hit him with? He wondered as he got up from the chair.

Jean Luc stood also feeling weak inside, for he knew that Black would surely notice that Aubrey was gone any minute now. What would he say? She went to the galley to eat breakfast? He was relieved to see Black pick up his hat and gloves and put them on.

"I trust all has gone well here?"

"Oui, all was fine," Jean Luc stammered.

"I want to leave here this evening and sail to the mainland of North America. I think that it is time we paid a visit to the port of Charlestowne," Black was saying as they went up the steps to the main deck. Jean Luc merely nodded, looking quickly down the corridor to see if Aubrey was in sight. There was no one around except Beaufort and he was headed the other way.

It was just a few moments later when the door to Jean Luc's cabin came open slowly. Aubrey checked in both directions before she slipped out into the corridor. She wished that she had not slept so late. When she had awakened to hear the movement of men and supplies overhead, she had leapt from the bunk. Now, with her boots in her hand, she returned stealthily to Black's cabin.

As quickly as her shaking hands could manage it, she made herself ready for the new day. She was just finishing brushing her hair and pulling it back in a ribbon when the door burst open. She turned suppressing a small cry of alarm. Rene Black stood in the doorway with a frightening gleam in his eye. She faked a smile. "Rene, you have returned."

He slammed the door behind him and advanced a few paces across the room toward her. His jaw was set and he made no reply. Not taking her eyes off him, she bit her lip and backed away, reaching behind her to keep from running into something or tripping in her retreat.

"Where have you been?" he asked in low even tones. She met his steady one-eyed glare with unblinking eyes, and she took a slightly defensive stance.

"What do you mean? You told me that I had free run of the ship." He advanced closer, throwing a chair out of the way. She watched wide-eyed as the chair crashed into the wall. Just as she looked back at him, he savagely reached out the remaining distance between them and grabbed a handful of the front of the shirt she wore.

"Free run of the ship does not mean whoring with the crew. Where have you been? You did not sleep in here last night."

She clutched at his hand, trying to pry herself free from him, "I did sleep here," she lied.

"It is nearly noon. I have been on board since nine. I came right to this cabin when I came on board. Now that I have had time to think about it, you were not in this cabin when I got back. I will ask you again, where have you been? In whose bunk did you sleep last night? I will cut out his heart." With that he threw her onto the floor. She got to her feet but did not answer his question. Instead she drew a small-bladed knife that Jean Luc had given her the night before. He had told her to keep it always to protect herself from Beaufort or anyone else who may chastise her. In return, she had secretly put her bracelet back into the pocket of his jacket as a token of her love.

Now she stood before Black brandishing the small blade. "I will not be manhandled by you," she said bravely.

He looked at the little blade and smiled without parting his lips.

"Where did you get that? Did he give it to you? Who is the man, Aubrey? Is it Jojoba?"

Her mouth dropped open. "Jojoba is my friend, nothing more." She moved toward the doorway, brandishing the weapon. He watched her as she opened the door.

"Where do you intend to go, Aubrey? I will find out who he is and he will die before your eyes. I hope that he was worth it. Then you will owe me," he chuckled evilly.

"I owe you nothing," she replied. She turned to leave as he lunged for her again. She ran down the corridor to the steps to the main deck. As she got halfway up the companionway, he grabbed her by the right ankle. She caught herself and kicked at him. He reached with his other hand to grab her at the knee but she struck out at him with the small blade. It cut into his forearm and with a roar of pain, he released her leg. She stumbled to the top and the blade slipped from her hand to clatter down the steps past him. Black was gathering himself up from the steps and saw her disappear out of sight as she ran onto the main deck.

Casting a glance around the deck, Aubrey set her eyes upon some nearby ratlines. She had seen the men climb up and down them before. It did not look that hard. She took off in a dead run to the ratlines. Setting one booted foot onto the ropes, she pulled up with all her might. It was not as easy as she thought. The distance between the lines was long and her legs barely reached. She struggled with every move as the lines swayed with her and the ship rocked on the seas. Glancing down, the height and the distance frightened her. Stopping to scan the deck to see where he was, she saw that Black had burst onto the deck and was looking for her.

It puzzled Black that she had gotten out of sight so fast. All the commotion had drawn the attention of some of the crew. He paused, looking at them, and then he followed the pointing fingers. Aubrey was halfway up to the fighting top on the foremast.

"Well, it becomes a monkey," he chuckled as he panted from the exertion of the chase. Black motioned for one of his men to climb the opposite ratline. As Aubrey pulled herself on to the wooden platform gasping for breath, she was distressed to find a man standing there waiting on her with his hands fisted on his hips and smiling at her.

Chapter 53

Jean Luc was at the stern of the ship when the commotion rose at the bow of the ship. He watched in disbelief as she started the climb to the fighting top. Then he saw Black storm angrily onto the deck behind her and stop. Fear clutched at his heart; they had been discovered.

Jean Luc began to make his way to the bow, pushing through the sea of curious men as they watched the scene unfold before them. He stopped for a moment to check on Aubrey. She was halfway up the lines, looking frightened and exhausted. Looking back at Black, he cursed when he saw the captain signal the man up the opposite side.

The man reached down and pulled Aubrey to her feet by one arm. She cried out in pain as he held her suspended over the edge by just her forearm. Effortlessly he brought her up to the planking of the fighting top. Despite the pain, fear, and exhaustion, Aubrey began to fight him as soon as her feet touched the wooden platform. Black called up from the deck below, "You might do well to be still, Mademoiselle. It is a long drop to the deck here and Michele might just let you go."

Now near the forecastle, Jean Luc kept an eye on Aubrey as Black walked up the steps to the quarterdeck. The pirate who held Aubrey called down in French to the captain, asking if he should bring her down.

Captain Black nodded, replying with a small smile, "Oh yes, please bring her down." He pulled his gloves on tighter.

The man on the fighting top put his arm around her waist. "You should not run from him, little one. It only angers him," Michele smiled. He tucked her against his side and reached out for a nearby line. He wrapped his foot and leg on the line and to her horror, he stepped off the fighting top. Their descent was fast and smooth. Michele carried her to Black, depositing her at his feet. Black stood over her, shaking his head and clicking his tongue. He poked her arm with the toe of his boot and tapped his long tapered fingers on the handle of his dirk.

"Should I cut you like you cut me with your ugly little blade? You never answered my question. Where did you get that thing anyway?" he droned in his deep voice. She scrambled to her feet and began to back away from him. Then he lunged forward and grabbed her by the front of the shirt again. He pushed her out at arm length. She felt the back of her thighs against the deck's side railing and she looked over her shoulder to see nothing but water below her. The ribbon in her hair, which had been worked loose in the

288

struggle, was caught by the wind and fluttered away into the sea. He spoke in English now as he shook her violently.

"You wanted to go overboard; then that is where I will put you, you little bitch." He held her in place by only the grasp of one hand.

"Put me over then, if you wish. You could hurt me no less by doing so. Better I should drown than surrender to you!" she told him defiantly.

He pulled her back toward him so closely that she could feel his breath on her face, and she could smell the rum that he had consumed in the cabin.

From behind him, she heard Jojoba easily plead for her. "Mon Capitaine, let her go. She is just a child." His voice was calm. Black seemed to ignore his first mate as he looked derisively over Aubrey.

"No, Jojoba, she is not a child, not anymore." Then he added in a low voice his eye caressing her partially exposed left breast. "Have you forgotten that you have already surrendered to me, Mademoiselle?"

"Have I then? Really?" she replied raising an eyebrow at him, the Irish drawl coming thickly.

"You belong to me and will be with no other man in this lifetime," he growled as he shook her again.

"I belong to no man, Monsieur," she replied evenly.

He took the back of his right hand and brought it up, striking her in the mouth. The blow he dealt her split her lip. With a growl, he threw her away from himself. She landed on the deck in a half-reclining position. He stood over her as she wiped blood from her lip and tried to scramble back away from him. Her retreat was cut short as she soon found herself tucked up under the gunwale of the ship and staring up at him with frightened hazel eyes. She looked at the blood on her hand. An unseen inner force took over and she started to rise.

"Bastard," she spat at him, droplets of blood spraying as the wound bled freely.

He reached out and pulled her up with his left hand this time. Jojoba came up the steps.

"Capitaine," he began again with a bit more firmness in his accented voice.

Black drew his pistol and pointed it at the Jamaican. "This is between her and me so I suggest you stay out of it. Or am I to assume that my suspicions are correct in that you are the one she has been whoring with?"

"Non, mon Capitaine, it is not I. I have not been with her," Jojoba said stiffly.

Black turned back to her and put the pistol away. He tore open the left front of her shirt, revealing the mark and thus exposing both breasts as well,

"This is the proof that you belong to me. Perhaps I should tie you to the mast for the day and put you on display for the benefit of the crew, so they are reminded to whom you belong. But then I will do that only after I have found your lover and tied him there as well, with his heart laying on the deck at his feet." She dangled in his grip like a rag doll. She had done something terrible. Jean Luc was in grave danger because of her. He shook her viciously once more. She looked up into his angry face with fear in her eyes now, a gripping fear that caused her response to freeze in her throat.

"Have you nothing to say now?" he bellowed. Suddenly, something made her say the words and she was alarmed at herself as they came out of her mouth so softly in the face of his rage.

"It is your mark, Monsieur, but you did not make the first mark to place it." He looked at her closely. She demanded herself not to reveal Jean Luc for the ruse, but she would not let Black go on with the thought that he had been the first to take her.

"No other man has marked you in this way," he finally said incredulously. Suddenly she was being thrown away from him. With the force, she fell onto the deck again. She scrambled to her feet, stumbling in her pain, as she moved to the steps that led down to the main deck. She clutched at the torn shirt with one hand to hold it closed against the many pairs of eyes that watched the scene.

Black cursed them in French and they disbursed to the lower part of the deck quickly, unwilling to invoke the anger of their captain on them. Jean Luc came up the quarterdeck steps purposefully and calmly. Black looked around at him as he drew nearer. There was a determined look in Jean Luc's blue eyes and he stepped up to where Aubrey knelt on the deck.

"What information can you offer me in light of this incident? You, who have been in charge of this ship in my absence? You, who seems to know all the comings and goings of the crew? Whom has she been whoring with?" Black growled.

Jean Luc was just a few feet from the man in black and said in a low voice, "Rene, let us take this discussion below."

"Non, we will not take this discussion below. We will discuss this here!" Black roared as he pointed a long finger at the deck to augment his demand. Jean Luc took a deep breath and he reached out to take Aubrey by the arm, gently pulling her to her feet. She continued to clutch at her shirt and she watched from one man to the other with apprehension. Jean Luc's voice was deep and quiet.

"I made the mark to give you the illusion that you had her. She does not want to be with you."

Black cocked his head and looked in disbelief at his quartermaster. His eye darted to the men on the decks below. They were watching in earnest, but did not appear to have heard the confession. Jean Luc gave Aubrey a gentle push past Black, taking her out of the close proximity of the enraged man.

Black was seething in the wake of the other man's words. He had claimed her as the Captain's woman–now he was told that his quartermaster had bedded her in his absence? This was a terrible embarrassment. Looking back, he noted that Aubrey was now pressed against the railing. Black turned back to Jean Luc and drew his rapier in one hand and his dirk in the other, nodding his head with a grim smile, "My own quartermaster, my friend. Where did this happen? In my bunk as well?"

Jean Luc merely stood his ground, looking from the drawn weapons, to Aubrey and then to Black.

"Whose whore does she want to be? Yours? I do not recall giving her the option," Black asked in deep-throated French.

"A whore is shared by many but she has chosen only one," Jean Luc said evenly and quietly as he met the angry look.

Black chuckled and readjusted the rapier in his right hand, looking at it thoughtfully. "Well, she made an unfortunate choice, n'est-ce pas, mon ami? Unfortunate for the pair of you." Jean Luc drew his own rapier for it was obvious that Black was serious in his stance. A movement in the corner of Jean Luc's eye showed him that Aubrey was on the move now.

"Rene, no," she gasped.

Aubrey was closing the distance between her and Black and Jean Luc noted that she had her hands out to shove at the captain from behind. Black saw Jean Luc's eyes dart to his left and braced himself. Aubrey slammed into him as if hitting a wall. With a growl, Black's left hand swung back to grab at her, forgetting that he held his dirk in the same hand. The point of his dirk caught and raked her just below the ribs on her right side, opening a slight gash.

Aubrey stepped back and away from Black. There was an odd burning sensation in her lower chest and she pressed her hand to that spot. Moving her hands and looking down, she let out a small cry of alarm. Her hands were covered in blood and a red stain was beginning to spread over one flap of the shirt that was now plastered wetly against her skin. Jean Luc watched in horror as her legs crumbled beneath her. She came to rest on her knees on the deck.

"Jean Luc," she whispered as she stared her bloodied hands.

Black turned his attention back to Jean Luc. "She is mine and when I

291

have finished with her, I will feed her to the sharks on the *Widow Maker*," Black said as he gestured to the men with his dirk that glistened in the sunlight with her blood.

"Then I will feed her to the ones in the sea," he finished. With a grim smile he added, "Unfortunately there will be one less 'shark' on board to feed since I suppose you have already been fed, mon ami," he glared down at Aubrey.

"Say adieu to Monsieur Pierne, my dear." With that, he lunged with his rapier at Jean Luc.

High in the crow's nest the lookout cried, "Ship ahoy! She flies the Union Jack."

With his weapon drawn, Jean Luc quickly parried the thrust by Black, but then something came down on the back of his head. Jean Luc crumpled to the deck as the blackness slowly replaced everything.

Black sheathed his weapons and reached down to grab Aubrey by one arm. As he pulled her to her feet he yelled, "Man the guns, turn her hard about. I do not want any broadsides." Handing Aubrey over to Jojoba, Black growled, "Take her below."

"Oui, mon Capitaine," the Jamaican replied as he picked Aubrey up into his arms.

"Put him in irons," Black ordered and jerked his head to indicate Jean Luc to some men near the quarterdeck steps.

There was the resounding crack of cannon fire and a ball crossed over the *Widow Maker*'s bow and splashed into the ocean.

Within minutes the pirate ship, out-gunning the British ship and moving twice as fast, had shortened the distance between the two and her guns were firing. As true to her name, the *Widow Maker* went to work to send the British ship and her crew to a watery grave.

Below, as the cannons rocked the ship, Jojoba tended to Aubrey. She was barely conscious from the loss of blood as he carefully pulled off the blood soaked shirt to survey the damage of Black's dirk. He drew his breath sharply through his teeth, "Oh ma petite, you should not have tested his rage."

The cut was fairly deep, but not fatal. After administering a tranquilizing herb to her, he cleaned the wound, stitched it and dressed it tightly with bandages wrapped around her to minimize the scarring. She drifted in and out of consciousness during the ordeal. Jojoba was pulling the covers up over her when Black came in, pulling off his gloves and taking off his hat.

"Will she live?" His question was uncaring as he poured a tankard of rum and took a long draught.

"Oui, she has lost a lot of blood and she will have a scar, but she will live," Jojoba replied. Black stood at the foot of the bunk, staring down at Aubrey.

"She is still just a child, Rene. She is a frightened child who tries every day to be brave. She feigned you off and chose another. You have had many women. Let dis one go, find Mala and..." Jojoba was saying.

"Get out," Black interrupted coldly. The first mate did as he was ordered, mumbling to himself in his native tongue.

"Jojoba," Black called out at the last moment, turning to the man.

"Oui, mon Capitaine?"

"Monsieur Pierne is to be marooned after we leave Bimini. The helmsman has the place marked on the charts where he is to be dropped."

"But he is your friend," Jojoba reminded him.

"Would you care to join him?" Black bellowed.

Jojoba clenched his teeth and answered, "Non, mon Capitaine."

"Then get out of here and do as you have been ordered!" Black growled. With a solemn nod, he exited the cabin, pulling the door closed behind him.

Chapter 54

Jean Luc awakened with his head pounding furiously. Even when he moved only his eyes, white-hot shards of pain coursed through his brain.

"Mon Dieu," he breathed as he tried to stand up. He was shackled at the wrists and ankles, pulled tightly against the bulkhead with only a foot or two of chain to spare. From the sounds and smells, he knew that he was deep in the bowels of the ship. He pulled against his entrapments then slumped back as the pain in his head overpowered him. His mind was fogged. Why was he here? How long had he been here?

The sight of Aubrey behind Black flashed in his mind. He remembered now. Black stood before him, enraged, brandishing his rapier and dirk. He saw Aubrey moving behind Black, and then she was on the deck, blood spreading over the front of her shirt.

"Aubrey," he moaned to the darkness. His mournful cry was answered by a low evil chuckle. Light from a hand-held lantern illuminated the area of his imprisonment.

"The last time I saw the little beauty, she was limp in the arms of that black bastard, Jojoba," came the smug monotone voice of Thomas Beaufort. Knowing of Jean Luc's dislike for the Jamaican man, Beaufort reveled at flaunting the information. Jean Luc did not want to feed Beaufort's need for chaos as he watched the man quietly. Beaufort set the lantern aside and informed him with a smile, "Black says if she lives, she is free game. She has scorned him and he no longer wants the bitch." Leaning lazily against the mast foot, Beaufort could feel the vibrations of the winds in the sails against his back as they traveled through this great mast that was sunk here deep in the bowels of the ship. He looked down upon Jean Luc with his close-set eyes and smiled cruelly.

"Was she worth it, Jean Luc? How many times did you lay her? Is she good?" Jean Luc clenched his teeth, determined not to answer. Beaufort leaned forward slightly, arms folded over his chest. "No need to answer that, I will find out myself. I will take her now, Jean Luc, and use her in ways that you never even dreamed of."

"She will not allow you!" Jean Luc exploded against the pain.

"She cannot stop me–little thing that she is," Beaufort smiled back with a shrug of his broad shoulders.

"I will not let you. I will spill your guts, Beaufort," Jean Luc growled.

"Indeed? From here?" Beaufort began with a chuckle. With arms crossed,

Beaufort leaned forward slightly and taunted, "Non mon ami, your gallantry will not help her this time. Why, you will not even be here to hear her squeal as she lies beneath me. And as for her newfound courage–that will not matter either. She will cower in my presence and will do whatever I tell her to. She does not have Black to run to anymore either." Jean Luc fought the chains to rise to his feet.

"Jojoba will protect her," Jean Luc growled, thankful that although he did not like the man, the Jamaican had seemed to take Aubrey under his protective wing as well with no returns required. With a guttural laugh, Beaufort kicked Jean Luc soundly in the stomach.

"Jojoba tends to her wound now, her rescuer as you say. Think about it, Jean Luc. He has his black hands all over her. But that is all right with me, I do not care because when she is up and about, I will kiss her scar for the pair of you. I will assume your position, both amid the crew and in the bed over her, while you rot on the island where Black puts you." Jean Luc raised pained blue eyes to stare at Beaufort.

"Non," he gasped.

"Aye–marooned, Jean Luc. That is the lot of the quartermaster for takin' the captain's woman to bed. But in a few days, she will belong to the new quartermaster–this quartermaster," Beaufort chuckled as he stabbed at his own chest with his thumb.

"I will kill you, you bastard!" Jean Luc spat as he struggled to his feet again.

"Indeed?" Beaufort sneered as he backhanded him. The blow sent Jean Luc's head slamming back into the bulkhead. Laughing, Beaufort picked up the lantern and left him in blackness again. Jean Luc went to his knees and hung his head, retching from the tremendous pain in the back of his skull. Slowly he slipped into unconsciousness again.

Jojoba had been tending to her wound for two days now. The crew had heard the reason for Jean Luc's imprisonment. Their knowledge had embarrassed and fueled Black's anger. He had been like a raging bull, throwing fear into the hearts of the crew by his mere presence.

"Jean Luc," Aubrey moaned painfully as he re-dressed the wound to her right side.

"Shh, ma petite. Do not call his name, it will anger de captain if he hears you," the Jamaican warned close to her ear.

"It hurts," she whimpered.

"I know, ma petite. Here drink dis," he soothed as he lifted her carefully and put a cup to her lips. She sipped the liquid and made a face. This would not have been his choice of medicines to give her, but he had been ordered to do so.

"Ah, Jojoba knows, it does not taste like de sugar cane but it will help to make you sleep."

She became suddenly active. "No! I do not want to sleep!" She was in tears.

He soothed her back down. "You do not feel de pain when you sleep, ma petite."

"No! I will not feel anything if I sleep. What if he comes? I am in his bunk–what if he..." Her pain-filled voice trailed off.

"Shh Aubrey. He will not do any'ting. You sleep now," Jojoba soothed as he covered her back up. The narcotic herb that he had given her as a tea worked quickly. Her eyes glazed over and she ceased to cry, slipping into a drug-induced slumber.

Black slammed into his cabin, banging the door against the wall upon his entry. The sound caused the relaxing Aubrey to jump even in her stupor. Jojoba clicked his tongue.

"Is she out?" Black growled.

"Oui, mon Capitaine, just as you asked," Jojoba nodded, his voice hinting of his disapproval.

"How long will she sleep like that?"

"She is so small, I was afraid to give her too much. She will sleep for de rest of de day and de night," Jojoba reported.

"Bon. Now, get out of here. Just before the next watch, gather all the crew on deck. There will be a vote for the new quartermaster," Black growled.

"Aye Capitaine, as soon as I pick up dis mess."

"Get out now, damn you!" Black bellowed.

The Jamaican left quickly, casting one last glance at his patient who was completely succumbed to the herb. Black had ordered him to drug her as deeply as he could and still keep her alive. Her breath came slowly, barely moving her chest up and down and her beautiful face was without expression. Jojoba moved through the corridor with sadness in his heart for her. Beaufort strode towards him and deliberately bumped against him as they passed.

"Watch where you are going, you black bastard," Beaufort growled. Jojoba offered him no reply save for a steady dark-eyed stare. A cold chill ran down his spine as Beaufort moved on–that would be the new quartermaster–and heaven help the frail little young woman in the captain's cabin when it came to pass. Beaufort had already spread the word about the ship that he had claimed possession of her.

Black took up his mug, filling it full with rum. He took a long draught and wiped his mustache. He stood at the foot of his bunk, staring dispassionately down at the unmoving body there. Jojoba had put a white shirt on her, but the front gaped open slightly and Black's eye rested on his mark on her left breast. The sight reminded him of Mala. Why had Mala rejected him? Why had Mala allowed him to believe that she was dead all this time? He had missed her beside him. She was the woman he wanted but she spurned him and her behavior in Bimini left him baffled, disconcerted and wounded.

Returning to the *Widow Maker*, Black found out that another woman had rejected him and had chosen Jean Luc, his friend. Unable to come up with answers concerning Mala's behavior as well as the embarrassment of being duped by Aubrey, Black could not think clearly. As the severely beaten Jean Luc was being dragged up on deck to be placed in the longboat, Beaufort had approached him to lay claim on Aubrey, but Black had not replied. For the first time in his life, Black was unnerved to find that he could not make a sound and quick decision. He had turned from the man with a growl and walked away.

Moving now to the great quarter gallery window, he watched with a grim look on his face as his longboat, the *Cay*, pulled away from the ship. Two men rowed the boat strongly on a course for the small island that lay just beyond. A third man held a pistol on the fourth man in the boat. Black looked upon the badly beaten face of a man that had been his friend for as long as he could remember and, with a deep sigh, he drained his mug and turned away from the window.

Two of the men dragged Jean Luc from the boat. They dragged him through the surf but the moment his feet hit the sand of the beach, he lashed out. It was not a matter of pride and honor anymore. It was a matter of survival–his survival. A swift punch in the stomach caused him to cease his fight. He was dumped onto the sand, face first. The third man laid items in the sand nearby and the three of them pushed the boat back into the surf, then hopped in.

Jean Luc struggled to his feet, watching the boat pull swiftly away.

"Do not do this, Rene!" he cried out to the ship. He watched as the boat grew smaller in the distance. Kicking at the sand, he cursed against the wind, "Mon Dieu, Rene! Do not leave me!"

With shoulders slumped in defeat, he watched as the sails unfurled on the ship and she started to tack away from the island.

"Aubrey, ma chérie, what have I done?" he moaned as he dropped back to his knees.

The vote was over and Beaufort was now the quartermaster by an almost unanimous decision. The man was in the galley, gloating over his success. With the help of Boulet and LaVoie, Beaufort managed to intimidate the crew to vote him as quartermaster.

Black sat at his desk putting down the day's events in his log. He had committed a sentence of death to his quartermaster–moreover–his friend. But there could be no change in heart or mind on the situation–pirate justice must prevail to keep his command. This would be the second of two burdens he would carry until fate dealt him death's hand. He looked over at the young woman in his bunk, remembering that a decision at the expense of another young woman had been the reason for his first burden.

Aubrey did not interest him in the least. When she was up and about, he would be rid of her. Mala was the only woman he wanted. Yet, now that he had found that she was alive, she scorned him. Finishing his entry in the log, he took up his mug and drained it. With a frown, he looked at his bunk and the young woman laying in it. He imagined her and Jean Luc lying together there and he snapped his logbook shut angrily. Casting his eye on Aubrey as he stood, he noted how she looked like a body laid out after death. Her face was nearly as white as the sheets she laid upon and she was completely without expression or movement. Putting on his hat and pulling on his gloves, he left the cabin.

Thomas Beaufort checked the location of his captain. Black was on the quarterdeck with the helmsman and the new navigator, looking at the charts. Beaufort watched as the dark-haired man raised a long glass to gaze in the direction of the island that grew ever smaller. Looking for the Jamaican, Beaufort found him on the main deck. A thin smile crossed over Beaufort's lips–she was alone.

Beaufort easily made his way to the companionway and slipped down the steps. At the doorway to the great cabin, he laid his hand on the latch and looked around to see if anyone was coming along before he slipped inside and shut the door quickly. The cabin was still and quiet as the sun streamed through the windows of the quarter gallery.

Jojoba had his patient nestled comfortably in the bunk on her back with her arms down along her sides. The sheet was tucked neatly around her slim frame, outlining it perfectly. Her breath came so easily that it was hard to tell from a distance if she was even breathing at all. Beaufort took in the scene before him as he slowly advanced toward the bunk.

Pulling off his gloves as his eyes surveyed her, he ran his knuckles along the line of her jaw on the right side of her face. She did not move. Beaufort noticed that she appeared to be heavily drugged. The backs of his long slender fingers skimmed down her throat and he caught his fingers in the lapel of the shirt. With a lewd smile on his face, he turned his hand palm down and ran it over her right breast beneath the shirt. Even in her drugged state, the nipple responded to the touch of his hand. He smiled in approval, slipping his hand over her chest to caress her other breast. Beaufort froze in place at the sound of a cocking pistol.

"What are you doing in here?" came Black's deep voice from the doorway.

Beaufort had not even heard the man enter. He removed his hand from her ever so slowly, hoping that his own body had blocked Black's view and that the dark haired man had not seen him touch the girl. He also hoped that he would not hear the unmistakable split-second click that preceded the firing of the weapon. Turning slowly, he smiled almost sheepishly, spreading his hands in explanation, "I–ah–heard her cry out, Captain. Thinking that she was in distress, I was coming to her aid. But then I find that she is only crying out in her sleep." Black watched him, still holding the pistol on him, as Beaufort casually pulled on his gloves. With a shrug, Beaufort continued, "I think that I heard her call out for Jean Luc."

Black's stolid gaze wavered and Beaufort could tell that his remark had struck a nerve. He smiled inwardly, pleased with his accomplishment.

"Get out of my cabin," Black growled. With a slight mocking bow and never taking his eyes off those of his captain, Beaufort strode out as if he had not a care in the world. Black stepped aside, still brandishing the pistol, and watched the man in his retreat out the door. Looking at Aubrey, he sneered and slipped the pistol back into his sash before moving to the desk.

Chapter 55

Three days later and no longer being drugged, Aubrey finally had enough strength to get up and move about on her own. Black refused to speak to her whenever he was in the cabin. When their eyes met, he would regard her with a cold stare and she returned it with look of defiance. Confined to the great cabin, Jojoba brought her meals and tended to her wound.

"Jojoba?" she asked after an extended silence between them.

"Oui, ma petite?" he answered as he finished the dressing.

"Where is Jean Luc?"

The Jamaican got up and began to gather up the items that he had used, but did not answer. She watched him in silent anticipation of his reply but when he did not answer, she caught his hand and asked again, "Jojoba, where is Jean Luc?" Her question came in worried tones.

"He is down below," he replied and his voice sounded unsure.

A look of panic crossed her face. "No, he is not! Rene killed him!"

"No, I have told you he is down below, the captain did not kill him, ma petite," he soothed. Jojoba hated to lie to her. Jean Luc would most certainly not survive on the island where Black had marooned him, but the captain did not kill him, not outright.

Aubrey sighed, drawing his attention back. "What will he do with me now?" she asked quietly.

Jojoba looked at her sadly. "I do not know. Capitaine Black, he is very angry. I best be getting back to my duties." Without another word, he left the cabin.

While she was alone in Black's quarters, Aubrey made use of the privacy by washing her hair and cleaning up after her five-day period of infirmary. She was brushing her hair when Black came into the room. He went straight to his desk and sat down, opening his logbook. The little bit of activity after such a long time of being down made her tired, so she lay on the bunk and closed her eyes. Finally, she opened her eyes again and looked up at the ceiling, asking aloud, "Why do you keep me here, Rene?"

"Because you are my property. You will remain on board my ship until I decide what I want to do with you," he replied coldly. She could tell that he did not even look up from his writing.

"I know that you keep Jean Luc below; let me have his cabin," she said as she still stared at the ceiling.

"Where do you get your information, who has been talking to you? Another lover perhaps?" he asked as he shut the log carefully.

"No, there is no lover and you know it. I am no more than a prisoner here and I have been in this bunk unable to move, thanks to you." she spat.

"Do not blame that on me. It was your choice that put you there. You are sadly mistaken if you think that I would honor your wish and give you quarters of your own. Do you think that you are so privileged?" Black said as he stood from the desk. As he neared the bunk, he continued, "While you have caused me great embarrassment in the eyes of my crew, you will remain here."

"They say that Monsieur Beaufort is telling everyone that I am to be his," she said in a small voice then added as she looked up at him. "Please do not give me to him."

"I have not made such an announcement. But when I make my decision, you will have to learn to live with it," Black replied coolly as he stood over her now.

"You may have back your bunk, Monsieur. Merci for the use of it during my recovery. Merci also for the lovely scar. I shall cherish it always," she said curtly. He chuckled evilly and like a flash, his hand shot out to catch her by the front of her shirt. He dragged her from the bunk and up onto her feet.

"To maintain your safety among the crew, and because I would not want anything to happen to you, you will stay in this cabin unless I take you out," he told her.

She struggled in his grasp. "Why should you care about me?"

"I no longer care about you but you will continue to share my bed as well to maintain the affirmation with the crew that you are my property." His voice hinted of anger as he ignored her question.

"I will not sleep with you. I had no choice before, because I was drugged senseless. But I will not get into that bunk beside you Monsieur!" she spat.

"Rest assured, Mademoiselle, although you will sleep with me, I have no intentions of actually bedding you. Surely you know the difference by now," he taunted.

"How would the crew know where I sleep once that door is closed? Or do you make it a habit to share your nocturnal business with them?" she spat in growing anger of her own. He dealt her an open-handed slap to her face for the reply.

"I do not believe that you understand, Mademoiselle. I hold your life in my hands," he began in warning. "Your scar is unfortunate, but I hope that it will not affect the price," he added smugly. Then he shrugged and continued, "But it is easily hidden until you are undressed." He released her

301

and moved back to the desk to sit down.

Aubrey tearfully dabbed her lip with the back of her hand where a cut bled freely.

"What do you mean? What price?" she asked carefully.

"The price I will be asking for you from the Captain of the *Artemis*," he replied calmly.

"The what?" Aubrey asked.

"The *Artemis*. She is a slave ship," he said as he dipped his quill into the ink well and began to write again.

"A slave ship? You are going to sell me to a slave ship?" she asked in disbelief as she approached the desk. Black merely raised his eyes to look at her then back down to his pages. His mind reeled with her questions. Dealing with a slaver was against his morals but it had been the only alternative.

"You bastard," she spat as she threw herself away from the desk.

Black set down his quill and watched her move away. She had grown a great deal from the polite young girl he had brought on board so many weeks ago. He mused on how he had been far more gentlemanly with her than with any other woman he had known with the exception of Mala. Aubrey had only been a distraction from his pining for the island woman. Mala!

A vision of Mala came to him like a haunting dream in the daylight hours. A fire burned through him at the thought of the island woman. The heat of desire pooled in his groin as he recalled the long nights and days long past of delicious intimacy between them. Mala had learned much from him and apparently had gone on to learn much more, for now she appeared to be a respected and revered pirate captain. For a few moments, he had forgotten that Aubrey was even there and had it not been for her movement, he may have gone on thinking and wondering about Mala for hours. Aubrey had sat down heavily on the settee.

"I will sleep here," she said firmly.

It was a sentence that had been spoken by her that first night on board and he had honored the wish. This time, he laughed at her. "Do you have a hearing problem that I am unaware of? You will sleep in the bunk as I have told you." Aubrey merely looked at him with a wounded expression on her face.

Several days later, Aubrey sat at the long table in the great cabin picking over her afternoon meal. Black was gone from the cabin, attending to their mooring in the cove of one of the islands back in the chain they called Bimini. Black had been telling her these past days about the *Artemis* and her captain. The man's name was Rosset and he was French. Aubrey wondered how she could get herself out of this predicament. The thought of yet another ship's captain scared her, but Black was not listening to her, either.

Sitting quietly at the table dressed in a beige silk dress that had come from some recent plunder, Aubrey shoved the plate away with a moan of distress. The door snapped open, causing her to yelp in mild alarm. Black entered and looked at her objectively, "That is much better. I would not want to take you to an audience with Captain Rosset dressed as a cabin boy. Come with me." Aubrey found herself being pulled to her feet as he caught her by the upper arm. She remained quiet until they reached the deck, hoping that he was only tormenting her with his threats.

Aubrey was distressed to see a small galleon moored across the cove. Her masthead was carved with a scene depicting hills in the background and trees in the foreground. *Artemis*–the Goddess of forests and hills. Aubrey thought to herself, it was a sign of the person who was captain of the ship. To decorate his ship so ornately was a clear sign of his apparent egotistical nature. Aubrey tugged at Black's sleeve as the long boat was being lowered into the water, pleading softly, "Rene, s'il vous plait, do not do this."

"Je regrette, Mademoiselle, but I cannot have you aboard any longer. Into the boat with you," he said with a grim smile. Aubrey's breath caught in suppressing a sob. She flinched then drew back as two men from the crew stepped forward.

"Mind your manners with the men, they mean only to put you in the boat, otherwise, you will answer to me. Also be warned that you will be no less than the proper young woman that you are when we are in the presence of Captain Rosset," he told her as he nodded to the railing. Aubrey gathered her skirts and moved closer to the railing. Two of the men assisted her over the side and held her until she had secured her footing on the rope ladder. She descended slowly and felt another man take her by the waist to pluck her from the ladder to set her on her feet in the boat. Black followed behind her and sat across from her in the small craft.

All too soon they were climbing the ladder of the other ship. Black had gone aboard first and he was at the side to bring Aubrey aboard. He held her against him as he and the Captain of the *Artemis* exchanged pleasantries. Despite her hatred of Black, Aubrey found comfort in the feel of his body against hers in this new and intimidating environment. She watched Captain Rosset in silence, thinking he was no more than two score years of age with dark short-cropped hair and brown eyes. He was not unattractive, but she did not like the way he looked at her. It reminded her of Monsieur Beaufort.

"Shall we go to my quarters, Rene?" the man was asking as he indicated a doorway set in the bulkhead of the quarterdeck.

The quarters were not nearly as grand as Black's as the two men seated with wine and Aubrey was stood at the right side of Black's chair. Speaking in French, Rosset began the conversation as he cast his eyes over Aubrey. "Shall I pour some wine for the lady?"

"Non," Black replied. Aubrey stood staring at the floor, wishing she were somewhere else.

"So, Rene, how is the pirating business?"

"Business is good," Black nodded.

"I am surprised that you have come aboard my ship," Rosset said with a thin smile.

Black easily tapped his gloves on his thigh and cast a glance up at Aubrey, "I have a business proposition for you."

"Vraiment? And what would that be? Do you have some natives in the hold of the *Widow Maker* that you wish to sell?" Rosset asked as he poured their now empty glasses full once more. Black downed the contents of his glass and Aubrey looked up to see the muscles in his jaw tighten.

"Non. I have brought with me what I wish to sell," he replied as he set down the glass and waved his hand to Aubrey.

Raising a brow with sudden interest, Rosset reassessed the woman. "She is a very attractive young woman, nice waistline and hips. Not very buxom though. Where is she from?"

"Her home was England, but she is of Irish blood," Black replied.

"Hmm, a Celt," Rosset muttered as he stood from his desk chair. Aubrey remained rooted in place next to Black as the man approached.

"How old are you?" Rosset asked. Aubrey looked at him but remained silent until Black cleared his throat, a definite signal for her to respond.

"Ten and nine years, sir–nearly a score," she replied, her voice replete with fear. Rosset leaned closer to her and she bit her lip, staring into his brown eyes.

"How nearly a score? You look like a little girl."

"In the winter, sir," Aubrey said tightly.

Rosset laughed and went back to his desk, and resumed the conversation in French, "She is very polite, Rene. Where did you get her, from a convent?"

Black chuckled as well, "Non, I took her from the merchant ship the *Gull* a few months ago."

Rosset's eyes lit up at the mention of the ill-fated ship, "Oh yes, one of the merchant ships from Peyton's fleet. I deal with him sometimes. They say the ship must have met with an unfortunate accident. She never made her destination to Africa." Aubrey silently watched the two men in conversation.

"Hmm, unfortunate indeed. She took on too much water about a week out of port and went right to the bottom. Much of her cargo was salvaged as we just happened to be in the area," Black replied. The two men looked at one another before laughing at the crude joke. Rosset pursed his lips as he looked at Aubrey.

"Just happened to be in the area, of course. But Rene, only one poor soul was saved?"

Black nodded with a feigned expression of remorse as well.

"Well then, she was the lucky one. You have had her aboard this long, Rene. Pray why do you wish to part with her?" Rosset asked as he leaned across the desk. Then he added, "She looks very fresh. Was she not good, Rene?"

Aubrey felt her face redden with embarrassment.

Black ran a gloved hand down along her lower back and over her bottom. "She was fine, James."

"Strong and healthy? Does not get seasick?" Rosset queried on.

"She is strong enough for a woman. She has never demonstrated a tendency to the illness. She has a fiery temper though and she pouts frequently–and I might add, James, she speaks French," Black reported as he continued to pat her bottom. He could tell by her posture that she wanted to explode with anger and move from his reach, but she stayed in her place as directed. Black chuckled low in his throat and patted her again just for spite.

"What is your asking price, Rene? If she is as good as you say, I may want her myself," Rosset said as he leaned back in his chair.

"I thought that you might. I am asking three hundred pounds for her," Black replied. Aubrey shot alarmed hazel eyes to look down at him. He was really going through with this!

"A steep price, Rene. Given your attitude toward slaves, I find it odd that you are marketing her as such. If you have tired of her, why not just give her to one of your crew? What about your quartermaster? That is to whom I generally give a woman when I have tired of her." Rosset said as he propped his feet up on the desk. Aubrey stared at the highly polished boots. She felt as Black's hand slipped farther down her skirts. His hand came to a stop at the back of her left thigh, and he crushed a handful of the satin material in his fist. She glanced down at him for the question had opened a deep wound between the pair of them.

"I cannot choose favorites on my ship. There is more than one man among my crew who would like to have her. To save a fight, I have decided to sell her," Black said thickly as he dropped the handful of material before he leaned forward to pick up his glass and drain it. Smacking his lips, he set the glass down and nodded at Rosset.

"That is my decision and my offer. Take it or leave it."

Rosset looked her over again, "Hmm. Why not leave her here the night and let me try her out. I will give you my decision in the morning." The comment was more than Aubrey could stand. She stepped back toward Black's chair a bit closer, her bottom now resting against the crook of his arm.

"Captain," she whispered hoarsely as she looked down at him with imploring hazel eyes.

Black pushed her slightly away with his other hand and stood, clapping on his hat, "Non, James, she will return to the *Widow Maker* with me. There will be no 'free sampling' of my property. If you decide that you want her for the price I have asked, send your quartermaster over in a longboat with the notes and she will be sent back with him." Aubrey thought that she might faint with relief.

Rosset stood and tugged at his waistcoat, chuckling, "Very well, Rene. I will give my reply in the morning."

Chapter 56

The ride back to the *Widow Maker* was a quiet one, for Aubrey felt sickened at the thought of being sold. She stared at Black in the growing darkness and she could not comprehend that he would go through with such an act. He remained seated in the longboat and waved a gloved hand for her to precede him up the ladder to the *Widow Maker*. Two men caught her under the arms and lifted her up to set her easily onto the deck.

Black allowed her to precede him into the cabin. As he shut the door and took off his hat and gloves, he looked up to see that she was slowly unbuttoning the front of the dress. He raised an eyebrow to her apparent undressing in front of him as opposed to hiding behind the screen as she normally did.

"Are you about to make me an offer for your freedom, Mademoiselle?" he asked with a thin smile.

"I am not a slave to be bought and sold," she said tightly as she peeled the dress down off her shoulders. He moved to the table, watching her from the corner of his eye as she removed the dress. Sitting in his chair and crossing his long legs, he cast his eye over her. She now stood before him in a cotton chemise. His dark eye came to rest on his mark that was clearly visible with the low neckline of the undergarment.

"Then what are you doing? You have never undressed yourself so blatantly before me, Mademoiselle," he said as he reached out to pour himself a tankard of rum.

"I am getting out of these clothes, Monsieur. Should Captain Rosset send his boat on the morrow for me, I will go dressed as I have lived on this ship," she replied as she left the dress in a heap in the floor and picked up her shirt and britches. Black chuckled as she finally went behind the dressing screen.

"Captain Rosset will make you wear dresses to show off your attributes even when he does not have them bared for his pleasure, which will undoubtedly be most of the time. He does not want a little boy."

"Well, apparently the way he talks, my attributes leave much to be desired in his eyes," she spat as she emerged from the screen tucking in the shirt. Aubrey flounced down onto the settee and Black came to his feet. She watched his approach and did not move as he sat easily beside her.

"A minor problem I am certain that he will get over. I would have." He reached out and stroked his fingers along the side of her throat. "James prides himself on how savage he is in his lovemaking. I think that you have a lot in store for you."

Aubrey angrily brushed his hand away and hissed through clenched teeth, "Leave me alone. You are all animals." Black chuckled and got up from the settee, leaving her in her own thoughts for the remainder of the evening.

The bell sounding for the change of the watch woke her. Aubrey inhaled deeply and looked around the darkened cabin. Black lay next to her, his back to her, sleeping soundly. Lightning flashed, illuminating the cabin for a split second. Aubrey loved thunderstorms, despite the terrible havoc they played on ships according to the stories that Black and Jean Luc had told. She slipped easily from the bunk and went to the quarter gallery windows to watch the storm.

A flash of lightning lit the cove as she peered into the following darkness; she knew that something was not right. Another flash illuminated the area. Aubrey's heart leapt, for the *Artemis* was gone and nothing but open waters lay all around them. Then a shudder ran through her body as she looked back to the bunk and the sleeping man. Had Black left her last night, she would be gone with the *Artemis* now. Slipping to her knees on the floor, she crossed herself and thanked God for her fortune–if it could be called as such. Silently, she slipped back into the bunk, laying awake for hours elated at the fact that she would not be sold as a slave to Rosset, but wondering now what Black would do with her.

Black roused from his sleep at his usual early dawning hour. Aubrey slept peacefully with her back turned to him. After shaving and dressing, he left the cabin to go to the main deck. The air was fresh and hinted of the rain the night before. He had not even heard the storm as he had slept. Inhaling deeply, he turned to look in the direction where Rosset's ship had been moored the day before while in the pit of his stomach he wished that it would not be there. His jaw dropped slack when he discovered that it was not.

"Jojoba! When did the *Artemis* weigh anchor?" he called to his first mate.

"I do not know. She was gone when I awoke dis mornin."

Black pounded his fist lightly on the railing. Had he left her there last night, he would have been duped today. Looking down at the water, a thoughtful look crossed his face. It was for the best that he had not left her because on the boat trip back, he had decided against selling her. As Rosset had pointed out, given his aversion to slave traders, he could not have gone through with the deal. He had planned to back out of the deal and tell Rosset that he had decided to keep her after all. He would then put her ashore somewhere and be rid of her in that manner.

The absence of the *Artemis* this morning made the matter much easier. He would tell Aubrey that he had changed his mind and it would look like his idea. Smiling to himself, he turned from the railing. The smile faded from his lips as he found himself staring down the barrel of a pistol. On the other side of the pistol stood a British Naval officer.

"Drop your weapons, Captain. By order of the King, you are under arrest for piracy against the Crown."

Rene Black had been here before. He surrendered his weapons without hesitation as he heard the officer order another officer, "Weigh anchor and drop her sails; bring this vessel and her crew alongside our ship."

Some British sailors stood guard over the crew as Black realized that he had been duped but in a different way. He would kill Rosset for this betrayal!

Black was ushered off his ship and into an awaiting longboat then they shoved off. The other officer left on the *Widow Maker* turned back to the small party of British sailors barking out orders.

One of the sailors held Beaufort by his arm as Jojoba stood at bay at the hand of another sailor with a pistol. The two pirates looked at one another then in unison, broke free of their captors, shouting to the men to come to arms and oppose the intruders.

The inexperienced young officer, frightened out of his wits, fell quickly under the hands of the much more seasoned and brutal pirates of the *Widow Maker*.

"Weigh anchor and drop our sails, bring her about as the British bastard ordered but when ya do, bear down on them with our guns. She will not take us or our captain without a fight!" Beaufort bellowed.

Aubrey stirred in her sleep. She opened her eyes as she laid facing Black's side of the bunk. He was gone–probably on deck. Stretching languidly she wondered what his reaction had been when he had gone topside and found that the *Artemis* was gone.

Suddenly the *Widow Maker* rocked to the percussion of her cannons. Aubrey sat bolt upright and listened to the silence of the lull. There was another thunderous sound and a cannonball skidded by the quarter gallery windows taking out a great portion of the top of them. Glass and wood showered the room and she leapt from the bunk with a scream. Grateful that she had slept in her clothing, she sprinted from the cabin, then out into the corridor with another shriek as another ball crashed into the room this time. On impact, fire was lit in several places about the cabin.

The deck seemed to be a mass of confusion. Both Jojoba and Beaufort were calling orders, and guns were firing. Aubrey ran to Jojoba, ducking and covering her head as pieces of metal from exploding balls rained on the deck.

"Jojoba! What is happening? Where is Captain Black?" she shouted in fear.

"Go below before you are injured!" he yelled at her as he tried to push her away.

"No! Where is the captain?" she pressed on as she hung on his muscular arm. Before he could answer, another ball whistled through the air close to them. Jojoba threw her down on the deck and fell over her, shielding her from the raining debris. They had no sooner hit the deck than he was pulling her to her feet, his face masked in deep concern.

"We have got to get you off of de ship," he said in a strained voice as he pulled her along to the railing.

"What?"

"We are out gunned, ma petite, it is no use," he moaned.

"But where is Rene? What about Jean Luc? He is still in the hold!" she asked as he came to stop at the port side with her.

"You have to go now. It is for your safety. Dey will not be kind to you if dey get you," he said as he picked her up into his arms.

"What are you doing?" she squealed clutching at him with her arms about his thick neck. Something warm, wet and sticky was on her arm. She drew it back to see that it was covered with blood. Touching her hand to the back of his neck with a look of horror on her face, she found that he was seriously wounded. He had taken a chunk of metal in the back of his neck when he had shielded her from the last blast.

"I will put you over de side, ma petite," he began as he held her over the edge.

"I cannot swim," she cried.

"You must now–for Jojoba. When you hit de water, kick your legs and pull with your arms. Dere are sandbars about. When you get to one, you run–run as fast as you can, Aubrey."

"Where is Jean Luc?" she cried one last time.

He shook his head sadly, kissed her tenderly on the cheek and let her drop calling weakly, "Swim, ma petite, swim."

Aubrey was at the mercy of the ocean. She had surfaced with a gasp. Somewhere high above and far away as if it were a voice from the Heavens, she heard Jojoba yell in a strained voice, "Swim, Aubrey! Kick your feet–reach with your arms."

She went under and resurfaced, trying desperately to do as he directed. She looked up one time when she surfaced but Jojoba was not there at the railing anymore. She felt herself being pulled now by the water. Clutching to a piece of driftwood, a sense of hopelessness descended upon her and Aubrey slowly gave in to the water, exhausted.

The surf was pushing her inland. She lost her hold on the wood planking and tumbled over and over, scraping and bumping along the sand. Suddenly a pair of hands plucked her from the water. Aubrey looked up at her rescuer breathlessly. He was a pirate no doubt, but not one that she recognized as being from Black's crew. He was considerably older with graying hair streaked with hints of red. The man pulled her further up onto the beach.

"There now lass, old Willie has ye now." She recognized the accent as Welsh. He held her gently as she went through the throes of coughing and throwing up seawater. Aubrey lay half in his lap as he sat on the beach. She looked up into his face and found eyes that were twinkling and kind. He seemed to be ignoring her as he scanned the sea.

"She be comin' fer us soon, now that the commotion is just 'bout over." He was talking almost to himself.

Aubrey exhaled in exhaustion. Please God, not another pirate ship. She had her fill of them now. Remembering the battle on the *Widow Maker*, she gathered up all the strength she could manage and pushed herself out of his arms. He watched her crawl shakily to her feet.

"Where are ye goin', lass?"

"The *Widow Maker*," she murmured. She could hear the resounding cracks of cannon fire over the pounding surf.

"Jean Luc," she muttered quietly as she went down on her knees in the sand with a mournful cry. A wave washed around her, almost knocking her down. Willie caught her as she tried to get up a third time, sputtering water.

"Here lass, ye been out to sea a long time. Ye ain't got yer land legs yet." He lifted her up to her feet and steadied her there.

"What are ye fussin about?"

"The *Widow Maker*," she said again.

"Aye, she still over there. What is left of her, Old Cap'n Black's ship. She was a might pretty one," he nodded. She followed the direction of his pointing finger.

"Was?" she echoed.

Just as she caught sight of the ship that had been her home and prison these past many weeks, she saw the big ship take a cannon blast from an oncoming British warship. Smoke belched from the side as the *Widow Maker* fired back. There was another blast from the warship and Aubrey watched in horror as the main mast of the *Widow Maker* cracked in two. It seemed that the mast and the sails fell in slow motion to the deck.

Aubrey fell to her knees despite the old man's hold on her and her voice was barely audible, "Oh my God, Jean Luc!"

Willie clicked his tongue and shook his head sorrowfully. "Broke her good they did, tis done fer now." Aubrey turned to look at him. Something on the ocean behind him caught her eye. Noting her gaze, he turned, then let out a yell of exuberance and his hand shot up into the air.

"Ahoy! Over here!" It was a longboat with six people in it. Four men rowed strongly and soon the boat was on shore and some of the people inside were walking toward them. Willie helped her up again.

"Ye see, what did I tell ye, lass? We be fine now, the Cap'n is here."

Aubrey wrenched herself free and stumbled down the beach, her eyes on the *Widow Maker* as she moved. The *Widow Maker* took hit after hit from the British warship until the pirate ship leaned to her starboard side.

"Stop!" she screamed at the British ship, knowing full well that they could not hear her but it was too late anyway. She finally collapsed to her knees in the surf again.

"Oh my God!" she cried out in desperation. A wave slammed into her but she managed to stay up as she watched the horrifying scene as it unfolded before her on the ocean.

Chapter 57

The party from the longboat was coming up the beach. Two men had broken away from the group and were coming toward her and the old man. Aubrey paid no attention to them, her eyes riveted to the ocean. Standing once more she set off stumbling further into the surf. The British ship still pounded the pirate ship although she was no longer firing back. The *Widow Maker* was almost flat on the sea on her side.

"Jean Luc!" Aubrey sobbed. Good, I will die with Jean Luc. Take me now. She thought to herself as she surrendered to the surf that rolled her again and again. As blissful unconsciousness began to seep over her, strong hands plucked her from the water again. Aubrey's eyes fluttered open to find a different man over her as he pulled her back onto the beach. Two other people were standing over her, but the sun shining from behind them prevented her from seeing them clearly. The rescuer cradled her as she coughed up water again. One of the two standing over her leaned down and reached out toward her but did not touch her.

"See Robert, I tol' ya twas Black's ship," came the drawl of a Scotsman's accent.

"Well, he is at the bottom of the cove now," came the British accented reply of the man called Robert as he held Aubrey.

"This is not a good sign, Mr. Deats," Robert went on as he nodded down to Aubrey. Her shirt was hanging open and off her left shoulder. Much of Aubrey's left breast was exposed to reveal Black's mark.

"Jesus Christ, how many of them has he marked like that?" the Scotsman spat as he looked down on the mark.

"If the Captain sees this..." the Englishman said as he began to pull Aubrey's shirt closed.

"Leave it, let the Captain see," Deats growled.

The conversation between the two men fell in faraway voices on Aubrey's ears. The sound of her pounding heart, the crashing surf in her head coupled with her physical exhaustion and her feeling of defeat pushed her into a mental abyss. Dear God, how she wanted to die!

The two men now directed their attention to another person who was coming down the beach toward them in a slower pace. The old man who had plucked Aubrey from the surf the first time was beside this new person. He was chattering with much animation, although the new person seemed to be preoccupied with watching the *Widow Maker* intently.

The big pirate ship had uprighted herself now as if she was rising from the dead. She held steady for several long moments. The two men on the beach watched the ship as well. Old Willie had stopped chattering and his wizened eyes shifted from the ship to the captain.

The ocean breeze caught wisps of long dark hair, making it undulate like the waves beyond the breakers. The wind-pressed red silk shirt molded like a second skin over shapely breasts. Mala's face was without expression as she watched the seemingly resurrected ship in the cove. But each blast the pirate ship took made her flinch inwardly.

Suddenly, as if pulled down by the giant hand of Neptune himself, the *Widow Maker* went straight down. With one last feeble flap, the Jolly Roger disappeared under the waves. Had any of the men been closer they might have seen the flash of sadness in the dark eyes or the slight quiver of the proud chin. But no one saw it and the emotion came so fleetingly. Mala did not want anyone to see. Deats, on the other hand, was smiling. The demise of the *Widow Maker* was a very pleasing sight to the Scotsman.

"Captain," the Scotsman called as he turned toward her, still smiling. The beautiful island woman closed her eyes and opened them slowly as if to compose a show of emotion that she refused to succumb to.

Mala took a deep breath, pulled her boarding gloves on a bit tighter and said, "Yes, Mr. Deats?" As she took a few steps closer, the Scotsman, now devoid of the smile, stepped aside and extended an open-palmed gesture toward Aubrey who still lay exposed and prone in Robert's lap.

Mala had noted that her men seemed to be hovering over a body on the shore. Now that she thought back on it, Willie had been prattling on about a young woman he had found in the surf. But Mala's head hurt today and her mind had been preoccupied with the battle between the two ships in the cove and she had not been listening to Willie.

Now with Deats' presentation, she was forced to check out the situation. She stepped a bit closer and gazed stoically down upon the auburn-haired woman who was draped in the lap of her second mate. Her dark eyes drifted to rest upon the mark on Aubrey's exposed breast. The Scotsman seemed to be fidgeting in his place in great anticipation of an order or reaction of some kind but Mala remained silent.

Finally, the wait and Mala's silence was more than he could stand. "What do ye wanna do with her?"

Agitating him more, Mala ignored him and looked at Robert instead. Her dark eyes met with his and asked, "Is she alive, Robert?" Robert opened his mouth to speak, but the Scotsman spoke up first.

"Captain, we must be getting back ta the ship before the British discovers the *Enchantress* and does the same thing ta her." He jerked his head toward the sea where the *Widow Maker* had gone down. Mala looked out toward the cove before looking back to Robert.

"Aye, she is alive," he told her with a nod. Mala turned on her heel, but not before casting one last glance at the spot out on the water where the pirate ship had gone down. Deats stood staring after her.

"Close her shirt, Robert, and put her in the *Witch*," Mala said over her shoulder as she continued away from them.

"Aye, Captain," Robert nodded as he pulled the shirt closed over Aubrey's chest and came up off the sand with the featherweight form in his arms. The Scotsman clicked his tongue and hurried to catch up with his captain.

"Mala," he began. The dark eyes darted sideways toward him, flashing an anger he knew all too well.

"Captain," he corrected gently through clenched teeth.

"I canna believe ye just dinna leave her here. She is near dead anyway," he protested. They strode toward the longboat that waited just up the beach line. Mala remained silent as Deats continued. "Ye dinna need a thing on the ship that connects ta him."

Mala splashed through the knee-deep water and threw a leg over the gunwale of the longboat.

"Be quiet, Deats," she finally growled in reply. As they reached the longboat, Robert turned to find Willie trailing behind.

"Willie! We are leaving!" he yelled to the old man. Willie nodded his capped head as he tried to move faster through the sand.

With a huge grin, the old man replied, "So leave!"

Robert stopped in mid-stride and turned slowly, still carrying Aubrey's limp form, to smile at the old man who had nearly caught up with the party as Robert said, "Without you? Never! Who would do all the cooking? Certainly not me!" he told the old man as Willie reached him.

The dark haired woman regarded the two men with an exasperated look and emphasized her readiness to leave with a deep exhale. When the men turned to her at the sound, Mala asked stiffly,"If you two are quite finished, I would like to leave now."

Remembering her urgency, the two had the grace to look chagrined. When she turned away, the other crewmembers in the longboat noticed the two grin mischievously. Willie had to cover his mouth to keep any sound from escaping.

"Let us be off, Mr. Deats," she ordered.

"Aye, Captain."

Not until Robert had set her in the longboat that they called the *Witch* did Aubrey fight against the mind numbing shock and exhaustion of her past ordeal. Clutching at the gunwale and looking around in distress and fear, she pushed herself from Robert's gentle embrace as he was holding her upright in the boat.

"Where is the *Widow Maker*?" Aubrey asked, more to herself.

"Gone," came Deats' sharp reply.

"Oh my God, is he really gone?" Aubrey said as tears began to stream from her eyes. She dropped her head in pointed remorse. Deats looked upon the display with a crooked smile, especially when he looked at his captain and saw the flash of anger in the dark eyes again. Worried hazel eyes looked around the occupants of the boat and Aubrey muttered, "More pirates."

Robert was the only one to hear her complaint. He chuckled at her easily and nodded, "Aye."

Aubrey's attention was drawn now to the other woman who sat in the front of the boat.

"Mala," she whispered to the wind.

Robert frowned down on her, wondering how she might know his captain. Although the name had been spoken softly against the wind, the dark haired woman turned her gaze upon Aubrey. The menacing look from the woman reminded Aubrey so much of...

"Where are you taking me?" Aubrey managed to squeak out as she darted a look toward Robert.

The Scotsman, who sat behind her, snorted. He had been observing Mala closely and saw the look of intensity in her dark eyes as she stared at Aubrey. Startled at the sound he made, Aubrey turned to look at him. He presented her with a leering smile. She turned her head quickly back to stare at the bottom of the boat at her feet.

As they had rounded the southern tip of the island, Robert tapped Aubrey's knee to draw her attention.

"We go there, Miss."

"Oh God," she breathed.

The *Enchantress* was moored in a back bay on the other side of the island from where the battle had taken place. Despite her new fears, Aubrey looked at it in fascination. Closer now than when she had first seen it, Aubrey thought that the ship looked even more magnificent. As they neared, a rope ladder was dropped and Mala went up the ladder first. As she passed Robert, she said, "Have a bath prepared in the great cabin and get her some clothes."

"Aye, Captain," he nodded as Deats went up the ladder behind Mala.

"Where are ye goin'?" the Scotsman asked of her as he came over the

316

gunwale on her heels.

Mala turned on him in a flash, her face close to his and her hand went to the hilt of her cutlass. She growled, "I do not believe that I need to answer to you, Mr. Deats." Turning from him, she strode away. Deats turned back, his face masked in measured anger. Robert was on deck now and had Aubrey by the arm as he helped her aboard.

"Captain says you are to get cleaned up," Robert was telling her as he took her in gentle tow.

Aubrey snatched her arm back from him. "Why? What are your plans for me?" As Aubrey stepped back in her retreat, she ran against yet another man. He placed his hands gently on her shoulders to steady her. In fear, and reminded of the initial encounter with Beaufort the day she was taken from the *Gull*, she whirled in his direction. Without further thought, she kicked the man soundly in the shin with her booted foot. He yelped in pain, clutching at his abused shin. Robert caught her by the shoulders and pulled her back.

"Easy there, Miss, no one is going hurt you." There was a slight chuckle in his voice as he cast his eyes to look upon the man she had attacked.

The man Aubrey had kicked straightened and looked down upon her with a painful frown before looking up to the man who held her. "What have you got here, Robert?"

"I found her in the sea, Morgan. She was tumbling along with the surf like a little shell."

"Hmm, not a mermaid. It has legs and it knows how to use them," the man called Morgan said as he now smiled down on Aubrey and cast an objective look over the length of her.

"Take her boots away from her. She is dangerous with those little leather things," he added with a mischievous grin at Robert.

"Ya will not be takin' anything away from me!" Aubrey hissed angrily with a touch of her Irish brogue. She strained against Robert's hold and kicked out again. Morgan laughed and backed away.

"Stop your folly, Morgan. She has had a bad mornin'," Robert said easily then he pulled gently at Aubrey.

"Pay him no mind, Miss. Morgan is the ship's jester and he delights in tormenting. Come along now, Captain's orders." Aubrey looked back at the man called Morgan as she went along with Robert toward the companionway. Delights in tormenting? Aubrey had a flash of Beaufort when he tormented her. Morgan presented her with a handsome smile and he winked a blue eye at her. She was forced to look away from him as she was escorted down the companionway steps. Morgan continued to watch with an amused smile until Robert disappeared below decks with the spirited young woman.

Mala and Deats were near the portside gunwale of the *Enchantress*. Morgan stepped up to them. He heard Mala order one of the crew who stood nearby, "Go to the top and tell me where those warships are headed." As he turned away, she grabbed the man's arm and added, "I am mainly interested in the *Majestic.*"

The man nodded and dashed off climbing the ratlines and up to the highest perch on the ship.

Mala looked at the point where she had last seen the *Widow Maker*. From the corner of her eye, she noticed Morgan standing near her.

"The *Widow* is gone, Morgan," she informed him softly. Morgan looked at her sharply as she added sadly, "The British bastard sank her." Neither Morgan nor Deats missed the sadness in her voice.

Since Mala was facing in Morgan's direction, he was privy to the grief-stricken look on her face and knew her pain. She closed her eyes to control the emotions churning within her. The sight of the *Widow Maker* going under filled her mind. Opening her eyes, she looked into Morgan's soft blue ones. Both of them missed Deats' glare. He heard her words and the tone in which they were said.

After a moment she looked upward, muttering in annoyance, "What the hell is he looking at up there?"

Deats stepped up to the woman and whispered, "Not this time, Mala. There will be a better opportunity to get her."

"If she is alone, this is the time," Mala gritted out between clenched teeth.

"And if she is escorting the other?"

Mala turned slowly to face Deats and the silence between them was intense. Deats recognized the expression on her face for he had seen it too many times before. He felt the chill as he always did when he saw the look and was thankful when it was not intended for him.

"Then she would not be alone, Deats," she answered finally. Deats had nearly forgotten his question. Mala looked upward again, awaiting word. After a few more moments of nothing, those near their captain heard her mutter, "Ame damne!" Then they were momentarily startled as she pulled out her pistol and shot upward.

Hastily a relay of the message was given to her. "The *Majestic* leaves with the other."

"Tell him to get down here!" she growled up to nearest man.

Calmly she took out her powder flask and began to reload her pistol. As she put the flask away, she glanced up to see the men warily climbing down.

As the man from the fighting top descended onto the deck, the Scotsman noticed that she had finished reloading and now held the pistol to her side. Looking to the men, Deats found them eyeing the pistol in her hand as well. When he faced the woman, she asked quietly,

"Why the delay?"

"She just sat there, Captain," the man answered quickly then took a deep breath thinking it to be his last. Mala's stern visage regarded the seaman for long agonizing moments before she turned that look on the other men from the relay. She found them returning her gaze and fidgeting.

"Did I hit you?" she asked the first man.

He nodded and looked to his leg. Mala noticed what appeared to be a flesh wound, barely grazing the leg. She had not expected any worse considering the height of the mast. She caught a glimpse of Willie coming up the companionway from her cabin.

"Have Willie see to that." she said as she turned back to the island in the direction of the ships. The man nearly fainted in relief that she was not going to kill him. With her attention away, the men dispersed quickly to their duties.

"We will have another meeting with the *Majestic*," Deats said to her as he regarded her profile.

"Aye, there will be another time," Mala said coldly then added with a menacing tone, "What little mercy I would have shown, he has taken away now." Before Deats could say more, she turned on her heel, ordering, "We go Santiago de Cuba, Mr. Deats."

Both Morgan and Deats watched her as she made her way to the quarterdeck, then turned to the men, barking out orders. Morgan could only guess what Mala meant with 'mercy' towards the British Navy. She had shown little to none thus far, but then the *Majestic* was different for some unknown reason. She would have treated that one differently, but with their involvement in the sinking of the *Widow Maker*, Morgan doubted that the *Majestic* would even know what hit them if Mala was given the chance.

Mala stood on the quarterdeck looking out to sea, her back to the deck. She pulled out a gold chain that was tucked inside her shirt and started caressing the medallion that hung on it as her mind raced. The captain and crew of the *Majestic* had destroyed yet another part of her life. For taking Rene Black's life, they would pay dearly. Their punishment would come without the slightest hint of mercy.

Mala closed her eyes as she thought back to her encounter with Rene Black at Bimini–his touch–his kiss. Her brows knitted together, trying to control the ache within her heart as she thought of how she would not feel his touch or kiss his lips again.

Her thoughts were interrupted as Deats stepped up to the quarterdeck. "Captain?"

Mala dropped the chain back inside her shirt before turning. Deats eyed her a second and found no grief although he was not sure whether to expect it or not.

"What about our passenger? Shall we drop her off at the next port?"

"She can tolerate us until we reach our next stop."

"But we could stop at..."

"No, we are off schedule as it is. Because of the unexpected change in course, I will have to better our time by a few days. So she stays with us."

Deats did not like reminder of what happened in Bimini in the first place. There would have been no delay if she had killed that blasted man as planned. Now 'we' are off schedule and have his latest mistress on board. Mistress! A small smile crept on Deats' face as the possibilities flowed end over end in his mind. This just may work for me. He thought. He gazed on the woman he had come to know and wanted to know more. As she spoke with the helmsman, Deats' eyes traveled down her slender form then back up to her face. Yes, this just may work.

"You have the helm, Deats. I am going below," Mala said, breaking into his thoughts.

"Aye, Captain."

Chapter 58

An hour later, Deats went down the companionway steps and stopped a passing crewmember to ask, "Have you seen the Captain?"

"Aye, sir. She is in the galley," the man replied.

Sitting at her table, Mala was turning a mug of rum idly in her hands and staring at it. There was a faraway and thoughtful look on her face as Deats sat down across from her carefully. Her dark eyes rose to look into his.

"Ye should have left her on the beach," he growled low in his throat. Mala continued to stare at him.

"We dinna need that kinda trouble on board," he went on as she took a long drink from her mug.

Setting the mug down firmly she asked, "What trouble?" Her speech hinted of the alcohol that she had consumed.

Deats put his forearms on the table and clasped his hands. "A woman on board."

The reply though softly spoken had very nearly been spat at her. Mala had just put the mug to her lips and taken another drink but it was all she could do to keep from showering him with the contents from her mouth. Given her nature and her state of inebriation, Mala could not resist the opportunity to chide him for the stupid remark.

Taking a deep breath and sitting back slowly in her chair, Mala swung her shapely legs, clad in tight britches and knee-high black boots up onto the corner of the table, crossing her feet at the ankles.

"Deats," she began as she raised her mug for another drink. He drank as well, with his brown eyes that followed the legs up, across her lap and leisurely over her breasts to her beautiful face. There was an immediate stirring in his loins that begged for attention–her attention.

"In case you have forgotten–I am a woman, you ass," she spat at him. Deats' mouth went dry and he clenched his teeth but not in anger of her insult, but with near rampant desire for her.

"There is no doubt in my mind," he managed to say huskily.

Deats had desired her from the moment he had laid eyes on her over a year ago. Mala, however, had refused all manner of advances from him. She was his captain and no more. He respected her for her position despite the unusualness of it, but he still desired her.

Mala drained her mug as he began his argument again. "I mean ye dinna need her on board. Ye saw what she was. Do ye rally wanna put yerself through that? Seein' her every day an' knowin' that she..."

"Tend to your duties, Deats," Mala interrupted quietly. He looked at her for a moment. Why was she showing any compassion toward this woman who had obviously been Black's whore? Deats looked on the presence of Aubrey as a constant reminder to Mala of her former lover. With such a reminder in her face everyday, Deats would be hard-pressed in his objective to erase the memory of Rene Black from the island woman's mind and make her his own.

After another moment's thought, Deats stood from the table, bristling, "Aye Captain, I suppose I best go make sure our guest is all right. Ye dinna see how Robert and Morgan was eyein' her," he began. Mala glanced up at him as he shrugged, "Ach, but the whore that she is, they will both be layin' her doon before the week is out."

"And they will both be swinging from my yardarm shortly thereafter," Mala growled, her boot heels scraping the tabletop as she removed her feet from the table and stood. Deats turned away from her, a smile spreading across his lips. He would like nothing more that to see Morgan Alcott dead. That young Englishman seemed to be the only man on board who Mala seemed to hold in her confidence, making Deats resent and hate Morgan.

Mala did not see the smile as she pushed past Deats forcefully. "Make certain we are on good course to Santiago de Cuba so we can finish business there before heading to Bermuda."

"Aye Captain," he nodded.

"Call Robert and Morgan to my cabin," she called over her shoulder as she exited the galley. Another smile crossed Deats' face as he had succeeded in instilling a touch of mistrust in her regarding the two men—especially Morgan. As he came out into the corridor, he came face to face with her again.

"You come, too." With that, she turned on her heel and headed for her cabin.

"Damn," he spat under his breath.

Mala strode into her cabin and was surprised to see the other woman standing at the windows of the quarter gallery staring out at the blue waters beyond. Upon her entrance, Aubrey whirled about in alarm. Mala stared at her stolidly, her dark eyes taking in the glistening trails of tears on Aubrey's cheeks.

Clenching her teeth as she drew a deep breath through her nose and blew out the air through slightly parted lips, Mala tried to calm herself.

Aubrey's hazel eyes followed her as she moved to her desk. She quickly swiped the tears from her face and cleared her throat. "Merci for saving me," she said in mixed French and English.

"You do not have to speak French on my ship. We are not French," Mala said firmly as she took up her quill and opened her logbook.

"Thank you for the bath and clothes," Aubrey began again quietly. Mala merely glanced up at her.

"How do you know of me?" Mala asked, the distrust evident on her face.

"I–I was told." Aubrey found herself stammering under the blatant hostile glare as the dark haired woman sat back slowly. The look was so reminiscent of Rene Black that Aubrey felt a sudden chill in the room.

"Who are you?" Mala asked as she cast a condescending eye over the auburn haired woman.

"My name is Aubrey Malone."

"Well, Miss Malone, your life aboard my ship will be much different than you have grown accustomed to on the *Widow*," Mala said with even firmness as she looked back down to her book.

"What do you mean?" Aubrey asked.

Before Mala could respond, there was a knock at the door.

"Come in," Mala said sharply. She rose from her desk and moved to the long table in the center of the cabin. Aubrey looked around the cabin again, noting that it was laid out very much like that of Captain Black's. Looking at Mala, Aubrey mused at how the man must have been a very strong influence on her during her time with him. Jean Luc had never given her any other information about the association between Mala and Black other than the fact that she had once been the lady of the captain. Aubrey's eyes drifted to the front of Mala's shirt to the mark she knew would be there.

"Sit down," Mala very nearly spat at her as she pointed to one of the chairs along the side of the table. Aubrey snapped out of her musing and eased herself down into the nearest chair. The three men she had already met came into the cabin. The man called Deats seated himself to the right of Mala. Robert sat at the end of the table and the blue-eyed man named Morgan sat next to Aubrey.

"Miss Malone, these are my officers," Mala began then indicated each one with a wave of her hand.

"Angus Deats, my Quartermaster. Robert Bates, my Second Mate, and this is Morgan Alcott, my First Mate and Head Gunner." Aubrey looked around the table at the faces. Deats appeared as if it would kill him to acknowledge her. Robert graced her with a gentle smile, as he had on the beach and now Aubrey found herself staring into the twinkling blue eyes of Morgan. He extended his hand to her.

"Welcome aboard, Miss Malone."

Aubrey looked down at his hand and then offered him a shy crooked smile. Welcome aboard indeed. Another pirate ship and he greeted her as if she were aboard a regular ship with a civilized crew and with a civilized course. Despite her thoughts, Aubrey found herself extending her hand. Morgan's touch was warm and gentle. Aubrey bit her lip and felt sorry now for having lashed out at him on the deck earlier. So far, nothing like the crude and frightening Beaufort.

"Miss Malone will require accommodations while she is with us. In addition, she will be educated in the business of being aboard the *Enchantress*," Mala was saying as she stood and went to a cabinet to take down a bottle of wine.

Facing them again, Mala added in a slow firm tone, "She is not here for the pleasure of the crew. I want that made clear first and foremost." She set glasses before them all, leaving Aubrey for last.

"You do drink?" Mala asked her stiffly.

"Just a small amount, please," Aubrey replied with equal stiffness. She looked up at Mala with a slightly angry frown on her face. Apparently this woman had some suspicions as to what Aubrey did on board the *Widow Maker*, and they did not sound very ladylike.

As if Mala could read her thoughts, she went on as she sat, her dark eyes resting on Aubrey, "While I am certain you men can imagine what her station or duty was on the *Widow*, there will be none of that on my ship." Deats seemed delighted at the reference that Mala made of their new guest who seemed confused. Aubrey hurt all over from her battle with the sea. She was hungry for a change, and she was heartsick for the loss of Jean Luc. Now with this woman making vulgar accusations of her in the presence of all these men, anger began to seethe in her as Aubrey came bravely to her feet.

"Captain Mala, what exactly are you saying? What exactly are you suggesting that I did on that ship? For your information, I was taken prisoner from a ship that they sank!"

Mala looked up at the other woman with hostile brown eyes. "Miss Malone, I know what women who are taken as booty aboard ships like that one are used for." Her dark eyes scanned Aubrey. With the exception of an old cut at the corner of her lip, the woman appeared to be pristine and well kept. Then, imagining the woman pleasing Black in his bunk, Mala's tone turned as menacing as her dark eyes. "I also know that often the woman is taken as a favorite by the Captain."

Aubrey's anger erupted without her control. "How dare you!" came the near-shrieking Irish-accented exclamation.

324

Deats nodded in approval of the confrontation. This was just what he had hoped for. Robert and Morgan exchanged glances as Mala drew an even breath and added, casting a warning eye among the men at her table, "Or sometimes she is the shared whore among the elite of the crew."

Aubrey's face went ashen. Once more emotions took over for her tired, confused and angry brain. She glared at the dark haired woman and said angrily, "How would you know of these things? Would it be from personal experience?"

Deats watched the dark eyes flash–the rift between the two women was widening by leaps and bounds. Robert stroked at his mustache and looked worriedly at his captain.

Morgan reached up and easily but firmly took hold of Aubrey's wrist. With a hushed voice he said, "Sit down."

Aubrey saw Mala's eyes dart down to Morgan's hold on her. She tried to jerk her wrist free to no avail. There was nothing to lose. Aubrey had wished to die back in the surf anyway. Jean Luc was gone.

"You know nothing about me. I did not ask to come aboard this ship. I would have been just as happy to die out there. How dare you sit there and presume to know what I did on the *Widow Maker*! Well let me tell you..."

Mala threw up a hand. "I do not want to hear it. Miss Malone needs quarters–somewhere to cool her temper." The dark eyes drifted over the men at the table.

Deats snorted, "She canna have my quarters!"

"And indeed I would not want them!" Aubrey spat.

Morgan tugged at her wrist as he still held it. "Sit down, please."

"I sleep on the gun deck among the crew. That is no room there for a woman, Captain," Robert said easily.

"She will not sleep among my crew," Mala said in quiet anger.

"I certainly will not!" Aubrey added with a violent shake of her head. Morgan tugged one more time and this time he succeeded in pulling her back down into the chair beside him.

Still holding her by the wrist, he leaned toward Mala. "Captain, there is an empty bunk in my quarters." He paused as Mala graced him with a firm stare. "Miss Malone can stay there," he finished with a gentle smile.

"And where in the bloody hell will ye sleep?" Deats spat.

"I have to share quarters with another man?" Aubrey blurted out. Mala's gaze moved slowly back to the other woman. The three men glanced quickly at one another and saw the dangerous look on their captain's face.

Morgan leaned forward easily and said, "Had you been listening, Mr. Deats, you would have heard me say that there was an extra bunk in my quarters. Miss Malone will have a bunk of her own and whatever privacy she requires. Trust me."

An audible squeak erupted from Aubrey with his last two words.

Morgan gave Deats a condescending smile, then turned his blue eyes to meet with Mala's dark ones. Deep in them he saw the twinkle of approval. They stared at one another for a few moments. Deats saw that singular friendship between Morgan and Mala, a trust that ran deep and could never be understood by any of the other men on board.

"Very well, Mr. Alcott, I leave Miss Malone in your charge and care—with no strings attached," Mala said with a slight nod.

"Indeed not, Captain. It will be my duty," he nodded in reply.

Aubrey rolled her eyes as she finally snatched her hand from his grasp. His duty? Was that not how she and Jean Luc came to be? Aubrey looked at Morgan as Mala now talked to her officers about sailing to Santiago de Cuba. No matter what, she would not slip into that place again—Jean Luc had been the only one for her. He was gone and she wanted no other.

Mala had moved back to her desk and the men were coming to their feet. Morgan drew Aubrey's attention and made a gesture for her to precede him.

"And close the door," Mala called sharply as they started out of the cabin.

Chapter 59

Deats stormed down the corridor without anyone noticing his irritation. Turning from the door, Robert leaned close to Morgan. His closeness caused him to hover over Aubrey who was much smaller in stature. "Such a gentleman you are."

"Aye, that I am," Morgan nodded with a smile.

"Captain's pet is what you are," Robert added with a knowing grin.

"That too," Morgan nodded. He looked down upon Aubrey who now stood most uncomfortably between the two men. "Shall I escort you to your new home?"

"Africa?" Aubrey asked hopefully.

Robert chuckled, "Africa!"

"No love, we do not sail those waters," Morgan chuckled as well.

"No, of course not," Aubrey muttered sarcastically.

"Why would a pretty young woman like you want to go to the wilds of that continent?" Morgan asked as they went down the corridor in a little group.

"To rendezvous with her husband no doubt. A strong handsome sea captain who will beat the hell out of the likes of you, Morgan Alcott!" Robert said in torment, making Morgan laugh.

Ignoring the question and the playful banter, Aubrey looked upon Robert and asked, "Why did you pull me from the water? Why not just let me drown?"

Robert's eyes searched her face questioningly. "Well, I could never do that Miss Malone. Seeing you tumbling about in the surf like that, I would never be able to live with myself if I had."

"But you are pirates, you do awful things. What would it matter?" she went on in puzzlement.

In an effort to change the foreboding discussion, Morgan said brightly as he opened the door, "Here we are. Nothing fancy, but I call it home. See you after the watch, Robert."

Grinning at the blatant dismissal, Robert nodded slightly, "Aye."

Aubrey looked around as Morgan lit a lantern, and noticed immediately the close proximity of the two bunks.

Shutting the door, he tossed his hat onto the bunk to their right and nodded at the other one. "That one is yours."

She sighed deeply and sat down far up toward the head of the bunk.

"I will tolerate nothing, Mr. Alcott." Her comment came coolly as she proceeded to pull off her boots. Propping herself up into the corner of the bunk, she pulled her knees up and put her arms around her legs.

Morgan pursed his lips and looked around the cabin. "Ah, are you hungry?" he finally asked.

Aubrey replied quickly, "Yes, but I would rather not go to your galley."

"I would be happy to go get you something," he offered with a small smile.

In the next instant, she was alone in the cabin. Looking around, the cabin was much smaller than what she was accustomed to. With no window, the space seemed even smaller. With a sad frown, she recalled how even Jean Luc's quarters had been larger than this. Jean Luc. With a sharp breath laced with a heaving sob, she threw herself onto the bunk and cried as flashes of the day's events went through her tired mind.

"Miss Malone?" Morgan called softly as he stood over her with the plate. She came up so quickly that he nearly fell backward to get away from the kicking legs.

"Whoa!" he yelled as he juggled with the plate to keep from losing it.

Aubrey settled immediately and looked at him sleepily and sheepishly, "I am sorry, Mr. Alcott. You scared me."

"You carry some dangerous little weapons with you there," he said as he nodded to her legs that she folded under her just as quickly as she had shot them out in defense.

"Have to kick many people on the *Widow Maker*, did you?" he asked as he handed her the plate. Hazel eyes regarded him, but she gave him no reply as he sat across from her on his own bunk.

He nodded to the plate and said, "Willie piled it up. He said you were too thin. He said they must not have taken good care of you over there. He said when he picked you from the water, you weighed little more than a starfish." Morgan offered her a twinkling-eyed smile and added, "I see nothing wrong myself. You look quite fine to me."

Aubrey poked at the food on the plate with her fingers and put a piece of it in her mouth. If he only knew! She was not fine by any means. She was devastated!

"How did you come to get off the ship anyhow?" he went on to ask.

Aubrey swallowed and picked at a piece of ham. "I was put off."

"Lucky for you," he said as he leaned back on his bunk, propping up one foot. Morgan got up and went to a small washstand. He poured a cup of water and returned, handing her the drink.

"If you need anything else, you just let me know."

"Thank you, Mr. Alcott," she nodded as she sipped the water. With a disdainful look at the plate that still seemed to be heaped with food although she was full, she said, "I cannot eat anymore, there was too much. I hope your cook will not be angry."

Morgan took the plate and made a scoffing sound. "Do not worry about him, he is just an old hen. Well, I bet he will just spoil the stuffin' outta you just like he does the Captain. He growls at the rest of us all the time but he dotes over the ladies."

"There are more?" Aubrey asked quickly.

"More what?" Morgan asked.

"Women? More women on board this ship?" Aubrey asked hopefully.

Morgan chuckled. "No, I mean he dotes over the Captain and now he has you." Aubrey's shoulders slumped in disappointment.

"I just do not think that your captain holds me in very high regard," Aubrey said stiffly.

Morgan chuckled pleasantly and said with a dismissive wave, "Give her time. It will be all right."

Aubrey thought about Mala's past association with Black and thought about the mark on her own breast. Shaking her head sadly, she said, "No, Mr. Alcott, I believe that there is not enough time in all the world for that."

Aubrey propped the pillow up in the corner of the bunk, sitting back against it with her legs drawn up closely with her arms around her legs. He watched her as she began to doze off.

"Miss Malone?" came Morgan's quiet voice.

Aubrey jolted awake to find him standing over her. "Yes, Mr. Alcott?"

"I have duties to tend to. You should lie down and get comfortable."

Aubrey was suddenly apprehensive at being left alone. She looked at the door as Morgan continued, "No one will bother you, but should you need anything, you can send any of the men for me." He smiled reassuringly at the wariness written on her face.

"Sleep well," he added as he headed for the door.

"Good day, Mr. Alcott," she said, trying to get rid of him.

"Please call me Morgan."

She did not reply, and he let it go at that.

The bell tolled eight calling for the first watch at 4am. Willie stepped into the galley to begin his day. Suddenly, he looked around as a sound from one from the tables stopped him. To his surprise, he found Captain Mala sitting at a table near the kitchen with two bottles before her, one empty and the other nearly so. He stopped and looked at her as she stared at a medallion dangling from her fingers on a chain. She took a drink from her tankard as she stared at the necklace. Once she placed the tankard back on the table, she took the medallion within the palms of her hands and rested her head on her hands as if in prayer.

Making his way as quietly as he could to the kitchen, Willie looked around to find that he had not disturbed her. She sat as before, but now he could hear her soft sobs. He shook his head as he disappeared within the kitchen, knowing that she would not want to be seen this way. Always the same whenever they sighted that big, black ship. She usually drank herself unconscious. But the tears were new. And now that Black's ship was gone along with her captain and crew, what was going to happen next? Willie thought to himself as he stood just out of her sight, but where he could watch the galley entrance. He would safeguard her privacy for as long as he could, just as he always had done.

To Be Continued...